DROUGHT

Graham Masterton

severn House

This first world edition published 2014
in Great Britain and the USA by
SEVERN HOUSE PUBLISHERS LTD of
19 Cedar Road, Sutton, Surrey, England, SM2 5DA.

Trade paperback edition first published
in Great Britain and the USA 2014 by
SEVERN HOUSE PUBLISHERS LTD.

British Library Cataloguing in Publication Data

Masterton, Graham author.
  Drought.
  1. Droughts–Fiction. 2. Environmental disasters–
  Fiction. 3. Social workers–California–Fiction.
  4. Suspense fiction.
  I. Title
  823.9'2-dc23

ISBN-13: 978-0-7278-8399-5 (cased)
ISBN-13: 978-1-84751-519-3 (trade paper)

Typeset by Palimpsest Book Production Ltd.,
Falkirk, Stirlingshire, Scotland.
Printed digitally in the USA.

'When the well is dry, we know the worth of water.'
Benjamin Franklin (1706–1790),
Poor Richard's Almanac, 1746

BOOK ONE
Act of God

ONE

Martin heard the screaming inside the house as soon as he pulled into the curb. He picked up his bulging folder of case notes and swung his legs out of his old bronze Eldorado convertible, but as he did so the frosted glass window in the front door cracked, sharp as a pistol shot. He could see that a woman in a dark red dress had been violently pushed against it from inside the hallway.

'*You whore!*' a man's hoarse voice was shouting. '*Two weeks I'm away and what do you do? Two weeks! You can't wait for me two weeks?*'

The woman was thrown against the front door a second time, even harder, so that a large triangular shard of glass crashed out on to the porch. Martin dropped his folder back on to the passenger seat and strode briskly up the concrete path.

'*You whore! You* pisona! *You piece of shit! I kill you!*'

Martin went up to the door, his shoes crunching on broken glass. Through the broken window he could see a woman sitting on the doormat with her back to him, sobbing, her black hair tangled into snakes. An unshaven Hispanic man in a filthy pink T-shirt was standing in front of her with both fists clenched, cross-eyed with rage.

'*Jesus!*' Martin shouted at him. 'Back off, Jesus, before you do something you totally regret! Leave her be!'

The man took no notice of him. He seized the woman's dress and heaved her up on to her feet, and then he punched her in the face, twice. Martin heard the cartilage in her nose snap, and blood sprayed in loops and squiggles all the way up the wall.

'*Jesus, leave her be!*'

But Jesus kept hold of the woman's dress and swung her from side to side. She was semi-concussed and her arms were dangling as if she were dancing a loose-limbed salsa.

'You go screw yourself!' he retorted. 'This is my business, nothing to do with social service! Go on, go screw yourself! *Vete a la verga!*'

Martin took one step back, and then he kicked the door so hard that the crossbar splintered. He kicked it again and this time the lock burst and it swung wide open, juddering on its hinges. Jesus let go of the woman so that she tumbled sideways on to the carpet. He retreated toward the kitchen, holding up both hands to fend Martin off.

'Don't you touch me! I warn you! Don't you fucking touch me! You – you work for the social service – you can't touch me! It's the law!'

Without any hesitation, Martin sidestepped around the woman and went after him. Jesus backed into the kitchen and frantically tried to close the door in Martin's face, but he was too late. Martin barged into the door with his shoulder and Jesus lost his balance and staggered back against a Formica-topped table crowded with smeary plates and empty Modelo bottles. Plates and bottles clattered on to the floor and smashed.

'Don't you touch me!' Jesus was so frightened now that his voice was more of a high-pitched, strangulated whine, like a dog straining at its leash. 'You touch me, I swear to God, you're going to lose your fucking job! I make sure of that!'

'Oh, yes?' said Martin. 'And how are you going to do that, when you're sitting in the slammer on a charge of assault?'

'Don't you touch me! Don't you touch me!' Jesus gibbered. He backed right up to the kitchen sink but Martin grabbed his wrist, twisted him around and forced both of his arms behind his back, right up between his shoulder blades. Jesus stank of beer and sweat and stale cigarettes, and the hair on his arms was so bristly that it felt like holding a large dog rather than a man. All the same, Martin found that Jesus was surprisingly weak.

'You can't do this!' Jesus protested. 'You can't do this to me! You work for the county! I know my rights! I have rights!'

'Sure you have rights. For starters, you have the right to remain silent, you sadistic scumbag. In fact, I insist on it.'

As if to emphasize his point, he rammed Jesus's arms up even higher between his shoulder blades. Jesus let out a girlish cry of pain.

Martin half-pushed and half-lifted Jesus out of the kitchen and back into the hallway. On the left-hand side there was a grubby cream-painted door with a discolored decal of a red rose stuck on to it. Martin turned his back to the door and kicked it open, and then forced Jesus inside. All of the houses along this side of East Julia Street were identical, and Martin knew that this was the restroom.

'What are you doing?' Jesus screamed at him. 'What are you doing, you fucking pervert?'

The restroom was small and narrow with a pale blue Venetian blind that looked as if it hadn't been dusted since it was first put up. A dried-up pot plant sat on the windowsill, and the mirror above the washbasin was smashed like a kaleidoscope. Around the toilet pedestal, the floor was cluttered with rancid sneakers and a rusty pair of roller skates, and balanced on top of the cistern there was an ashtray overflowing with cigarette butts. The toilet itself was filthy, its bowl streaked in fifty shades of dark brown, its water still amber with stale urine.

'You can't!' screamed Jesus. 'You can't do this! It's against the law!'

Martin didn't answer him. He forced Jesus to kneel down on the floor in front of the toilet. Then he gripped the back of his neck and pushed his head down into the bowl, as far as it would fit. Martin heard the sides of his skull knocking against the porcelain.

'Oh, no! *No*! Holy Mary Mother of God! No!'

Martin yanked down the cistern handle and the toilet flushed. Jesus struggled furiously as water cascaded over his head. Martin kept him kneeling until the flush had finished, and then pulled him up. Jesus spluttered and coughed and blinked, and for the first few seconds he couldn't speak.

'Well?' said Martin. 'Not so tough now, are we?'

'You *can't* – you can't fucking do this—'

'I can and I will and there's not a goddamned thing you can do about it. You're not even supposed to *be* in this house, Jesus, you worthless waste of space, and you know it. You're not even supposed to be anywhere near this neighborhood. How do you think little Mario would feel if he saw you hitting his mother like that? You think he'd respect you?'

'That's my son! How do you think he's going to respect *her*, his own mother, if she screws around with other men, right in front of him? Of course I hit her. She's a whore. She was asking for it.'

'From now on, Jesus, you're going to leave her alone. The court says you have to and I say you have to.'

'Well, screw you,' Jesus spat at him. 'She's my wife and that makes her my property and no court is going to keep me away from her and neither is no *caca palo* from social services.'

Martin rammed Jesus's head into the toilet bowl again and pulled down the handle. This time, however, the handle clanked down loosely, and no water came out. Martin pulled it again, but the cistern wasn't filling up. He dragged Jesus up again.

'So what's it to be?' Martin demanded. 'Are you going to stay away from Ezzie, or not?'

Jesus spat out water and wiped his mouth with the back of his hand, and then spat again.

'Yes? No?' Martin coaxed him. 'If it's a no, Jesus, I can shove your head down there for a third time, no problem. And more, if necessary. I'm willing to go on shoving your head down there as long as it takes for you to change your mind.'

Jesus looked down into the dirt-encrusted toilet bowl. There was no water in it now. He spat into it, and then he looked back at Martin and shook his head. 'OK,' he said. 'You win, you bastard.'

'You're sure you don't want one more lucky dip?'

Jesus shook his head again. Martin released his grip on the back of his neck, and Jesus stood up, almost losing his balance and tilting against the wall. The first thing he did was go to the washbasin and turn on the faucet, but only a dribble of water came out. He smacked the faucet in frustration.

'No fucking water! What the fuck?'

'Maybe Ezzie didn't pay her water bill.'

'It's you. The C-fucking-FS. *You* are supposed to pay for her water bills.'

He smacked the faucet again but it was no use. He had to content himself with rubbing his hair with the gray, mildew-smelling hand towel that hung beside the basin. As he did so, he stared at his own reflection in the shattered mirror and said to Martin, 'If I catch some lethal infection, you – you will be a dead man, I promise you.'

'No, Jesus . . . if you catch some lethal infection, *you* will be a dead man, and the world will be a better place without you, believe me. Now, where's Mario? I have to take Ezzie to the hospital.'

He stepped back into the hallway. Esmeralda was sitting up now, her back against the wall, dabbing her bleeding nose with the hem of her dark red dress. Her curvy brown legs were dappled with bruises – some red, some purple, some yellow.

'Jesus was just leaving, weren't you Jesus?' said Martin.

Jesus had appeared from the toilet with his wet hair sticking up. He said nothing to Martin, but as he passed Esmeralda on his way to the broken front door, he stopped, and spat at her, and said, '*Pisona!*'

'Hey!' said Martin. 'You want another dive down the U-bend? Be happy to oblige you!'

Jesus stalked out of the house without saying anything else. A few seconds later, he drove past them in his bright yellow turbocharged Mustang, blasting his horn in defiance.

Martin hunkered down next to Esmeralda and examined her face. Both of her eyes were already crimson and swollen so that she could hardly see out of them, and her nose looked like a large maroon plum. Her upper lip was split, too. He couldn't tell which was blood and which was sticky red lipstick.

'Come on, Esmeralda,' said Martin, gently. 'We need to get you to the ER. Where's Mario?'

'Mario is staying with his friend Billy today. I'm so glad he wasn't here when Jesus came. That Jesus. He's the devil.'

Martin helped her to climb to her feet. Before they left for the hospital, he tore a piece from a cardboard tomato box which he found in the kitchen and stuck it over the broken window in the front door with duct tape. Then he managed to wedge the door shut with another piece of cardboard so that at least it looked as if it were locked.

'Don't worry, Martin,' said Esmeralda, in a blocked-up voice. 'I don't have nothing which is worth nobody stealing. Apart from Mario, I don't have nothing worth nothing.'

Martin opened the Eldorado's door for her. He looked up at the sky and it was cloudless. It was June ninth and it hadn't rained since November twelfth, and even then less than a tenth of an inch had fallen. He remembered the date because that was the day that Peta had walked out on him, taking Ella and Tyler with her. He had stood on the sidewalk watching them drive away and it had started to rain, very softly and very quietly, and even then it was the first time in over a year.

He climbed in beside Esmeralda and said, 'Listen to me, Ezzie. We all have something, more than we know. Most of the time, though, we just don't appreciate it. What does that song say? "You don't know what you've got until you lose it all again."'

TWO

He waited forty-five minutes with Esmeralda in the Urgent Care department of San Bernardino Community Hospital, sitting next to an elderly man who reeked of stale garlic and who groaned loudly every two or three minutes. After each groan he croaked out, '*Madre de Dios!*' and crossed himself, again and again. At least it was cool inside the hospital, although the sunlight shining through the window was reflected so brightly by the white walls and the white marble floor that Martin felt as if he were sitting in an over-exposed photograph, and put on his Ray-Bans.

Esmeralda dabbed her nose with a tissue and said, 'I sleep with Jorge because Jorge is always good to me, always helping me. He is married but I don't know his wife. It is wrong, I know that. But sometimes I feel so much alone.'

Martin said, 'You can sleep with anybody you like, Ezzie, just so long as you're discreet about it with little Mario. So far as I'm concerned, Mario's well-being is my number one priority – and he should be yours, too, *and* Jesus's.'

'Mario doesn't know about Jorge and me sleeping together. It only happens when he is at playschool. I don't want him to find out. Jesus is still his father, even if he is a *tapado*.'

At that moment a wide-hipped Hispanic nurse in a pale blue uniform came up and said, 'Mrs Rivera? If you'd like to come this way, please, Doctor Varga can see you now.'

Martin and Esmeralda stood up. Esmeralda took hold of Martin's hand and said, 'I see you later maybe, Martin. You are a good man, bless you and bless you. Not like any other social worker I ever know before.'

Martin smiled and shook his head. 'There's not much that's good about me, Ezzie. In fact I'm not so different from your Jesus. I'm only on the side of the angels by accident.'

'You should be careful of Jesus. He never forgets. Never. If he thinks you have done him wrong, he will do to you twice as bad as you have done to him, even if he has to wait for years.'

Martin watched the nurse take Esmeralda away to the Urgent

Care Department. As he did so, his cellphone played the opening bars of 'Mandolin Rain'.

'Martin?'

'Oh, hi, Peta. Listen – I'm in the community hospital right now. Let me take this outside.'

He walked out into the hospital parking lot. It was just past midday now and the temperature was well over a hundred and ten. The flag outside the hospital entrance hung lifelessly, and ripples of heat rose off the tarmac so that it looked as if water were running across it. Martin was wearing only a short-sleeved white shirt and khaki chinos, but by the time he had reached the shade of the walkway that led to the ambulance parking zone, his forehead was beaded with perspiration and his shirt was clinging to his back.

'Martin, we have no water. All of our faucets have run dry and the toilets won't flush.'

'I had the same thing on East Julia Street, downtown, about an hour ago. What about your neighbors? Do they have water?'

'No. Nobody does. I've tried calling the water department but their phone is always busy. I looked at their website, too, but it makes no mention of water being cut off. I just wondered if you knew anything about it.'

'No, nothing. I'll try to find out what's going on and get back to you. I expect a couple of water mains have burst, that's all. They'll probably have them fixed by the end of the day.'

Peta said, 'I'm worried about Ella, that's the trouble. She has a temperature of ninety-eight-point-eight and she says she's feeling shivery. I don't want to be stuck without water if she's not very well.'

'Did you call the doctor?'

'I don't think I need to, not yet, anyhow. I've given her some Tylenol and put her to bed. It's probably nothing worse than period pains.'

Martin didn't respond to that. Ella had always been his favorite little girl and the thought of her becoming a woman when he wasn't around to take care of her was constantly hurtful. But he knew that it had all been his own fault, his marriage to Peta splitting up. No woman could be expected to put up with black moods like his, and his unpredictable bursts of temper. He called them his 'Djinn Days', after the devils who were supposed to appear in dust storms in Afghanistan, and make everybody depressed or mad.

'I'm going back to the office now,' he told Peta. 'I promise you I'll look into this and get back to you. How's Tyler, by the way, is he OK?'

'Tyler is just fine. When he's not asleep or at school he's stuck in front of his laptop but all his friends are the same.'

'OK, Peta. Like I say, I'll get back to you.' He was tempted to add, 'I love you,' but he knew that would only irritate her.

If you love me so much, why did you shout at me and push me around and try to make feel so small? Why didn't you get yourself some help, if you were so disturbed by what happened to you in Afghanistan?

THREE

On the way back to the office in Carousel Mall Martin switched on the radio in his car. According to the weather reporter on KTIE, there was no foreseeable prospect of what he called 'measurable precipitation'. In other words, no rain was expected for the next four days at least. Temperatures would reach 100–107 degrees during the day, and drop only to between seventy-five and eight-three degrees by night.

'San Bernardino's Municipal Water Department is asking every citizen of San Bernardino to conserve as much water as possible. Over the past three years the lack of any significant rainfall has brought us close to crisis point. You should think twice, folks, before washing your vehicle, and make sure you check the watering index online to decide how much water you're going to use to irrigate your plants.'

Martin parked his Eldorado in the basement parking lot and went up in the elevator to the office. As he pushed open the glass door with *San Bernardino County Children & Family Services* stenciled on it in silver letters, Brenda the receptionist gave him her usual glower, peering at him over her thick-rimmed spectacles. Martin had always thought Brenda would be quite attractive if she didn't wear such schoolmistressy glasses and didn't clench her hair in the tightest of French pleats, like a coil of copper wire. He sometimes wondered if she was always so scathing to him because she thought *he* was attractive, too.

'Arlene wants to see you in her office,' she told him.

'OK, Brenda, thanks,' he said, and started to walk down the corridor toward the soda vending machine.

'I think she wants you in there right *now*,' said Brenda. '"Just as soon as he comes through the door," that's what she said.'

'I'll be sure to tell her you gave me the message,' said Martin. He continued to the end of the corridor, pushed a dollar into the soda vending machine and noisily bought himself a can of Dr Pepper. Brenda continued to glower at him as he walked back past her desk.

'Brenda, have a heart. My throat was as dry as a camel's back passage.'

She pursed her lips but didn't say anything. As he reached Arlene Kaiser's office, however, and knocked on the door, he glanced back and he was sure that he caught her smiling. *Women*, he thought. *If only they would come out straight and tell you how they felt, and stopped making you guess.*

'Come!' called out Arlene Kaiser, in her usual high-pitched screech, and he opened the door and stepped into her office. Arlene was the Deputy Director of Children & Family Services and so she had a gray steel desk the size of an aircraft carrier and a corner office. Out of the windows she enjoyed a view of orange-tiled rooftops and gleaming new office buildings and scaffolding and tower cranes, and the distant San Bernardino mountains, hazy and wavering in the afternoon heat, like mountains seen in a dream.

'Ah, Martin!' Arlene shrilled at him. 'At last! Didn't you get my text?'

'*Text?*' Martin blinked at her.

Arlene was short and bulky, with close-cropped gingery-brown hair and an oddly cherubic face for a fifty-five-year-old woman, with bright blue eyes and a bulbous nose. She was wearing a mustard-colored nylon blouse and a gingery-brown pleated skirt which matched her hair, and a necklace of shiny green beads which looked like olives.

'Well, anyhow. You're here now. This is Saskia Vane, from the water department, and her associate—'

'Lem Kunicki,' said a pale, thirtyish man sitting in the corner. In his pale lemon polo shirt and pale gray linen pants he was almost invisible, like a chameleon. He even had bulging eyes like a chameleon.

Saskia Vane, however, was far from invisible. She was sitting cross-legged beside Arlene's desk, dressed in a scarlet suit with a short matador jacket and a very short skirt, and high-heeled Louboutin shoes with bright red soles. Her hair was black and glossy and cut in a severe geometric bob, which emphasized the sharp angles of her cheekbones and her slanting, catlike eyes. She had full, pouting lips, which had been glossed in scarlet to match her suit. Underneath her jacket she was wearing a black scoop-neck T-shirt which revealed a deep suntanned cleavage. Between her breasts dangled a necklace which looked like a shark's tooth set in gold.

She raised her hand toward Martin in an undulating motion, as if she were trying to demonstrate to him how dolphin swim. He took it, and briefly shook it, and smiled at her. She didn't take her eyes off him as he pulled up a chair and sat next to her, but she didn't smile back. She was wearing a strong jasmine perfume with musky undertones, the sort of perfume a woman wears to mask the smell of recent sex.

Martin said, 'So, Ms Vane, you're from the water department? That's a lucky coincidence. You're just the person I wanted to talk to.'

'Please, Martin, call me Saskia. And I don't actually represent the water department itself. I'm a member of a special emergency team which Governor Smiley has put together. Our brief is to advise local government officers on how to deal with the ongoing drought situation.'

'Oh! In that case, I think you're *exactly* the person I want to talk to. My wife just called me from Fullerton Drive to say that her water's been cut off. And this morning, when I was dealing with a case on East Julia Street, there was no water supply there, either. So what gives?'

Saskia gave him one of those queasy smiles that politicians give when faced with a question they don't really want to answer. 'I'm afraid I'm not personally familiar with those particular locations, Martin, so I couldn't possibly give you a specific response to that. But I can answer you in more general terms.'

Martin glanced across at Arlene but Arlene simply nodded toward Saskia as if she were telling him to let her have her say, because this was critical.

Saskia said, 'The reason I've come here today to talk to you is because we're faced with having to consider rotational hiatuses in service.'

'Excuse me? "Rotational hiatuses"? That sounds like some kind of skin complaint.'

Saskia kept on smiling that slightly nauseated smile. 'Let me tell you this, Martin. Water reserves nationwide are lower than they have been in almost fifty years.'

'Sure, I know that. But I can't see *this* city running dry, can you? We're sitting right on top of more underground water than we know what to do with. I mean, that was the whole reason the city was built here in the first place. And what about Arrowhead Springs, up in the mountains? San Bernardino *exports* water, for Christ's sake.'

'Well, sorry, but not right now you don't. You'll have seen for yourself on the TV news that reservoirs are nearly empty and rivers and lakes are down to the lowest levels ever recorded. This is happening all across the country, Martin, coast to coast, especially in California and the Midwest. Even here in San Bernardino, I'm afraid to tell you. You used to have one hundred fifteen million gallons of water stored in your reservoirs, and your groundwater wells used to hold more water than Lake Shasta, but now they've dropped to less than a fifth of that. Demand is outstripping supply, by a very long way, and continuing to do so, and that's one of the reasons I'm here.'

'OK,' said Martin. 'But you still haven't told me what "rotational hiatuses" are.'

'Martin – this is strictly restricted information which is being given to selected individuals only – local government administrators, emergency services, the police and military. If we made it public we could be risking a national panic. The drought situation is very much more severe than you've seen on the news. Crops have been devastated, especially corn and soy, and if it carries on like this we're going to be facing food rationing as well as water restrictions.'

'Go on,' said Martin. He had a long-standing aversion to being lectured, especially by women, but he knew he would have to listen to this.

Saskia said, 'We've already been forced to start rotational hiatuses in San Bernardino, both city and county. That means we've been cutting off the water supply on a strict rota basis, first one neighborhood and then another, and we've been doing it without giving those neighborhoods any prior warning.'

'That's kind of drastic, isn't it?'

'Yes, I agree. But if you give people notice that their water supply is about to be cut off, they immediately fill up buckets and bathtubs and any other container they can lay their hands on, which puts an even greater strain on what limited reserves we have left.'

'So how long is each of these "rotational hiatuses" going to last?'

'Hopefully, no longer than forty-eight hours.'

'Forty-eight hours, in this heat?'

'Well, we're hoping it won't have to be longer.'

'Yes, but come on! How are people going to wash, and cook, and everything else you need water for?'

'I'm afraid they'll just have to get by.'

'That's easy enough to say. But what about local businesses? How are restaurants and laundries going to cope? And what about hospitals, and clinics, and retirement homes? In forty-eight hours, believe me, people won't just be thirsty, they'll be dying. I saw droughts when I was serving in Afghanistan, and it didn't take more than a couple of days without water before old people and children were dropping like flies.'

'Martin,' said Saskia, 'you just don't get it. Take San Bernardino alone. The average rainfall here is usually sixteen-point-four-three inches per year, and that's pretty low by any standard. Over the past three years you've had less than a tenth of that, one-point-five-two, which is disastrous. We can't supply people with water that we simply don't have.

She paused for a moment, and lowered her voice, as if she were making an effort to be reasonable. 'I came here today to talk to you at CFS because you need to be aware that many families which are already dysfunctional are going to be under even greater stress when they find that they have no water, especially in this heatwave. You need to know what the situation is so that you can keep them calm – explain to them that the San Bernardino Municipal Water Department is doing everything it can to share out water fairly, and that protesting about it is not going to do them any good – in fact it's going to be severely counterproductive. You have to persuade them that this drought is an act of God, and not the fault of the county, or the state, or the federal government for that matter.'

'And this is your remit, is it?' Martin asked her. 'You're here to tell us that we have to keep a thirsty sweaty resentful underclass from running riot?'

Saskia raised her eyes again and looked at Martin steadily. 'It's in everybody's best interests, Martin. Especially all of those children you care for.'

'So what do we say to them? "Let them drink cola?" As well as wash in it, cook in it, and spray it on their lawns?'

'Not even that, Martin. All soda manufacturers have been ordered to stop production until further notice.'

Arlene tilted her chair forward and gave Martin her most serious frown. 'Saskia tells me that Governor Smiley has been keeping a very tight lid on this, Martin, and now you can understand why.'

'Oh, for sure. It's coming dangerously close to inhumanity.'

Arlene ignored that. 'I'm not sharing what Saskia has told us with everybody in the office, Martin, believe me, and I'm only sharing it with *you* because you're in charge of some of the city's most deprived districts, which have a much higher risk of social disorder. We're right on the front line, here at CFS, you know that. We have to do our best to keep at-risk families from boiling over and falling apart, with all the damage that could do to their children.'

Martin shrugged. 'All right, Arlene, if you say so. I don't quite understand how you can boil over and fall apart both at the same time, especially if you don't have any water. But at least I know what's going on now. I'll call my wife and tell her.'

He stood up, but Saskia reached up and caught hold of his tan leather watch strap. 'I'd rather you didn't, Martin.'

'You'd rather I didn't what? Tell my wife? It's OK. She's only my *ex*-wife, as it happens.'

'I'd prefer it if we kept this information on a need-to-know basis only, if you don't mind. Like I say, we could be right on the brink of a national panic. It only takes one spark to start a forest fire.'

'With respect, Saskia, I think my ex-wife has a need to know. My daughter has a high temperature and she has no water.'

'Martin, please. Just tell her that the water is coming back on again very soon, if she can just hold on. I'm not supposed to advise anybody to do this, because supplies are so low, but tell her to go to her nearest supermarket and stock up on as much bottled water as she can, if she hasn't done that already – and if there's any left.'

Martin looked down at Saskia's hand, still holding his watch strap. Her fingernails were polished red to match her suit and her lips. She was wearing a single large ring with a red agate in it, but no wedding band. He was prepared to admit that he didn't always understand women, but they never frightened him. All the same, there was something about Saskia Vane that put him off balance, although he couldn't understand exactly what it was. Maybe it was that pungent post-coital perfume; or the way that she looked at him with eyes as bright and hard as nail-heads. He may not have been frightened of her, but then it was obvious that *she* wasn't frightened of *him*, either.

'OK,' he said. 'But you'll need to give us a schedule. Which neighborhoods you're planning to cut off, and when. Then – if we do get any trouble – at least we'll be prepared for it.'

'I can't do that, Martin. That really *is* restricted information. If it got into the wrong hands . . . believe me, it would be disastrous. All hell let loose. Some neighborhoods have much higher and more critical needs than others, and you can imagine the resentment if some were disconnected for a shorter period than others.'

Martin didn't know what to say to that. He looked across at Arlene again, but all Arlene could do was shrug. 'Don't see what else we can do, Martin. We're here to keep families together and protect children from harm. Starting a riot isn't going to help any.'

Martin lifted his arm a little and Saskia released her grip on his watch strap.

'It was very good to meet you, Martin,' she said. 'Look – take one of my cards. If there's anything else you need to know, just get in touch. Do you have any further questions for now?

'No,' said Martin. 'I don't think so. Or – yes, maybe one. Can I ask you what qualifications you have? I mean, what does it take for somebody like you to be appointed to a drought crisis advisory team?'

Saskia kept on looking at him unblinking and for quite a long time Martin thought that she wasn't going to answer him, or else she was going to tell him to mind his own business.

Instead, she said, 'Good looks, Martin, and a natural flair for diplomacy. And a doctorate in environmental management from UCLA, that helped. And a law degree. And connections in some very high places.'

'I just wondered, that's all,' Martin told her. 'I find it hard to picture you, when you were an innocent little girl, dreaming of telling everybody in California not to flush their toilets so often.'

Saskia looked away from him, but as she did so, she said, 'I was never an innocent little girl, Martin.'

Martin hesitated. If this had been a cocktail bar, and he had been coming on to her, he could have thought of some smart and provocative response to that. But it was Arlene's office, and Arlene was listening intently.

He smiled at Saskia as if to say '*touché*', and then he gave Arlene a salute and turned to leave. On his way out the pale man in the pale lemon shirt bobbed up from his chair and held out his hand.

'Lem Kunicki,' he said. His palm was chilly and damp and Martin thought that it was like shaking hands with somebody who had recently died.

FOUR

Peta put down the phone and went through to the sunlit living room, where Tyler was sprawled on the couch with his laptop, playing *Alien Armageddon IV.*

'Tyler? I was just talking to your dad. He says the water's going to be staying off for at least two days and we should stock up on as much bottled water as we can lay our hands on.' Pause. Silence. '*Tyler?*'

Tyler couldn't hear her, with his headphones in his ears, and he kept on frantically playing.

'*Yessss!*' he said, clenching his fist, as he blew up another alien cruiser.

Peta went up to him and snapped his computer shut, catching his fingers in it. He looked up at her in hurt and astonishment, as if she had just slapped him.

'*Mom* – what did you do that for?' he protested, taking out his headphones. 'I was up to my highest level ever!'

'I need you to run an errand for me, that's why.'

'Oh, *shoot*, Mom, can't it wait? That was my highest level ever!'

'Your dad says we should do it as soon as we can.'

'Oh, I see! My *dad* says! I thought you didn't even *like* my dad.'

'Of course I like him. As a matter of fact I love him, but that doesn't make him any easier to live with. He says our water's going to stay cut off for at least forty-eight hours and some expert from the water department has told him to stock up on bottled water, as much as we can get hold of.' She dangled her car keys in front of him and said, 'Take my truck and go to Ralph's and see how much you can manage to buy. Here, look, here's a fifty. If there's any change you can keep it.'

Tyler tossed his laptop on to the couch. At times he not only looked like his father but sounded like him, which Peta found quite disturbing, as if Martin had gone but left a clone of himself behind, to keep an eye on her. Tyler was tall and wide-shouldered but very skinny, with blond hair that stuck up like a porcupine and a long, chiseled face. He even walked like his father, with that brisk aggressive stride that made people feel that he was coming up to hit them for no reason. He was wearing tight blue rolled-up jeans and a maroon Cardinals T-shirt.

'Listen,' she said, 'I'd go myself, but I can't leave Ella. I think I may have to take her to the doctor if she gets any worse. I'm just hoping it's not West Nile fever or anything serious like that.'

'Oh, come on, Mom! Ella *always* has something wrong with her, you know that. She's a hypo-con-artist, whatever you call it. She only does it for attention.'

'She's *sick*, Tyler. She has a very high temperature and she can't keep anything down. Now, please.'

Tyler reluctantly snatched the car keys from her. She followed him out through the front door to the driveway in front of their single-story house, where her turquoise-blue Hilux was parked. The day was cloudless and baking hot, and the concrete driveway was so dazzlingly white that she raised her hand in front of her face to shield her eyes. When she checked the thermometer by the side of the front door she saw that it read 112. Behind the rooftops of the single-story houses on the opposite side of the road, the brown San Bernardino mountains were almost invisible behind a haze of heat, and buzzards were circling over them, around and around, without having to flap their wings even once.

'Just drive carefully!' Peta shouted after him, as Tyler backed down into the road. 'And call me if you have any problems!' She held up her hand to her ear to mime talking on a cellphone, in case he had already put in his iPod earplugs, and couldn't hear her.

Tyler turned left at the end of Fullerton Drive, and headed for University Parkway. He was listening to Rihanna singing 'Where Have You Been', and he was singing along with her, tunelessly, under his breath. As he came around the curve toward the parkway, he saw that it was unusually jammed with slow-moving traffic in both directions. He managed to edge his way in front of a people carrier filled with anxious-looking old women, but after that it took him almost ten minutes to cover the short distance to Ralph's, stopping and starting every few yards. Every now and then there would be a barrage of horn-blowing but that did nothing to make the traffic move forward any faster.

It was only when Ralph's came into view that Tyler could see what was causing the delay. Red-and-white barriers had been set up across the entrance to the supermarket parking lot, and at least half-a-dozen police officers were directing traffic to keep moving. He put down his passenger-side window as he came closer and called out to one of the cops standing by the side of the road. 'What's the problem, officer?' He could see his own reflection in the yellow lenses of the cop's sunglasses.

'Store's closed until further notice, son. Keep moving.'

'I'm only looking to buy some bottled water.'

'Sure, you and everybody else in San Berdoo. People started fighting over it, so they had to close.'

'Any idea where I can get some?'

'Even if I knew, son, I wouldn't tell you, but I don't, so I can't.'

Tyler closed the window again because uncomfortably warm air was starting to flow into the Hilux from outside. He had to stay on the parkway until the next exit, but then he turned off and headed for North E Street. It was a scruffy blue-collar neighborhood, but at the intersection with West 33rd Street there was a Thrifty gas station and a tattoo parlor and a small grocery store called Dan's Food & Liquor. Tyler's mother never shopped there, but Tyler regularly dropped by on the pretext of buying gum or sodas because Maria Alvarez often served behind the counter after school.

Maria was in Tyler's class at Arrowhead High and he was hopelessly in love with her. Tyler thought that she was amazingly beautiful, but he had never asked her out on a date. This was partly because he had never managed to summon up the nerve, and partly because she already had a boyfriend, Ken Rigsby, who played tight end on the Arrowhead football team. Ken Rigsby was highly possessive and aggressive and probably would have beaten up on him if he had taken Maria out. In fact he probably would have beaten up on him if he had known that he visited the store so frequently to talk to her.

When he pulled into the parking area in front of the store, however, Tyler saw that the folding security grilles had been closed, and there was a sign in the window saying SORRY CLOSED. The Thrifty gas station was closed up, too, and there were padlocks on all of the pumps.

He was about to back out of the parking area when he caught sight of Maria's father inside the store. He climbed out of the truck and went up and knocked on the window. Maria was inside the store, too, emptying out the cash register and counting out change.

Maria's father waved his hand dismissively and shook his head, but Maria came up and shouted through the window, 'Sorry, Tyler! We're closed! We had some trouble in here this morning! We're going to stay closed until the water comes back on!'

Tyler spread his arms wide and pulled an appealing homeless-puppy face. 'I just need a few bottles of water, that's all!'

Maria turned to her father, although Tyler couldn't hear what she was saying. He flapped his hand again, as if to say that no, he wasn't going to open up for anybody. Maria looked back through the grille at Tyler and shrugged and shook her head

'My sister's real sick!' Tyler shouted. 'I have to find some water for her!'

Maria turned to her father again. Tyler could tell that he wasn't very happy about it, but he came over to the front of the store with his keys and unlocked the front door. Then he reached through the grille and unlocked the padlocks that fastened that, too, and slid it back just enough for Tyler to be able to squeeze inside.

'Totally, thank you,' said Tyler. 'I went to Ralph's first but it was all closed off because they had customers fighting over water.'

Maria's father was a short, stocky man with a bald nut-brown head and a heavy gray moustache like a yardbroom. He was wearing a red polo shirt with Dan's Food & Liquor printed on it, in white, and a blue apron around his waist. Tyler saw that his left cheekbone was bruised crimson and his eye was beginning to close.

'I'm just doing you a favor here, son, because of Maria. We had some nasty business here this morning, kids trying to take water without paying for it, and other stuff, too. I chased them off with a baseball bat and then I called the cops but the cops said they was too busy, on account of the water being off.'

'I totally appreciate this, sir. I mean it.'

'Well, fill up a couple of baskets quick as you can. Maria – help your friend, will you?'

The store was very cramped, with narrow aisles, but its shelves were crowded with everything from cans of catfood to bug repellent to dried lima beans. Packets of nuts and beef jerky and dishwashing brushes hung down everywhere, so that it was like walking through a small and aromatic forest. Maria led Tyler to the refrigerated shelves at the back of the store.

'Be careful,' she said. 'The floor's still wet where they were fighting over the water.'

'I totally appreciate this, Maria.'

Maria handed him a wire basket and smiled at him. She was very petite, with black flicked-up hair like a TV star from the 1960s and a heart-shaped face with huge brown eyes. Tyler loved her little upturned nose and the way her lips pouted as if she were almost on the verge of crying, and he loved her wrists which were so thin he could have clasped his hands all the way around them. He had surreptitiously taken photographs of her in class with his cellphone, and he had six or seven of them stuck on to the back of his bedroom closet door. More than anything else he was intoxicated by the smell of her. She always seemed to smell of vanilla, and roses.

'Is you sister very sick?' she asked, as she stacked two-liter bottles of Arrowhead into one of the baskets.

'She has this really high temperature, that's all. We're not sure what it is.'

'Well, I hope she gets better soon. And I hope the water comes back on soon. It was so scary this morning. We had around ten of them in here, and they were taking bottles of water and candy bars and anything else they could lay their hands on and just running out without paying. When my dad tried to stop them they hit him with a mop-handle.'

'What – was it a gang?'

'Not one of the proper gangs – not like any of the Bloods or the Sun Crazie Ones or one of those. Just local kids. But they were really going wild.'

'I should've shot them,' her father put in. 'The trouble is, you do that, you shoot some punk, you get into trouble yourself, just for defending your own property.'

Once they had filled two baskets with bottles of water, Tyler hefted them up and carried them across to the counter. 'Thanks, Mr Alvarez. How much do I owe you?'

Maria's father was totting up the number of bottles when there was a deafening crash at the front of the store. They all looked up in shock to see three or four young men in hoodies kicking at the security grille. They kicked at it six or seven times before they suddenly woke up to the fact that although the grille was drawn all the way across the front of the store, Mr Alvarez had left the padlock unlatched after he had let Tyler inside.

With whoops and shouts, they started to shake and rattle and yank the grille open.

Mr Alvarez picked up the phone from behind the counter and handed it across to Maria. 'Call the cops,' he told her, tersely. 'Don't take no for an answer. Tell them if they don't come, somebody's going to get themselves shot. Tyler – take Maria into the back of the store. Take this.' He reached under the counter and handed Tyler a baseball bat with duct tape around the handle. Then he ducked down a second time and came up with a sawn-off shotgun.

Maria said, 'Papa – *don't!*'

But Mr Alvarez snapped, 'Get in the back, Maria, you hear me? This is my store – my property! Nobody breaks in here and takes what is mine!'

Tyler took hold of Maria's arm and said, 'Come on, Maria! Just dial nine-one-one! Your dad can handle this!'

'Papa!' said Maria, as the hoods wrenched the grille back far enough to open up the door. They came strutting into the store, whooping and whistling, pushing over displays of cookies and cakes and baby-food, and dragging their hands all the way along the shelves so that scores of cans clattered on to the floor.

'Papa, don't shoot them!'

But Mr Alvarez was already pointing his shotgun at the hoods, and flicking off the safety-catch with his thumb.

'You get out! All of you, get out now, or else!

'Oh, Papa, don't *shoot* them!' mimicked one of the hoods, in a falsetto voice.

'You hear me? I count to three, then I shoot!'

'Oh, *please*, Papa, please don't *shoot* them!' crowed the hoodie, and danced around in front of the counter with his arms spread wide, as if he were inviting Mr Alvarez to pull the trigger. At the same time, more hoods were crowding into the store from outside, at least another six of them. They swaggered down the aisles, pulling even more cans and jars and packages off the shelves so that the floor was littered with dented cans and broken glass and burst-open bags of flour and peanut butter and strawberry jelly. To add to the mess, they stamped on cereal boxes so that cornflakes and Cheerios were scattered everywhere.

'Water!' shouted one of the hoods. 'Get all of that freaking water, man!'

Crouching low behind a Coca-Cola display unit so that the hoods wouldn't see them, Tyler pushed Maria through the door at the back of the store and into the cramped little room which Mr Alvarez used as an office. They hunkered down on the floor next to Mr Alvarez's battered old desk. It was unbearably stuffy and hot in there and smelled of stale cigar-smoke. Maria handed Tyler the phone and said, 'Here, please, you call the cops, I can't breathe!'

Just as Tyler punched out 911, they heard a shattering *boom*! as Mr Alvarez's shotgun went off, but it was immediately followed by hoots and shouts of hilarity. Tyler could only guess that Mr Alvarez had either missed the hoodie he was aiming at, or else he had simply fired his gun into the ceiling to try and scare all the hoods away.

'Oh, God,' said Maria, pulling at the sleeve of Tyler's T-shirt.

'San Bernardino nine-one-one, what is your emergency?'

'All of these guys have broken into the store, they're wrecking the place. The owner has a shotgun and we just heard it go off!'

'What is your location, caller?'

Tyler was about to tell the emergency operator where they were when the shotgun went off again, with a different sound this time, more muffled, *boooomffffff*! as if it had been fired into a pillow. There were more triumphant whoops, and this time they heard one of the hoods scream out, 'Got him! Got the bastard! Fucking-A, man! Got the bastard!'

Maria stood up and called out, 'Papa!'

Tyler grabbed at her arm and tried to pull her back down again. 'Sshhh!' he told her. But she twisted herself free and went back out of the office door and into the store. Tyler heard the hoods whooping and whistling again, and then he heard Maria scream.

'Papa! Papa! Oh, God, you've killed him! You've killed him you monsters you've killed him *you've killed him*!' Her voice rose higher and higher in a hysterical scream until it sounded almost like a piercing whistle.

In response, the hoods started laughing and cat-calling and mocking her. 'You've killed him you monsters! You bad bad monsters! Look at my poor old daddy with his guts hanging out! No candy for you, you naughty monsters!'

'Hey!' jeered one of the hoods. 'Maybe we can learn her to *like* monsters!'

'Yeah, maybe we can give her a monster good time! *Monstaaaaahh*!'

'Come on, baby, how about it, pretty baby? Come on, baby your Papa can't help you now! What you crying for? Ain't no use in crying, is there? You know what they say . . . no good crying over spilt guts!'

There were more whoops and guffaws and Tyler heard Maria screaming, 'Get off me! Don't you touch me! Get off me, you monsters, let go of me!'

Tyler slowly stood up. His heart was beating so hard against his ribcage that it was painful, as if somebody were rhythmically and viciously punching him from the inside. He could hardly move. If these hoods had already killed Mr Alvarez, and simply laughed about it, why should they have the slightest compunction about killing *him*, too?

But he couldn't leave Maria at their mercy. What kind of person would he be if he let all these hoods attack her, and continued to hide? They knew that he was here, anyhow, because the first few hoods who had forced their way in had seen both of them. *Once they've finished with her, they'll probably come after me, because they don't want any witnesses.*

Oh dear God help me, he thought. Right at that moment he wished that his father were there beside him, because he knew that his father would beat the living hell out of these hoods. *But Dad isn't here. It's just me.* And then he heard Maria scream again, and a roar of approval from the hoods. He could guess what was happening and he felt sick to his stomach as well as frightened. *Please God, don't let me be the only one who can save her, because I know I can't save her and they'll probably shoot me, too.*

'*Tyler!*' screamed Maria. '*Tyler, help me! Tyler!*'

The hoods immediately took up the cry. '*Oh, Tyler!*' they shrieked, in a nightmarish chorus. '*Help me, Tyler! Come on Tyler you lily-livered chickenshit! Help me!*'

Tyler closed his eyes for a moment although he couldn't think of a prayer. Then he picked up the baseball bat that Maria's father had given him and stepped out of the office and into the main store, his sneakers crunching on broken glass and cereal.

The hoods were gathered around the front of the store, beside the counter. All that Tyler could see behind the counter was one upraised hand leaning against the wall and a feathery plume of blood that went almost up to the ceiling, spattering the face of the clock and a poster for Farmer John Bacon.

A green-and-blue plaid picnic blanket had been ripped out of its packaging and spread out on the floor, and Maria was lying spread-eagled in the middle of it. Four hoods were kneeling, one at each corner, gripping her wrists and her ankles. Some of them had now pulled back their hoods, and were openly leering at her, and Tyler could see them now for what they were. Not terrifying faceless demons, but ordinary pasty-faced teenagers with grade-one haircuts and wispy moustaches and splotches of bright red acne on their cheeks. Two or three of them he was sure he had seen before, at the Del Rosa bowling lanes.

One was much taller and bulkier than the rest, in a soiled gray hoodie. As Tyler cautiously made his way toward the front of the store, he was standing with his back to him, blocking the center aisle. But when as Tyler came closer Maria lifted up her head from the blanket and gasped out, '*Tyler!*' and it was then that the big, tall hoodie turned around and saw him.

He was Hispanic looking, with a broad flat nose speckled with blackheads and frog-like eyes, but even under his hood Tyler could see that his hair had been dyed a dark shade of ginger. Tyler approached him with his baseball bat raised.

'Hey now, bro, *you* must be Tyler! The knight in shining armor, come to rescue the damsel in distress! What you aiming to do with that bat, bro? How about I stick it up your ass? How about I stick it up your ass *sideways*?'

Tyler lunged forward but the hoodie immediately seized the bat and wrenched it out of Tyler's hand. He tossed it to one side, and then he reached out and snatched at Tyler's T-shirt and pulled him in so close that Tyler could feel his spit on his face when he spoke.

'You know what they call me? Big Puppet, that's what they call me. And you don't want to find out why.' Tyler could smell marijuana on his clothes and a strong, sour body odor.

Tyler twisted his head around and looked down at Maria and his heart thumped even harder. The hoods had pulled up her flowery cotton dress until it was bundled up under her neck, like a scarf. Then they had cut off her bra and tossed it to one side, and dragged her pink cotton panties down around her ankles. Her figure was boyish, tiny-breasted and narrow-hipped, with dark brown nipples like dates and a little black soul patch between her legs.

'You can't do this,' said Tyler, although his throat was constricted with fear.

'What do you mean, bro? We can do anything we like, and who going to stop us? Not her poppa. He dead. How about you? *You* going to try to stop us? I don't think you got it in you, bro!'

Big Puppet cackled in Tyler's ear, *hah-hah-hah-hah!* and then he shoved him away, so that Tyler stumbled and fell heavily against the shelving, bringing down a noisy cascade of aerosols and cans of polish and kitchen scouring pads. He managed to regain his balance, but as soon as he did so, his left sleeve was snatched by another hoodie, and yet another gripped his right shoulder, so that there was no chance of him getting away.

'Do you see what we have here, brothers?' Big Puppet called out, stretching out both of his arms as if he were a preacher. 'What we have here is a fine *piruja quinsenánera*, and she's going to be good to us, aren't you, baby? You going to be good to *all* of us!'

'Let go of her!' Tyler shouted at him, hoarsely. 'She never did anything to you! Let go of her!'

'You *so* right, bro,' said Big Puppet. 'She never did nothing to me. But here today, with the situation being what it is, we can put that right, can't we? Now she can do something to me. Like give me a little *mamada*.'

He stepped over all the cans and packages that littered the floor until he was standing right over her. She stared up at him, wide-eyed. '*Tyler*,' she whispered, but both of them knew that Tyler was powerless to help her. Big Puppet unfastened his belt-buckle and then popped open the fly buttons of his low-slung jeans. He scooped out his brown, half-erect penis and lasciviously rubbed himself, swaying his hips from side to side as he did so.

Tyler struggled and pulled and tried to tug himself free, but the two hoods were holding him too tight, and the one who was gripping his shoulder punched him hard in the side, right under the ribs, bruising his liver. He had never known anything hurt so much, ever, and his mouth was flooded with bile and half-digested cereal.

Big Puppet pulled his jeans halfway down his thighs, and then he sank to his knees next to Maria and held out his stiffened penis. She shut her eyes and closed her mouth tight and turned her face away, but one of the hoods who was holding her down took hold of her head and forced her to turn back toward him. Big Puppet grinned at her wolfishly and then he pressed the dark purple head of his penis right up against her lips. She stared up at him in fear and disgust and fury, and still kept her mouth resolutely closed, but he reached down and pinched her nostrils between finger and thumb.

'Let her go, you fucking *animals*!' Tyler shrilled at them, almost choking on his own sick. 'Let her go!' But the hoodie punched him in the liver again, and this time he doubled over in pain, with tiny white sparks floating in front of his eyes.

Maria held her breath for as long as she could, but her eyes were bulging and it was obvious that she couldn't keep her mouth closed any longer. She arched her back in desperation and tried to turn away, but the hoodie who was keeping her head still had his fingers dug deep into her scalp, and she couldn't move without tearing her own hair out. She opened her mouth and screamed for air, and as she did so Big Puppet forced the side of his left hand between her teeth.

He leaned forward and stared her directly in the eyes. 'You listen to me, baby. You going to be good to me and you ain't going to bite. You understand me? I feel your teeth in my *pirula* just once and I'm going to cut off your teentsy little tits and take them home and feed them to my pet piranha.'

There was a howl of laughter from the rest of the hoods but Big Puppet's expression was deadly serious. Tyler could see Maria staring back at him, and she didn't blink once.

'Just give me one nod for yes,' Big Puppet told her.

There was a long pause, and then Maria nodded. Big Puppet took his hand out of her mouth and patted her cheek and smiled. He turned around and grinned at all of his fellow hoods and held up both of his thumbs. 'In the war of man versus spitch, man won!'

He knelt over her, with his knees in her armpits. She closed her eyes and reluctantly parted her lips but then he gripped her jaw between finger and thumb and pulled it downward, opening her mouth wide.

'*Gaaaaaggh!*' she choked, as he lifted his hips and forced his penis as far down her throat as he could. She retched, and bucked up and down, but the four hoods who were holding her wrists and ankles kept her pinned to the blanket, and Big Puppet relentlessly thrust himself in and out of her mouth, grunting as he did so.

Tyler looked away, his chin still smothered with bile and bits of breakfast and his eyes so crowded with tears that he was almost blind. He had never felt so powerless, or so weak. The hoodie who was gripping his shoulder said, 'Hey, dude! You're missing all the action! Look at that baby *suck*, dude! It's like she's swallowing his whole fucking *pitote*! Hey! I got to get me some of this!'

With that, he released his grip on Tyler's shoulder and started to unbuckle his belt. He pulled down his jeans and stepped out of them, and then pulled down purple spotted shorts. He stripped off his hoodie so that he was wearing only a black T-shirt and sneakers, and then he dropped on to his knees on the blanket, in between Maria's thighs.

Big Puppet turned his head around and said, 'What the fuck you doing, K-Bomb?'

'Riding the bitch seat!' K-Bomb retorted, and the two of them whooped and high-fived each other.

The two hoods who were holding Maria's ankles levered her legs even wider apart, and K-Bomb pushed himself into her, his T-shirt riding up at the back, his narrow white buttocks jerking up and down like a dancing marionette. Tyler tried not to look, but if he turned his face away it was just as bad, because he could still hear Maria gagging and the hoods panting and 'oh-yessing!' and saying 'here it comes, baby! Ready for this, spitch?'

He didn't know how long it went on. It seemed like hours. All he knew for sure was that the shadows slowly moved across the floor, and that each one of the hoods took Maria in turn, and some of them twice. She lay on the blanket as if she were dead, her body jiggling from side to side only because one of the hoods was thrusting himself into her. They no longer had to hold her down, because she made no more attempts to struggle or turn away. She simply stared at the ceiling, her arms and her legs spread wide.

They no longer had to hold Tyler, either. He knelt between the shelves, his head lowered, numb with shock and overwhelmed with his own helplessness.

'That's it, bro, time we split,' said Big Puppet, at last. 'K-Bomb, you want to take all them bottles of water out to the truck? And all them smokes, and all them six-packs, and all those bottles of liquor. And grab some of them Hungry Man dinners, and some of them pizzas, but none of them fucking pineapple ones.'

He approached Tyler and stood over him, his fly buttons still undone. 'Pretty girl that, bro. She your girlfriend or something? You want to take better care of her, know what I mean? You wouldn't want eleven other guys fucking her, would you? I wouldn't let that happen to *my* girlfriend, no way.'

Tyler lifted his head and looked up at him. He would never have imagined it possible to hate another human being as much as this. He was trembling uncontrollably, right on the verge of jumping up and trying to tear the hoods to shreds with his bare hands. He knew, however, that he didn't stand a chance against them, and that they would almost certainly kill him, if they weren't going to kill him anyhow. He stayed where he was, kneeling on the floor, saying nothing.

Big Puppet turned away, but almost immediately he turned back again and pointed at Tyler and said, 'You know something? We ain't been fair to you, bro.'

Tyler didn't answer. Whatever Big Puppet was talking about, he didn't like the sound of it.

'No, we ain't been fair you at all! K-Bomb! Joker! Buzzy! We ain't been fair to this poor guy! We all been taking a piece of his girlfriend and never let him have none! Like disrespectful or what?'

Tyler opened and closed his mouth. His throat was so dry that he could barely speak. He swallowed twice, and then he managed to croak out, 'She's not my girlfriend.'

'That's not the point, bro! Like, she ain't *our* girlfriend neither! But there we all was, taking a piece of her like, and you didn't get nothing! That's just not respectful! We got to put that right, bro!'

'What – what do you mean?'

Big Puppet beckoned to K-Bomb and between them they took hold of Tyler's arms and heaved him up from the floor. He could barely stand, and his knees kept giving way, but they kept him on his feet while the hoodie called Buzzy came forward, grinning, and unfastened his belt. Tyler tried to collapse on to the floor, but Big Puppet and K-Bomb wouldn't let him drop. Buzzy levered off his sneakers, and then he dragged off his jeans and pulled down his white Calvin Kleins.

'Come on, bro!' Big Puppet urged him. 'It's your turn now!'

Big Puppet and K-Bomb manhandled him into a kneeling position between Maria's wide-apart thighs. He could see Maria staring at him dully, but all he could do was stare back at her. To his shame, his penis was sticking up erect. He couldn't imagine why, unless he had been aroused by fear and humiliation and embarrassment.

'Don't mind a little cream pie, do you, bro?' Big Puppet asked him. 'Come on, now, get in there, my man, have a little *chon chon*, enjoy yourself!'

Tyler tried to twist himself free, but K-Bomb wrestled him back down on his knees. Big Puppet said, 'Hey, *güey*, don't tell me you're refusing this fine young lady I'm handing you on a plate right here? If you're refusing her, maybe you think she ain't good enough for you, and if she ain't good enough for you, then maybe we should just dispose of her. Joker – go find that shotgun. I saw some shells there, too, right under the register.'

Joker went around the counter and came back with Mr Alvarez's sawn-off shotgun and a cardboard box with three or four pink shotgun cartridges in it. Big Puppet said, 'Load it,' and Joker ejected the two spent cartridges and pushed in two fresh ones.

'Now, take her out,' said Big Puppet.

Joker pointed the shotgun at Maria's head. Maria turned her head away and closed her eyes tight, but she didn't utter a sound.

'Look at her,' said Big Puppet. 'I think she even knows what a worthless spitch she is.'

'Stop it!' said Tyler. 'Please! Stop it! I'll do it!'

Big Puppet smiled at him and patted him on the head. 'Glad you saw the light, bro. Glad you saw the light!'

Tyler leaned over Maria and guided himself into her with his hand. After a few seconds, Maria opened her eyes again and looked up at him. He kept up a slow, persistent rhythm, trying to be as gentle as he could, but all he could see in her expression was a weary disappointment, as if she were saying *you too, Tyler?*

'Come on, bro, get your ass moving!' said Big Puppet. 'What's all this sloppity-slippety-slop? You supposed to be the knight in shining armor, riding to the rescue! How about you ride a little *harder* to the rescue?'

Tyler could feel himself shrinking inside her. He tried to keep going, but he simply fell out. Big Puppet said, 'What's happening, bro? Don't tell me you a *faggot* or something? Don't go for girls?'

Big Puppet stood up. He was clearly bored with this game now. He took the shotgun from Joker and pointed it directly at Tyler's face. He held it so close that Tyler could smell the burned cordite from the shot that had killed Maria's father. He started to cry. He couldn't help himself. He had wanted to be brave but it had been impossible. There were too many of them, eleven against one, and now they were going to kill him. He had never imagined that his life would end this way, kneeling on the floor in some neighborhood store, with his head blown off his shoulders,

'*Dad?*' he sobbed: but at that instant a police siren let out a high, weird whoop right outside the store, and Tyler saw red flashing lights shining against the window.

Immediately, there was a mad scramble for the door. Big Puppet threw down the shotgun so that it clattered and bounced across the floor and then he barged his way toward the door, too, pushing his fellow hoods out of his way. From the parking lot outside, Tyler heard a cop shouting out, 'Stop! Hold it right there! Stop! All of you!'

He reached over and picked up the shotgun. All he could think of was Big Puppet forcing himself into Maria's mouth, and taunting him while he did it, and making him feel completely emasculated. Now he had a chance to get his revenge for Maria, and Maria's father, and to show Big Puppet and all the rest of these punks that he was a man, and an angry man, too.

He pulled open the door and stepped outside. A silver Caprice was already squealing away from the parking-lot in a cloud of burned rubber. Big Puppet was about fifty feet away, running toward a red Toyota pick-up. Three other hoods were close behind him, but Tyler didn't care if he hit all of them. He raised the shotgun, but as he did so a cop yelled, 'Drop it, kid! Drop it! Drop it, or else I'll drop you!'

Tyler hesitated. His hesitation was long enough to allow Big Puppet to clamber into the pick-up, followed by the other three hoods. They roared off along West 33rd Street with the passenger door still swinging open.

Tyler was left alone, standing in the doorway of Dan's Food & Liquor.

Two cops came toward him, crouching slightly, both of them pointing guns at him. He raised his left hand as a sign that he was surrendering, and then he bent down and carefully laid the shotgun on the ground. He had some fragmentary memory of a movie in which a criminal had dropped his shotgun on to the sidewalk and it had gone off, prompting the cops immediately to shoot him.

'Assume the position!' shouted one of the cops. 'Face down, arms and legs spread!'

'Officer – I was only trying to stop those guys from getting away.'

'I said, assume the position!' the cop almost screamed at him.

Tyler lay down on the hot, gum-speckled sidewalk. One of the cops came up and picked up the shotgun, while the other gingerly pushed open the door with his shoulder and checked inside the store.

There was a moment's pause, and then he called out, 'Rick! We need back-up! Plus a bus and a meat-wagon! We got ourselves a dead guy in here, plus a two-six-one by the looks of it!'

'Don't you move,' said the cop who was standing over Tyler. 'Don't even fucking *breathe*, you got it?'

FIVE

When Martin walked around to the back of the Murillo house, he found the whole family sprawled out under the shade of their verandah.

The four younger Murillo children were lying in a tangle of arms and legs on two rusty recliners, looking hot and lethargic. Mina the youngest was three and the oldest Mikey was eleven. On the steps next to them sat their twenty-one-year-old half-sister Susan. She was wearing a sweat-stained yellow dress, unbuttoned at the front, and she was flapping herself with a folded-up newspaper.

Santos, their grandfather, was sitting in the far corner in monotonously creaking rocking chair, sucking at an unlit stogie. He was dressed only in a T-shirt and red-striped boxer shorts and a Panama hat.

'I rang the doorbell,' said Martin.

'We heard you, Wasicu,' said Santos, in his dry, cracked voice. 'We figured it was you, and if it was you, then you would know where to find us. If it wasn't you, then you would go away and leave us in peace. Today is too hot for answering doors.'

'Is your water off here, too?' asked Martin.

'Since this morning,' said Susan. 'I can't do the laundry. I can't wash the kids. All we have left to drink is half of a bottle of Dr Pepper. I went to the store for water and soda but the store is closed, and somebody had busted open the soda machine and stolen all the soda. I mean, like, what's happening, Martin? When are they going to turn the water back on?'

'I'm sorry, Susan, I don't have any idea. They've set up a special team of people to deal with the drought, and they've been shutting off the water by rotation. First one neighborhood, then the next.'

'You don't know for how long?'

'Forty-eight hours each neighborhood, that's what they told me. But I can't tell you for sure. It may not be as long as that.'

'Forty-eight hours?' Susan protested. 'We could all have died of thirst by then! What are we supposed to drink? How do we take a shower? The toilet is all blocked up already!'

'I don't understand it,' said Santos. 'San Bernardino is a city that was built on water. That is what brought us Yuhaviatam here in the first place.'

Martin sat down on the steps next to Susan and opened his folder of case notes. 'From what I've been told, even the groundwater wells are running dry, which gives you some idea of how bad it must be in other parts. Right now, though, there's nothing I can do about it, except ask you to try and be patient.'

'Patient? Why should we be patient? Whose water is it? It was our water long before you people came. Who discovered the Arrowhead Springs? Not the white people. It was us.'

'Yes, well, I know that. But I can't change history, Santos, even if it is unfair. Now, how are the kids coming along? Mikey – how are you doing at school now, feller?'

'Mikey's been barred from school,' said Susan, without pausing in her newspaper-flapping.

'Oh, come on, Mikey, not *again*!' said Martin. 'How long have they barred you this time?'

'This time they don't want him back, ever.'

'What did you do, Mikey?'

Mikey shrugged and looked away. He was thin and underweight for a boy of eleven, with long black greasy hair that almost reached down to his shoulders and three silver earrings in his left ear. He was bare-chested, but wearing a baggy pair of cargo pants that were two sizes too big for him.

'He started a fire in the gym,' said Susan. 'He didn't want to do no PE so he torched the changing rooms.'

'That wasn't very smart, Mikey,' Martin told him. 'Why didn't you just tell the teacher you had the mud thunder, or something like that?' He turned to Susan and said, 'I'll have to see if I can get another school to take him. I can't say that I'm all that hopeful, with his record.'

'School sucks, anyhow,' said Mikey. 'All the other kids kept calling me Tonto.'

'So what? You're a Native American, you should be proud of it. And Johnny Depp plays Tonto in the movie, and he's cool. Your people were here in San Bernardino long before theirs were. At least they can never accuse you of being an illegal.'

'It still sucks. Who needs to know about some stupid kid chopping down some stupid cherry tree and then being stupid enough to say that he did it?'

'Did you admit that it was you who torched the changing rooms?'

'I didn't have to. The janitor caught me doing it. But if he hadn't, I wouldn't. I'm not stupid like that cherry tree kid.'

'*Ha!*' said Santos. '*Ha!*' Martin didn't know if he was ashamed that Mikey was so ignorant, and so immoral; or if he agreed with him that the young George Washington should have had the nous to keep his mouth shut.

'Your mom home?' he asked Susan.

Susan jerked her head sideways to indicate that her mother was indoors.

'How is she?'

'How do you think? It's the middle of the afternoon.'

'OK if I go inside?'

Susan shrugged. 'Why not? She won't care.'

Martin pulled open the dilapidated screen door and went into the house. There was no air conditioning so it was insufferably hot and stuffy, and there was a strong smell of bad drains and cooking fat and stale urine.

He found Rita Murillo in the living room. The sagging orange drapes were drawn, so the room was gloomy. Above the fireplace there was a fifty-inch plasma TV. On the opposite wall hung a reproduction of an amateurish painting of a Serrano encampment in the mountains, its large communal lodges covered in snow.

Rita herself was lying on her side on the sagging white leatherette couch, her short brown dress rucked up around her waist, snoring. On the floor beside the couch lay three empty Coors cans and an empty UV vodka bottle.

Martin crossed the gray rag rug and stood beside her. He watched her sleeping for a while, and then he said, 'Rita?'

She didn't stir so he bent over and shook her fat, sweaty shoulder. 'Rita, are you awake?'

She snorted, and then she opened one eye and peered at him suspiciously.

'Are you awake?' he repeated.

'No. Can't you see I'm asleep. Go away.'

'I need to talk to you, Rita. It's about Mikey.'

'Mikey's a pain in the ass. Go away.'

'Rita . . . Mikey's been kicked out of school.'

'Well kick the little shit back in again.'

'I can't, Rita. They won't have him back. I need to talk to you because we may have to take him into care.'

'Good. Fine. Take him. He's a pain in the ass. Always has been, like his father.' She suddenly sat up. She picked up the vodka bottle and frowned at it, but when she realized it was empty she dropped it back on the floor. Then she shook each of the Coors cans in turn, and dropped them back on the floor, too. 'I need a drink,' she said. She had chaotic bleach-blonde hair that was thinning at the top and a squashed, puglike face that might have been qtuite pretty when she was younger and before she started drinking. She had no front teeth at all.

'There's nothing to drink, Rita. You've drunk it all, by the looks of it.'

She reached down into her cleavage and produced two ten-dollar bills, limp with perspiration. 'Here,' she said, waving them at him. 'Go to the store and buy me two bottles of vodka.'

'Store's closed, Rita. All the stores are closed.'

'I don't believe you.'

'We need to talk about Mikey, Rita.'

'I need a drink. For God's sake, Martin, I really need a drink. At least get me a glass of water.'

'I can't even do that, Rita. I'm sorry. The water's turned off. I think Susan has a little soda left.'

'I need a drink, Martin. Anything. I got me such a raging thirst.'

'Let me see what I can do.'

Martin went back out on to the verandah. Nathan, seven, was listlessly kicking a ball around the dusty back yard, but none of the others had moved. Three-year-old Mina's cheeks were flushed and her eyelids were drooping as if she had a fever; and George, who was five, was industriously picking his nose.

'Well?' asked Santos, still without removing his stogie.

'Well, nothing for now. She's too drunk to talk any sense about Mikey. I'll have to come back tomorrow morning, when she's sobered up. But I need to talk to the water department, and I need to talk to them urgent. There's people like Rita are going to die if they can't get water. And look at poor little Mina here. She's burning up.'

'You tell them it's our water, and they have no right to shut it off. Wasn't it bad enough they sent their militia here and shot us, in our hundreds, because they wanted our land? For thirty-two days they hunted us down and shot us. Now they want us to die of thirst?'

'Santos, I'm very sympathetic, but that was nearly a hundred and fifty years ago and I don't think the water department is deliberately targeting Native Americans. Everybody's having their water shut off, no matter what their ethnic origins.'

Santos waved his hand dismissively. 'That's what they say. So a few beaners die of thirst, too? What do they call that? Collateral damage. So long as they kill off the Yuhaviatam. Finish the job they started in eighteen sixty-six.'

As if to emphasize his point, they heard sporadic knocking sounds from the front of the house, and two or three young boys' voices raised in an ululating war cry.

'Those gang kids, tossing rocks again,' said Santos. He made no attempt to get up out of his rocking chair. 'Last week they took young Mina's doll pram and smashed it up. Ripped the head off her favorite doll. Week before they sprayed graffiti all over the front door.'

'What's their beef with Serranos?' asked Martin. Serranos was the Spanish name for Yuhaviatam, and the name the CFS staff usually used around the office.

'Who knows?' said Santos. 'I guess they don't like anybody who's not as dumb as they are.'

Martin heard three or four more knocking sounds as the boys continued throwing rocks, and then he heard a smash, as a front window was broken. Immediately, he stood up, dropped his folder on the verandah steps, and ran around the side of the house. Out on the sidewalk there were five Hispanic boys, about fifteen or sixteen years old, as well as two young girls in short sparkly shorts. Two of the boys were circling around and around on bicycles while the other three were collecting up lumps of concrete from the curb.

Martin said nothing, but stormed toward the nearest and the biggest of the boys, an overweight kid in a green T-shirt and Hawaiian-style shorts with palm trees on them. The boy lifted his right arm as if he were going to throw a rock at him, but Martin was advancing on him so fast and with such determination that he staggered backward and tripped over the curb, landing on his backside in the road.

'*Don't hit me!*' he screamed, but Martin grabbed hold of his arm and heaved him back on to his feet. Then he seized his podgy thigh, as well as his arm, lifting him clear off the ground. He swung him forward, and then back, and then threw him directly into the dried-up flannel-bush hedge that separated the Murillo's property from the house next door. The boy screamed again, and struggled his way out of the hedge, his arms and legs covered in criss-cross lacerations. The other boys immediately dropped their lumps of concrete and started to back away, and the two cyclists pedaled off as fast as they could.

The girls stayed where they were on the opposite side of the street, holding hands and nervously laughing, unsure of what to do, but then Martin began to walk briskly toward the other boys and they both shrieked and ran away.

'Look at me, you *mamon*!' protested the boy he had thrown into the hedge. 'I'm all over scratches! I'm going to call the cops on you, man! I'm going to have you arrested, man – assault and battery!'

'You just do that,' said Martin. 'But if I catch you or any of your sorry-ass friends around here again, tossing rocks, I'm going to be guilty of something much worse than throwing you into a hedge. In fact, you'll be *begging* me to throw you into a hedge.'

He stayed in front of the house with his arms folded while the boy limped away down the street. He didn't really know if he made a mistake, chasing the boys away like that. There was every likelihood that when he had left, they would return to harass the Murillos even more. But it simply wasn't in his nature to stand by while defenseless people were being attacked. He had suffered too much in that jail in Kabul to tolerate bullies.

He checked the front of the house. One of the lumps of concrete had left a large hole in the middle of the kitchen window and it would have to be temporarily patched up. Like Esmeralda, the Murillos probably had no possessions of any value, apart from their plasma TV, but in this neighborhood anybody would take anything if it wasn't nailed down.

He returned to the backyard, where the family looked at him with almost no interest at all. They were all too hot and thirsty to care about vandalism.

'So . . . what happened?' said Santos.

'I chased them away for you, Santos. But they've broken your kitchen window.'

'That's OK. I have a friend who mends windows. He won't charge us too much.'

Martin picked up his notes and checked his wristwatch. If he didn't leave now, he was going to be late for his next appointment.

'Did you ever think about relocating?' he asked.

'For sure. Many times. But how could we afford it? And where would we go? Mind you, if this drought goes on much longer, maybe we will have to. Maybe we will have to go back and live where the Yuhaviatam used to live, even before they found the Arrowhead Springs.'

'Oh, yes? And where was that?'

Santos sucked on his stogie and then took it out of his mouth and stared at it, as if it held the answer to everything.

'I shouldn't tell you this,' he said.

'OK, then don't. I don't want you letting any tribal cats out of the bag.'

'No,' said Santos. 'What you did for us today has proved that you are one of the people, one of the Wa'am. You do not have to be born one of the people to become one.'

'Forget it, Santos. I just did what anybody else would have done. Don't make me out to be some kind of hero, because that's the one thing I'm not.'

Santos continued as if he hadn't heard him. 'My grandfather told me this, and it was told to him by *his* grandfather, who was actually there, when he was a boy. When my people first came out of the Mojave Desert, seeking a new place to live, they found a sheltered valley in what we now call the Joshua Tree National Park. When they arrived there, they made camp. One of their girl children went missing, and her mother was wailing and crying. But the girl soon reappeared, and showed the people that she had discovered the entrance to a hidden cave. Inside the cave was a huge underground lake, of the purest water. They named it the Lost Girl Lake.'

'Never heard of it,' said Martin.

'Well, you wouldn't, because most of the Wa'am wanted to continue the journey west. Their shamans had told them that the Great Spirit had made them a sign, a giant arrowhead on the side of a mountain, which would point to the place where they were supposed to settle, and they weren't going to be satisfied until they had found it. But . . . a few of them decided to stay at Lost Girl Lake and start a small settlement there, including my great-great-grandfather. The valley was sheltered and there was plenty of game and seeds and prickly pears to eat and of course there was always fresh water. I don't know for sure if it's true, but my grandfather told me that there were some years when the Arrowhead Springs almost ran dry, but the Lost Girl Lake never did.'

'So what happened? There's no settlement there now, is there? Like I say, I never even heard of it.'

Santos sucked at his stogie and shook his head. 'They lived there maybe five or six years, difficult to say. Not too long, anyhow. But then a party of militia came across them, more by accident than anything. They raped the women and then they shot them all. Only my great-grandfather and another man called Broad Face managed to escape, because they were out hunting for deer when it happened. My grandfather and Broad Face left Lost Girl Lake and came to join the rest of their people here in San Bernardino. They never spoke of Lost Girl Lake again, not only because of their grief, but because they believed that they had been punished by the Great Spirit by not following his direction to settle at Arrowhead. But . . . the lake is still there, even though most of the Yuhaviatam have forgotten it, and no white man has ever found it.'

'Have *you* ever been there?' Martin asked him.

'Once,' said Santos. His dull gray eyes widened, and seemed to grow brighter. 'Before I died, I was going to tell my grandchildren where it is, but children these days . . . they are no longer dutiful, like they used to be. They don't care about the old ways. Not only that, I don't have too long.'

'What's wrong with you, Santos?'

'Prostate. Too late to do anything about it now. I got maybe a year if I'm lucky.'

'Hey, I'm sorry.'

'Don't be. If the Great Spirit thinks that it's time for me to go, there's nothing that I can do about it. I have been waiting for a long time to find a man I trust, so that I could share my secret. Somehow I think that today is the time, Wasicu, and that you are the man.'

'I'm flattered,' said Martin. 'I don't have to tell you that I won't be trumpeting this particular piece of information from the rooftops. It stays with me.'

Santos reached out and took hold of Martin's hand. His fingers were leathery and claw-like, with large silver rings on every one, and he clutched Martin so tightly that it hurt.

At that moment, Martin's cellphone played 'Mandolin Rain'. He carefully pried himself free from Santos' grip and said, 'Excuse me for just one moment, Santos.'

He could see that it was Peta calling him. 'Peta? What's up? Everything OK?'

She was crying so much that she could hardly speak. 'It's Tyler,' she told him.

SIX

'So, how's my favorite persuader?' asked Governor Smiley, coming up behind her and leaning over the back of the white leather couch with his usual predatory grin.

'Oh, Halford, you've arrived,' said Saskia, setting aside her laptop. 'I thought I heard a helicopter. Where's Mona? Didn't you bring Mona with you?'

'Mona's gone to one of her charity bashes. Don't ask me which one. Spoiled Trophy Wives For One-Eyed One-Legged Tibetan Orphans, something like that. Besides, why would I bring Mona with me when I'm meeting you?'

'For a threesome?'

Halford came around the end of the couch and sat down very close to her. He was a big man – over six feet three, with broad shoulders and a large rough-cast head. He had tight curly gray hair and an overhanging brow, underneath which his eyes glittered like the eyes of a wolf lurking in a cave. He was wearing a white suit with an orange shirt, and orange alligator shoes, with no socks.

He wasn't particularly handsome, but he had almost palpable charisma, which could make the backs of women's necks prickle, and forget what they were going to say next. One woman delegate from San Diego confessed that after Halford had sat next to her all evening during a fund-raising dinner, her gusset had been soaking. 'He gives off pheromones like some kind of funky animal.'

Saskia, however, had known him for a long time, and although she was still aware of how virile he was, she also knew what a self-serving, blustering, untrustworthy man he really was. He even had his own way to describe lying to his electorate: he called it 'telling the creative truth'.

Saskia herself was wearing a short Zuhair Murad dress in a slightly paler orange than Halford's shirt. Apart from being short it was very low cut and he stared into her cleavage and never raised his eyes once.

'Mona?' he said. 'Mona wouldn't go for a threesome. She's much too possessive. She believes in all this "to have and to hold, till death us do part" stuff.'

'You don't regret marrying her, do you, Halford?'

'I don't regret marrying her money. I just wish that she hadn't come along with it.'

Saskia smiled and shook her head. 'If it hadn't have been for Mona, you never would have made Governor, you know that. Everything you want in life has its price, and Mona was yours. Now, what are you going to say to the good people of San Bernardino about the drought situation?'

'Have you eaten?' asked Halford.

'Yes, I have. Tuna salad. I don't recommend it.'

'Then how about a drink? I could really use a drink.' He looked around the lounge and spotted a waiter in a yellow coat talking to one of the golf club members. Saskia didn't know how he caught the waiter's eye because he didn't even raise a finger, but the waiter immediately saw him looking toward him and excused himself to the man he was talking to. He came hurrying over and said, 'Yes, your honor, what can I get you?'

'Bring me a double Knob Creek on the rocks, would you, and this desirable lady will have a glass of Krug.'

'Well?' asked Saskia, when he had gone.

'What am I going to say to the good people of San Bernardino? I'm going to be straight with them.'

'That'll be a first.'

'Come on, Saskia, they're dumb but they're not stupid. They already know that we're suffering the worst nationwide drought since records began, so there's no point in trying to hide that from them, is there? What they *don't* know is that it's a hell of a lot more serious than we've been telling them, and it's not just the lack of rainfall that's to blame.'

Saskia raised one eyebrow. 'Don't tell me you're going to admit that we've been turning a blind eye to decades of chronic mismanagement and underinvestment in the water supply business, and right now the infrastructure is so darn rotten that our pipes are leaking more water than is actually reaching people's homes?'

'God, Saskia, you're such a goddamned lawyer. No, I'm not exactly going to put it like that.'

'Don't tell me you're going to warn them that the little water that *is* getting through is five times more polluted than it's ever been? Or that the water in at least nineteen cities in California is pretty much poisonous? Did you see the latest tests from the water department? Every glass of water you drink in California contains agricultural pesticides and toxic chemicals from factories and mines, not to mention untreated domestic sewage.'

'I'm not exactly going to say that, either.'

Saskia smiled. 'I didn't think you would, Halford, not for a moment. You'll tell them one of your creative truths, won't you? Just like the creative truth I've been telling the county departments about your wonderfully egalitarian scheme for rationing water neighborhood by neighborhood.'

'That's your job, Saskia. That's why I appointed you. Governing a state like California involves a whole lot more than looking after people's welfare. Now and then, God gets pissed with us, for one reason or another, and He shakes us up with an earthquake, or brings us a three-year dry spell, like He has now. When that happens, and it's simply beyond our capabilities to supply everybody with all the vital services they need, we have to keep people calm, and optimistic. We have to make it clear to them that we're doing everything we can, but most of all we have to make them understand that it's not our fault. I mean, whose fault was Hurricane Katrina?'

The waiter brought them their drinks, as well as a bowl of wasabi nuts and a selection of cheese straws. Halford immediately tipped out a handful of nuts and then clapped them into his mouth. 'Haven't eaten since breakfast, and that was only muesli. Mona's got me on this goddamned health regime. I mean, do *you* think I've put on weight?'

Saskia said, 'Nobody blamed the federal government or the New Orleans city administrators for Hurricane Katrina. What they *did* blame them for was the cack-handed way they handled it. The same is going to happen to you with this drought, unless you're careful.'

Halford swallowed whiskey and clapped some more nuts in his mouth. He crunched for a while, looking at Saskia and saying nothing. Eventually, though, he swallowed, and coughed, and said, 'Like I told you, sweet cheeks, I'm going to be straight with them. I'm going to tell them that we have no choice but to shut off the water supply, neighborhood by neighborhood, and people will undoubtedly suffer. But everybody in every city in the state will suffer equally. We're all in this together. I'm even going to shut off the water supply to my own home in Brentwood for forty-eight hours.'

'You're such a liar, Halford.'

Halford shrugged, as if even his predilection for lying wasn't really his fault. 'No, I'll do it. I'll really do it. Admittedly, I'll probably stay at the Hyatt Regency in Sacramento until it's turned back on again, but I often have to stay there anyhow, and I couldn't really govern the state of California without taking my daily shower, now could I? Don't want them calling me Governor Stinky.'

'Some people call you that already, Halford.'

Halford was about to snap back at her, but he had just helped himself to another mouthful of wasabi nuts and at the same time his cellphone rang, a loud old-fashioned telephone jangle.

'Smiley,' he coughed, spitting out bits of nut. He listened for a moment and then he closed his cellphone and said, 'He's arrived.'

'Who's arrived?'

'The man I asked you to come here to meet. His name's Joseph Wrack, and he's going to be working alongside of the drought team from here on in, or at least until it starts to rain again.'

'Excuse me? Joseph *Wrack*? "Wrack" as in "wrack and ruin"? I never heard of him. And what exactly do you mean by "working alongside" . . . ?'

Halford stood up. He picked up his cut-glass tumbler of whiskey, and Saskia's champagne flute, too. 'Come outside and meet him. He can explain it a whole lot more clearly than I can. In fact you'll have only to look at him and you'll know what I mean.'

He led the way out of the lounge and through the open door that led out on to the golf club verandah. Twenty or thirty golf club members were sitting under green striped parasols, talking and laughing and drinking and eating. Most of them sported bright-colored polo shirts and lurid checkered golfing pants. But it was the tall, gaunt man at the very far end of the verandah who imme-diately caught Saskia's attention. He had an iron-gray flat-top buzzcut, and he was wearing a black long-sleeved shirt and black pants and he was leaning over the railing, smoking a long thin cigar. As far as Saskia knew, there was a no-smoking rule out on the verandah, but it looked as if none of the waiters had summoned up the nerve to tell him to put it out.

'Is that him?' she asked.

'That's him,' said Halford.

'He looks pretty mean to me. Like a gunslinger out of one of those Spaghetti Westerns.'

Halford nodded. 'Yeah, you're right. That sums him up exactly.'

They walked across the verandah with several of the golfers

swiveling around in their chairs to stare at Governor Smiley and to admire Saskia's figure. The only person who didn't turn to look at them was Joseph Wrack, who continued to stare into the distance, blowing out occasional clouds of smoke, which hurried away from him like frightened ghosts.

'Joseph!' called Halford.

Joseph Wrack stood up straight. His face was Slavic, almost skull-like, with a high forehead and a sharply-chiseled chin. He had deep lines in both of his cheeks, and pursed-up lines around his mouth. In spite of that, his eyes were large and brown and liquid, which made Saskia feel as if he was much more sensitive than he appeared at first sight – more like a starving poet with an ax to grind than a gunslinger.

'Hallo, your honor,' he said, in a harsh voice that was little more than a whisper. He made no attempt to hold out his hand. He looked at Halford for a moment as if he were making a critical assessment of his white suit and his bright orange shirt, and thinking how the fuck can the Governor of California come out in public dressed like the owner of a second-rate Reno casino? But then he turned his attention to Saskia and she could immediately tell that he liked the look of her.

'You're Sasha, then?' he whispered.

'Saskia.'

'What kind of a name is that?'

'Czech, originally, although some people think it's Dutch. It means "protector of mankind".'

'That's appropriate.' He transferred his panatela to his left hand and held out his right. 'Great pleasure to make your acquaintance, Saskia. You're a beautiful woman.'

'And you're a very scary-looking man.'

Joseph almost managed to smile. 'I like to think so. It's part of my job description.'

'So what's the job, Joseph, and why do you have to look scary for it?'

Joseph pointed across the golf course, to the second green, where sprinklers were busily jetting water across the emerald-green grass. 'You see that?' he said. 'It's not going to be long, and that's going to need protection. Like, *physical* protection.'

'I'm surprised the sprinklers are even going at all,' said Saskia.

'Hey, that's bent and poa annua grass,' said Halford, as if he were surprised at her ignorance. 'Have to keep it well-watered.'

'What was that you said about "we're all in this together"?'
Saskia retorted. 'I know you're planning to allocate a more generous
water supply to some districts than you are to others. I wasn't born
just before breakfast. But to irrigate a golf course, Halford, when
you have hundreds of vulnerable people with nothing to drink and
no way of washing themselves or flushing their toilets . . .'

Halford gave another of his dismissive shrugs. 'Look around you,
Saskia. You see these guys sitting here, having their lunch? They
have money, they have influence. So far as they're concerned, they
keep the local economy going. Without them, the less advantaged
people in this county would have no jobs, no homes and no social
security. They wouldn't even have access to a faucet, let alone have
any water coming out of it. These guys having their lunch here
rightly feel that they deserve special treatment. They've worked
their rear ends off all of their lives and they've given more to the
community than anybody else, so they expect to get more back out
of it. You can't say that isn't fair.'

'What you really mean is, they've donated more to your campaign
funds than anybody else, and you owe them, big time.'

'Come on, Saskia. Stop being so cynical. These guys are wealth-
creators. They're philanthropists. They give millions to charity. If
they want to continue to play golf, then they shall. It's the least we
can do to show how much we appreciate everything they've done
for this community.'

'Halford – San Bernardino is officially bankrupt. It's the second
poorest city in the nation, after Detroit. What have these vultures
done for it?'

'I know how bad things are. You only have to look at the place
from the air. But without these guys, believe me, things would have
been a whole lot worse.'

'Maybe you're right,' said Saskia. 'But if the thirsty masses see
that thousands of gallons of precious water are being sprayed on to
a golf course, they might start getting a little restless about it, am
I right? And this is why you've called in Joseph?'

'It's pointless having an austerity program if you can't enforce
it,' said Halford. 'Just ask the President. Now, Joseph here is director
of public safety at Empire Security Services. You must know ESS
. . . they employ over two thousand four hundred security guards
and they handle everything from cash transportation to guard duties
to crowd control.'

'ESS – oh, yes, I know all about ESS.' said Saskia. 'Two of your security guards were accused of randomly shooting three innocent bystanders during that Chase Bank siege in Rialto last February. I know. I represented the bereaved family of one of them. "Trigger-happy to the point of psychotic," that's how the judge described your ESS men.'

Joseph hadn't taken his eyes off Saskia once. 'That bank siege really was a one-off, Saskia. I hope it doesn't mean that you and I can't work in harmony together.' His voice soft but abrasive, like somebody rubbing a pillow with glasspaper, and he made 'harmony' sound like some kind of devious conspiracy.

'I'm totally confident that you can mollify the masses, Saskia,' said Halford. 'But if things *do* start getting out of hand, you can call at any time on Joseph and his people to supply any extra protection that might be required. It's just a precaution, sweet cheeks. The thing of it is, the police have enough on their plate already, and a large number of officers live in neighborhoods where the water supply will be quite severely restricted, so I'm not one hundred percent confident that we can rely on their wholehearted support.'

'Well, you may be a liar, Halford, but you're a realist, I'll give you that.'

'This woman,' grinned Halford, shaking his head and giving Joseph an unwelcome nudge with his elbow. 'I love her. I do. I love her.'

They sat down at one of the tables and talked for another twenty minutes, then Halford lifted his wrist and peered at his weighty Rolex watch. 'Well, time I was gone, my friends. I have a meeting with some oil people before this pesky TV broadcast. Saskia, can I have a private word with you before I go?'

'Sure,' said Saskia. She stood up and Joseph stood up, too. He held out his hand again and said, 'An unexpected pleasure to meet you, Saskia. Till the next time.'

'Joseph?' said Halford. 'I'll see you later on, my friend. *Semper fi.*'

As they went back inside the golf club building, Saskia said, 'You weren't in the Marines, were you, Halford?'

'Are you serious? Of course not. But Joseph was. He was invalided out for some reason or another. Insanity, probably. No – only a joke! But I know for sure that he was at Abu Ghraib – that prison where the GIs were torturing Iraqi prisoners.'

They were halfway along the corridor that led to the reception area when he suddenly opened a door on the left-hand side and peered inside. 'Empty. Good. This'll do.'

Saskia looked inside, too. The room was windowless and airless and smelled of new carpet and leather. There was a long mahogany table in the center of it, with chairs all around. Halford held the door open wider and said, 'After you, sweet cheeks.' Once they were inside, he turned the key. 'Don't want anybody disturbing us, do we?'

'What do you want, Halford?' Saskia challenged him.

'Maybe I'd like some reward for being so tolerant. You're the only woman I ever allow to speak to me the way you do, and yet you have less of a right to do that than any other woman I know.'

'You're a pig, Halford. And the trouble is, you know you are, and you just don't care. In fact you wallow in it, don't you?'

Halford came up close to her and laid his hands on her shoulders, rhythmically squeezing them. 'You know how serious this is, Saskia. One way or another, a whole lot of people are going to die. The only question is, *which* people. Somebody has to make the decision and I was elected to make life-or-death decisions so that's what I'm doing. I can't stop people from dying. But it's my judgment that they're better off not knowing in advance. Otherwise, what's going to happen? Anarchy. And then even more people are going to die, the worthy as well as the worthless.'

With that, he turned her around, so that she had her back to him, and he pushed her forward until her thighs were pressed up against the edge of the table. She didn't resist him, but then she didn't make it easier for him, either.

'Supposing I tell the media what you're doing?' she said.

'You won't. Any more than you'll quit from my specialist drought team. You'll do what I want you to do because you can't face the alternative. Apart from that, you're the best at what you do, and you take pride in that, don't you? Forget the ethics, forget the morality. You're the queen of friendly persuasion.'

He was standing so close behind her now that she could feel his hardened penis through his pants. She started to twist herself away, but he clamped his left hand around the back of her neck and forced her face-down on to the table. Then, quite casually, he lifted her floaty orange dress at the back, right up to her waist, baring her buttocks.

'I was wrong to call you a pig, Halford,' she told him, with her cheekbone pressed against the surface of the table.

'Glad to hear it,' he replied. She could hear him tug open his zipper.

'Calling you a pig, that's an insult to pigs. I never knew a pig who blackmailed every other pig he knew, just to make sure that he always got his own way.'

'It's not blackmail, sweet cheeks. It's insurance.'

'Insurance?' said Saskia. He was parting the cheeks of her bottom with his thumb now. 'You just don't have the stones.'

'Oh . . . I have the stones, Saskia. You know that already.'

He tugged aside the thin white elastic of her thong and slid inside her, right up to the open zipper of his pants.

'I hate you, Halford,' she said, breathlessly, as he pushed himself into her again and again, more and more forcefully each time.

'That,' he gasped, 'that – is – *beside* – the – fucking – point.'

He rammed himself into her harder and harder, and started to grunt with every thrust. He was keeping Saskia's head pressed against the tabletop, which hurt. His penis was so big and hard she felt as if she were being forced wide open, and that he was burying himself inside her so deeply that its tip was almost nudging her heart.

Somebody rattled the door-handle, trying to get into the conference room. After a few rattles they knocked, and called out, 'Anybody in there?'

This doesn't deter Halford at all. He kept ramming and ramming and at last he suddenly said, 'Kiiiii-*mota!*' He took himself out of her and ejaculated all over the cheeks of her bottom and her dress.

She stayed bent over the table with her face against it for almost half a minute, despite the fact that Halford was no longer holding her down. Eventually she stood up straight, and adjusted her thong, and straightened her dress. Halford had already zippered himself up and was combing his hair.

'OK,' he said. 'We have my local TV broadcast this evening. That's at seven, isn't it?' He was breathing loudly through his nose, and there was perspiration on his upper lip, but apart from that he showed no indication that he had just been forcibly having sex with her.

Saskia didn't answer. Her teeth were clenched tightly together and she couldn't bring herself to open them.

'Who's next on *your* agenda?' he asked her.

He was just about to repeat the question when she said, 'Which son-of-a-bitch am I going to allow to rape me next? Is that what you mean?'

He smiled and tilted his head to one side and tried to lay a consoling hand on her shoulder but she jerked away from him.

'Come on, Saskia, you know what I mean. Which city department are you going to work your magic on next? You must have almost wrapped everything up here in San Bernardino, haven't you? When do you move on to Palm Springs?'

'Open the door,' she told him.

'Saskia . . . sweet cheeks.'

'Open the fucking door, Halford.'

'I just need to keep abreast of your progress, Saskia. That's all.'

'I'll text you,' she said.

He unlocked the door and opened it and she walked straight out without saying anything else to him. She left the golf club building and crossed the hot, glaring parking lot until she reached the silver Traverse that she had rented for her stay in San Bernardino. She climbed into the driver's seat and switched on the engine to start the air conditioning, but she didn't immediately drive away. She sat clutching the steering wheel, her mouth puckered, doing everything she could to stop herself from crying, while the wetness between her legs grew colder and colder.

SEVEN

When Martin arrived at San Bernardino police headquarters on North D Street, he found that the steps that led up to the front doors were crowded with hot and angry people, and that police officers were standing outside, preventing anybody from going inside.

'What do we want?' the crowd was chanting. 'Water!'

Martin managed to force his way up through the struggling throng until he reached the front doors. A young police officer with fiery red cheeks held up his hand and said, 'Headquarters is closed right now, sir. We're asking everybody please to leave peacefully. There's nothing the police department can do about the water supply.'

'I haven't come here about the water supply. My son's been arrested and charged with homicide. My wife tells me that he was brought here.'

'You'll have to show me some ID, sir. What's your son's name?'

Martin reached into his shirt and lifted out his CFS identity badge. 'Tyler, that's his name. And I have a lawyer coming in maybe twenty minutes, David Lemos.'

The young officer frowned at the ID badge for a moment, and then said, 'OK, sir. Follow me.'

He opened one of the doors and as he did so the crowd surged up the steps behind Martin, as if they, too, expected to be allowed inside. Two officers with nightsticks immediately moved across to hold them back.

'What do we want?' the crowd kept on chanting. 'Double-yah! Aye! Tee! Ee! Ar! – *water!*'

Martin stepped into the chilly air-conditioned reception area. Once the door had been closed behind him, and the noise of the crowd was muffled by bombproof glass, it was eerily quiet in here, with only the squeak of rubber-soled shoes on the polished marble floor, and the muted warbling of three or four unanswered telephones.

'That kid they brought in from Baker Division,' the young officer told the desk sergeant. 'This is his dad.'

The desk sergeant was bulky and bald, with eyebrows that joined in the middle and a large brown wart on the side of his nose. He looked across at Martin with deep suspicion, as if Martin had deliberately fathered Tyler with the express intention of giving him extra work to do.

'Makepeace? OK. So far as I know your son is still here.'

He picked up a phone and punched out a number. When he was answered, he cupped his hand over the receiver so that Martin couldn't clearly hear what he was saying. Eventually he paused, and sniffed, and said, 'OK.' Then he looked up at Martin and said, 'Won't be too long, sir. Take a seat.'

Martin waited for over fifteen minutes, sitting down at first on a very hard plywood chair, and then pacing up and down, and looking out through the windows at the restless crowd outside.

He noticed that there was a water cooler on the opposite side of the reception area, and that officers and other staff were frequently stopping by to help themselves.

He was still staring out of the window when he heard the squeaking of shoes behind him, and somebody coughed. He turned round to find himself facing an earnest-looking detective in a short-sleeved shirt and tan linen pants. He must have been only about thirty-six or thirty-seven, with a smooth oval face and a triangular nose like a sundial pointer. His dark brown hair was cut very short and parted on one side like a character from a 1960s TV comedy like *Bewitched.*

'Mr Makepeace?' he said. 'Corporal George Evander, sir. Detective, Northwest Division.'

Martin found it hard to keep his voice steady. 'My wife says that you've brought in my son for shooting some storekeeper.'

'That's correct, sir, yes. Your son was arrested in possession of a loaded firearm at Dan's Food and Liquor on West Thirty-third Street, and the body of the store's owner Emilio Alvarez was subsequently discovered behind the counter.'

Martin shook his head. 'You've made a mistake, detective. My son could never have shot anybody. It's just not possible.'

'I'm sorry, sir. He was in the company of numerous other young men, but he was the one who was holding the weapon.'

'What other young men? He's never gone around with a gang. He spends all of his time shut in his room playing video games.'

'We don't yet know the identity of his companions, sir. They all fled the crime scene when our officers arrived, and so far we haven't been able to trace them. Your son has given us a couple of gang names, but none of our patrol officers has heard of them, so it may be that he's simply invented them to protect his friends.'

'He's talked to you? Did you read him his rights?'

'He's over eighteen, sir. He's legally an adult, and of course we read him his rights. He said he was anxious to clear things up.'

'His attorney isn't even here yet.'

Corporal Evander shrugged. 'If a suspect volunteers to talk to me, sir, there's not a whole lot I can do about it.'

'Listen – I've told you. Tyler doesn't *have* any friends. Well, only the kids he hangs around with at school. He doesn't have any *street* friends, for Christ's sake.'

'Maybe he's never told you about them, sir. Parents always think they know everything about their kids, but you'd be surprised how often they don't know half of what they get up to. The point is, though, that he was caught holding what appears to have been the murder weapon, a double-barreled shotgun, which had been discharged twice and then reloaded. The storekeeper had been shot at point-blank range in the stomach, and probably died instantly.'

Martin said, 'I still don't believe he did it. Not Tyler. He doesn't have a single mean bone in his body.'

'Our investigation isn't complete yet, sir, not by a long way. Our forensic people are still examining the crime scene, and we'll be holding an autopsy, too. And of course your son will have every chance to defend himself in court. However, I've formally detained him on a charge of felony murder. As soon as we can we'll be booking him into the West Valley Detention Center in Rancho Cucamonga to await a preliminary hearing.'

'Wait a minute,' Martin interrupted him. 'Felony murder? Isn't that when you kill somebody while you're carrying out another crime?'

'That's correct, sir.' Corporal Evander ticked them off on his fingers. 'Murder while engaged in robbery, or kidnapping, or rape, or sodomy, or sex with a juvenile, or oral copulation, or burglary, or arson, or train wrecking or carjacking.'

Martin stared at him in disbelief. 'So which one was it?'

'Which *two*, sir, as a matter of fact. Robbery, and rape.'

'*Rape*? Who the hell is he supposed to have raped?'

Corporal Evander took a notebook out of his shirt pocket and flipped it open. He frowned at it for a moment and then said, 'Maria Alvarez, sir. The store owner's daughter, seventeen years old. She was sexually assaulted numerous times, possibly by all of the suspects involved, including your son. She's in the hospital right now, but so far she's been too traumatized to tell us anything.'

Martin had to sit down. 'I just can't get my head around this, detective. Tyler – shooting a storekeeper and raping his daughter? That is so totally out of character. I know he *liked* the girl, for Christ's sake. He told me about her a couple of times, but he always said that he didn't have the nerve to ask her out.'

Corporal Evander didn't answer that, but Martin glanced up at him again and he could guess what was going through his mind. He probably thought that while Tyler and his companions were robbing the store, he had seen his chance with Maria, and taken it. Martin had seen young enlisted men forcing themselves on village girls in Afghanistan, even though they were probably as shy as Tyler when it came to dating the girls back home. But he couldn't believe that Tyler would have done such a thing to Maria. Apart from anything else, he wasn't stupid, and he would have known what the consequences were. Not just the legal consequences, but the consequences if Martin found out about it.

'You can see him now if you want to,' said Corporal Evander. 'We won't be taking him to West Valley for a while. We're having some delays with transportation.'

'My lawyer will be here soon,' Martin told him. 'You'll make sure that he gets in here OK, won't you?'

At that moment, they heard shouting in the street outside, and a brick or a lump of concrete was thrown against the doors.

'Getting a little hairy out there,' said Corporal Evander. 'Let's hope we get some rain before we have a full-scale riot on our hands.'

The chanting grew louder and louder, and when he stood up Martin could see that the crowd in the street had swelled by at least another hundred protestors since he had arrived here. The police officers were now standing with their backs pressed against the doors, and there was a sharp rattling sound as they were showered with coins and bottles and pebbles and fragments of broken brick.

'What do we want? *Water!* What do we want? *Water!* What do we want? *Water!*'

* * *

Corporal Evander led Martin along a shiny gray-painted corridor to the holding cells at the rear of the building. A black female officer was standing guard at the end of the corridor, and when they approached she lifted the bunch of keys on her belt and walked toward them, rhythmically shaking her keys like maracas.

There were only two prisoners there. One was Tyler, wearing orange detention-center coveralls, and the other was a middle-aged man with wildly messed-up hair, two black eyes and only one shoe. Tyler was sitting on his bed looking pale and frightened. As soon as he saw Martin coming he stood up and came toward the bars.

'Dad!'

The guard unlocked his door and allowed Martin to step inside. Corporal Evander said, 'I'll let you two have some time together, OK? As soon as your lawyer shows up, I'll bring him through.'

'Thanks,' said Martin, although he wasn't feeling very thankful for anything.

The guard locked the door behind him and he opened out his arms and hugged Tyler tight. Tyler burst into tears and he was quaking as if he had a fever.

'Dad, I didn't do it! It wasn't me! I swear to God, Dad, it wasn't me!'

Martin held him close for over a minute, without saying anything. Eventually Tyler stopped sobbing and took a step back and pulled up his T-shirt to wipe his eyes.

'It wasn't me, Dad,' he repeated. 'I wasn't me, I swear it. I only went to the store to buy some bottled water like Mom told me to. I was in back when they shot Mr Alvarez, I didn't even see them do it. There was this one guy who was like in charge of them all and he said his name was Big Puppet. I think it was probably him who did it because he was going to shoot me, too. One of the others was called K-Bomb and another one was called Buzzy.'

'Who were they, these guys? They weren't friends of yours, were they?'

Tyler said, 'No – *no!*' He was so desperate that he sounded like a small boy again. 'I didn't know any of them! I think I recognized one or two of them from the Del Rosa bowling lanes, when me and Sandy went there, but I don't know their names or where they come from.'

'And what about Maria? They've charged you with raping her.'

'He *made* me, Dad. Big Puppet forced me do it. He said that if

I didn't he was going to shoot her, too. I *had* to – or he would have killed her.'

Haltingly, he told Martin what Big Puppet and his gang had done to Maria. When he had finished, Martin said, 'Damn it. I mean, damn it! If only I hadn't told your mom to stock up on water, this never would have happened.'

'Dad, you couldn't have known. I wanted to stop them, but I couldn't. There were too many of them. And if the cops hadn't showed up when they did, I think they would have shot Maria and me, too.'

Martin put his arm around Tyler's shoulders and gave him a reassuring squeeze. Just then, Corporal Evander came along the corridor, accompanied by Martin's lawyer, David Lemos.

David Lemos was rotund and round-shouldered, with a shiny gray comb-over and wobbly cheeks and dark rings under his eyes. He was wearing a double-breasted suit in pale-green linen that flapped as he walked.

The guard unlocked the cell for him and he stepped inside and shook Martin's hand. Then he turned to Tyler and said, 'So – you're Tyler.'

'Yes, sir,' said Tyler.

'I won't beat around any bushes, Tyler. You are in very deep shit.'

Martin spent an hour with Tyler and David Lemos, going over every detail of what had happened in Dan's Food & Liquor again and again.

David Lemos made Tyler give him exact descriptions of as many of the gang members as he could – what they said, what they were wearing, what kind of vehicles they used to make their getaway. He recorded it all on his iPad, but when he had finished he said, 'Keep on thinking about it, Tyler. I know how disturbing it is, to go over it again and again. But each time you recreate it in your mind's eye, you'll think of something that you thought you'd forgotten, and that may be the one clue that saves your life.' He paused, and then he said, 'You *do* realize that felony murder potentially carries the death penalty, don't you, or a minimum of twenty-five years in jail?'

Martin took hold of Tyler's hand and gripped it tight. 'Don't you worry, Tyler. It won't come to that. I'll find this Big Puppet character, I swear to you, and the rest of those animals, and I'll make damn sure that they pay for what they did.'

Tyler, teary-eyed, gave him a nod; although he didn't look convinced.

* * *

He almost had to fight his way out of the police headquarters because the crowd had grown so large and so angry. He guessed that there were at least four hundred people gathered here in North D Street, most of them blue-collar or poor by the look of them. Some of them were now waving improvised cardboard signs that said WATER! and WE'RE THIRSTY! and U R KILING US!

The street was blocked now and Martin could see more vehicles arriving in the parking lot opposite. Obviously the protesters had called for more people to join them.

As he crossed the street back to his own car, he saw that the police officers who had been standing at the top of the steps were now disappearing inside the front doors. They were being replaced almost immediately by fresh officers in full black riot gear, carrying plastic shields. The crowd roared their disapproval, and started to throw an even more furious blizzard of coins and rocks. A group of them started to use car jack handles to break away the red-painted curbstones that had EXCEPT FOR POLICE VEHICLES stenciled on them.

Only a half mile further south on North D Street, Martin heard another roar, almost as loud. An even larger crowd was gathered outside the Civic Plaza, where the Water Department building was located. He could see bricks and debris flying in the air there, too, and a billow of black smoke. It looked as if a white panel van had been set on fire.

He climbed into his Eldorado and pulled out of the parking lot with his tires squittering on the molten tarmac. He headed west on 4th Street to Carousel Mall, back to the office. The streets downtown were unusually deserted, with hardly any traffic and only a few people on the sidewalks, and most of those seemed to be hurrying in the direction of D Street. He could almost have believed that a UFO had landed, and abducted everybody except a last few stragglers.

When he had parked in the basement and gone up in the elevator, he found that the office, too, was oddly quiet. There was no Brenda behind the reception desk, scowling at him; and when he knocked on Arlene Kaiser's door and opened it, there was no sign of Arlene, either. A cold cup of coffee stood on her aircraft-carrier desk, next to a half-eaten donut.

In the large open-plan office at the back, he found Shirelle Jackson, sitting at her desk and squinting at her laptop as if she were trying to decipher a message in Egyptian hieroglyphs. Shirelle was skinny and black with upswept spectacles and beaded dreadlocks and teeth like a horse.

The only other person in the office was Kevin Maynard, a plump and officious CFS employee who was always ready to take children away from their dysfunctional parents, no matter how much their children loved them. He was talking on the phone in a nasal, repetitive tone to somebody who obviously didn't agree with him.

'Yes, you can, Vera. You can. I promise you, you can.'

'Shirelle, hi, where is everybody?' Martin asked her.

Shirelle blinked at him as if she didn't recognize him, and then she flapped her hands as if she were drying her nail polish. 'Oh – *Martin* – it's all gone *crazy*! We've had so many emergency calls! Everybody's had to go out! Well, except for me! It's like Armageddon out there! You've had a whole bunch of messages, too! I did try to contact you, I promise!'

Martin took his cellphone out of his pocket. He had been requested to switch it off while he was at police headquarters and afterward he had deliberately kept it switched off, because he knew that he would have to field countless calls from anxious and beleaguered families.

Shirelle flicked through her notepad. 'Here – this one came from Tanisha Belling – she's that woman on North Lugo with seven kids in one bedroom, isn't she? She says they have no water and she's run out of diapers and she can't cook the kids anything to eat. Not that she ever did. But now her microwave's busted, too, because her little boy tried to broil his Batmobile.'

'And – here – Madeleine Kusnick called you. She doesn't have water, either, and her two cats look like they're in a coma because of the heat and because of *that* her two kids won't stop howling. She's worried they're going to be permanently traumatized. The kids, I mean, not the cats.'

'Oh – and somebody called Jesus left a message? He said he wouldn't forget today, ever, so don't go thinking that he ever would. Do you know what he meant by that?'

'Yes,' said Martin. 'I know exactly what he meant.'

EIGHT

He didn't return any of his calls. He had something more important to do first. He went to the office kitchen, opened up the storeroom, and lifted out two five-gallon containers of water. He grunted with effort, because they weighed over forty pounds each.

He knew that it was wrong for him to take them. But he left three containers where they were, and he reckoned fifteen gallons would be enough water to keep the CFS office in coffee for a day or two, if their supply was shut off, and even to wash their hands now and again. Before Shirelle or Kevin could come out and discover what he was doing, he lugged the containers out through reception, out through the front doors and down in the elevator to the basement. He stowed them in the trunk of his car, looking around to make sure that nobody was watching him, and that he was obscured by one of the concrete pillars from the CCTV.

He drove north out of the city center to Fullerton Drive, and again he was aware how empty the streets were. Even after he had joined the freeway, he passed only three or four semis, a clapped-out Winnebago, and a small V-shaped formation of Hell's Angels, who looked more glum than menacing. Around Lionel E. Hudson Park the neighborhood was deserted. No children were playing on the slides or the swings. The trees were turning yellow already and the grass was scattered with fallen leaves. He slowed down and all he could hear was a distant airplane. It was almost eerily peaceful. When he pulled up outside Peta's house, however, and looked back toward the downtown area, he saw more black smoke rising into the hazy late-afternoon sky.

He came up the driveway with a five-gallon water container swinging from each hand. As he did so Peta opened the front door and said, 'Thank God.'

She was wearing a pink strapless top and white shorts. She was small and skinny, but very pretty in a Scandinavian way, with denim-blue eyes and little ski-jump nose with freckles across it. Every time Martin saw her he wished that they could get back together again, or try to, at least; but he still wasn't sure that he had exorcized his djinns, and that he wouldn't end up hurting her. It wasn't that Peta didn't trust him. He didn't trust himself.

'Water, thank God,' she repeated, as he stepped inside the house. 'Ella's no better at all.'

'Did you call Doctor Lucas?'

'The line's always busy and I can't get through. I tried the medical center's website but that seems to be frozen. You press to make an appointment but nothing happens.'

Martin carried the water containers into the kitchen and lifted them on to the table. 'OK if I go in and see her?'

'Of course, yes. Did you see Tyler? Is he all right? What's happening? They said they were going to send him to the West Valley Detention Center. I mean, who is he supposed to have killed?'

Martin walked down the corridor to the door of Ella's bedroom. Before he opened it, he said, quietly, 'Tyler is charged with shooting Mr Alvarez at Dan's Food and Liquor while he was robbing his store. He's also charged with raping his daughter Maria.'

Peta pressed her hand against her mouth in shock. Then, 'He *raped* Maria Alvarez?' she said. 'He *raped* her? The police told me that they were charging him with killing a man but I thought it was maybe some kind of an accident. But Tyler wouldn't *rape* anybody!'

'He says he was forced to. He says a gang broke into the store and shot Mr Alvarez and then they all took it in turns to rape Maria and they forced him to do it, too, otherwise they threatened to shoot her, too.'

'Oh my God. Oh, Martin.'

Martin put his arms around her and held her close. 'Listen,' he said, 'Tyler swears that he didn't shoot Mr Alvarez and my lawyer thinks he can get him off of that charge. The CSIs tested his hands for gunpowder residue and if he didn't fire it then they'll be able to tell for sure. As for rape, he only did it because he feared for Maria's life and his own life, too. Maria's not talking yet, but when she does, you'll see, he'll get off that, too.'

Peta shook her head. 'It's still like a nightmare. I just can't believe that it's true.'

Martin gave her another hug, and then he pointed his finger at Ella's door and said, 'OK to go in?'

'Sure. Of course. I'll bring her a drink of water.'

He tapped lightly on the door but when there was no answer he opened it and went inside. The cream cotton blinds were pulled right down but even so the bedroom was still glowing with sunlight. Martin saw Ella's reflection first in her dressing-table mirror, so that she looked like a framed picture of herself. Her eyes were closed and she was lying in bed propped up on pillows, covered by only a single sheet. Her cheeks were flushed, and her long mousy-brown hair was bedraggled and damp. She looked so much like her mother had looked when he had first met her that it was hard for him to believe that she didn't remember all the things that he and Peta had done together: walking in the mountains, dancing and playing pool in the downtown nightclubs, or simply sitting together by the pool, staring at each other, and each one of them thinking how lucky they were.

Martin sat down on the chair next to Ella's bed and took hold of her hand. It was chilly and moist, even though she looked so hot. He leaned over and kissed her forehead and said, gently, 'Hallo, baby. It's your Daddy.'

Ella opened her eyes and blinked at him, and then she smiled. 'Daddy. You came.'

'I brought some water for you. Here – Mommy has it now.'

Peta came in with a large glass of water and sat down on the bed to help Ella drink it. Martin propped her head up while she gulped it down. Occasionally she stopped and gasped for breath, but she managed to finish all of it.

'Could I have some more?' she asked.

Martin lowered her head back on the pillow and grinned at her. 'What are you, a camel?'

'I'm just so thirsty, Daddy. I feel like my throat is full of dust.'

Peta gave Ella some more water to drink and plumped up her pillows and then she and Martin went back into the kitchen.

'I really think we need to get her to a doctor,' said Peta. 'She doesn't have a rash, and she's not vomiting or anything, but then all she's eaten all day is a piece of dry toast and half a cup of chicken soup.'

'Maybe you should try calling the medical center again.'

'I can try,' said Peta. She took the phone off the wall and punched out the number but before she even handed it to him, Martin could hear the busy signal.

'I'll drive down there myself,' he said. 'If they're really so busy I don't want to take Ella with me. Maybe I can persuade one of the doctors to make a house call.'

He went to the door. Peta caught his sleeve and said, 'What about Tyler? He must be so frightened!'

'We have a good lawyer for him, sweetheart, that's all we can do for now. The detective who's in charge of his case promised to call me when they're ready to send him over to Rancho Cucamonga.'

He turned to go but she still kept hold of his sleeve.

'Martin—' she said.

He waited, but she simply said, 'Nothing. But call me, won't you, when you've found out what's happening at the medical center?'

Highland Medical Center was ten minutes' drive south-east, through quiet, wide, well-kept streets, and each street that Martin passed was even more affluent than the street before, with larger houses and more expensive vehicles parked in their driveways.

Like everywhere else, though, the streets were empty, and he drove for over five minutes before he passed another car, a Lincoln Town Car, heading in the opposite direction. The driver had dyed black hair and a papery, sun-mottled face, and as he passed he stared at Martin with undisguised suspicion.

Only a few streets further on, however, he took a right turn toward the medical center, and he saw a pot-bellied man in a baseball cap and khaki shorts, watering the plants on either side of his driveway with a hosepipe.

He pulled in to the side of the road and called out, 'So – you have your water back on? When did that happen?'

'Never been off,' the man told him. 'I saw on the news they cut it off in some neighborhoods, but not here, not so far. Not too sure they'd dare. Too many council members live around here!'

'Yeah, maybe you're right,' said Martin, watching the man fill his terracotta plant pots until they were flooded, and thinking of the Murillo children, listlessly sprawled out on their verandah, with only a half bottle of Dr Pepper left to drink, and that was probably long gone by now.

He drove on. He was only three streets away from the medical center, however, when he saw a battered black Dodge Ram parked at a diagonal across the road in front of him, and an old silver Caprice pulled up on the sidewalk. Both the car and the SUV had their doors wide open, and five or six young Hispanic men in sleeveless black T-shirts were milling around them. As Martin came closer, he saw that there were at least three more young men in the front yard of one of the houses, and he heard angry shouting, and then a woman screaming, too.

He pulled into the curb. Now he could see what was happening. The young men were filling up a variety of plastic bottles and large plastic containers with water from the outdoor faucet at the side of the house. Two of the young men had the house owner pinned up against the wall of the house. He was a big man, with curly gray hair and a jazzy red Hawaiian shirt, but although he was big he had the blueish lips of an angina sufferer, and in spite of his obvious anger he was staying silent, and making no effort to break free. His wife, however, was standing next to him in her housecoat and hairnet, almost bent double, screaming at the young men to let him go.

I don't believe this, thought Martin. *These punks are actually stealing water. More than likely they're aiming to take it back downtown and sell it.* For a split second, he thought: *why not let them?*

But then the woman furiously started pummeling one of the young men with her fists. 'Let my husband go, you punks! You let my husband go!'

Another member of the gang shoved her in the small of the back, so that she tumbled face-first on to the wet brickwork drive, hitting her head. She tried to climb back on to her feet, but then he kicked her with his shin, so that she toppled sideways on to the dried-up lawn.

Martin climbed out of his car and walked up toward them. 'Hey,' he said.

The gang all stared at him. One of them was wearing mirror sunglasses and at least six gold chains around his neck, and by the challenging way he looked back at him, Martin guessed that he was their leader. He said, 'What?'

'I'll tell you what,' Martin told him, glancing back down the street as if he were expecting reinforcements to arrive at any second. 'You just assaulted this lady, which counts as battery, and you're holding this gentleman against his will, which at the very least is false imprisonment, and at the same time you're trespassing on private property, not to mention taking water which you haven't paid for.'

The gang member in the mirror sunglasses looked around at his four companions, and then said, 'Are you a cop?'

'No, I'm not. But I'm a council official, and I know the law.'

'Are you carrying?'

'No, I'm not.'

The gang member frowned, as if he were thinking seriously about this. Then he said, 'You're not a cop. You're not carrying. In that case, fuck you.'

Martin came further up the drive and helped the woman back on to her feet. She had a large crimson lump on her forehead and she was obviously concussed, because she nearly fell over again. Martin led her over to the front steps of the house and sat her down. 'Just stay there for a moment, ma'am. OK?'

The husband meanwhile stared at Martin with bulging eyes but he was clearly too frightened to say anything. It was only when Martin turned back to face the gang members that he saw that one of the young men who was pressing him up against the wall was holding a shiny double-edged knife up to his chest.

Always go for the guy with the weapon first. He expected that all of the gang members were carrying knives, but this one had a blade that was out and ready, and probably wouldn't think twice about using it.

Without warning, he kicked the gang member in the mirror sunglasses very hard between the legs. When the young man soundlessly bent forward, his mouth wide open, his sunglasses flying off his face, Martin heaved him over backward, so that he staggered into the arms of his friends. Then, with no hesitation at all, Martin stalked up to the gang member who was holding the knife, seized his hand and bent his wrist backward so forcefully that he could hear his tendons crackle. The young man screamed in a piercing falsetto and dropped the knife on to the brickwork. Martin kicked the knife underneath the gate at the side of the house and then seized the young man's ears, which were both pierced with six or seven earrings each. He twisted both of the young man's ears around in opposite directions, first one way and then the other, ripping at least half of his earrings out. The young man dropped to his knees on to the driveway, stunned, and with his ear-lobes in bloody rags.

Martin had taken out their leader; and the one with the knife. Now he turned around and faced the rest of them. He saw one of them pulling up his T-shirt at the front, as if he might be going for a weapon that was tucked into his belt. Martin couldn't actually see a pistol-grip, but he shouldered two of the other gang members out of his way, and went for him. He grabbed his wrist with his left hand and punched him hard in the mouth with his right. There was a deafening bang, and the legs of the young man's jeans were suddenly flooded with blood.

The young man stared down at himself, and spat out two teeth. Smoke was rising out of his waistband. He looked back up at Martin and his face was white with shock, all except for his burst-open lips, which made him look as if he were holding a blossoming red rose in his mouth.

'You fucking shot me, man,' he bubbled. But then he pitched over backward and lay on the driveway with his eyes rolled up into his head and his legs twitching.

Martin bent over him and wrestled the gun out from under his belt. It was a Sig-Sauer compact 9 mm automatic with frayed duct tape wound around the grip. He held it up and said to the rest of the gang, 'One of you give me a knife. I have to see how bad this wound is. Come on, right now! Give me a knife! And handle first, OK, if it's all the same to you.'

A skinny gang member with a wispy black moustache took a clasp knife out of his jeans and held it out to him. Martin took the knife, opened it up, and then knelt down beside the young man lying on the driveway and cut open the left leg of his jeans, all the way up past his knee. His thigh was smothered in blood, but Martin could see by the puckered wound just above his kneecap that the bullet had missed his femoral artery.

He folded up the clasp knife and dropped it into his pocket. Then he said, 'Time for you morons to hit the bricks now, wouldn't you say? You'd better take your buddy down to the ER, and quick.'

Three of the gang lifted up their wounded friend and carried him over to the Chevrolet. The gang member who had been wielding the knife shuffled past Martin nursing his swollen wrist. He gave Martin a glare of venomous hatred, but he didn't say anything. Last of all, with his hand still cupped between his legs, the leader of the gang picked up his mirror sunglasses and put them back on, even though one of the lenses had dropped out, and Martin could see his left eye. They climbed into their vehicles and roared away in clouds of burned rubber, leaving tire tracks all the way along the street.

The homeowner had been leaning over to comfort his wife, but now he came up to Martin and said, 'I don't know how I can thank you, sir. You took one hell of a risk there. One hell of a risk.'

'What happened?' Martin asked him. He looked up and down

the street and he could see that the man's neighbors were beginning to emerge from their houses. 'Why did they pick on you?'

The man shrugged and shook his head until his jowls wobbled. 'They came driving past and I guess they just saw me watering my plants and they decided that I was an easy mark. They stopped and asked me if they could fill up all of their containers but I said no way.'

'Why not? It's only water.'

The man stared at Martin as if he had spoken in a foreign language. 'Well, sure, but it's not just any water. It's *my* water. I pay for it. Why should I give it to some gang of hoodlums? Those people, they never pay for anything. They're all on welfare and who pays for that? I do, out of my taxes. I don't have any choice in that, but today I had a choice and I said no.'

'Yes, all right,' said Martin. He wasn't going to argue about it.

'Ralph? Are you OK?' called a podgy, white-haired man from across the street.

The homeowner lifted his arm in acknowledgement and called back, 'We're fine, thanks, Leland, thanks to this gentleman here. I didn't think they made Good Samaritans any more, but I was wrong.'

NINE

When he turned the corner, he found that the road outside Highland Medical Center was crowded with vehicles, and that a large crowd was gathered outside, at least two or three hundred people. He had to park five hundred yards away and then walk. The crowd weren't shouting or tossing rocks like the crowds downtown, but it was edging close to 120 degrees and everybody was clearly suffering from heat exhaustion and growing restless.

Martin maneuvered his way through to the front of the crowd. A barrier had been lowered across the entrance to the medical center's parking lot, and it was guarded by five men in dark blue police-style combat uniforms, with peaked caps. Martin recognized who they were without having to check out the badge on their sleeves: a rising sun with the letters ESS embroidered on top of it. *Empire Security Services.*

He approached one of them and said, 'What's going down here?'

'Do you have an appointment to see a doctor here, sir?' the security guard asked him. He had bleached-blue eyes and clear drops of perspiration on his upper lip.

'No, I don't. I tried to make an appointment but the phone's always busy and the website's not working. I need to see Doctor Lucas. My daughter's sick.'

'Well, your daughter and a whole lot of other folks, I'm sorry to say.' He was carrying a clipboard under his arm and he lifted it up and folded back the first two or three pages. 'Want to tell me where you live, sir?'

'My daughter lives at sixteen-oh-five Fullerton Drive. She's registered with Doctor Lucas. She's been on his list for two years at least.'

The security guard licked the ball of his thumb and turned over another sheet of paper. 'Fullerton Drive . . . Fullerton Drive . . . oh, yeah, here we are, Fullerton Drive. I'm sorry, sir, but no.'

'What do you mean, "no"? What difference does it make where she lives? She's sick. She has a fever.'

'Don't waste your time, buddy,' said a man in a 66ers baseball cap standing close behind him. 'My wife has diabetes and they won't let her in to see Doctor Grove. Just because we live on West Kendall Drive.'

'I'm sorry, sir,' the security man repeated. 'The medical center can't deal with any patients from hiatus areas.'

'You mean neighborhoods where the water supply has been shut off?'

'That's correct, sir. The doctors simply can't handle the demand from those areas.'

'But the people from those areas are the people who need treatment the most. You heard this gentleman. His wife has diabetes. I'm not a doctor but I do know that it's dangerous for a diabetes sufferer to get dehydrated.'

The security man had heard some shouting on the opposite side of the medical center and he turned his head to see what was happening. 'I'm sorry, sir,' he said, abstractedly. 'The hiatus period in your area is only expected to last for another twenty-four hours. Then *you'll* get priority medical care and the people from other areas will have to wait, the same way that you're having to wait now.'

'This is insanity,' Martin protested. 'The council is cutting off people's water but when they get sick they're actively preventing them from seeking treatment – even though it was them who made them sick in the first place?'

'The way I understand it, sir, each hiatus is only going to last forty-eight hours. Even the sickest person can survive without water for forty-eight hours.'

Martin stood very close to him, face to face, so that his chest was actually touching the security man's clipboard. 'Are you going to let me in to see Doctor Lucas, or what?'

'No, sir. I'm not.'

'Do you know who I am?'

'No, sir, I don't.'

'My name is Martin Makepeace and I'm an officer with Children's and Family Services. So I represent the council even more than you do. Apart from that I served three years in Afghanistan and other places east and they trained us to eat little shits like you for breakfast, just to keep our bowels moving.'

The security guard remained impassive. 'I'm sorry, sir. I'm not allowed to admit anyone domiciled within a designated hiatus zone during the period of hiatus.'

'OK,' said Martin. He had to concede that this security guard had neither the imagination, the authority or the inclination to use his initiative. The British squaddies he had met in Afghanistan would have called him a 'jobsworth,' as in, 'I can't let you do that, it's more than my job's worth.' He turned away and walked back to his car. He was so angry now that he felt deadly calm. He knew exactly who he needed to talk to now, and that was Saskia Vane.

As he backed out of the street with squealing tires and softly-bouncing suspension, he thought: maybe it's time for a little arm-twisting, Ms Vane. You asked me to help you out, now you can return the favor.

Behind him, he thought he heard more shouting, and two shots.

As he was driving back to Fullerton Drive, his cell played 'Mandolin Rain'. It was Corporal Evander, calling him from police headquarters.

'Just wanted to let you know, sir, that we'll be sending Tyler over to West Valley Detention Center tomorrow afternoon. Right now we're kind of short-staffed, on account of the demonstrations we're having to deal with.'

'OK, Corporal. Good of you to let me know.'

'Well, I've been talking to Tyler again, sir, completely informally, and between you and me I think he's probably telling the truth.' He paused, and then he added, 'Just don't quote me on that.'

'Is that something you'd stand up and say in front of a judge and jury?'

'In front of a judge and jury, sir, I can only answer the questions that are put to me, and I can only answer those questions with the facts. Detectives aren't paid to have opinions.'

Martin parked outside Peta's house and rang the doorbell. It was so hot now that the mountains appeared to be melting.

Peta came to the door. 'What's happening?' she asked him. 'He's not going to come, is he?'

'This whole drought situation is a lot worse than they're telling us,' said Martin. 'They have security guards outside of the medical center and they won't treat anybody who lives in an area where the water's shut off.'

'What? That doesn't make any sense. Surely those people need the treatment most.'

'Can I see her?' he asked.

'Of course.'

He opened Ella's bedroom door and looked inside but Ella was asleep, her cheeks flushed pink. Martin turned to Peta and said, 'They're not moving Tyler to Rancho Cucamonga until tomorrow afternoon. I'll go see him then.'

'Do you want to stay for something to eat?'

Martin shook his head. 'No, thanks. I'd like that a lot, but I have some business to attend to. I want to find out why my son had to go out foraging for water and my sick daughter isn't allowed to see a doctor, and I want to hear it from somebody who knows what the hell is really going on.'

'Martin—'

'What?'

Peta reached out and touched him, almost as if she were bestowing a blessing on him. 'Be careful,' she said, with her eyes lowered.

Martin headed due south on I-215 to Riverside. Again, the freeway was almost deserted, and he drove for almost three miles before he passed another car. Off to his left, a pall of black smoke was still hanging over the city center, over two hundred feet high. It had taken on the shape of the Grim Reaper, with a long pointed hood and a scythe over its shoulder, and two police helicopters were circling around it, which made it look as if its cloak was swirling.

He had heard Governor Smiley's media conference being advertised on the radio this morning, and that was how he had guessed where he could find Saskia Vane. Governor Smiley would make a statement on KNBC at six p.m., and then he and members of his drought emergency team would answer questions in front of a studio audience. Martin was almost one hundred percent sure that Saskia Vane would be there.

He switched on his radio now to listen to the latest news. The headline story was that the San Bernardino City Council were considering closing three fire stations for ten days every month on the same rotational basis as the water supply, in order to save three and a half million dollars. They were also thinking of outsourcing their trash collection.

'We're flat-busted,' said the City Attorney. 'San Bernardino is over forty-five million dollars in the red and at some point we have to start making some drastic cuts.'

'Well, leaving the city to burn to the ground should save quite a few bucks,' retorted the Acting Fire Chief.

Martin arrived at the KNBC studio on Chicago Avenue and found a place to park outside a dry cleaner's two blocks away. Three shiny black Escalades were already lined up outside the studio, which was a white-painted single-story building with a red shingle roof. Four security guards in the caps and dark blue uniforms of Empire Security were standing by the entrance. It looked like Governor Smiley had already arrived, and maybe Saskia Vane had, too.

Martin approached the tinted glass doors and as he did so one of the security guards immediately stepped forward, holding up his hand.

'Sir? You want to show me your pass?'

'I have an appointment to see Ms Vane.'

'She arranged to meet you here?'

'Not exactly,' said Martin, but he produced Saskia's card from his shirt pocket and held it up so that the security guard could read it. 'She said any time. And now is "any time", wouldn't you say?'

'Sorry, sir. Access to this evening's event is by invitation only, and for that you need a pass, which would have been emailed to you.'

'I know Ms Vane personally and she said that any time I had a question I could ask her.'

'Sorry, sir. Those are my instructions. No pass, no access. Period.'

Martin's skull was still aching from that devastating head-butt. He was hot and sweat was sliding down his back and if anything his anger was even greater than it had been before. He closed his eyes for a moment to control himself, because he knew that if he didn't the next words he tried to speak would be completely incoherent.

When he opened his eyes again, however, he saw that the tinted glass doors were opening and Saskia was stepping outside. Saskia, smiling. She was wearing a light gray suit with a very short skirt and light gray shoes with perilously high heels.

'Martin! It *is* Martin, isn't it? What are *you* doing here? I thought you'd be out in the field somewhere, you know, trying to calm people down.'

'That's not so easy, I'm afraid,' said Martin. 'Maybe it would be easier if *I* was calm. But I'm not. I need to talk to you. I'm very, very far from being calm.'

She came up to him and laid her hand on his shoulder. 'It's all right,' she told the security guard. 'Martin's with me. I'm sorry, Martin, I forget your second name.'

'Makepeace.'

'Very appropriate,' she said. He could smell that perfume again. She had something else about her, too, apart from her scent. Her fingers were barely touching his shoulder and yet he felt as though she was lightly caressing him, rather than simply guiding him toward the door.

They went into the reception area. It was crowded with more security guards, as well as harassed young women with iPads and bored-looking TV technicians with headphones and at least four Councilmen that Martin recognized. The noise of self-important men trying to out-shout each other was deafening.

'I can't spare you very long, I'm afraid,' said Saskia, leading Martin past the reception desk and along an empty corridor with a gleaming yellow floor. 'What seems to be the problem? Well, I don't know why I'm asking you, really. I know what the problem is already. We thought that people would be irritated if we shut off their water for forty-eight hours. We didn't realize that they would start to stage violent demonstrations, and almost immediately. We misunderestimated them, to quote George W. Bush. And very badly.'

'You'll have to call this off, this hiatus thing,' said Martin. 'If you don't, people are going to die.'

Saskia had been walking along the corridor quite quickly, her heels rapping on the vinyl tiles. Now, however, she abruptly stopped, and looked into Martin's eyes with an expression that he had never seen on any woman before. It was partly arrogance, partly impatience and partly pain. *I have to act like this, because that's the kind of person I am, and I don't have any choice, no matter how much it's hurting me.*

'I know people are going to die,' she said, in little more than a whisper. 'But it's about time we realized that our resources are finite. We don't have enough money so we can't afford all of the social services that people need. We don't have enough water so we can't afford to drink. It's simple math and simply physics. You can't create something out of nothing.'

Martin tried to keep his voice level. 'Saskia, I have an eleven-year-old daughter back home who's burning up with fever. I managed to steal some water from my office which I shouldn't have done but so far as I'm concerned charity begins at home. I went to Highland Medical Center but one of these Empire Security Service goons told me that the doctors wouldn't see patients from neighborhoods where the water was shut off.'

Saskia looked down at the floor. 'That's true, I'm afraid. That's part of the rotational hiatus. Medical services are restricted, as well as water, otherwise all of the emergency rooms and clinics would be totally overwhelmed.'

'So it's a double whammy. No water, and no doctors? What kind of people are you?'

'I've admitted it, Martin. People are going to die. People die in earthquakes. People die in floods. People die in tornadoes and epidemics. They're all natural disasters and so is this. There's nothing we can do about it except to share out our limited resources of water as fairly as we can, and rotational hiatus is the only way.'

She looked back up but Martin returned her look with his eyes narrowed.

'You're not telling me everything,' he said.

'I don't know what you mean. There's nothing more to tell you.'

'Yes, there is. There was definitely a "but" in there somewhere. "People are going to die," you said. OK, people are going to die. But, *what?*'

She took hold of his watch strap, the same way she had in Arlene's office, when she was trying to dissuade him from telling Peta about her water being cut off. 'Why don't you come and meet the governor? Maybe *he* can put your mind at rest.'

'Oh, you think so? As it happens, there's something a whole lot worse than my daughter having a fever. I told my wife to stock up on bottled water, just like you suggested, and she sent my son out to buy some. When he got to the store he found himself mixed up in a robbery – some punks trying to steal water, would you believe? The storekeeper got shot dead and his daughter got gang-raped.'

'My God,' said Saskia. 'That's terrible.'

'Oh, you think? It gets worse. When the cops arrived, all of the punks managed to run away, but my son was caught and charged with felony homicide. Felony homicide, for doing nothing, except trying to buy some bottled water, just like you suggested.'

'Where is he now, your son?'

'He's still at police headquarters. They're shipping him over to West Valley tomorrow afternoon.'

'Do you have a lawyer?'

'David Lemos. You know him?'

'Yes, I know David. He always looks like Neil Sedaka after a heavy night out, but he's good. Listen, though, I'll tell you what I can do for you. I'll talk to some of the people I know in the District Attorney's office.'

'And what good will that do?'

'If a gang was responsible, and not your son, they'll make sure the gang gets what's coming to them. The DA's office is very hot on gangs these days. They've even been serving civil process against gangs, like the Cuca Kings in Rancho Cucamonga. They'll move heaven and earth, Martin, don't you worry, especially for me.'

Martin said, 'I ran into another gang this afternoon, stealing water from a house in Shandin Hills. Like, they were stealing water from this couple's house at knifepoint, would you believe? You can't let this go on.'

'Come on,' said Saskia, soothingly. 'Let me introduce you to the governor.'

Again she laid her hand on his shoulder and guided him gently along the corridor to a door at the end. A security guard was standing outside but all Saskia had to do was give him one of her toothy smiles, and he opened the door for her.

Inside, Halford Smiley was sitting in front of a make-up mirror with a white gown around his neck, while a plump blonde girl was patting orange foundation on to his face. Perched on the dressing table next to him was Joseph Wrack, sucking at an unlit panatela and looking sour. Lem Kunicki was standing in the far corner, as pale and chameleon-like as he had been before.

'Halford,' said Saskia. 'I'd like you to meet Martin Makepeace. He's one of the leading lights in San Bernardino's Children and Family Services. Martin, this is Governor Smiley, and this *non-smiley* gentleman is Mr Joseph Wrack, of Empire Security Services.'

Halford's hand appeared from under his gown to give Martin what he obviously considered to be a power handshake. Martin could have scrunched every bone in his fingers but decided it would be more diplomatic not to.

'Martin is concerned about our rotational hiatus policy,' said Saskia. 'It's impacted on his own family as well as the families he cares for.'

Although she was talking to Halford, she didn't take her eyes off Joseph Wrack, and Joseph Wrack didn't take his eyes off her.

'I'm truly sorry to hear that you've had problems, Martin,' said Halford, furrowing his brow and putting on his best concerned-politician voice. 'I'm sure that Saskia here will do everything she can to help you deal with them.'

'I appreciate that, your honor,' said Martin. 'But I don't think you realized how seriously people were going to be affected by cutting off their water for forty-eight hours, especially the young and the elderly and the sick. What's worse is that you're denying them medical help. Like I said to Ms Vane here, people are going to die. A lot of people are going to die, and these are people I'm sworn to protect.'

'And what did Ms Vane say to that, if you don't mind my asking?'

'She admitted it.'

Halford turned around in his chair and pushed the make-up girl to one side. 'The reason she admitted it, Martin, is because it's true. We're facing hundreds of fatalities, if not thousands. The springs are all drying up, the groundwater wells are almost empty, Lake Arrowhead reservoir is now less than thirty feet deep at its deepest point, instead of a hundred eighty-five, which it should be. Millions of acres of crops of all kinds are withering for lack of irrigation. But all we can do is manage the situation as best we can, and try to keep public order. That's where people like you come in.

'What I'm telling you, Martin, is strictly confidential, and the reason it's confidential is because a citywide panic would only make matters a whole lot worse, and potentially even more lives would be lost. We're having to make some very difficult choices here. In the final analysis, it's not so much a question of how many people are going to die, but who.'

Martin glanced at Saskia, although Saskia still had her eyes fixed on Joseph Wrack. That was the 'but' that Martin had sensed in her voice when she had confessed that 'people are going to die'. Not how many, but *who*?

'I'm not so sure I understand what you're saying,' said Martin, even though it was obvious. He just wanted to hear Governor Smiley spell it out.

Joseph Wrack took the unlit cigar out of his mouth and said, 'Governor – maybe you've said enough on the subject.'

'Not at all,' said Halford, expansively. 'Martin here is one of us, aren't you, Martin? If he works for Children and Family Services, then believe me he's a realist. He's seen for himself those people who can help themselves and help others and people who can't.

'The plain unvarnished truth, Martin, is that forty-three-point-two percent of the population of San Bernardino is on welfare, and we're having to dish out more than five hundred and three million dollars annually on cash benefits, Medi-Cal and food stamps.'

'So what are you talking about?' asked Martin. 'Using this drought as a *cull*?'

Halford shook his head and laughed. '*Cull* is kind of an extreme way of putting it, Martin. But let's put it this way. In this life, you get what you pay for, and if you can't afford to pay for it, you can't have it. How can we justify cutting off the water to those people who religiously pay their taxes and their water bills, while continuing to supply those people who have never paid a bent cent for either?'

'I see where you're coming from,' said Martin. 'Some neighborhoods are going to have their water cut off less frequently than others? And some neighborhoods won't have it cut off at all?'

'We don't have a choice, Martin. If we were running a gourmet restaurant, we wouldn't let penniless bums come in and eat just because we felt sorry for them. You said that you're sworn to protect the children in your care, and that's admirable. But the best way that you can protect them is to make sure that their families stay calm and that civil unrest is kept to a minimum. Make them understand that they can't make it rain by rioting.' After he had said this, he actually laughed, and even repeated it. 'Can't make it rain by rioting. I'll have to remember that one.'

Martin said nothing, but he was aware now that Joseph Wrack had taken his eyes off Saskia and was staring at him, and there was no doubt about what that stare was trying to convey. *You misuse anything that Governor Smiley has told you here in confidence, you make a single word of it public, and you're going to regret it.*

Halford beckoned to his make-up girl and said, 'Come on, let's get on with it.' He turned around to grimace at his bright orange face in the mirror and didn't even bid Martin goodbye. Saskia opened the door for Martin and led him back down the corridor to the reception area.

'Call me tomorrow morning,' she said. 'I'll talk to my contact in the DA's office and see what I can fix for your son.'

Martin said, 'Surely you don't go along with this rotation thing. It's inhuman.'

'I'm just doing my job, Martin. Like I said before, it's a natural disaster and we're just trying to cope with it the best way we can.'

'You mean it's like the Holocaust without having to go to the expense of buying Zyklon-B?'

'My hands are tied, Martin. Apart from that, between you and me, I owe Governor Smiley big time.'

'Surely you don't owe him your common humanity?'

Saskia gave Martin another one of her inexplicable expressions. 'Yes,' she said. 'I think I probably do. Call me tomorrow, OK, about ten?'

TEN

Martin arrived back home at his apartment just after ten forty-five p.m. After leaving Riverside, he had first driven back to the office to collect all the folders he needed for the following day's calls, even though he suspected that he would have to cancel his afternoon visits if he went over to the West Valley Detention Center.

He had only two visits marked in his afternoon diary: a seventeen-year-old single mother with two children by two different men, now living with her incontinent grandmother in a rundown house on West Spruce Street, opposite the Salvation Army; and a family with eight children who lived not too far away on West Temple Street, in a two-bedroom house that was alive with bed bugs.

Normally, he wouldn't have considered that either of these visits was urgent. But both families were located in one of the neighborhoods where the water had been shut off, and he was anxious to see how they were coping. If he couldn't make the appointments himself, because he was over at Rancho Cucamonga, maybe he could persuade Shirelle to drop in and see them, or maybe Dana.

Before he had driven back home, he had made a detour to East Julia Street to call on Esmeralda. She came to the door with an immense white plaster covering her nose, like a cartoon character. 'I'm OK now, thank you, Martin,' she had told him, in a blocked-up voice. 'Bless you, bless you for being a saint.'

All the same, she didn't invite him in, and she didn't open the door wide enough for him to be able to see inside. He could hear soft mariachi music playing and smell marijuana smoke, and so he guessed that her lover Jorge was paying her a visit.

'OK, Ezzie. *Asta.* Watch out for that Jesus.'

'You too, Martin. Take care.'

At last Martin pulled into the parking lot at Hummingbird Haven and wearily climbed out of his car. The fluorescent light over his parking space was intermittently flickering and buzzing. He walked across the dry, balding grass until he reached his apartment home. It was identical to all of the other one hundred and fifty apartment homes in this development – a two-story tiled house built of ocher-colored brick, and set in what had once been described as a 'lavishly landscaped' garden. Over the years, however, Hummingbird Haven had become increasingly shabby. The concrete surrounding the swimming pool was looking blackened and diseased, the net across the tennis-court was sagging, and the sandbox in the 'tot lot' was empty, except for a few sun-faded plastic buckets. But none of this bothered Martin much. He never swam or played tennis here and didn't have any small children to amuse. He was hardly ever at home, except to sleep, and at least the rent was cheap.

He climbed the steps to his second-story apartment. The night was noisy with cicadas and moths were swarming around the light above his door. He let himself in and he could smell bacon from this morning's breakfast. The living-room lights were on a time switch, so they were on already, but he went into the kitchen first. His frying pan was still in the sink, waiting to be washed, and his half-empty mug of coffee was standing on the draining board beside it.

On the fridge door he had stuck individual photographs of Peta and Tyler and Ella, as well as a picture of the family all together, smiling and hugging each other, on the seashore at Solana Beach. He stared at them for a moment, gently touching the family picture with his fingertips, before he opened the fridge and took out a bottle of beer.

He went through to the living room, swigging his bottle of beer as he went, and switched on the TV. He was just in time to see a repeat of Governor Smiley's statement on KNBC News. Governor Smiley looked even more orange on the screen then he had in the make-up room; and his orange shirt only intensified the brightness of his face.

'I'm not going to try to downplay this, folks. This drought is one of the worst natural disasters that the state of California has ever faced. It is far, *far* more severe than any earthquakes that we've suffered, because it affects not just those communities built on fault-lines, but *all* of our communities, from north to south, and from west to east. Because of that, I am asking each and every one of you to share the discomfort that a critical shortage of water is inevitably going to bring us. I have appointed a special drought crisis team to manage the fair and equitable distribution of what limited water is available to us, and I trust you will understand that when they shut off your water supply for a controlled period of time, they are acting in the best interests of all of you.'

Martin took another swig of beer and shook his head. *God*, he thought, *you're such a liar.* He had always taken it for granted that politicians lied, but it was still shocking to hear Governor Smiley come out with such a blatant untruth, when he had already told Martin that deprived neighborhoods would suffer much longer water shortages than affluent parts of the city. *In this life, you get what you pay for, and if you can't afford to pay for it, you can't have it.*

He switched off the TV and went into his bedroom, where his bed was still unmade, the red-and-green Navajo-style blanket thrown back at an angle. He undressed in front of the mirrored wardrobe doors. He thought he looked exhausted, his dirty-blond hair messed up, his gray eyes hooded. He had a pattern of red bruises on his arms, which he had probably sustained when he was struggling with the gang who were stealing water.

His body was still sculptured and muscly even though these days he didn't work out as much as he knew he ought to. Across the right side of his chest, at a sharp diagonal, there were five white parallel scars as if he had been ripped across the nipple by a mountain lion. He had similar scars across his back and his buttocks and there were no nails on either of his big toes. There were two V-shaped burn marks on either side of his scrotum.

He couldn't help thinking about Saskia Vane, and what she had said to him about owing Governor Smiley 'big time'. He couldn't help wondering how a strong woman like her could be so much indebted to a man as crass as him, even to the point of forfeiting her sense of humanity.

He went into the bathroom, dropped his shirt and his shorts into the laundry basket, and reached into the shower cubicle to turn on the water. Nothing happened. He went over to the washbasin, and tried both hot and cold faucets. Nothing. The water supply was shut off.

For the first time that day, he understood exactly why the crowds on North D Street had been so angry.

By the time he woke up the next morning, the sun was already beating down out of a cloudless blue sky. He pushed back the covers and rolled out of bed, and went through to the living room to turn on the TV News and weather forecast, as if he couldn't guess already what Craig Fiegener would be telling him about today's temperatures.

'By midday, the IE is going to experience triple figures yet again, maybe in excess of one hundred twenty. Cloud, nil; precipitation, nil. And now over to Jacob Rascon for news about last night's protests against the rotational shutting off of water supplies in San Bernardino County – Jacob?'

Martin went to the bathroom and tried the faucets again. There was still no water. He lifted the lid of the toilet cistern and saw that there was just enough water for one flush, so he took a pee but decided not to pull the handle until later.

There was no water for brewing coffee so he drank Pepsi instead, straight from the bottle. Usually it didn't bother him if he didn't make coffee, and when he did he rarely finished it, but now that he had no choice he found himself really craving for it.

Back in his bedroom he was pulling on his pants when his cell played 'Mandolin Rain'.

'Mr Makepeace? Good morning, sir. This is Sergeant Wosnicky from police headquarters downtown. Corporal Evander asked me to call you and inform you that your son is going to be transported to West Valley Detention Center at two p.m. this afternoon. He should arrive there about two thirty. Once they've booked him in there you'll be allowed fifteen minutes to talk to him, but you should call them in advance to make an appointment. Do you want me to give you the number?'

'Fifteen minutes? Is that all?'

'Fifteen minutes is the usual permitted visiting time, sir. His defense lawyer will be able to see him for longer before his arraignment hearing. So far as I know that's scheduled for tomorrow sometime.'

'OK. Thank you, Sergeant.'

He called Peta. Sergeant Wosnicky had already told her that Tyler was going to be moved to Rancho Cucamonga that afternoon, and she was in tears.

'It's going to be OK, Peta. He didn't do it and they won't be able to prove that he did. In any case I'm going over there this afternoon to see him. How's Ella?'

'A little better, thank God. Her temperature's almost back down to normal, and she managed to eat some cereal for breakfast.'

'How about your water? Your water back on yet?'

'No, not yet. I tried to call the water department to find out how much longer we were going to be cut off, but the line's always busy, and there's been nothing about it on the local news.'

Martin said, 'It's the same here, in my apartment. Do you know
something, after I talked to Governor Smiley yesterday, I'm beginning to think that they've shut our water off for good, or at least
until it rains, which won't be for weeks. Or months, even. Who
knows?'

'They can't do that. Can they?'

'It wouldn't surprise me. Governor Smiley and his gang seem to
think that anybody on welfare doesn't deserve squat.'

'But we can't live without water, Martin.'

'Maybe that's the idea.'

When he drove downtown, Martin found that the streets were almost
completely deserted and most of the stores were shuttered. Broken
bricks and other debris were strewn across the sidewalks and traffic
signs had been uprooted. At most of the major intersections, black-
and-white squad cars were parked, but he was disturbed to see nearly
as many dark blue Explorers with the ESS logo on their doors, from
Empire Security Services. Both squad cars and security vehicles
had their engines idling to keep their air conditioning on. Although
it was only nine a.m., the temperature was already up to ninety-two
degrees, and the weather forecast on his radio warned of 120 by
noon.

Most mornings when he didn't feel like cooking his own breakfast
he stopped at Molly's Café on the corner of North D Street for
Polish sausage and scrambled eggs, but Molly's was shuttered, too.
Further along West Court Street, he saw more squad cars parked
diagonally across the street, and more ESS Explorers, too, and at
least twenty riot police standing around with the sun reflecting from
their plastic shields, as well as uniformed security guards. A siren
was whooping three or four blocks away, and there was a feeling
in the air that something ugly was about to happen.

He drove to the office, parked, and went upstairs. Brenda the
receptionist pulled a face at him as if she were disappointed that
he had actually come in early, and she had no cause to complain
about him. 'Arlene's having a team meeting,' she said. 'Don't worry.
It hasn't started yet.'

'What? Me worry?' said Martin. He went through to the kitchen
first, where a jug of coffee was brewing. He filled his mug, took a
couple of Anna's Orange Thins from the tin on the counter, and
went through to Arlene's office. Shirelle Jackson was already there,

as well as Kevin Maynard and Dana Suykerbuyk, a plump young woman with a mass of dry blonde curls, a huge bosom and a bottom to match, and a fondness for lime green sweat pants with loops under the feet.

Arlene looked up and said, 'Ah, Martin, you're here! We're still waiting for Karen and Michelle, but we might as well begin. The thing is that this drought situation has suddenly escalated and the police are expecting some very serious trouble as the day goes on. The water was supposed to come back on in the first neighborhoods that were affected by mid-afternoon, but the drought crisis people think it may have to stay off for a little longer.'

'Exactly how long is "a little longer"?' asked Martin.

'They're not entirely sure.'

'Oh, I'm sure they *are* sure. They're just not *telling* anybody, is all. So what are we supposed to say to our families?'

'As always, Martin, our first concern is the safety and well-being of the children in our care. So what we need to do is to keep our families calm and try to minimize any risk of civil protest. We don't want any of our children getting hurt in a riot.'

Martin put down his coffee mug on her desk, which he knew she didn't like. 'If you think that I'm going to do Governor Smiley's dirty work for him, Arlene, you'd better think again. You might as well know that I talked to the governor yesterday and he openly admitted to me that he has a deliberate policy of depriving the poorer neighborhoods of water while maintaining supplies to the wealthier districts.'

'Aw, come on, I can't believe that,' put in Kevin Maynard. 'Governor Smiley made a specific promise in his statement on TV last night that everybody would get their fair share.'

'He's a politician, Kevin, for Christ's sake. President Obama promised that he would reduce the nation's deficit.'

'That's different. This is a natural disaster, not a man-made one.'

Martin was about to tell Kevin that a broken promise was a broken promise when his cellphone rang and he saw that Saskia Vane was calling him. He excused himself and went outside into the reception area.

'Martin?' said Saskia. She sounded as if she were in a diner somewhere, with plates clattering and people laughing in the background. 'I've spoken to Bill Schiller in the DA's office. Your son's arraignment is tomorrow but Bill has promised me that he'll look at the possibility of not contesting bail. Your son has no previous criminal record and the circumstances of his case are still very iffy, which are both in his favor. And, well, Bill owes me one.'

'You mean they might let Tyler out?'

'I'm not sure yet. Even if they do, it's still going to take two or three days at least to arrange bail and Bill doesn't know how much we're going to be talking about. It could be fifty thousand. It could be much more. It's highly unlikely that the judge will let him out on OR.'

'Well, thanks for trying, Saskia. I appreciate it.'

Saskia hesitated for a moment and then she said, 'There's something else you need to know, Martin.'

'OK. What's that?'

'I shouldn't be telling you this, but I think you're one of the good guys.'

'Oh, yes? After everything I've said to you?'

'Maybe I deserved it. I'm the best in the business, but you only get to be the best in the business by making other people believe in you, especially when you're lying. Sometimes the only way to do that is to convince yourself that you're telling the truth.'

'So what are you going to tell me now?' Martin asked her. 'The truth, or a lie, or a lie that you've convinced yourself is true?'

'This is true, Martin. We had a meeting of the drought crisis team at seven a.m. this morning, mapping out the areas where we're going to be shutting down the water supply. All of those neighborhoods that we've already shut down are going to stay shut down, at least for another twenty-four hours.'

'They're going to *stay* shut down? And you expect me to tell people to keep calm about it?'

'Martin – we just don't have the water! The average citizen of San Bernardino uses two hundred twenty-six gallons of water every single day. We've cut off only thirty-two thousand people out of a total population of two hundred thirty thousand, but that means we've managed to save fourteen million gallons of water already.'

'Well, hallelujah! Now you sound like you're trying to convince me that you and Governor Smiley are the saviors of the planet.'

'Listen to me, Martin, this is serious. We're cutting off the water supply at West Valley Detention Center.'

'What?'

'That's right. From noon today. I don't know for how long.'

'That's insanity. You can't deprive prisoners of water. Apart from the fact that it's inhuman, you're going to have a riot on your hands that makes all this chanting and rock-tossing we've had up until now look like playschool.'

'I know, Martin. But Halford won't be budged on it. "The inmates of West Valley Detention Center knowingly broke the law, but still the long-suffering taxpayer has to pay for their upkeep," that's what he said. "Why should we give them the same privileges as everybody else?"'

'Water isn't a privilege, Saskia. Water is necessary for human beings to stay alive.'

'That's why I'm telling you. I personally think this almost amounts to genocide. But most of all I don't want your son to get hurt.'

'Well, great, thanks. But they're taking him to West Valley whether I like it or not. What can I do about it?'

'I really don't know. But I just thought I ought to warn you.'

'Saskia?' he said. 'Saskia?' But her line had gone dead. He tried calling her back but she had switched off her cell and all he heard was her recorded message.

He stood in reception, his hand pressed to his forehead, trying to think what to do. Brenda stared at him, but she didn't ask him why he hadn't gone back in to join Arlene's team meeting.

She didn't even speak when he walked straight out of the office without saying where he was going or when he might be back.

ELEVEN

As he drove out of the city center, he could hear shouting and screaming coming from the direction of Meadowbrook Park, and more sirens scribbling and whooping, followed by the sporadic popping of tear-gas guns. A police helicopter was slowly circling around City Hall, its white reflection wavering across one glassy wall after the other, the clatter of its rotors echoing from street to street.

His cell played 'Mandolin Rain' over and over. He glanced at it and saw that Arlene was trying to get in touch, but he didn't answer it. After five minutes of repeated calling she gave up. He didn't like to let her down – or the families that he was supposed to be visiting that morning – but this was too urgent. He didn't have time to argue, or to justify himself.

He drove west of the city center to the suburb of Rialto. The streets were quiet here, and so he guessed that the water supply hadn't yet been cut off. Mothers were driving past in SUVs, taking children to school. A mailman was delivering letters. A young dogwalker was taking seven assorted dogs for a walk along West Alru Street, ranging from a St Bernard to a Shiatsu, and straining to keep them all in check.

South Beechwood Avenue was deserted, but then it usually was – a long, straight street with neat single-story houses on either side, silently baking under the mid-morning sun. Martin reached the 600 block and parked on the corner, outside a white Mexican-style house with arches over its front verandah and a stack of logs outside the garage. The Stars and Stripes hung limply from a flagstaff, as if it were suffering from heat exhaustion.

He climbed out of his car and went up to the front door. He could hear a TV playing loudly inside and a woman talking. He rang the doorbell and waited. Nobody answered so he rang it again.

The door was opened almost immediately. Martin found himself confronted by a young round-faced Hispanic woman in a sleeveless red dress and a red checkered apron. From inside the house behind her came a strong smell of frying onions.

'Hi, there. Is Mr Bonaduce at home?'

'Mr Bonaduce? Who wants to know?'

'If he's at home, tell him it's Angel.'

'Angel?' The expression on the girl's face clearly said, you don't look like any kind of angel that I've ever seen. But she went back inside and Martin heard her say, 'Mr B! You have a visitor! Calls himself Angel.'

There was a moment's pause and then the girl reappeared and now she was smiling. 'Mr Bonaduce says to come on in.'

Martin stepped inside and went through to the living room. Sitting in a high-backed brocade armchair in front of the TV was a fortyish man with gray slicked-back hair and a round, homely, Italian-looking face, with bags under his eyes. He was heavily built, with a bulging belly and swollen thighs. It was only when he held out his left hand in greeting that it was obvious that his right arm was missing, and that his empty sleeve was folded and pinned to the side of his dark maroon shirt.

'Charlie, how are you?' said Martin, shaking his hand.

'Bored, sex-starved,' said Charlie. 'Haven't seen you in a coon's age, Angel. Take a load off why don't you?'

Martin sat down on the end of the couch next to him. 'Sorry it's been so long, Charlie. We've been three team members short these past six months, so we've all been working our asses off.'

'You want a beer? Rosa, bring us a couple of beers, will you, my darling? Only domestic, I'm afraid. I know you like that Indian stuff. This drought affecting you much? I saw on the news that there's some kind of a riot downtown, on account of people having their water shut off.'

'I just came from there,' Martin told him. 'The whole thing's turning into a full-blown disaster movie. And it's affected me person-ally. My son, anyhow. That's one of the reasons I'm here, Charlie. I really need your help.'

'I might have known. And here's me thinking you came here just to talk about pussy and baseball and give me an excuse to get drunk. Not that I need one.'

Martin told him how Tyler had been arrested for murder and rape, and how he was scheduled to be taken to West Valley Detention Center. He also told him that the water supply to the prison was going to be cut off in less than two-and-a-half hours' time.

'They're really going to do that?' asked Charlie. 'How the hell did you find that out?'

'I know this woman who's working for Governor Smiley's drought emergency team.'

'Oh, yeah? How well do you know her?'

'Not *that* well. But well enough for her to give me the heads up.'

Rosa came in with two cold bottles of Rolling Rock. Martin didn't usually drink before the evening, these days, but today was different. Charlie clinked bottles and said, 'Here's to swimmin' with bow-legged women! So where do *I* fit into this?'

'You still have those two Colt Commandos and that RPG-Seven?'

Charlie was about to take a swig from his beer bottle but now he slowly lowered it. 'Hey, now. Hold on here. What exactly do you have in mind, Angel?'

'I don't want Tyler locked up in that jail. It's as simple as that.'

'So what are you planning to do? Blow a hole in the prison wall, and then go in with all guns blazing?'

Martin shook his head. 'I'm going to make sure that he never even gets there.'

'Oh, really? And how do you intend to do that? Jesus, Angel, you always were a psycho, even back in Camp Leatherneck.'

'Listen,' said Martin, 'the cops have told me that they'll be driving him away from police headquarters around two p.m. They'll be heading along the Foothill Freeway because that's the quickest and the most direct route. That means that approximately fifteen minutes later they'll be passing the intersection with North Alder Avenue.'

'Go on,' said Charlie, swallowing beer and wiping his mouth on the side of his sleeve. 'What are you going to do? Wait on the bridge till the prison bus comes past and then jump on top of it?'

'Who do you think I am? Spiderman? I'm going to do what we used to do with those Taliban trucks in Helmand. I'm going to blow out their tires just before they reach the intersection so they have to take the off ramp up to North Alder Avenue.'

'Supposing they don't?'

'They'll still have to stop, even if they stay on the freeway.'

'But then what?'

'That's when I confront them with the RPG and tell them to let Tyler off the bus or else.'

'Supposing they say no? Supposing they say, "You won't blow this bus up so long as your son is on board"?'

'They won't. People don't think like that when they're being threatened with a weapon. You know that. They just want to get themselves out of danger.'

'OK . . . supposing they do let him go. Then what?'

'I hightail it south on North Alder Avenue and then I take a left on Baseline and keep going until I hit downtown.'

'And you don't think the cops will have put out an APB on you?'

'That's why I'm heading downtown. The cops will be too tied up with the water riots to worry about looking for me.'

Charlie thoughtfully finished his beer, and called out, 'Rosa! Bring us another two beers, will you?'

'Not for me,' said Martin. 'I need to keep a very clear head for this.'

'OK,' said Charlie. 'Supposing I don't own those weapons any more. Supposing I sold them. Like, what use are two sub-machine guns and an RPG to an old fart like me with only one arm? If I tried to fire them – *shit* – I'd only spin around in circles.'

'Charlie, you still have those weapons because they're part of your life. Those weapons are a testament to the fact that you were a fighting man once, and not just a one-armed cripple.'

Charlie look at him narrow-eyed. 'Well, you're right, of course. I forgot that you were trained in all of that psychiatric shit. OK, you can borrow them. But only *borrow*, and don't go killing anybody, OK? If you kill anybody I'm going to say that you took them from me without my knowledge, because there's no way I'm going to prison for facilitating no murder, no way. Not with one arm, and not in a prison with no fucking water.'

Martin checked his watch. 'Thanks, Charlie. I don't have any idea if this going to work but you know what they say about desperate times.'

Rosa came in with another beer for Charlie, but before she could give it to him he said, 'No, Rosa. On second thought, put the top back on it. I'm going to need a clear head, too.'

'What, for watching *The Young And The Restless*?' Martin ribbed him.

'No,' said Charlie. 'I think you're going to need back-up. I'm coming with you. It's about time I got out of this goddamned chair and did something that takes a bit of nerve. The hajjis may have left me with only dickskinner but my balls are still intact.'

* * *

He phoned Peta. He was already formulating in his mind what he was going to do, and even though he knew it was extreme, he couldn't think of any alternative for protecting his family. When he was in the Marines he had earned a reputation for coming up with tactical solutions that appeared at first to be madness, but which had almost always saved lives. That was how he had earned the nickname 'Angel'.

His motto had always been *'Don't hope that the worst thing that you can possibly imagine isn't going to happen, because it will, and a whole lot sooner than you think.'*

'Sweetheart,' he told Peta, 'we're going to have to leave, like today.'

'Leave? Why? What are you talking about? We can't *leave*. Ella's still sick and Tyler's being arraigned tomorrow.'

'Is your water back on?'

'No, not yet, but we still have plenty of that bottled water you brought us.'

'Peta, I don't think your water is ever going to come back on. Not until it starts raining, and even then it's going to take weeks for the aquifers to fill up again.'

'So what are we supposed to do?'

'First off, I'm going to go get Tyler.'

'I don't understand you. They're taking Tyler to prison.'

'Not if I have anything to do with it, sweetheart.'

Martin explained to her what Saskia had told him and what he was planning to do. She listened in silence, but when he had finished she said, 'You're crazy. Do you know that? You're totally, utterly crazy.'

'All right, I'm crazy. But what else can I do? Watch my family dying of thirst, or worse?'

'They'll arrest you as well, and then you'll be stuck in that detention center along with Tyler, and then *you'll* die of thirst, too.'

'Peta, I survived three tours of Afghanistan. I think I can handle myself. Besides, Charlie Bonaduce is going to help me.'

'Charlie Bonaduce? Charlie with only one arm? Now I *know* that you've lost it.'

Martin said, 'Peta, please trust me, just this once. Pack a few things for yourself and Ella and have yourselves ready to leave by four p.m. at the latest. If I don't show, then you'll know that it's all gone wrong. I know this sounds insane, but it's the only way we're going to survive, I promise you.'

There was a long pause, and then Peta said, 'Aren't you forgetting something?'

'What? I don't think so.'

'Aren't you forgetting that we're not married any more? I never did allow you tell me what to do when we *were* married, and I'm certainly not going to let you start now.'

'Peta, I love you. You know that. I never stopped loving you. In fact I probably love you more now than I did when we were married.'

Another long pause. Then, 'I'll think about it, Martin. If you can bring Tyler safe home this afternoon, well – I'll see how I feel then.'

'Peta, this is nothing to do with all of those fights we had. This is a matter of survival. And I mean *our* survival. Mine, yours, Tyler's and Ella's.'

'I'll see you later, Martin,' said Peta. 'And Martin—'

'Yes?'

'Be safe, Martin. Please. For my sake.'

TWELVE

Charlie led him into the spare bedroom. He rolled back the faded blue Chinese rug, and then he handed Martin a long screwdriver.

'You'll find them under there. Don't go splintering those floorboards any, will you?'

Martin knelt down and levered up three of the dark oak floorboards. Underneath, wrapped up in heavy-duty polythene and silver duct tape, were Charlie's two Colt Commando sub-machine guns with five spare thirty-round magazines and a Russian-made rocket-propelled grenade launcher, with two grenades.

'All clean, oiled, and in perfect working order,' said Charlie, proudly.

Martin lifted them out and laid them side by side on the bed. 'You don't have to get yourself involved in this, Charlie. You know that.'

'Oh, you try and stop me, Angel. My life is so fucking boring these days I feel like taking out one of these babies and blowing my brains out. The only one reason I don't is Rosa. I wouldn't like to give her all of that mess to clear up afterward.'

Martin said, 'You can come along with us, if you like, after we've rescued Tyler. You still have water here for now, but I don't know how long it's going to be before they cut you off, too.'

Charlie laid his hand on Martin's shoulder. 'Thanks for the offer. I'd love to come with you, but it's not just my arm that's fucked, remember. That shrapnel I took in my gut . . . I still have a bag. You don't want to have the Colostomy Kid slowing you down, now do you?'

Martin unwrapped the Colts and checked them over. Their weight and their shape and the smell of them was so familiar that he could have closed his eyes and felt as if he were still in Afghanistan, especially on a hot day like this. He had never handled an RPG but if Charlie said that it was in perfect working order, then he believed him. When he had still had an arm, Charlie had been a sniper, and he could strip and reassemble any weapon, American or foreign, in total darkness.

'That magazine with the red tape on it, be careful with that one, it has tracer rounds in it,' said Charlie.

'OK. I don't think I'll be needing those. I'll be doing this in daylight.'

Charlie reached down under the floorboards and came up with two spherical, khaki-colored hand grenades. 'Want to take these along, too? Don't know why I kept them, to tell you the truth. Not much you can do with an M67 frag grenade except pull out the pin and blow yourself up with it, if life ever gets too boring.'

'OK, let's take them anyhow,' said Martin. He checked his watch. 'It's too early to go yet. I don't want us to be noticed, hanging around the intersection. What are you going to do, take your own truck?'

'Sure. It'll be easier for both of us. You can make a clean getaway and I can head straight back home. Meanwhile . . . how about some chow? Rosa! How much longer is that chili going to take? You need to try some of Rosa's chili. That's my second reason for staying alive.'

After they had finished eating, Martin carried the two Colt Commandos out of the house and laid them on the passenger seat of his Eldorado, covering them up with a blue hand towel. He lifted the RPG into Charlie's dusty black Dodge Ram. The Ram had a knob on the steering wheel which allowed Charlie to steer with one hand, and he could operate the direction indicators and the horn with his left foot.

Before they set off, Charlie took hold of Martin's hand and squeezed it and said, 'If this all goes to shit, Angel, at least we tried. Never stop fighting, that's what you always used to say, even when there's nothing left to fight.'

'Did I say that? I think I've learned more sense since then.'

They climbed into their vehicles. It was so hot now that Martin could barely touch his steering wheel. He wished he could put up the top and turn on the air con, but for what he was planning to do he needed the roof down. With Charlie following close behind him he drove northward to join the Foothill Freeway. In fact Charlie was uncomfortably close behind him, what the Marines used to call 'nuts to butts.' He waved his hand to indicate that Charlie should back off a few feet, but all Charlie did was let go of his steering wheel and wave back.

As he crossed over the freeway, Martin saw that the traffic was light to moderate, with most of it heading due westward to Rancho Cucamonga and probably beyond, to Pasadena and LA. It looked as if people were getting out of town, and he could hardly blame them. Looking back toward the city center he could see smoke rising from several different locations, and helicopters glinting as they circled over the downtown area.

He checked the time again. It was 2.02 p.m. There was no way of knowing if the prison bus taking Tyler to West Valley was going to be dead on time, or if it was going to be delayed by the riots. All he could do was wait for it to appear, and then improvise. He drove down the ramp to join the freeway, but after only two hundred yards he pulled over on to the shoulder and switched on his hazard lights. Charlie steered his Ram in close behind him, with his lights flashing, too.

Fifteen minutes passed, and there was still no sign of the prison bus; or the police van; or whatever vehicle they were using to transport Tyler to West Valley Detention Center. He saw red, white and blue lights flashing in his rear-view mirror, and started up his engine, ready to set off in pursuit, but then a Highway Patrol car sped past him, its siren wailing, with only two officers in it. He turned off his engine again, and looked around at Charlie, and shook his head.

It was 2.28 before he peered into his side mirror and saw a likely looking vehicle approaching. It was a dark blue bus, and as it came nearer he could make out the silver letters ESS on the front. He knew that Empire Security Services had a contract to carry inmates from prison to court and back again, and now that the SBPD were having to cope with riots, it was logical that they would call on them to take Tyler to Rancho Cucamonga.

He fired up his engine, and gave a whirling-finger signal to Charlie to do the same. The old Ram started up with a whistle and a hefty roar, and Charlie revved its engine up again and again, like a dragster driver who couldn't wait to get off the starting-line.

The dark blue bus came closer and closer. It was traveling at less than forty miles an hour, at most, so that when it passed him, Martin could see through the horizontal bars that lined the windows. He glimpsed two security guards, both of them wearing peaked caps, two white men with shaved heads, a black man with a woolly cap on, and right at the back of the bus, Tyler's blond hair, looking even more porcupine-like than usual.

He stepped on the gas and swerved off the shoulder on to the highway, trying not to drive too dramatically, in case he alerted the bus driver before they reached the North Alder Avenue flyover. Charlie followed, although he kept his distance this time. He knew what Martin was planning to do, and he didn't want to catch any ricochets.

Martin pulled out into the center lane, so that he was driving just behind the bus, matching its speed. Charlie stayed where he was, in the right-hand lane, about fifty yards back.

The bus driver obviously wasn't aware that Martin was close-tailing him, because he didn't slow down or increase his speed or try to take any evasive action, and neither of the security guards turned around to look at him. The bus kept going, mile after mile, with Martin keeping pace with it, his speedometer just nudging forty mph, until he could see the North Alder Avenue flyover up ahead.

This was going to take some calculation. He had attacked Taliban trucks dozens of times before, but in Afghanistan the roads were rough and rocky and the vehicles had usually come bouncing to a halt within only a very short distance – apart from which their drivers had known they were going to be shot at, and had immediately jumped down from their cabs and run away.

He waited until they were just over half a mile away from the flyover, and then he lifted off the towel that was covering the two Colt Commandos, and hefted one of them up. He leaned across the front seat and rested the barrel on top of the passenger door, lodging it between the side mirror and the windshield to steady it.

Through the barred window at the side of the bus, he could see the back of one of the guards' heads; and through the rear window he could just see Tyler's hair. He still had a choice. He could drive away, and let Tyler be taken to prison. But he still believed that motto he had always used in Afghanistan, about the worst thing that you can possibly imagine, and he knew that he had to act now, or he would regret it for ever.

He fired two shots in quick succession, and then a five-second burst. The noise of the gun was deafening, because this was one of the old Colt Commandos before they suppressed them. The bullets tore into the rear offside tires, ripping them into blackened shreds, so that they flapped against the road surface like a witch's cloak.

The bus slewed to the left, and then to the right, its remaining tires howling. Martin saw the security guard swivel his head around and stare at him through the bars, his mouth wide open in shock; but then he touched his brakes and swung the Eldorado behind the bus, its long hood softly dipping, and then accelerated again, so that he was coming up on its nearside.

He shifted the sub-machine gun to his left hand, steering with his right. Tucking the butt into his left armpit, he fired another nine or ten ear-splitting rounds into the bus's back tires. A blizzard of torn black rubber burst all around him, thumping against his windshield, while the bus tilted from one side to the other, its steel hubs screeching on the blacktop and showers of sparks cascading from its wheel arches.

It seemed to take forever before the bus stopped careering from side to side. The driver managed to pull it over on to the shoulder, only about twenty yards shy of the off-ramp that led up to the North Alder Avenue flyover. It came to a grating halt, rocking slightly on its ruined suspension, and a large piece of twisted metal chassis dropped on to the ground with a clatter. Martin overtook the bus, parked his Eldorado on the shoulder in front of it, and climbed out, pointing the Colt Commando at the door.

Charlie parked behind it, and walked around to join Martin, holding up the RPG. He was grinning.

'That was real fancy shooting, Angel,' he called out 'Haven't had so much goddamned fun in years!'

Traffic was still streaming past them on the freeway, cars and semis and even a tow truck from the Freeway Service Patrol. Martin could see most of their drivers turning their heads to stare at him, but none of them slowed down He had counted on passers-by not wanting to get involved in any situation that could be dangerous, especially if they saw men with large guns. Maybe some of them might call 911, or a trucker might report it on his CB radio, but by the time the police could respond they would be long gone.

Martin walked up to the bus and banged on the door with his fist. 'Open the door, now, or you're going to get blown to kingdom come!'

Charlie was standing right behind him with the RPG launcher resting on his shoulder, still grinning. One of the security guards said something in a muffled voice, and then the door opened up with a sharp pneumatic hiss.

'OK, out of there, all of you!' said Martin. 'And you two guards – if either of you goes for a weapon, believe me, it'll be the last thing you do!'

The bus driver stepped down first, and put his hands on top of his head. He was followed by the two security guards, and then the two white prisoners, and the black prisoner in the woolly hat, and finally by Tyler.

Tyler was wide-eyed and obviously shaken, but at least he had the good sense not to shout out 'Dad!'

Martin stepped forward, popped the studs on the security guards' holsters, hooked out their pistols with his forefinger and then slung them left-handed into the dry brown scrub at the side of the shoulder. Then he said, 'Cellphones, too.'

They took out their cells and threw them after their guns. Neither of them spoke, not even to ask him why he had shot out their tires, or what he wanted. One was middle-aged, with a broken nose like a boxer, and no front teeth. The other was much younger, Hispanic, with a shadow of a black moustache and a large mole on his chin. The older one, oddly, looked almost bored, as if he just wanted to get this over with.

'Tyler,' said Martin, 'go sit in the car. The rest of you guys, get back in the bus. Stay there, because my friend here is going to keep you covered until I'm gone, and my friend's RPG could punch a hole through an armored personnel carrier, leave alone a bus.'

'Whatever you say, buddy,' said the older security guard. 'I'm not risking my neck for some punk kid, believe me.'

The three inmates climbed back on to the bus, followed by the driver and the younger security guard, with the older security guard taking up the rear, his hands still held on top of his head. Martin backed toward his car, keeping his sub-machine gun lifted, but when he reached it and opened up the driver's door, he tossed the gun on to the back seat.

He climbed in and started up the engine, turning around to wave goodbye to Charlie. Charlie was still keeping the bus covered, the RPG mounted on his right shoulder, his left hand holding the pistol grip. The older security guard was now mounting the steps into the bus, taking both hands off the top of his head so that he could grasp the rails. Charlie turned to Martin and called out, 'Mission accomplished, Angel! *Yee*-ha! You did it again, man! Just like the old days!'

Suddenly, though, the older security guard used his grip on the rails to push himself backward, and jump down on to the tarmac. He rolled over, underneath the bus, so that he was out of Charlie's line of sight. Charlie stepped to the left, ducking down to see where the security guard was hiding himself. Martin shouted out, '*Charlie! Watch out!*' and immediately reached down for the second Colt Commando, which Tyler had taken off the passenger seat and laid in the footwell.

He lifted up the Colt and opened his door, but even before he could climb back out of the driver's seat the older security guard appeared from underneath the front bumper of the bus. He was lying on his side, grimacing, and he was holding a small-caliber pistol in both hands. Martin thought: *hideaway gun, shit, why didn't I think of checking his ankles?*

He raised the sub-machine gun but everything seemed to be happening in slow motion. Charlie must have seen the security guard's pistol because he teetered sideways and backward and with that forty-pound rocket launcher on his shoulder, he began to lose his balance, especially since he only had one arm. As he did so, the security guard fired three shots at him, and then another two shots in Martin's direction. With a hollow bang, one of them hit the trunk of Martin's car, but the other missed, even though Martin heard it whizz past his ear.

Charlie, however, was staggering further and further backward, with the rocket launcher tilting upward, and then downward.

Martin fired two loud shots at the security guard under the bus, but the security guard had disappeared again, like a rat disappearing under a baseboard, and he wasn't at all sure that he had hit him.

'*Charlie!*' he yelled, and started to run toward him.

The rocket launcher was pointing down toward the ground now, and it looked as if Charlie was trying to disentangle himself from the shoulder strap. But his index finger must have been caught in the trigger guard, because he was tugging at it furiously, and as he did so one of the grenades went off. Within a split second of each other, there was a sharp whoosh as the projectile ignited, and then a devastating explosion as it hit the ground.

The world was turned inside-out. Martin heard nothing at all, and saw nothing but blinding white light. He was hurled backward against his car, jarring his shoulder against the trunk and knocking his forehead against the sharply angled tail lights.

He lay on the ground, staring at the tarmac in close-up, and the inside of his head was singing and singing and wouldn't stop. Very faintly, he heard Tyler's voice saying 'Dad! Dad, are you OK? Dad! Can you hear me? Dad!'

He raised his head a little and saw the scuffed-up toes of Tyler's blue-and-white sneakers. Then he managed to raise it a little more, to see that Tyler was crouching down next to him, his eyes wide with worry.

Gradually, he managed to drag himself into a sitting position. There was a crater in the tarmac where Charlie's grenade had exploded, with smoke still rising from it. The force of the explosion had blown the windshield and all of the windows out of the bus and forced the whole vehicle sideways, so that its front wheels were up on the scrubby embankment and its rear end was sticking out into the right-hand lane of the freeway. Martin couldn't see any of its passengers.

He couldn't see Charlie, either. He looked around, his head still singing and bright green after images still swimming in front of his eyes, but there was no sign of Charlie anywhere. It was only when he looked down at his own clothes, and at the back of his car, that he began to realize what had happened. His khaki chinos and his white shirt were finely sprayed with blood, and so was his car. The blast from the grenade had been so powerful that Charlie had been vaporized.

Several cars had stopped on the freeway now, and more of them had slowed right down to a crawl. A large Peterbilt semi had pulled up behind Charlie's truck and the driver was climbing down from his cab.

Tyler said, 'Dad – I think the police are coming!'

'What?'

'I can hear sirens. I think they're getting closer!'

Martin listened intently, cupping his hand to his ear, but all he could hear was that persistent singing. 'OK,' he said, 'I think we need to get ourselves out of here, and fast. Come on.'

'Dad – we can't!'

'No "can't" about it, Tyler. We have to. This whole country is going to hell in a handcart and we'll be going with it unless we go now.'

'Dad—!'

Martin bent down and picked up his Colt Commando. He threw it back into his car with a clatter and then opened the passenger door and pushed Tyler inside.

The truck driver was approaching them now, and he called out, 'Hey! What happened here, fella? What's going on? Hey, there's blood all over!'

Martin didn't answer him, but climbed behind the wheel, started the engine, and accelerated up the off-ramp with rubber smoke billowing behind him. Once he reached the top of the ramp, he turned left with a screaming chorus of tires, crossed the flyover and headed south.

Tyler was looking at him, white-faced and bewildered. 'Why did you do that, Dad? That man was blown up! Who was he? Was he with you?'

Martin kept his foot flat on the floor and blasted his horn as a panel van tried to pull out in front of him.

'That man was Charlie Bonaduce. He and I served in the Second Marine Expeditionary Brigade in Afghanistan together. He lost an arm to a roadside bomb.'

He swerved in and out of a slow-crawling line of cars, and then he said, 'Charlie said that his life wasn't worth living any more and he wanted to blow his brains out, but he didn't because it would make a mess, and his maid would have to clear it up.'

He slewed left into Baseline Avenue, running a red light and provoking a furious fusillade of horn-blowing from other drivers.

'*Asshole!*' screamed one of them.

Martin ignored him. He turned to Tyler and said, 'Seems like Charlie found a way round that particular problem.'

THIRTEEN

He kept his foot down and didn't stop for anything – not red lights nor yield signs nor traffic snarl-ups. At the intersection with Mount Vernon Avenue he avoided a long line of cars waiting to turn left by swerving into the exit of Walgreens parking lot and careering out again through the entrance.

'*Dad*,' said Tyler, gripping his armrests tightly to stop himself being thrown from side to side.

'Sorry, Tyler, I don't mean to scare you but things are getting critical, and a whole lot sooner than anybody's prepared to admit.'

'Dad, I didn't shoot Mr Alvarez and like I told you that Big Puppet made me do what I did to Maria. He would have *killed* her if I hadn't, he would have shot her right in front of me. She'll tell the judge that, I know she will. Mr Lemos said they would have let me out on bail, for definite.'

'Listen, I know that,' said Martin. 'But this afternoon they're going to cut off the water supply to West Valley Detention Center, just like they've cut it off to all off the poorer districts downtown. Come on, Tyler, prison is bad enough as it is. Can you imagine being locked up in a place like that without being able to take a shower or flush the john or even have a drink of water? You're talking hell on Earth.'

'Are you serious? They're going to cut off the water? They can't do that!'

'They can and they're going to. Not only that – I don't think they have any intention of turning it back on again, not until this drought is over, and when *that* will be, God alone knows. They keep talking about rotating the water rationing from one neighborhood to the next but that's B.S.'

'How do you know that?'

'I have it on good authority from someone on the Governor's special drought team. It's survival of the wealthiest, dude. Welcome to the wonderful world of the haves and the have-nots, and the way things are going, the have-nots are *never* going to have it. Look up ahead of us. See all that smoke downtown? That's a water riot.

That's people who haven't been able to have a drink of water or wash for two days.'

'I heard the cops talking about it in the police station. Even some of them were saying that you can't blame people for protesting if they don't have any water.'

'Of course not. But as soon as people riot, the authorities can accuse them of civil disorder, and that automatically puts them in the wrong. We're supposed to have free speech in this country, but that depends on who you are and what you say.'

'So what are we going to do?' said Tyler. He turned around in his seat to see if anybody was following them, but the nearest vehicle was two blocks behind them, and it was a bus. 'The police are going to be looking for us, aren't they?'

'The police are kind of busy right now, so I'm taking advantage of that to get us out of town – me, you, your mom and Ella – and some other people, too. Some people who can help us to survive, with any luck.'

'What people? Where are we going?'

'If I knew that, exactly, I wouldn't need anybody's help. But right now, I do.'

'Dad – your friend Charlie—'

'I know,' said Martin, glancing down at his blood-spattered shirt and pants. The blood had dried now, and turned a rusty brown color. 'Just try not to think about it, OK? That was the way Charlie would have chosen to go, believe me. Not with a whimper, but a damn great bang.'

As they drove nearer and nearer to downtown, they could hear sirens screaming in chorus and a pattering sound that sounded like rain, except that it hadn't rained in over a year. They also heard intermittent popping and crackling, a mixture of fireworks and gunfire.

As they crossed over 3rd Street and looked westward to North D Street they could see almost nothing but thick gray smoke and a scattering of small orange fires burning on the ground, which Martin guessed were the shattered remains of home-made gas bombs. Red and blue police lights were flashing through the gloom, and they could see scores of people running, although the smoke was so thick they looked like ghosts. It was their feet that were pattering like rain.

Windows had been broken and cracked all the way along the

street, including the Bank of America, and there was debris strewn everywhere – chairs, newspaper stands, railings, bricks, even a giant fiberglass ice-cream cone, lying on its side.

Tyler said, 'What do they *expect* people to do, if they cut off their water?'

'I think they expect them to lie down obediently and die,' said Martin. He could smell tear gas in the air, and so he shifted the Eldorado back into drive and took the next left, away from the city center. 'In fact I think they've forgotten that people on welfare are as human as they are, even if they're poor. They're just, like, inconvenient statistics. They use up x amount of water every day, but they never pay for it. Therefore, they're not entitled to any.'

He turned right, and then left, and then right again. The rundown suburban streets leading to the Murillo house were hot and empty, their tar melting and their concrete cracking and their parched bushes decorated with candy wrappers and torn sheets of newspaper and dented cola cans. There was nobody in sight, only a mangy brown-and-white dog trotting along the sidewalk with its tongue hanging out, rasping for breath.

They parked and Martin stowed the two Colt Commandos in the trunk, making sure that he locked it. Then he led Tyler around the side of the house. All of the Murillo children were still there, lying in the shadow of the back verandah, except for Susan, who was inside, banging and clattering in the kitchen, although what she was able to cook without any water was anybody's guess. Mikey was playing a game on his iPhone while Nathan was using a toy truck to run over ants and squash them. George and Mina were asleep, and their grandfather Santos Murillo was asleep, too, his Panama hat covering his face, his flaccid belly hanging over the withered elastic of his boxer shorts. From inside the living room came the overenthusiastic sound of a TV shopping program.

People are dying of thirst, thought Martin, *and they're still trying to sell them crystal bead drop earrings.*

He stepped carefully over one of the sleeping children and shook Santos' shoulder. Santos let out a sharp bark of surprise and lifted his hat, trying to focus on Martin with misted-up eyes.

'What is it? You scared the shit out of me. I was having a dream about buzzards, trying to peck out my eyes.'

'They still haven't turned your water back on?'

He coughed, and sniffed, and sat up straight. 'Another twelve hours, that's what they said on the news. Well, ten now because that was two hours ago. But I won't believe it until I see it pouring out of the faucet with my own eyes.' He paused, and looked Martin up and down, and then said, 'What the hell happened to you? You been creosoting a fence or something?'

'Something like that. But you see all that smoke? That's people rioting about the water, because they don't believe it's ever coming back on.'

'I was right, then. They want us dead. But what we can we do?'

'We can get the hell out of here.'

Santos stared at him, licking his lips with a tongue as gray and as dry as a lizard's. 'I do believe I know what you're thinking, Mister Children-and-Family-Service man.'

'Go on, then. Tell me. What *am* I thinking?'

'You're thinking about what I said the last time we talked. You're thinking about Lost Girl Lake. You want me to take you there, don't you? There's always plenty of water at Lost Girl Lake.'

'Very astute of you, Santos. But not just me. All of us. My family, and *your* family, too. Rita, and Susan, and Mikey, and all the rest of the kids. There's plenty of room for them all in that old Suburban of yours, isn't there?'

'Unh-hunh. Rita won't come. Rita won't go anyplace where she isn't two minutes away from a discount liquor store. Besides, it would probably kill her if she stopped drinking cold turkey. And she would never let us take the kids. She may be a drunk but she loves the kids almost as much as she loves her booze.'

'What about Susan?'

Santos shook his head. 'No way. Susan won't come without her brothers and sisters. She's like their mother.'

'This *city*, Santos – this county – this entire state – maybe this whole goddamned country for all they're telling us – it's Armageddon, Santos. People are going to start dying in their thousands.'

Santos reached across to a rusty metal ashtray and picked up his half-smoked stogie. 'Oh, well. Maybe it's retribution time. Maybe at last the Great Spirit has decided to take his revenge on the people who killed our women and children and took our land away from us.'

'You don't believe that any more than I do,' Martin retorted. 'Come on, Santos. I need you. How can I find Lost Girl Lake without you?'

Santos sucked thoughtfully on his stogie, although he didn't light it. Almost half a minute went past before he said, 'Give me one good reason why I should.'

'Because once this drought is over I'll make sure that Rita goes into rehab and that the kids get everything they need, and more. A private education. Health care. You name it. I'll also make sure that you get the best palliative treatment for your prostate cancer.'

'So why didn't you do all this before?'

'Because I wasn't trying to bribe you before.'

Santos couldn't stop himself from smiling. 'You know something, Wasicu, for a bacon stealer, you're very, very honest.'

For Santos to call Martin 'Wasicu' was a long-standing joke between them. 'Wasicu' was a Lakota word for 'white man' but it was often confused with 'wašin icu' which means 'steals the bacon' or 'greedy,' and even many Native Americans thought that was why the white men had been given that name.

'So can you show us how to get there?' Martin asked him.

'I can. I could. But Lost Girl Lake, it's only a daydream, these days. A place I think about when the pain gets worse.'

'Santos, I'm seriously asking you to be our guide.'

'Don't you have satnav?'

'Lost Girl Lake isn't marked on any satellite maps. I know. I looked for it.'

'I'm too sick, my friend. What I said to you before about relocating . . . that was wishful thinking, that's all.'

Martin looked down at the children sprawled all around them. 'Santos, if you take us to Lost Girl Lake, I will guarantee that I will have somebody from CFS come here and take all of your family someplace safe. Somewhere where the drought is not so serious and they can start all over. I have contacts in family services in Portland, in Oregon. I also have contacts in Vancouver, in Canada. I'll pay for it myself.'

'So why don't you just take your own family there?' asked Santos.

Martin looked across at Tyler, who was sitting on the steps at the end of the verandah, bouncing Nathan's ball. Nathan himself was sleeping on one of the sunbeds, breathing harshly through his mouth and twitching from time to time as if he were having a nightmare.

'My son Tyler here got into some trouble with the law. I've just sprung him from a prison bus. We couldn't go near an airport or a major highway without risking him getting caught again.'

'What's he supposed to have done?'

'The cops think he shot somebody but he didn't.'

Santos nodded, reflectively. 'That happened to one of my boys once. John, his name was. Only trouble is, he didn't even get a trial. The cops shot him dead on the spot.'

Santos laid his hand on little Mina's head. Her eyes were half-closed and her lips were swollen and cracked.

'Granpa,' she whispered. 'Granpa, I'm so thirsty.'

'It's OK, sweet thing,' said Santos. 'Mikey . . . bring your sister some of that Mountain Dew, will you?'

Mikey got up and went into the house. Santos said, 'Him and Nathan went out last night and came back with three big bottles of soda. We didn't ask them where they found them. We were just glad of the drink.'

'Santos,' said Martin, 'these kids are going to die unless we do something. I still think your best option is for your whole family to come with us. There's no rain forecast and things are only going to get much, much worse.'

Santos thought for a moment longer, and then stood up, wincing as he did so. 'OK, I'll go talk to Rita. Don't be surprised if you hear some yelling and cursing. But I'm the head of this family, after all, when it comes down to it, and Rita knows that, even when she's drunk as a skunk.'

Less than forty minutes later, Rita and all the rest of the Murillo family were crowded into Santos' faded green Chevy Suburban in the front driveway of their house, all eight of them. They had packed some changes of clothes into black plastic trash bags and cardboard boxes.

Santos started up the Suburban's engine with a shriek of its fan belt and a cloud of black smoke. Martin walked across the scrubby, sunburned lawn and said, 'Don't know how you managed to persuade her, Santos, but congratulations.'

Susan was sitting in the center, and Rita gave Martin a finger-wave from the right-hand passenger seat. 'You're a good man, Martin!' she crowed. 'I always said so, didn't I? You're simply the best, better than all the rest!'

Santos leaned out of his window, cupped his hand over his mouth and said, very quietly, 'I told her that you had a case of Smirnoff Blue Label at your house. I said that if she agreed to come with us, she could have it all to herself.'

'I see,' said Martin, grinning at Rita and giving her a wave of his hand in return. 'What happens when she finds out that she's been bamboozled?'

'You were in the Marines, weren't you? I am sure that you know all about crossing bridges when you come to them.'

Martin walked back to his car and sat down behind the wheel. As he started up the engine, Tyler said, 'This is insane, Dad.'

'Of course it's insane. But life is insane. If there's one thing I've learned, it's that the only way to survive is to out-insane it.'

It would have been far quicker for them to go back through the city center and join the northbound freeway by the 5th Street on-ramp. But as they reached the end of the street they could see that even more fires had broken out downtown and now they could hear repeated crackles of gunfire, as well as people screaming.

Thick brown smoke was pouring from the upper floors of the nine-story Vanir Tower. It was billowing in front of the sun, so that the afternoon had become prematurely gloomy.

Tyler looked at Martin wide-eyed. 'Jeez, Dad. It's like a war.'

'It *is* a war,' said Martin. He turned around to Santos, who had stopped close behind them, and indicated that he was going to turn right, away from the city center, and make his way north through the suburbs. He would probably take North Mountain View Drive, if it was clear. It was a divided highway for most of the way, and even though the speed limit was only forty he doubted if there would be many traffic cops around.

He was right. When they turned into it, he could see that North Mountain View Drive was wide and empty, all the way to the Foothill Freeway. He put his foot down and headed due north, with Santos' Chevy rattling only a few feet behind him. He just hoped that Santos' brakes weren't as worn out as Santos was.

He turned on the radio, but all he could find was country-and-western music and AllWorship contemporary Christian rock and some Spanish-language station discussing burritos. When he tried to tune in to the news, there was nothing but a loud hissing sound.

'Maybe the rioters have broken into the radio stations,' Tyler suggested.

'Either that, or the powers-that-be don't want us to know what's happening, and they've jammed them.'

He was still punching repeatedly at the buttons on the radio when his cell rang. He heard a woman say, '*Martin?*' and then something else, but at first her voice was distorted and blurry.

'Hallo?' he said. 'I can't hear you. Who is this?'

Suddenly he could hear her very clearly, almost as if she were sitting next to him. 'Martin? It's Saskia – Saskia Vane. I need your help. I think I'm in serious danger. I don't just *think* it . . . I know I am.'

'Right now, Saskia, we're *all* in serious danger.'

Saskia said, 'I know, but this is something different. I've been specifically threatened. It's Joseph Wrack, from Empire Security Services. He's their director of public safety, so-called, which really means that he's in charge of making sure that anybody who causes trouble for any of their clients suffers a very nasty accident, very often fatal.'

'But you're supposed to be on the same side, aren't you? ESS works for Governor Smiley and so do you.'

'I do. Or at least I did. But I tipped you off about them cutting off the water at the West Valley Detention Center, didn't I? Maybe I was naïve, but I didn't realize you were going to rescue your son in quite such a spectacular way. Joseph Wrack's gone apeshit. One of his top security guards was crushed underneath the prison bus, and seriously injured. His back was broken and it looks like he's going to lose one of his legs.'

'Listen to me, Saskia. That so-called top security guard shot my old service buddy Charlie right in front of me, in cold blood. He only got what he asked for.'

'Maybe, but Joseph Wrack doesn't see it that way. He's out to get me.'

'How do you know that?'

'One of Governor Smiley's PR girls happens to be a friend of mine. After Wrack saw me and you together at KNBC she overheard him telling Governor Smiley that he thought we were acting "too familiar". From then on, Wrack's people tapped all of my cellphone calls and all of my emails. Wrack's paranoid like that, so my friend says. So he knew at once that I gave you the heads up about them cutting off the water at the West Valley Detention Center – and according to my friend he blames *me* for his security guard getting hurt and his bus being wrecked. She heard him tell Governor Smiley that he's going to nail me.'

'And what did Governor Smiley say to that?'

'Nothing, apparently.'

'You told me that you *owed* Governor Smiley. Big time, that's what you said. So what do you owe him?'

'I can't talk about that now, Martin. I just need to get out of San Bernardino before one of Wrack's people finds me. I was hoping you could help in some way.'

They were driving over the freeway now. Below them, the east-bound lanes were solid with stationary traffic, while the westbound lanes were almost empty. It looked as if everybody was trying to escape from the city, although Redlands and Palm Springs and Palm Desert were probably just as short of water as San Bernardino. The mid-afternoon sun was so intense that the vehicles were shimmering with heat. Martin could see that scores of people had left their cars and were sitting under the flyovers to find some shade.

'Where are you now?' he asked Saskia.

'I'm down in the lobby of the Hilton Hotel, on East Hospitality Lane, which is where I've been staying. I'm using their house phone so that Wrack doesn't know I'm calling you. I didn't want to go back to my room in case there was one of his people waiting for me.'

Martin thought for a moment, and then he said, 'Me and my family, we're getting away from the city right now. I can't tell you exactly where because I don't know exactly where.'

'Can I come with you?'

'How do I know that I can trust you?'

'I told you about the water at West Valley Detention Center, didn't I?

'True. But maybe you just want to find out where I am, so that you can tell Joseph Wrack, and do a deal to get him off your back.'

'You have a *very* suspicious mind, Martin Makepeace.'

'I didn't stay alive in Afghanistan by believing everything that everybody told me.'

Tyler was frowning at Martin now, wondering who he was talking to. They had reached West 34th Street north of the freeway and Martin spun the steering wheel with the flat of his hand to take a wide left-hand turn. Santos followed inches behind in his Suburban. He was so close that Martin could hear Mina and George both crying.

Saskia said, 'Please, Martin. I'm really begging you now. If I stay here or if I try to go back to LA, Wrack will get to me. And Halford Smiley won't do anything to protect me, either.'

'All right,' said Martin. 'So long as you promise me one thing
. . . that one day you'll come out and tell the world what kind of
a man Smiley really is.'

'Oh, that would be a pleasure, Martin, believe me.'

Martin checked the time. 'OK,' he said, 'do you have
transport?'

'I have a rental, with satnav.'

'If you can get to Lionel E. Hudson Park by four thirty and wait
on North Park Drive by the swing sets, I'll meet you there. Don't
worry if I'm a few minutes late.'

'I won't forget this, Martin, believe me.'

Martin tossed his cellphone on to the seat beside him. He knew
that he could be making a serious mistake by inviting Saskia to join
them. In the past, however, he had found himself in several life-or-
death situations when he had needed to ask for help from people
he didn't particularly like. But if they hadn't helped him, he probably
wouldn't be here today.

'Who was that?' asked Tyler.

'That was the woman who pretty much saved your life.'

'Is she going to come with us?'

Martin nodded.

They drove in silence for another few minutes, and then, through the
dreamlike rippling of heat, two vehicles came toward them in
the opposite direction – a silver Caprice, followed closely by a red
Toyota pick-up. Both of them were traveling at no more than twenty-
five miles an hour, so that as they came nearer Martin could see
that at least seven young hoods were sprawled in the back of the
pick-up, hooting and laughing and waving beer cans.

'Dad, that's *them!*' said Tyler, urgently, laying his hand on Martin's
arm. 'Those are the guys who shot Mr Alvarez and raped Maria!'

He turned around as the pick-up passed them by, and said, 'There
he is! That's Big Puppet! And the other one with him, that's K-Bomb!'

Martin twisted around, too. 'You're sure about that?'

'Hundred percent! It's them, Dad! Those are the same two cars
they got away in – that Chevy and that red pick-up truck!'

Martin immediately signaled and pulled into the side of the road.
He beckoned to Santos to pull up alongside.

'What's wrong?' Santos shouted. Mina and George were still
mewling, and Rita and Susan were arguing about something.

'Keep going straight ahead until you get to Brookfield Street!'

Martin shouted back at him. 'I think it's the third or maybe the fourth turning on your left. There's a sign there for Lionel E. Hudson Park. Wait for me there, at the park, OK?'

'Where the hell are you going, Wasicu? These kids are getting real tetchy. You're not going to be long, are you?'

'Not if I can help it.'

With that, Martin gunned the Eldorado's engine and U-turned across the road in a cloud of rubber smoke. He put his foot flat down on the gas pedal and headed back the way they had come.

Tyler was wide-eyed. '*Dad*? You're not going after them, are you?'

'You think I'm going to let them get away, after what they did? If it hadn't been for them, Charlie Bonaduce would still be alive and you wouldn't have been accused of felony murder. Those punks turned my life upside down, as well as yours. You just try to stop me from going after them!'

FOURTEEN

After less than two minutes, the red Toyota pick-up came into view around the curve ahead of them, and then the Caprice. Martin stamped his foot down even harder and the Eldorado surged up to ninety miles an hour. He had no particular plan in mind, and he was well aware that he was acting recklessly, even stupidly, but law and order was falling apart all around them, and if he wanted justice to be done he felt that he had to do it himself. Who else would do it? The cops were too busy beating and tear-gassing innocent people because they wanted water.

'That's him, Dad,' said Tyler, as they came closer and closer to the back of the pick-up. 'The guy in the light gray hoodie, with the dyed ginger hair.'

Big Puppet was sitting right at the back of the pick-up, in the left-hand corner, with both of his arms stretched out along the sides. K-Bomb was sitting right next to him, his long greasy hair flapping like a raven's wing.

Martin could hear rap music playing, and all of the hoods were nodding their heads in time to the beat. They didn't notice how quickly his Eldorado was gaining on them until Martin and Tyler were less than fifty feet away. It was only then that Big Puppet turned around and stared at him and gave K-Bomb a shove on the shoulder. Martin saw him mouth, 'Hey, what the f—?' or something similar.

The hoods all stared at him. Martin didn't know if Big Puppet recognized Tyler or not. Apart from being dusty, the Eldorado's windshield was sharply raked back, and the sun was probably reflecting from it. All the same, Big Puppet flapped his hand at them as if he were telling them to back off and stop tailgating, and some of the other hoods gave them the finger.

In reply, Martin blasted his horn, which made them all jump. Big Puppet gave them the finger with both hands and started to scream obscenities at them. Martin blasted his horn again, which unsettled the pick-up's driver, because he suddenly swerved from side to side, and the hoods in the back had to grab the sides to stop themselves from losing their balance, or even falling out.

Martin flashed his headlights to tell the driver to pull over, but instead the Toyota began to pick up speed. Big Puppet kept on shouting and gesturing at him, but now he had to sit down and use one hand to hold on tight. Martin flashed his headlights again, and then again.

'*Dad*,' said Tyler, but Martin was too hyped up with adrenalin now to let the hoods get away. He blew his horn and nudged the Toyota with his front bumper, pushing it just hard enough and long enough to make the driver momentarily lose control of his steering. The hoods in the back shouted in chorus as the pick-up veered wildly to the left, crossing over to the opposite side of the road, and then veered back again, so that its nearside tires ran off the blacktop altogether, on to the verge, throwing up a cloud of dust and a machine-gun rattle of rocks.

In front of the Toyota, the gang member who was driving the Caprice clearly couldn't understand what was happening right behind him, because he gradually slowed down and began to pull over toward the side of the road. With a dull thump of rubber and metal, Martin nudged the Toyota again, and this time the Toyota driver accelerated as hard as he could, swerving to the left and overtaking the Caprice.

Both vehicles were traveling now at more than seventy miles an hour, and the hoods in the back of the Toyota had stopped cursing and gesticulating and now they were all hunched down like a family of monkeys, desperately gripping the sides of the pick-up and holding on to each other, too. Big Puppet's face was tight with fury, and Martin could see that he was mouthing something, over and over, and he didn't have to hear it to guess that it wasn't a prayer.

The flyover that crossed the freeway was coming up fast. They were touching eighty-five miles an hour because the road was dead straight, but Martin could feel himself calming down now. His djinn moment was fading and he was beginning to think that he couldn't keep up this pursuit for much longer. What would he do, even if he managed to force these hoods to stop? He had two Colt Commandos in his trunk and plenty of ammunition, but he couldn't really line them all up by the side of the road like a one-man firing-squad and shoot them, could he? Besides, he had to think of Santos and his family, and his only family too. It was no good allowing his rage to get the better of him, no matter how righteous it was.

He glanced at Tyler and he could see that Tyler was feeling the same way. At least they had managed to frighten his tormentors half to death, which was some kind of retribution for what they had done to him.

Martin pressed his foot down again and the Eldorado rammed the back of the Toyota one more time. Its tires screaming, the Toyota slewed toward the concrete retaining wall at the side of the flyover, but instead of colliding with it and bouncing back, it was traveling so fast that it burst right through the wall and the guard rail on top of it, and flew out over the freeway.

Martin slammed his foot on the brakes. The Eldorado howled around one hundred and eighty degrees before coming to a stop, but at the same time he saw the Toyota pick-up virtually frozen in mid-air as it ran out of momentum, sixty feet above the westbound lanes of the freeway. The hoods were tumbling out of the back and into the air, their arms and legs waving like acrobats. It looked more like a spectacular circus performance than a traffic accident.

He could have sworn that for almost five seconds there was silence, and that the pick-up and the hoods who had been sitting in it were motionless.

Then there was a deafening crash as the Toyota nosedived into the reinforced steel rails of the median strip, and a soft complicated series of thumps as the hoods fell on to the tarmac roadway.

Martin and Tyler climbed out of the Eldorado and hurried across to the guard rail. Two more cars stopped behind them, and two men and a woman came over to join them. In the middle distance, however, Martin saw that the silver Caprice was U-turning and heading back north.

'Holy Moses,' said one of the men. The eastbound side of the freeway was still jammed solid, and people were emerging from underneath the flyover and climbing out of their cars. They were hunkering down beside the spreadeagled bodies of the hoods, but it didn't appear to Martin as if there was much that anybody could do for them. None of them was moving and there was blood sprayed all the way across the road.

The woman crossed herself. 'May God have mercy on their souls,' she said.

Considering where those punks are headed, I don't think God will get the chance, thought Martin. He put his arm around Tyler's shoulders. 'Come on,' he said. 'I don't think there's anything more that you and me can do here.'

He shaded his eyes and looked toward the city center. Smoke was piling up in thick black curds now, and at least three helicopters were circling around.

'Time to go, Tyler. Come on.'

'We *killed* them,' said Tyler, turning back one more time to look at the bodies of the hoods lying on the freeway. He was so shocked that his voice was thin and breathless, almost like a girl's. 'I can't believe it, Dad. We *killed* them.'

They drove back up West Kendall Avenue in silence. When they reached the park they found that the Murillo family were waiting for them under the trees. Mikey and Nathan were playing on the swing sets but the smaller children were too tired and too hot, although they had at least stopped crying.

Rita was finishing the last of a half bottle of Jack Daniel's. When it was empty she held it up and squinted at it and shook it hard, as if it would magically refill itself.

'What happened?' asked Santos, as Martin and Tyler walked across the grass to join them. He pointed to each of his eyes in turn and then pointed at them, as if to show them that he had special powers of perception. 'Something *bad* has happened, hasn't it? I can tell by your faces.'

Martin said, 'I don't know, Santos. Guess it depends on your point of view. Let's just say that the Great Spirit moves in mysterious ways, His wonders to perform, and because of that some very unpleasant characters got what they deserved.'

'Very well,' said Santos, with a shrug. He didn't ask any more questions. 'And now we should leave, yes? We need to be well into the mountains before it gets dark.'

Martin led them the short quarter-mile distance to Peta's house. As soon as they parked outside, Peta opened the front door and came hurrying out to meet them. She hugged Tyler as if she never wanted to let him go again, ever, and she looked at Martin tearfully over Tyler's shoulder, shaking her head as if to say, *you shouldn't have done what you did, but thank you.*

Santos and Susan and the children all climbed out of the Suburban, although Rita stayed where she was, her head tilted back and her mouth open, snoring. Santos came up to Peta and held out his hand.

'Peta – this is Santos Murillo,' said Martin. 'Santos knows a place where we can hold out until the drought's over.'

'What kind of a place? Where is it?'

Santos said, 'I won't lie to you, dear lady. It is a place in the mountains where we will have to survive in the way that my Yuhaviatam ancestors used to survive. But we will always have water, and food, and we will be safe. There are caves there, and we can build shelters, but if you have any tents, so much the better.'

Peta obviously didn't know what to say. She turned to Martin and then she looked at the Murillo children with their grubby T-shirts and worn-out sneakers with no laces in them. Mikey had his finger up his nose.

'The water's not going to come back on, sweetheart,' Martin told her. 'There *is* no water – not unless you're one of Governor Smiley's chosen few.'

Peta said, 'This is the USA, Martin, not Ethiopia. This is the twenty-first century. The federal government is not going to let thousands of people die of thirst.'

'You think? It makes no difference what country we're in, sweetheart, or what century it is. No government has the power to produce water out of thin air. Only God can do that.'

Peta looked along Fullerton Drive, with its neat brown-shingled houses and its well-trimmed hedges and all of the shiny cars and SUVs parked in its driveways. Martin could tell by her expression what she was thinking. *This is my home, this is my security, this is where my friends live. This is daytime TV and chicken dinners and church on Sundays. How can you expect me to give this all up and go to live in the mountains like some primitive pioneer?*

'These poor children look like they could all use a drink,' she said. 'I still have one bottle of that water left that you brought me from work.' She beckoned to the children and said, 'Why don't you come on inside, kids? You can have a drink and some rocky road ice-cream. Tyler, can you sort that out for them?'

'Sure, mom,' said Tyler, and led the children into the house. Susan followed, giving Tyler the shyest of smiles.

'Thank you,' said Santos. 'I have been very worried for them.'

Peta said, 'Do you really think the situation is so bad we have to leave?'

'People are rioting downtown,' said Martin. He nearly put his arm around her, but then made out that he was simply stretching.

'The cops are using tear gas on them. They may even be shooting them for all I know. That woman Saskia Vane I was telling you about, she thinks things have gotten so critical that she's going to be coming with us.'

He didn't tell her that Saskia was much more afraid of Joseph Wrack hunting her down than she was of having no water. He didn't want to complicate matters.

'As a matter of fact, I already have everything packed,' said Peta, and she nodded toward her Hilux, parked outside the garage doors.

'You do?'

'Clothes, food, and those two tents we took to Yosemite.'

'Really?'

She smiled at him wryly and laid her hand on his arm. 'Martin, for all the arguments we had, for all of those times I hated you, I still trust your judgment when it comes to something as serious as this.'

'Is Ella any better? Will she be OK?'

'She's still feeling very tired and she doesn't have her appetite back, but her temperature's back to normal, and otherwise she's fine. I wouldn't think of taking her if I didn't think she was up to it.'

'OK. Great. Thank you.' He leaned forward to kiss her, but as he did so he saw Rita climbing awkwardly down from the back seat of Santos' Suburban. Rita's scraggly bleach-blonde hair was sticking up even more wildly than usual and her purple cotton dress was creased and stained down the front. She stood blinking at her surroundings, keeping one hand on the Suburban's door to steady herself, and then she turned around and frowned at Martin and Peta as if she had just arrived on the surface of Mars and they were two aliens.

'This is Rita, the kids' mother,' said Martin. 'Rita is what you might call a non-recovering alcoholic.'

'And she's coming with us?'

'I didn't have a choice. She wouldn't have let us take the kids, otherwise.'

Rita came up the driveway, walking stiff-legged. She patted Martin on the shoulder and said, 'My hero. He's simply the best. Better than all the rest.'

Peta said, 'Hi, I'm Peta.'

'Peta? How about that? You look like a girl to me.'

'It's Peta with an "a". Not an "er".'

'Well, thank the Lord for that. The number of times I've been taken to ER. Fractured my ankle the last time.' She patted Martin on the shoulder again and said, 'My hero.'

'I'll go in and make sure that everybody's ready to leave,' said Peta. She went inside while Rita stood next to Martin, swaying slightly and clinging to his sleeve to keep her balance.

'Santos said you had a case of vodka,' she said slowly, and with special emphasis on the word '*vod*-ka.'

'I do, Rita. I'll load it into the trunk of my car, so that we can take it along with us.'

'It would be good to have a taster. I have to tell you, Martin, I'm jonesing for a drink.'

'Listen, Rita, you sit down here on the bench and I'll see what I can do.'

He helped Rita to ease herself down on the low marble bench beside the front door, and then he went into the house. In the kitchen, the Murillo children were gathered around the table, clattering their spoons as they ate their ice-cream. Tyler and Susan were standing by the sink, talking. Tyler looked pale but Susan was blushing.

'OK?' asked Martin. 'Nearly ready to hit the bricks?'

He went along the corridor to Ella's bedroom. Ella was up and dressed in a pink checkered blouse and jeans. Martin came into the room and gave her a hug.

'You're sure that you're up for this?' he asked her.

'Daddy, I'm fine. I think it was maybe a flu bug, that's all.'

'You still look a little washed out, if you don't mind my saying so.'

'Daddy – I'm *fine!*'

Martin went into the living room. He opened the cupboard doors underneath the TV, and there it was, untouched since the day that he had left this house, a bottle of Maker's Mark whiskey with only one measure taken out of it. He had taken that drink as a regretful toast to the past – a past that he had always hoped was going to be his future. He had meant to take the bottle with him, but just then Peta and Tyler and Ella had arrived outside, all ready to move back in.

He went back outside and handed the bottle to Rita. She stared at the label for a long time before she said, 'I'm not complaining, Martin, but this doesn't look much like vodka.'

'I've already stowed the vodka in the car. We can crack that open later. Now, we need to be leaving, Rita. And for Christ's sake don't drink that all now. At least take a breath or two, in between swallows, OK?'

He checked his watch. Saskia should have reached the park by now. He helped Rita and the Murillo children to climb back into the Suburban, while Tyler and Susan got into Peta's Hilux and Ella joined him in his Eldorado. They started their engines and Martin could see several neighbors coming out of their houses to see what all the commotion was about.

Martin was just about to back out of the driveway when two black Cadillac Escalades with tinted windows came up the road and drew up nose-to-tail by the opposite curb. He gave Ella what he hoped was a confident smile and said, 'Hold tight. I think we may need to get the hell out of here somewhat *prontissimo*.'

He had backed only halfway across the road, however, before the Escalades' doors all opened and seven men climbed out. Three of them stood in front of him holding up their hands while the other four stood behind him to prevent him from backing up any further. Two of them wore light gray suits, white shirts and dark blue neckties, while the rest of them were dressed in the dark blue uniform of Empire Security Services.

One of the suits approached him. He had cropped gray hair and a squarish head, and he walked with the rolling gait of the very fit and the very muscular. He reminded Martin of one of his drill instructors in the Marines.

'Misterrr Makepeace?' he demanded. He didn't stand too close, and Martin could see his eyes darting from side to side as he tried to take in what was happening here – Santos' Suburban blowing out exhaust fumes and Peta's Hilux all ready to back out behind him.

'What if I am?'

'It happens that I *know* you are, sir, and what I need you to do is turn off your engine, exit your vehicle and come with us.'

FIFTEEN

'Oh, really?' said Martin. 'On whose authority?'

'Empire Security Services, sir, with posse authority from the San Bernardino Police Department.' The agent reached into his inside pocket and produced a black leather wallet. He flipped it open so that Martin could see his silver-and-blue enamel badge.

Martin looked around. He was going to have to play this very carefully. There were so many innocent people around, including his own children, Tyler and Ella. All five of the uniformed security agents were openly carrying sidearms, and he could see by the bulges in their coats that the two agents in suits had shoulder holsters, too.

'OK,' he said, raising both hands so that the agents could see them. At the same time, however, he turned to Ella and said, 'As soon as I get out of the car, pop the trunk, OK? You know where the button is, don't you, in the glove box?'

Ella nodded, her eyes wide with alarm. Martin opened his door.

The agent in the gray suit said, 'Please keep your hands up, Mr Makepeace, and walk across to the vehicle on your right. Curtis! You want to open the door for Mr Makepeace, if you would?'

One of the uniformed security agents went over to the second Escalade and opened up its rear passenger door. Martin, still with his hands held high, glanced over his shoulder. Whatever he did now – even if the security agents took out their guns and started shooting at him – Ella and Peta and Tyler and the Murillo family would all be out of their line of fire.

'Just keep walking, sir,' said the agent in the gray suit.

But Martin took only one more step before he half-bent his knees and then hurled himself backward, so that he collided with the agent in the gray suit and both of them fell heavily on to the roadway. For Martin, most of the impact was cushioned by the agent's body, but the agent himself struck the back of his head on the tarmac, and he let out a hoarse, high-pitched wheeze as all of the air was knocked out of him.

The other security agents began to reach for their weapons, but Martin was too quick for them. He rolled over on to the fallen agent's right side and hooked his left arm around his neck to throttle him. At the same time he reached inside his coat and wrenched his gun out of his shoulder-holster. He cocked the gun, jammed the muzzle into the agent's right ear and shouted out, '*Freeze*! Drop your weapons or I'll blow his head off!'

Two of the security agents already had their guns lifted, but Martin pulled the fallen agent even closer, so that he was at least half-shielded by him, and the agents could see that if they opened fire there was a high probability that they would hit their own man, too.

'I said drop them!' Martin repeated. 'Put 'em down – now!'

There was a moment's pause, but then the other gray-suited agent genuflected as if he were in church and laid his automatic on the ground. He looked around at the other agents and made a flapping sign with his hand. They hesitated for a few seconds, but then they followed his example and laid down their guns, too.

Martin guessed that they were probably carrying hideaway guns strapped to their ankles, like the agent who had shot Charlie, but he wasn't going to give them the chance to go for them. He climbed to his feet, heaving the agent in the gray suit up with him, and then circled around to the back of his car, keeping his arm around the agent's throat and his gun pressed hard into his ear.

'Go easy, will you?' said the agent, in a strangulated voice. 'Believe me, you're not worth getting killed for. I have kids.'

'You should have thought of that before you came looking for me,' Martin retorted.

Ella had unlocked the Eldorado's trunk, so Martin released his hold on the agent's neck and raised the lid. He reached inside and lifted out one of the Colt Commandos. Then he shoved the agent out in front of him, tossing his automatic into the trunk and raising the sub-machine gun.

'I need you all to get back into your vehicles!' he shouted. 'Do it now and don't try anything creative! Like your friend here just said, I'm not worth getting killed for!'

Again the agents hesitated for a few seconds, but then the agent in the gray suit said, 'Do like he says, OK?'

All seven agents backed away across the road and climbed back into their Escalades. All of them were scowling.

'Close the doors and don't try to open the windows!' Martin told them. 'And don't try to drive off, either! Stay right where you are if you want to get out of this alive!'

Once the agents had slammed all of their doors shut, Martin called out over his shoulder, 'Tyler!'

'Dad?'

'Come and pick up all of these guns! Drop them into the trunk of my car, OK?'

Tyler climbed out of Peta's Hilux and jogged over to collect up all of the weapons that the agents had laid down in the road. Once he had done that, Martin walked across to the two Escalades and slowly swung the Colt Commando from side to side, as he if were preparing to rake both vehicles with bullets.

Tyler was climbing back into the Hilux now. 'Dad!' he called. 'Come on, Dad!'

Martin raised his left hand to indicate that he had heard him. He guessed that by now the agents had already put in an emergency call to their headquarters and asked for a back-up team, but since the ESS were helping the police to handle the riots downtown he doubted that they had the manpower to respond very promptly, if at all.

He took two or three paces backward, and then he fired a burst into the leading Escalade's front tires and into its engine compartment. The bullets made a series of satisfying bangs as they penetrated the SUV's front fender.

He fired another burst into the rear tires, and then he turned to the second Escalade, and shot its tires out, too. He finished with three single shots into its radiator grille. He couldn't see the expressions on the agents' faces because of their darkly tinted windows, but he could imagine their tightly closed eyes and their tightly clenched teeth. He had been in a Buffalo armored personnel carrier in Afghanistan when it was hit by Taliban machine-gun fire, so he knew from experience that you just grit your teeth and pray.

He climbed back behind the wheel of his car although he kept the sub-machine gun lifted in his right hand in case any of the agents took it into their heads to fire any retaliatory shots at him as he drove away.

Ella was still pressing her fingertips into her ears. 'My *God*, Dad! I think you've made me deaf.'

Martin reached across with his left hand, started up the engine and shifted the Eldorado into gear. He blew his horn twice to alert

Peta and Santos that they were leaving now, and he backed up to allow them to reverse out of the driveway. As they headed off down the road, he saw the driver's side window in the leading Escalade drop down three or four inches, but he aimed his sub-machine gun at it and it was quickly closed up again.

He followed Peta's Hilux, but he kept glancing in his rear-view mirror from time to time, just to make sure that it hadn't occurred to the ESS security agents to commandeer a vehicle from one of her neighbors and come after them.

'Dad,' said Ella.

'What is it, sweetheart? Are you OK?'

'I'm OK. I'm really OK. It's *you*.'

He gave a last quick look in his mirror. There was nobody following them so he lowered the Colt Commando on to the floor behind the passenger seat.

'*Me*?' he said, deliberately pointing to himself like Robert De Niro in *Taxi Driver*. 'What about me?'

Ella shook her head, although she was smiling, too. 'Don't you ever get *scared*? I mean, what happened back there, they could have shot you, those men, and you could have been killed.'

'You can't go through life being scared of dying, Ella. That's one of the things I learned in Afghanistan. If you go through life being scared of dying, you'll never live. Not properly – not the way God meant you to live. And the sad part about it is, you're going to die anyhow, sooner or later.'

They had reached the end of Fullerton Drive, and Martin could see a green Buick LaCrosse parked beside the children's playground in Lionel E. Hudson Park. He flashed his lights and blew his horn to tell Peta and Santos to pull over, and then he pulled over himself, in front of the Buick, and climbed out of his car.

He walked back to the Buick and as he did so the door opened and Saskia climbed out. She was wearing a black silk blouse and tight black jeans and very high-heeled black ankle-boots, and when she came toward him she strutted almost like a model on a catwalk, one foot in front of the other.

They stood facing each other for a moment, not saying anything. Martin couldn't read Saskia's expression at all. Her chin was lifted and her lips were slightly pursed and even though she was looking him directly in the eyes she was repeatedly blinking, as if she had lost the power of speech but was trying to give him a coded message.

'Are you OK?' he asked her. 'We're leaving now . . . heading for the mountains. Are you sure you want to come with us?'

Saskia nodded. She had appeared to be so confident and professional when he had first met her – scathing, even – but now she sounded as if she were falling to pieces. She grasped the shoulder of his shirt and said, 'I'm *scared*, Martin. I've never been so scared in the whole of my life.'

Martin went back to talk to Santos. As Santos put down his window, the children all stared at Martin in awe. Mikey pretended that he was holding a sub-machine gun and spraying bullets in all directions.

'That was *so* cool, the way you shot up those SUVs! That was unbe-*lieve*-able!'

'Yes, well, thanks, Mikey, but that wasn't supposed to be a lesson in how you should normally deal with a sticky situation.'

'Shit – I wish I'd of had that machine gun when I was in my math class! "Mikey – what's nine times thirteen?" "Who gives a shit, Mrs Terman?" *Brrrrrp-brrrrrrp-brrrrp!*'

Rita turned around in her seat and said, slurrily, 'You watch your language, Mikey, you little prick!'

Mina whispered, 'I'm *thirsty*. And I'm *hungry*.'

'Me too,' said George.

Martin said to Santos, 'Do you know your way from here?'

'I'll be OK once we get to the Rim Of The World Highway. But I'm running pretty low on gas.'

'There's a gas station on the way, at Wildwood Plaza,' Martin told him. 'Go back the way we came, but hang a left when you get to West Fortieth Street. It's only a couple of miles.'

'This other woman is coming with us?'

'Saskia, yes. I'll introduce you when we stop for gas.'

'You can trust her?'

'What makes you ask?'

Santos pointed to his eyes and then pointed to Saskia, the same way he had pointed to Martin and Tyler when they had rejoined him after ramming Big Puppet's pick-up.

'Even as a child, I could see things when others were blind. Many of my people have that gift.'

'Oh, yes?'

'That woman is not only dressed in black. She has a dark shadow around her.'

Martin turned around. Saskia was standing under the trees but apart from that he couldn't see any shadows.

'Let's worry about that later,' he said. 'Right now I think we need to get out of here. You go first, then Peta and Tyler will follow you. I'll bring up the rear, just in case any more of those spooks come after us.'

'Whatever you say, Wasicu.'

Martin knew that Santos had called him 'Wasicu' to make a point. It was to emphasize that he was a white man, and didn't have the sensitivity to see the auras that surround not only people, but animals, and birds, and even trees. He didn't say anything, but patted the roof of Santos' Surbuban and went back to join Saskia.

'Let's go,' he told her. 'It'll make things a whole lot easier if you leave that rental car here and come with me.'

He introduced Saskia to Ella. Ella, guardedly, said, 'Hello,' and then, 'I'll go sit in the back.'

Martin gave a wagons-roll! wave of his hand and Santos drove off, closely followed by Peta in her Hilux. As Martin pulled away from the curb, Saskia said, 'You know that Wrack isn't going to let up. He's going to do everything he possibly can to find us. He's that kind of person.'

'You don't have to tell me,' said Martin, and he described how the ESS agents had tracked him down to Peta's house, and how he had shot up their SUVs.

'Oh my God,' said Saskia. She pressed her hand against her forehead as if she were starting a migraine. 'It's not just Joseph Wrack, either. It's Halford Smiley. Once Halford finds out that I've run out on him, *he's* going to want me out of the way, too, just as much as Wrack, if not more.'

'So what is it between you and Governor Smiley? If anybody had asked me, I would have said that you were a woman who wasn't afraid of anybody.'

Saskia glanced at Ella, who was now sitting in the back of the Eldorado, leaning her elbows on the seats in front of her, her hair blowing across her face. 'I can't tell you now, Martin,' said Saskia. 'Let's just say that I'm much more afraid of me than I am of him. The me that I used to be, anyhow.'

Martin was about to ask her what the Saskia that she used to be had done to frighten the Saskia that she was now, but decided against it. It was clear that she didn't think that it was suitable for the ears of fourteen-year-old girls.

They were approaching Wildwood Plaza, at the intersection between East 40th Street and North Waterman Avenue. As they neared the intersection they passed a McDonald's Drive-Thru and a Del Taco restaurant and a Starbucks. Outside McDonald's a large cardboard sign announced NO WATER SORRY CLOSED TILL FURTHER NOTICE. Del Taco and Starbucks, too, were both closed, their doors shuttered and their interiors in darkness.

Saskia was looking around and frowning. 'This isn't right. We weren't supposed to rotate this area for at least three more days. We had a hiatus schedule meeting only yesterday afternoon, and we weren't going to cut off the water in this neighborhood until the middle of next week, if at all.'

'Maybe something's happened that you don't know about.'

'I still have the schedule. Arrowhead, then Ridgeside, then Nena. Shandin Hills was going to be the very last to lose its supply, and even then we were only going to cut if off for twenty-four hours, because of the golf club.'

'My God. You people are all heart, aren't you? Who cares about babies dying of dehydration, so long as the golf courses get watered?'

'Well, I happen to agree with you about that. But you just try to tell that to Halford Smiley. Babies don't have a vote; and babies don't pay taxes or make generous donations to the Halford Smiley re-election fund.'

They reached the Chevron gas station on the corner. With its suspension squeaking, Santos turned his Suburban into the forecourt, and Peta followed him. Martin parked beside him and climbed out of his car. The gas station was deserted and all of the pumps were fastened with padlocks. There was nobody inside the office or the small food mart attached to it. It was late afternoon now and the shadows were lengthening, but the air was still baking hot; and although they were only two or three miles to the east of them, the mountains were barely visible through a haze of heat.

Santos came over to Martin, stretching his arms and sniffing. 'So what do we do now?' he asked. He lifted up one of the padlocks and said, 'I don't have any bolt-cutters on me, how about you?'

'Let's take a look inside,' said Martin. He walked across to the office and peered in through the glass door. He couldn't see any keys hanging up but he doubted if the staff took them home with them, so they were probably kept in a drawer, or in the cash register. He would have to force his way into the office in any case, to switch on the pumps.

Santos took hold of the door handle and shook it. 'See. All locked up. Maybe Gitche Manitou is trying to tell us not to go. Maybe we should just go back and try to survive like everybody else. My ancestors suffered much worse than this.'

'Don't chicken out on me now, Santos. I can't go back, and neither can Tyler, or Saskia, and you're the only person who can take us to Lost Girl Lake.'

Santos smeared the sweat from his deeply creased forehead with the back of his hand. 'I'm tired, Wasicu. I'm tired and I'm hurting.'

'Do you have any painkillers?'

'Forgot to bring some, like a fool.'

'Well there's plenty of Tylenol inside of that store. I can see it from here.'

'I don't know. This whole expedition is crazy. What if we get to Lost Girl Lake and find that it's all dried up, just like all of the other lakes?'

'Come on, Santos. You know that it won't be. Your ancestors went through times much harder than this, didn't they, and they stuck at it until they got where they were going.'

'Oh, for sure. And then *your* ancestors came and wiped them all out.'

Martin walked back to his Eldorado, reached into the back and picked up the Colt Commando. Ella said, 'What's happening, Daddy? What are you going to do?'

'The gas station is closed, sweetheart, but we're all running out of gas so Daddy has to open it up again.'

'With *that*?' said Saskia, looking at the sub-machine gun.

'If I had a key, I'd use it. But I don't, so this is the next best door opener I can think of.'

He walked back to the gas station office. He could see his dark reflection approaching in the glass door, his weapon raised. It was like seeing a ghost of himself, the way he used to look in Afghanistan. Santos, who had been standing close to the door, didn't need to be told to back away.

He fired three ear-splitting shots and the door exploded into sparkling fragments, which dropped to the floor in a heap. Immediately, an alarm bell began to shrill, but Martin stepped without hesitation into the office, his shoes crunching on the broken glass, and went behind the counter. He pulled open one drawer after another, looking for the padlock keys, but all he found were dog-eared notebooks and business cards and half a tube of fruit-flavored Lifesavers.

In one drawer, however, he discovered a large screwdriver, and he used it to pry open the cash register. There was no money in it, but the padlock keys were all there, underneath the coin tray, each of them neatly tagged with their pump numbers.

The alarm continued to jangle, and Martin reckoned that it was only a matter of time before the police or an ESS patrol or some local vigilante came to find out what had set it off. He turned around to the control panel on the wall and flicked on all of the pump switches, and then he went back outside to unlock the pumps.

They filled up all three of their vehicles. As they did so, fewer than twenty cars and trucks passed through the intersection, most of them heading south. Some of them slowed down when they heard the gas station alarm ringing, and their occupants stared at them with beady-eyed suspicion, but none of them stopped.

They were almost finished when they heard the *flacker-flacker-flacker* of a helicopter. Martin stepped out of the shadow of the gas station's canopy and shielded his eyes with his hand. A helicopter was heading in their direction from the south-west, flying unusually low and very fast. Martin backed into the shadow again, just as the helicopter flew past them. He recognized it at once: a Robinson R44 Raven in the distinctive dark blue livery of Empire Security Services. It looped around the intersection and then it returned to hover over the parking lot on the opposite side of the street. As it came down it blew up a storm of grit and waste paper, and it clattered and droned so loudly that Martin could hardly think straight.

Saskia screamed, 'My *God*, Martin, they've found us already!'

Tyler had just finished filling up Peta's Hilux. Peta came over to Martin and shouted, close to his ear, 'What are they going to do? What *can* they do? They're not going to shoot at us, are they? We have children with us . . . they must know that!'

Martin turned around. Santos had climbed back into his Suburban now, and Tyler was hanging up his gas pump nozzle. 'Just get ready to go,' he told Peta. She lifted her head and even though she didn't say anything he could see in her eyes the look that she used to give him when they were first married, before he was sent out to Afghanistan.

He could see trust, and confidence, and he hadn't seen those in her eyes for a very long time. He could almost have believed that it was love.

He lifted the Colt Commando out of the back seat, and then he walked out from under the gas station canopy and across the sidewalk, holding the sub-machine gun with its muzzle pointed skyward. The dark blue helicopter continued to dip and dance over the parking lot, hovering so low that Martin wondered if the pilot was preparing to touch down.

Its cabin windows were tinted but he could see that there were four security agents aboard it, including the pilot. Although the agents would all be armed, the helicopter itself was fitted with no external weapons, and so they would have to land and climb out before they could take a shot at him.

He crossed the intersection, ignoring the four or five cars which passed him, blasting their horns, and then he hopped over the low wire fence around the parking lot. As he approached the helicopter, he had to narrow his eyes against the blizzard of dust, and his shirt and pants were furiously flapping like yacht-sails in a force-eight gale. All the same, he walked right up to it and stood in front of it. He hefted up his sub-machine gun in his right hand until it was pointing at the pilot. Then he held up his left hand with his fingers folded.

'One,' he mouthed, and stuck up his index finger.

He could see the agent sitting next to the pilot lean over and grip his shoulder as if he were saying, '*What's he doing? What the hell is he doing?*'

'Two,' said Martin, and held up his middle finger.

The pilot nudged the helicopter lower, and tilted it forward, so that Martin could feel the rotor blades whistling only five or six feet above his head. The noise was almost unbearable, and the flying grit was stinging his eyes. He felt that he was going to be blinded and deafened for the rest of his life.

'Three,' he said, and raised his third finger, holding back his pinkie with his thumb.

Again the pilot tried to intimidate him by pushing forward his collective lever and tilting the helicopter toward him, but Martin knew from his service experience that even if he landed it, the rotors would still be ten feet clear of the ground. His hair was being wildly blown about and the slipstream was drumming in his ears, but there was no danger of him being beheaded.

'*Four*,' he mimed, holding up four fingers.

The security agent sitting next to the pilot was furiously gesticulating now that he should land. He had even taken out his gun and was jabbing it in Martin's direction as if he were prepared to shoot at him through the cockpit bubble.

Martin lifted his thumb, and he didn't even have to say '*Five*,' because the pilot ignored the security agent's rage and lifted the helicopter up and away in the fastest spiral climb that Martin had ever seen, so that its rotors screamed like some horrified choir. Within seconds it was high above the treetops and well out of range of his sub-machine gun; and as soon as it was high enough, it angled back toward the south-west, where it had come from. Within less than half a minute it had gone, and all Martin could hear was the droning of its engine.

He lowered his gun and stood for a moment in the middle of the parking lot with his eyes closed. He felt drained, in the same way that he used to feel drained after a firefight in Afghanistan. He had never been able to describe the feeling to anybody who hadn't been through it. He had never felt triumphant that he had beaten the enemy. He hadn't even felt elated that he was still alive. He had felt as if all of his humanity had been emptied out of him, as if his soul had been bleached by fear, and he was nothing but a ghost of what he once was. He had felt transparent, as if nobody could see him any more.

He turned and walked back across the intersection to the gas station. They were all waiting for him. Even the children had climbed out of the Suburban and were standing by the pumps.

'That was some face-off,' said Santos, giving him one of his eagle's-claw handshakes. 'I never saw nothing like that in the whole of my life.'

Peta was standing by the open door of her Hilux with her arms folded, but she was giving him a tight, proud smile. As he returned the Colt Commando to the trunk of his car, though, Saskia turned around in the passenger seat and said, 'They'll come after us again, though. They won't give up. There's no way that Wrack is going to let us get away now.'

'Let's worry about that when it happens,' said Martin. 'Meanwhile, since we're already guilty of vandalism and larceny, let's raid that food mart and load ourselves up with some supplies. It doesn't look like they have any water, but there's plenty of soda.'

Little Mina came up to him and held out her hand. Her nose was running but she was looking less flushed than she had before. 'Can I have some Oreos?' she asked him, solemnly.

Martin said, 'Sure you can.' At the same time, from the direction of downtown, they heard a deep, resonant boom.

'What was *that*?' asked Ella.

Santos said, 'Sounded like a bomb, or a gas main blowing, who knows?' He paused, and then he said, 'Whatever it was, it sounded like a reason for us to keep on going.'

Martin pointed to the inside of the store and said, 'Painkillers, Santos. Go get them. Make sure you get plenty. Who knows how long we're going to be away.'

SIXTEEN

They drove eastward on the Rim of the World Highway, which twisted its way higher and higher up into the mountains. Behind them the sun was touching the horizon, and it had become bloated and elliptical, like a huge orange face with features made of drifting smoke. It made Martin feel as if they were being watched impassively by God, and that God was not going to help them because they were getting what they deserved.

In his rear-view mirror, he could see that three or four more major fires were burning downtown. Otherwise the sky was clear but that in itself was ominous. There were no criss-cross vapor trails, as there usually were, which meant that no planes were flying in and out of San Bernardino International Airport, nor any of the municipal airports around it, like Redlands or Riverside or Ontario.

Saskia kept turning around and shading her eyes with her hand. 'No sign of them yet,' she said.

'I can't see them sending a helicopter after us up here,' said Martin. 'They probably haven't even figured that we've come this way. Even *I* haven't figured why we've come this way. I thought Santos was taking us to the Joshua Tree National Park. This road takes us to Big Bear Lake and then turns up north toward the Mojave Desert. If we keep on going we'll end up in Barstow or even in Vegas.'

'Didn't you *ask* him why we're taking this route?'

'I trust him. Sometimes you just have to trust people.'

'I don't trust anybody.'

'Well, you should. Being too cynical is just as dangerous as being too gullible.'

'You don't know Halford Smiley.'

The higher they climbed, the more dramatic the scenery around them became – mountains covered with grayish-green chaparral and shadowy valleys and mile after mile of pine forests. The air was unusually warm for this altitude, but it was much fresher than it had been in the city, and the breeze was light for this time of year. In the fall, hot, dry Santa Ana winds would frequently come down from the high desert at anything up to eighty or ninety miles an hour, bringing depression and sickness to people in the city, and fanning wildfires in the canyons. Martin knew about both of those effects from bitter experience. Santa Ana winds always made him feel moody and quick-tempered, but apart from that he had bought a small cabin eight years ago just outside Running Springs where he and Peta and the children could spend weekends. During the wildfires of October 2007, the cabin had been burned to a blackened skeleton. That had been yet another reason for him to believe that God had turned his back on him.

They reached the western end of Big Bear Lake, and Martin could see that even here, where the lake was at its deepest, the water level had dropped dramatically. The sun had gone down now, and although it was still light the sky had turned a deep shade of violet. He flashed his headlights and blew his horn to tell Santos to pull over by the side of the road.

He walked up to Santos' Suburban and looked inside. Nathan and George and little Mina were asleep, and so was Rita, whose head was resting against the window. The bottle of Maker's Mark was lying on the seat beside her and it was nearly empty.

Susan said, 'Can't we stop here for the night? The kids are beat, and so am I. There must be someplace that will have us.'

Santos looked at Martin and said, 'It could be a risk. If those friends of yours know that we have come this way, they will soon catch up with us.'

'So what were you planning on doing?'

'Driving for another hour into the mountains. There are many places where we can turn off the main highway and settle ourselves down for the night. Old campsites, places like that. I have one particular place in mind. If we do that, nobody will know where we have gone.'

'I'm not surprised. Even *I* don't know where the hell we're going. This highway turns north, doesn't it, into Nevada? I thought Lost Girl Lake was pretty much off to the east.'

Santos tapped the side of his nose with his finger. 'Don't forget that this is *our* country, the Yuhaviatam. You bacon stealers know only the roads on your maps, and on your NeverLost. But in the same way that I can see shadows that you cannot see, I can also see roads which to you are invisible.'

'So you're going to tell me which route we're taking?'

'No. You will have to wait until you see it with your own eyes. I am prepared to take you that way, but not to speak of it.'

'What if something happens to you? Like you get sick or something?'

'Then you will have to find your own way.'

'Why are you being so inscrutable, for Christ's sake?'

'Because your people took our land and left us with nothing but our knowledge of it. This land is our mother. Why do you think our people would never grow crops? Because we would no more push a plow-blade into the soil than stick a knife into our mother's breast. In the same way, we would never tell your mother's most intimate secrets to a stranger.'

Martin stood up straight. 'Do you know something?' he said, 'I think you're totally nuts. But, respect.'

Mina woke up and started almost immediately to whimper. Susan put her arm around her and said to Martin, 'Please – can't we find someplace here to stay? I need to give them something to eat and they need a proper sleep.'

'Well, maybe we could risk it,' Martin told her. 'Let's drive further into town, anyhow, and see if we can find anything.'

'I still think it is a risk,' said Santos. 'If we stay here overnight, it will be much easier for them to find out where we are. How do you think so many of my people managed to escape when your militia came to shoot them all in eighteen sixty-six? They disappeared into the forests like ghosts, because our mother hid them. Our mother, this land.'

'Granpa, *please*,' Susan begged him. 'Mina's soaking, I have to change her.'

'All right,' said Santos. 'We can ask. But if those people catch up with us, we will know who to blame.'

Martin said, 'Who? You're talking about Saskia? You think *she's* going to tell them where we are? Why would she? She's terrified of them, and they're just as keen to get their hands on her as they are on me.'

'So tell me,' asked Santos. 'How come they found us at the gas station so quick?'

'You're being paranoid, Santos. More than likely they used their heads. They knew roughly which direction we were heading in, and then a gas station alarm was set off. All of those alarms are connected to their local police switchboard, and the ESS are right in there at the moment, helping the police so they put two and two together.'

Santos shrugged, as if to say that he wasn't going to argue.

Martin walked back to his car. Ella said, 'What are we going to do? I'm starving!'

'I'm going to try and see if I can find us someplace to stay. There are plenty of bed-and-breakfast places here in Bear Lake. Santos doesn't think it's a good idea because he's convinced that Wrack's people will find out where we are, God knows how. But we all could use a rest.'

'It's me, isn't it?' said Saskia. 'Your Native American pal thinks that if I can get near a landline, I'm going to put in a call to Empire Security Services and tell them where we are. I wouldn't be surprised if he believes that I tricked you into letting me come along with you, so that they could track you down.'

Martin smiled and shook his head. 'Saskia – he's an old-school Serrano, and you know what happened to them, even if it was a hundred and fifty years ago. He doesn't trust any of us.'

'Well, let's go find a bed and breakfast, just so's I can prove him wrong.'

They drove a half mile further along the lakeshore, until they came to a three-story Bavarian-style building with a carved wooden shingle hanging outside saying *Tyrol Bed & Breakfast*. Martin blew his horn again and they parked outside. Lanterns were shining along the hotel's verandah and all of the windows were lit but there were no other vehicles in the parking lot, and when they switched off their engines, they could hear no voices or music or people laughing.

In fact, the whole city of Big Bear Lake was unnaturally quiet, with only the distant barking of a dog and the warm breeze whispering in the trees.

'Give me a couple of minutes,' said Martin, opening his door.

'I think this place is spooky,' said Ella. 'It's like something out of one of those horror movies.'

Martin climbed the steps and pushed his way in through the hotel's front door. There was nobody behind the front desk, only a stuffed elk's head hanging on the wall, staring down at him in glassy-eyed panic. He could faintly hear a television in another room, but otherwise there was no sign of life. He went up to the desk and called out, 'Hallo? Anybody at home?'

There was no answer, so he picked up the brass bell beside the register and jangled it loudly.

'Hallo?' he repeated. Then, 'Hallooooo!'

He heard a door close, and measured footsteps. After a few moments a large red-faced man appeared, his greasy hair parted in the center like Oliver Hardy. He was wearing a red checkered shirt buttoned up to the neck and red suspenders. As he crossed the reception area he was slowly and meticulously wiping catsup from around his mouth with a crumpled paper napkin.

'Yes?' he said. He was plainly irritated at being interrupted in the middle of his meal.

'Hi. Are you the manager?'

'Brett Vokins. I'm the owner.'

'I was wondering if you have any rooms free for tonight?'

'Rooms?'

'There's twelve of us altogether, eight adults and four kids, but it's only for the one night.'

'I'm closed,' said the owner. His eyes had the same unblinking stare as the stuffed elk just above his head.

'You're sure you can't open up just for us? The kids are dog tired. We wouldn't even expect anything to eat. Just beds to sleep in.'

'I'm closed because the water supply has been cut off,' the owner told him, speaking very slowly and very precisely, as if he had been obliged to explain this over and over. 'If I was to let you stay here without my having an approved water supply and sewage disposal system then I would be breaking every regulation in the book, and then I'd be closed for good and all.'

'You're right on the shore of a damned great lake. How can you have no water supply?'

The owner continued to stare at Martin as if he couldn't believe his ignorance. 'The lake water isn't drinkable. The city pumps all of its water from underground wells, and there's never enough to go around even when it's been raining, which you've probably noticed it hasn't been doing a whole lot of, lately.'

'Oh. OK.'

'I'll tell you,' the owner continued, as if he were determined to make sure that Martin understood what he was saying. 'Big Bear Lake has some of the strictest regulations on water abuse in the whole state of California. If your home address ends in an odd number, you can only water your plants on odd-numbered days, and you can't water them at all on public holidays.'

'All right, but we don't need to water any plants. We don't even need anything to drink and we don't need to wash. All we need is a few hours' sleep.'

'So what do I do with all of your soiled laundry, after you're gone?' the owner asked him. 'And don't tell me that out of eight adults and four kids, none of you is going to need to go to the bathroom. More important, supposing the place catches fire? What am I going to put it out with?'

Martin said, 'I can't appeal to your better nature then?'

The owner didn't even blink. 'When you run a bed and breakfast, mister, you can't afford to have a better nature. You have to smile, but there's no law that says you have to smile because you mean it.'

'So what do you suggest I do?'

'I have no idea. There's plenty more B and Bs in town, and hotels, too, but you won't find none of them prepared to take you in. The whole city's water supply has been shut off for thirty-six hours already and it don't look like there's any prospect of it coming back on again any time soon. Folks have been leaving in droves, although who knows what the point of that is. According to the news, every place is just as dry as every other.'

'Oh, well. Thanks for your humanity.'

'No need for no remarks like that, mister. This is my livelihood, this business, and my family's livelihood. Charity begins at home.'

Martin left the red-faced owner behind his desk and went back outside.

'Well?' asked Saskia.

'The water's off here, too. They can't take us in because it's against health and safety regulations. It looks like we're going to have to spend the night in the woods after all.'

He went across to tell Santos that the hotel was closed. Although it had been Santos' original plan to camp out overnight, he was looking gray and strained and he seemed almost as disappointed as Susan and the rest of the children. All the same, he nodded and twisted the key in the Suburban's ignition and said, 'Let's go. The sooner we set up camp, the sooner we can give these kids something to eat and settle them down.'

'Are you OK, Santos?' Martin asked him.

Santos grimaced and gave him an almost imperceptible shake of his head.

'Do you want to give this up, and go back? Saskia and me, we can always take our chances.'

'No,' said Santos. 'I think I was always meant to do this. Like it's my destiny. One day you'll be able to look up Lost Girl Lake on Wikipedia and you will see my name there too. Santos Murillo, the man who showed that the Yuhaviatam still know their own land better than the bacon stealers who took it from them.'

They drove out of Big Bear Lake and continued eastward. The night was warm and black and moonless but it was thick with stars. Lightning was flickering in the distance, although Martin doubted if the storms would bring any rain. The air was so dry and so heavily charged with static that it made the hairs on the back of his neck prickle.

After about forty minutes Santos slowed down and signaled that he was turning right. He led them down a narrow road which had been tarmacked for the first three-quarters of a mile but then degenerated into nothing but a rutted, dusty track. Their three vehicles jostled and jolted like three small boats in a choppy sea. Martin could see nothing ahead of him but the rear of Peta's turquoise-blue Hilux, and nothing on either side but grayish-green chaparral and a few scrubby knobcone pines.

'My God,' said Saskia, clinging on to her doorhandle. 'Where's he taking us?'

'Your guess is as good as mine. Are you OK in the back there, Ella?'

'I feel sick,' said Ella.

'Do you want to stop?'

'No, I'm all right for the moment. But I'll tell you if I need to barf, I promise!'

The track rose steeper and steeper, and they found themselves climbing at a sideways angle, too, their suspensions squeaking and banging with every deep rut that they had to drive over. On their left-hand side, the pines grew increasingly dense and close together, and then they began to crowd into their right-hand side, too, until they were engulfed by forest.

Just when branches were beginning to scrape and scratch against the fenders of Martin's Eldorado, Santos turned to the left. They followed him and saw in their headlights that they had reached a wide and level clearing, thickly carpeted with brown pine needles. Seven small wooden cabins were clustered around it in a semi-circle, and a broken wooden sign said *Camp Knobcone*.

Martin took his flashlight out of the glovebox. Then he folded his seat forward and helped Ella out of the back seat. 'How are you feeling?' he asked her, putting his arm around her.

She took three or four deep breaths. 'Better now. But I felt so pukish. It was all that jiggling about and all of those exhaust fumes.'

Everybody was climbing out of their vehicles now. Santos came over and Martin said, 'Camp Knobcone. It's not exactly Day's Inn but I guess it's better than sleeping in a tent. How did you know about this place?'

'My uncle used to take me hunting up here,' said Santos, stretching and looking around. 'Then, when I was older, I used to take girls up here. So . . . it has some good memories.'

Martin went to the nearest cabin. The door wasn't padlocked but it had jammed solid so he had to kick it open. He shone his flashlight inside and saw that there were two wooden bunks, one on each side, and a table in between them. The cabin smelled musty, and there was a dented collection of empty Coors cans under the table, but apart from that it was reasonably clean. Peta came up to him and laid her hand on his shoulder. 'I brought plenty of blankets,' she said. 'We should be all right for tonight, anyhow.'

Martin looked at her. He couldn't tell by her expression if she was suggesting that they should sleep together. Before he could say anything she turned away and went to talk to Ella.

Along with Santos and Tyler, he went from one cabin to the next, pushing and kicking the doors open. They wanted to make sure that no raccoons or skunks had made themselves at home there, and that no snakes were hiding beneath the bunks. The roof of one cabin had collapsed and it was filled with debris and two old birds' nests, and in the cabin next to it they found the remains of a long-dead coyote, so gray and mangy and decayed that it was hardly recognizable.

'Poor creature probably came inside to take a look and the wind slammed the door shut,' said Santos. He peered down at it, and then he said, 'Either that, or it was some guy who pissed off a Yuhaviatam shaman, and got turned into a *wa ya ha* to teach him a lesson.'

'Oh, for sure,' said Martin. There was a folded copy of *The San Bernardino County Sun* on the table, so yellow that it must have been as old as the dead coyote. 'And I suppose he was reading the sports pages when it happened.'

Santos said, 'You should never mock magic, my friend. What is this drought, but the Great Spirit, punishing us with weather magic? You even half believe that yourself.'

Martin looked at him sharply. He was tempted to say, '*How the hell did you know that?*' but he decided to leave it. He was never sure if Santos were ribbing him or not.

SEVENTEEN

They lit a fire in a natural hollow in the rocks. From the soot-blackened granite and the heaps of ashes they could see that campers had lit fires in this hollow many times before, because it acted as a natural hearth. For them, though, the greatest advantage was that nobody on the highway would be able to see it, and it was sheltered by so many trees that it would be difficult to spot from the air.

'Before dark tomorrow we should reach Lost Girl Lake,' said Santos. He had taken three Tylenol with the coffee that Susan had brewed, and now he was sitting upright and his eyes were brighter. 'To start with we can make a camp in the cave there, and then we can think about building a better shelter.'

They grilled hot dogs in front of the fire on sticks, and heated up cans of baked beans and vegetable soup by burying them in the embers. When they had eaten, Peta and Susan made up blanket-beds for the younger children in one of the cabins so that they could settle down to sleep. The moon had risen over the treetops, and Camp Knobcone was now illuminated by a hard white light.

For Rita's sake, they had taken nine six-packs of Budweiser from the Chevron food mart, and she had already managed to drink five cans. None of them had been happy about bringing along so much alcohol for her, especially Peta, who never drank; but even Peta understood that if Rita suddenly stopped drinking altogether, she was liable to suffer from hallucinations and tremors and even a stroke or a fatal heart attack.

'Let's sing something!' said Rita. 'Here we are, sitting around a campfire, we should sing something! How about *Great Green Gobs of Greasy Grimy Gopher Guts*? We always used to sing that when I was at camp! Come on, all of you! Join in!'

She started to sing, shrill and off-key, waving her beer can from side to side so that it sprayed into the fire.

> '*Yankee Doodle went to town a-ridin' on a gopher*
> *Bumped into a garbage can and this is what fell over:*

Great green gobs of greasy, grimy gopher guts,
Mutilated monkey meat, chopped up parakeet.
French-fried eyeballs rolling down the street.
Oops, I forgot my spoon!'

After she had finished, there was silence, except for the crackling of the pine branches on the fire. She looked around her – at Martin and Peta and Saskia and Ella and Tyler and Santos and Susan, and Mikey, too, because Mikey had been allowed to stay up later.

'Do you know something?' she slurred. 'You are the stuff – I mean, you are the stuffiest people I have ever come across – ever – in my life. And I mean *ever*. But do you know something else? I love you. I love all of you. I love you from the bottom of my heart.'

Susan put her arm around her and said, 'Come on, Mom. I think it's time you hit the sack. It's going to be another long day tomorrow.'

Rita took a last swallow from her beer can and then tossed it into the flames. 'You're right,' she blurted. 'You're absolutely right.'

She allowed Martin and Susan to lift her up between them, and then she staggered with Susan to the cabin where she would be spending the night.

'You don't mind sharing with her, do you?' Martin asked Saskia. 'She'll be dead to the world for the next eight hours.'

'Me too, probably,' said Saskia. 'I don't think I've ever felt so exhausted in my life.'

'Can't we have a ghost story?' asked Mikey. 'I never went to a camp before, and aren't you supposed to tell each other ghost stories?'

'Aren't you scared enough already?' Tyler asked him.

'Me? Nah. I'm not scared of nothing.'

'OK,' said Martin. 'Once upon a time there was a boy who really hated school. One day he drew a picture on the chalkboard of his teacher Mr Wolfe looking like some kind of a monster, and underneath he wrote "Werewolf". Well, actually he spelled it wrong and wrote "Where wolf".'

Mikey pulled a face. 'That's not a *ghost* story. That's about me. You know that. The principal asked you to come to the school and he showed it to you.'

'Just hold on,' said Martin. 'I'm not finished yet. Not too long after, this boy who really hated school spent the night in a cabin, way up in the mountains. That same night, back in the classroom, when the moon came up, it shone through the window on to the chalkboard. The chalk drawing of the werewolf came to life. It jumped down from the chalkboard and it left the school and it ran through the streets with its chalky claws scratching on the sidewalk. It followed the boy up into the mountains.'

'Now that *is* scary,' grinned Santos.

'When the boy was asleep, the chalk werewolf crawled through the gap under his cabin door. It could do that, because it was only a drawing. It tippy-toed over to the boy's bunk and it used its claw to write on the wall – "*Where* wolf? *Here* wolf!" When the boy woke up in the morning and saw what the werewolf had written right above his bunk, his hair turned as white as chalk.'

'Hey,' said Mikey. 'That's a really cool story. Nobody ever put me into a story before.'

'Maybe *you* could,' Martin suggested. 'Maybe that's what you could be one day. A story writer, with you in all of your stories. The continuing adventures of Mikey Murillo.'

For a fraction of a second, Martin saw in Mikey's eyes a flash of that enthusiasm that he always looked for when he was trying to give difficult children a reason to behave and to knuckle down to their studies. But then Mikey said, 'Nah. You have to learn all of that spelling. I couldn't even spell "werewolf" right. That was the whole point of that story, wasn't it, me not spelling right?'

As midnight approached, and the fire was dying down, they retired to the cabins. Peta was sharing a cabin with Ella, while Saskia went in with Rita, who was already deeply asleep. Tyler and Mikey took the next cabin together, and Martin shared with Santos.

'Goodnight, everybody,' called Martin, but not too loudly, in case he woke up the children. Peta was standing by her cabin door, under the moonlight, as if she were a character in an amateur stage play. She looked at him but she didn't say anything and she didn't wave. She just went into her cabin and closed the door behind her.

'"Goodnight, everybody"?' said Santos, who was already pulling up his blanket over his shoulders. 'You sound like *The Waltons*.'

Martin closed the cabin door and eased himself back on his bunk. It was hard, of course, but he had slept in much more uncomfortable places in Afghanistan, like the back of a Buffalo, or a trench so narrow that his arms had been pinned to his sides all night.

'We *are* doing the right thing, getting out of the city like this?' he asked Santos.

'Are you asking me if I think that you are a coward, for running away?'

'Not really. But maybe we should have stayed there and toughed it out, like everybody else.'

'My people learned a very hard lesson, when your people came to steal our land. It may be brave to face up to adversity, but it is no disgrace to survive.'

Martin turned over to face the wall. Every muscle in his body felt bruised, almost as badly as when he had been beaten by the Taliban. Even his brain felt bruised, as if he just couldn't think any more. But he did think about Peta, standing in the moonlight looking at him. Had she been wondering if they could possibly start over, and live together again? Or was she simply resigned to the fact that he would never change?

He slept for about two hours and then he was woken by a soft groaning sound. He opened his eyes and lifted his head a little. The moon must have gone down because the interior of the cabin was completely black. There was silence for a while and then the groaning sound was repeated. At first he thought the wind might have risen, because the cabin door was rattling, too.

The next groan, however, was very much louder, and ended in a thick, phlegmy cough.

'Santos?' he asked.

'I am sorry, Martin. I did not want to wake you.'

Martin found his flashlight and switched it on. Santos was perched on the edge of his bunk. His shoulders were hunched like a vulture's wings and his face was glossy with sweat.

'So much pain,' he said. 'I never thought that such pain could exist.'

'Do you want to take some more Tylenol?'

He nodded. 'I will have to. I left them in my truck.'

'I'll go get them for you. Where are they?'

Santos shook his head. 'I will get them myself, and maybe stay in the truck for the rest of the night. You have all of these people to look after. Your wife, your children, my grandchildren, too. You need all the sleep you can get.'

With that, he stood up and wrapped his blanket around his shoulders. Martin stood up, too, and helped him out of the cabin, shining his flashlight across the clearing so that he could see where he was going. Santos reached his Suburban and laboriously climbed inside. Martin waited until he had closed the door and given him a salute, and then he went back to his bunk.

Santos had been right. It was no disgrace to survive. But sometimes survival could be more than anybody could bear.

After another twenty minutes or so he managed to sink back to sleep again. He dreamed that he was sitting in a bare room in Afghanistan, with a single high window covered by a cotton blind. There was a desk in the opposite corner of the room, and a black-bearded man in a black turban and salwar kameez was sitting at this desk, engrossed in writing.

Martin could even hear his pen scratching. *Scritchety-scritchety-scritch.*

Eventually the man set down his pen. He studied what he had written for a while, and then he stood up and came over to where Martin was sitting, holding up the sheet of paper in front of him. He held it much too close to his face, so that Martin found it hard to focus on it. He could see that it was covered in Pashto characters, although he couldn't understand any of it. To him, Pashto writing had always looked like nothing more than a procession of black wriggling worms.

'You know what this means?' the man demanded.

Martin's mouth was so dry that he could hardly manage to say 'No . . . I don't have any idea . . . they just look like worms to me.'

'This is because they *are* worms!' the man snapped back at him. He gave the sheet of paper a violent shake and all of the wormlike writing dropped off it and fell on to Martin, squirming and convulsing. He had worms in his hair, worms down the back of his shirt, and worms all over his clothes.

He twisted around and slapped at his sleeves, gasping in panic and disgust. Somebody, however, seized hold of his wrists to hold him down, and breathed hotly into his face. 'Sshh, *sshh*! You're having a nightmare, that's all. Ssh!'

He stopped struggling. Somebody was sitting on the bunk next to him, still gripping his wrists. It was still dark, but it must have been growing lighter outside because he could make out a silhouette. It was a woman, and he could smell a woman's perfume, too, jasmine and musk. It was Saskia.

'Are you OK now?' she asked him. She sounded sympathetic, but also amused. 'That must have been some scary dream you were having. It wasn't about chalky werewolves, was it?'

She released his wrists and he sat up. 'What's wrong?' he said. 'Rita's not sick, is she?'

'Rita's fine, except she's been snoring all night like a cow elephant on heat. I haven't been able to sleep at all.'

'Oh, I'm sorry. You can stay in here if you like. Santos didn't feel too good so he's gone to sleep in his truck.'

Saskia looked across at the opposite side of the cabin, and then she said, 'Great. Thank you.'

Instead of going over to Santos' bunk, however, she lifted Martin's blanket and climbed in close beside him, putting her arm around him and crossing her left leg across his thighs. He had taken off his shirt and his chinos and was only wearing shorts, and he could feel that she had taken off her pants, too, and was dressed in nothing but her blouse.

For a moment, he thought about telling her that this wasn't what he had had in mind, but then she snuggled in even closer to him and pressed her breasts against his chest and she felt so warm and smelled so womanly that the words just wouldn't come out.

'Santos doesn't trust me at all, does he?' she said.

'I don't think he trusts any white people. He doesn't even trust *me* all that much, but he knows that I'll take care of his family, mainly because it's my job.'

'How about you? Do you trust me?'

'Do I need to? We're both in the same boat, aren't we, so trusting each other is kind of irrelevant. It's a question of mutual self-preservation.'

'I like that,' she said, and spontaneously kissed him on the cheek. 'It makes us sound like Adam and Eve. A man and a woman, running together from the wrath of God.'

He turned his face toward her, and as he did so she kissed him again, on the lips this time. He kissed her back, and then she slipped her tongue into his mouth. They kissed again and again, with increasing passion, scarcely pausing for breath. When Martin pushed his tongue into her mouth, she teasingly bit it, and wouldn't let it go. As she did so, she reached across and took hold of his penis through his cotton shorts. It was already half-stiff, and she needed only to rub it up and down three or four times before it was totally hard. In fact he felt that it had turned to bone.

Neither of them spoke. They didn't need to pretend that they needed permission for what they were doing, or that they loved each other, or even that they liked each other. Saskia took hold of the waistband of Martin's shorts and wrestled them down around his thighs. He lifted up his knees so that she could pull them off altogether and drop them on to the floor.

She ran her hands all over his chest, feeling the five diagonal scars on his shoulder.

'What are these?' she asked him.

'Nothing.'

'Did somebody hurt you? Who was it?'

'War wounds. Afghanistan.'

She took hold of his penis again and slowly massaged it, probing into the hole with her sharp, manicured thumbnail. 'My battle-scarred soldier,' she breathed, and bit his shoulder, too.

He started to unbutton her blouse, and she sat up a little to make it easier for him, but the only time that she relinquished her hold on his penis was when he had to tug her arm out of her sleeve. When he had managed to wrestle her blouse right off her, he reached behind her with his right hand and slid open the catch of her bra. Her breasts, now that they were bare, seemed very much bigger, and he could feel their weight and their warmth in the palm of his hand. Her nipples were tightly knurled, and he lifted up each breast so that he could suck them, and roll them with his tongue against the roof of his mouth.

When he nipped one of her nipples with his teeth, however, she dug her fingernails into the shaft of his penis and said, '*No*, Martin! I do the biting.'

With that, she dragged the blanket aside, and turned herself around to kneel astride him, facing away from him. He ran his hands down her long smooth back, and felt the wide flare of her hips, and then he reached around and cupped both of her breasts. Then she bent forward and took the head of his penis into her mouth, licking it and gently sucking it, but every now and then biting at it. Every bite hurt, but only for a split second.

Martin was gripped by a tension that he had never experienced before. Usually, as he came close to ejaculating, he felt a pleasurable tightness gradually mounting between his legs. But what Saskia was doing to him made him feel as if his whole existence was building up toward a climax that would blow him apart like a bomb, body and soul.

She bent over him even more, lifting her hips so that her open vulva was right in front of his face. He opened her lips even wider with his fingers, and she was so wet and slippery that he could have washed his face in her juices. He licked her, and slid his tongue inside her, and even though she had his penis deep in her mouth she let out a muffled moan.

Now she began to bite him even more viciously, and the combination of pain and pleasure made him feel as if he were losing his sanity. It was that pain again, the same pain that he had endured as the Taliban whipped him with wire and beat him with canes, and yet for the first time since he had left the Marines, Saskia seemed to be making sense of that pain.

He pulled the cheeks of her bottom even wider apart, so that he could poke the curled-up tip of his tongue into her anus. She flinched at first, and her anus tightened, but then he could feel her deliberately opening herself up to him. Next, very slowly, he slid his tongue down to her clitoris, teasing her at first with occasional flicks, but then licking it faster and faster, trying to arouse her as much as she was arousing him.

She gave his penis one last lascivious suck, circling her tongue around it. But then she ran the tips of her teeth down the side of its shaft and sank her teeth into the skin of his scrotum, so hard that he gasped out 'ahh!'. She didn't let go, though. With her teeth clenched together, she stretched the skin upward as far as she could, and worried it from side to side. He couldn't help it then. It was impossible to stop himself. He shot warm semen everywhere, all over her face and her hair and her hands, and his own thighs, too. His climax seemed to go on and on, and he felt blinded and deafened and lost to the world.

Afterwards, she lay very close to him, still massaging his penis, and smearing his semen over his stomach until it dried.

'You needed that, didn't you?' she told him. 'I could tell that was what you needed from the very first moment I met you in your boss's office.'

'Oh, yes? And how could you tell that?'

'I saw it in your eyes. I can always recognize people who have suffered pain. What most people don't realize is that you need more of it. Your suffering defines you. It helps you to understand who you are.'

'You're a very interesting woman, Saskia Vane. I think I misjudged you, that day.'

She lifted her head so that she could kiss him lightly on the lips. 'Maybe you did and maybe you didn't. You don't know anything about me. Quite possibly, you never will.'

'Tell me about you and Governor Smiley.'

Now she sat up and kissed him again. 'No,' she said. 'You've had enough time to recuperate. I want you to fuck me.'

BOOK TWO
Sins of Men

ONE

It was still dark when Bryan heard the doorbell chiming, again and again, and then somebody knocking at his door and shouting, 'Bryan! Bryan!'

Next to him, Marjorie stirred and snuffled and then said, 'What's all that noise?'

Marjorie could usually sleep through anything, even a late-night barbecue next door, or the most catastrophic of thunderstorms, but the chiming and the knocking and the shouting were so persistent that even she had woken up.

Bryan switched on his bedside lamp. 'Sounds like Luis,' he said. 'What the hell does Luis want, at this hour?' He frowned at his alarm-clock and saw that it was only three twenty-one in the morning.

The knocking and the shouting continued. 'Bryan! Bryan! You need to wake up! It's happened to *us* now!'

Bryan eased himself out of bed and went across to the chair by the window to pick up his maroon cotton robe. Marjorie said, 'Whatever it is, Bry, take it with a pinch of salt. You know how excitable Luis can get.'

Bryan lifted his hand in acknowledgement and then walked along the corridor to the front door. There was a frosted glass panel in the top of the door, and he could see Luis bobbing up and down behind it.

He switched on the outside light, slid back the security chain and opened up. Luis was standing in the porch in a baggy blue tracksuit and slippers, his shock of black hair standing up on end as if he had suffered an electric shock. His eyes seemed to be bulging even more than they usually did.

'They've done it to *us* now!' he announced.

'Done what, Luis? Do you know what time it is?'

'Of course I know what time it is! They must have done it sometime after midnight, because I was working late on my accounts and it was OK just before I went to bed.'

Bryan sniffed. He could smell smoke in the air. From the city center, which was only three miles away, he could hear warbling sirens and the popping of what sounded like gunfire.

'They've cut off our water!' said Luis. 'I went to the bathroom and flushed the toilet and it flushed only once, and didn't refill. I turned on the faucet and what did I get? *Nada!*'

'Well, the water department said they might have to,' Bryan reminded him. 'They said they were going to do it by rotation. First one neighborhood, and then the next.'

'That's what they said, for sure! But you hear all that noise downtown? The rioting, it's still going on! So I just call my cousin in Seccombe Lane and they *still* don't have any water after three days now. There's no rotation, Bryan! It's all BS! They're cutting us off permanent, one neighborhood after the other!'

'You'd best come on in,' said Bryan. 'I need to make some phone calls.'

'That's another thing,' Luis told him, stepping into the hallway. 'I can't use my cell. There's no signal. I tried Carla's cell, too, and Roberto's, but nothing. Just this noise like *ssshhhhhhh!* It's like we're being jammed.'

Bryan led the way into the living room and switched on the lights. Even though the air conditioning was rattling, and it was the middle of the night, the room was still airless and uncomfortably warm. 'Here, sit down,' he told Luis, pointing to one of the heavy brown overstuffed armchairs. Then he picked up the phone and sat down himself.

He punched out a number and it rang and rang for a long time before anybody answered.

'Corben? It's me, Bryan. Listen, I'm sorry to wake you, but Luis has just found out that the water department have cut off our supply.'

He waited for a few moments, listening and nodding, but then he said, 'No, Corben. I don't believe they're keeping their promise. They still haven't restored the supplies to any of the Westside neighborhoods or any of the east side neighborhoods downtown.'

He listened a little longer, first of all nodding and then shaking his head. 'I don't believe they're keeping their promise, and that's because they *can't* keep it. They've run out of water, Corben, and it's simple as that. I know that. I know. They've been mismanaging our water supplies for decades but it's too late to worry about that now. My friend Walter Johnson said he drove past the Lake Perris Reservoir about a week ago and it almost looked like you could walk across it and you wouldn't be any deeper than your knees.'

Again he listened and nodded, and then he said, 'I'm calling a committee meeting to see what we can do about this. It's causing chaos downtown and we don't want that happening here in Muscupiabe. I can hear gunfire and that could mean that people are being wounded or even killed. Yes. But who knows for sure? They had a report about protests on the TV news yesterday afternoon, but since then there's been nothing, not a word. It's like it's not even happening. And all the cellphone networks are dead. Is yours dead? Well, try it. I think you'll find that you don't have a signal.

'Corben – I'm the chairman of the Muscupiabe Neighborhood Association and I am the elected representative of the residents of Muscupiabe and as such I have a right to go the authorities and demand to know what's going on.

'Come around here at noon, say. I'm going to call around and get the rest of the committee together. OK. OK, good. I'll see you then.'

He put down the phone. Luis said, 'What can you do, Bryan? What can *any* of us do?'

Bryan stood up and as he did so he caught sight of himself in the mirror over the red-brick fireplace. A balding overweight fifty-five-year-old realtor with bushy gray eyebrows and a fleshy nose and two double chins. He knew he didn't look like much of a champion, but he had fought for seven years to improve the quality of life in his neighborhood, a triangle of residential homes between the intersection of three freeways – the Mojave Freeway, the Foothill Freeway and Route 259.

Muscupiabe's crime rate was still too high, but it was nearly twenty percent lower than neighborhoods like Roosevelt or Las Plazas; and Bryan had worked tirelessly to beautify Muscupiabe, too, with tree-planting and landscaping and fencing and lighting, and organizing teams of volunteers to fill in gopher holes and to clean off graffiti as soon as it appeared.

'We're not going to riot, Luis. Not here in Muscupiabe. When you riot, you only end up destroying your own neighborhood. But we're not taking this lying down, neither. No, sir.'

Marjorie appeared in the living room doorway with her hair in curlers. 'Would you men care for some coffee?' she asked.

Bryan said, 'Yes, I'd love some.' But then, 'No . . . On second thought, I think we need to conserve all of the water we can.'

TWO

As dawn began to lighten the streets downtown, Lieutenant Henry Brodie pushed open the door of police headquarters and came briskly down the steps on to North D Street, accompanied by Sergeant Hector Perez Gonzalez and closely followed by seven officers in full riot gear.

The warm morning air still smelled acrid, although Lieutenant Brodie had been told that most of the serious fires had now been brought under control by the fire department or had simply burned themselves out.

He could see that smoke was still drifting from City Hall, three blocks further south, and that even thicker smoke was rising from the Vanir Tower, over on G Street. The roadway was littered with broken glass and lumps of concrete and overturned trash cans, and every vehicle in the parking lot opposite police headquarters had been burned to a blackened shell. There were even two burned-out squad cars blocking the West Seventh Street intersection, and halfway down the next block, a police van was lying on its side, with all of its windows smashed.

'We lost control of this, Sergeant,' said Lieutenant Brodie. 'That was inexcusable.' He was a tall, clear-eyed, gray-haired man with a squarish, chiseled face, and rather large ears. If he hadn't always looked so sour about the state of the world around him he might have been quite handsome. As it was, men found him intimidating and women thought that he was humorless and cold, even his wife Sylvia.

'We just didn't have the manpower, sir,' said Sergeant Gonzalez. 'Even with all of those security guards to back us up, there was no way that we could cope with so many protestors in so many different locations, not all at once.'

'That's because we got the psychology all wrong, right from the get-go.'

'Sir – these people had no water. They *still* have no water.'

'I know that, Sergeant. And I'm sure that this probably started off as a perfectly legitimate demonstration. Most of these civil disturbances do. But it never takes long before a criminal element joins in, and uses them as a cover for violence and looting and criminal damage. This has happened so many times before and we *still* haven't learned the lesson, have we? It's Watts, all over again. Monkeys in the zoo.'

They heard sirens in the distance, and more crackling sounds that could have been automatic gunfire.

'Do you know what our worst mistake was?' said Lieutenant Brodie. 'We felt sorry for them. Instead of allowing them to demonstrate, we should have dispersed them immediately, and collared anybody who wouldn't go.'

'Yes, sir,' said Sergeant Gonzalez. 'What do you want to do now, sir?'

Lieutenant Brodie irritably checked his watch. 'Are they bringing around those Humvees or not?'

'Yes, sir. They should be here any second now.'

'Good. Like I told you, I want us to undertake a slow and systematic tour of the whole division, street by street. Slow and systematic. I want people to see us. I want to show them that we've completely regained our control of the situation, and I also want to make it clear to them that if these riots kick off again we're going to come down on them like a shitload of bricks.'

'Yes, sir,' said Sergeant Gonzalez. 'But, you know, before we start off – maybe we could contact the water department and find out when they're going to turn the water back on. If we could tell people that, it could calm them down some.'

Lieutenant Brodie shook his head. 'It's too late for that. They tried calming people down in Watts and it didn't work there, either. Once the looting's started there's nothing you can do. If people believe that they're justified in running off with a flat screen TV just because they're socially hard done by, you've lost the battle.'

Two khaki Humvees appeared around the corner and parked in front of police headquarters. The SBPD had bought them at a military surplus sale in Barstow, three years ago, for use in emergencies, but so far they had been used only twice, both times in flash floods in the Riverside district, after tornadoes.

Lieutenant Brodie climbed into the leading hummer, but before he could close the door Sergeant Gonzalez received a message on his radio. He held up his hand to indicate to Lieutenant Brodie that he should wait.

'OK, sure,' he said. 'We can get down there in ten.'

'What is it?' snapped Lieutenant Brodie, impatiently.

'Rioters have broken into the Inland Center mall, even though it was closed. Maybe as many as two hundred of them. They've broken almost every store window in the place and now they're looting Macy's.'

'Right, then. What are we waiting for? What's the situation in East Valley? The latest report they gave me, it was pretty quiet there now. See how many men they can spare us at the Inland Center as backup. And ask ESS if they have any personnel who can help us out.'

'Yes, sir.'

They drove down toward South E Street, to the Inland Center. Even from nearly a mile away, it looked like a war zone already. Two of the large anchor stores, Sears and Forever 21, were already on fire, and at least twenty automobiles in the huge parking lot were burning. As they approached, a Jeep Cherokee blew up only twenty yards from them, and was thrown up into the air before landing on its side with a deafening crash, blazing fiercely.

Young people with their faces hidden by hoods or bandannas were running in all directions. Some of them were carrying 3D televisions in cardboard boxes and laptops and Xboxes and clothes which they had looted, designer jeans and leather jackets. Others were throwing bricks and lumps of concrete and metal fence-posts at a small group of police officers in riot gear who were huddled in the corner between Forever 21 and the eastern wing of the shopping mall. The police had parked five squad cars at different angles to give themselves some protection from the hail of missiles, but the cars' windshields had already been smashed and their roofs and hoods badly dented.

When the two Humvees were still a hundred yards away from the Center, Lieutenant Brodie ordered them to stop. There was very little that he could do to control a rampaging mob of rioters with only seven officers, but at least he could assess the situation before backup arrived, and plan how he was going to deal with it.

He climbed out of the Humvee and the first thing that struck him was the noise. The barrage of missiles that were being thrown at the riot police were clattering and banging against their squad cars like a West Indian steel band. There was shouting and screaming and whooping, but most of all there was an ugly endless roar, which was the sound of human voices, some elated, some angry, some just carried away with the thrill of wanton destruction.

The air reeked of wood smoke and the fumes from burning plastic, which made Lieutenant Brodie's eyes water and seared his nostrils. He had dealt with public disorder situations before, several times. Mostly, they had been short-lived disturbances sparked off by somebody from an ethnic minority being arrested for some petty infringement of the law: like some kid pulled over for driving with a faulty brake light and then found to have marijuana in his glovebox, or two jealous women fighting in the street over the same feckless man.

He had usually found that a rapid zero-tolerance response was the best way to deal with them – snatch arrests, baton charges, and tear gas if necessary to disperse the crowds. But this riot was on a far greater scale than anything that he had faced before, and it had already become much more violent. What with the fires and the smoke and the screaming and the roaring, he felt that he had arrived in the parking lots for hell.

'Sergeant – tell them we need that backup five minutes ago. *All* the backup that they can spare. Urgent.'

'Yes, sir.'

At that moment, with their sirens wailing and their horns blaring, two bright red fire engines and a heavy rescue truck turned into the parking lot. Sergeant Gonzalez hurried out to flag them down, so that they wouldn't go too close to the rioting crowds before they could give them police protection. The sound of their sirens, however, had attracted the attention of twenty or thirty of the rioters, and some of them picked up pieces of broken concrete and brick and started to run toward them.

'That's it,' said Lieutenant Brodie, turning to the officers in riot gear. 'Spread out, and don't hesitate to use your batons if you have to. Tasers, too, if it's necessary.'

He could see the alarm on the officers' faces, so he barked at them, '*Now*! Spread out! If any single one of these firefighters gets hurt, then I'm holding *you* responsible!'

He turned to face the rioters as they came running through the parking lot, dodging their way between the parked cars. At the same time, with a loud ripping sound, a Ford Explorer exploded on the far side of parking lot D, which set fire to two other cars parked next to it.

Lieutenant Brodie unholstered his nickel-plated SIG-Sauer pistol and pointed it unflinchingly at the three leading rioters, his arm rigid. As soon as he did that, they slowed down, although they didn't stop. They kept on coming, but much more cautiously, weaving from side to side like hyenas as if they were stalking him.

When they were less than thirty feet away, he shouted, 'Hold it! Hold it right there! Drop all those rocks! Do it now!'

As if to punctuate his order, the seven officers behind him cocked their carbines. Three or four of the rioters dropped their half-bricks and pieces of curbstone on to the ground, but the leading rioter held on to his, a large pyramid-shaped lump of concrete, which he kept jiggling up and down in his hand as if he were weighing it. He was short and skinny, wearing a blue hoodie and baggy black sweatpants with a crotch that came almost down to his knees, and what looked like brand new Nike sneakers, so new that he hadn't even had time to put laces in them yet.

'We need water, man,' he said, in a hoarse Hispanic accent. 'You turn the water back on and we'll go home.'

'Taking all of your ill-gotten goods with you, I suppose?' Lieutenant Brodie retorted.

'Resti-*too*-shun, man, that's all we was lookin' for.'

'Put down the rock, kid.'

'You turn the water back on, man. We're dyin'.'

'Dying to watch your new plasma TVs, you mean. Now put down the rock.'

The young man lifted the lump of concrete even higher, and arched his back as if he intended to throw it. Lieutenant Brodie fired a shot into the air, only just above his head. The young man immediately dropped the concrete pyramid and started to back away, his hands held up in the air. His friends all backed away, too.

Whether they heard the shot or not, only a few of the rioters who were still pelting the riot police next to the mall appeared to take any notice. They carried on shouting and whooping and running in and out of the mall's main entrance like swarms of termites running in and out of a termite mound, carrying away their loot. Even from so far away, Lieutenant Brodie could see that they were stealing anything they could, even ironing boards and deckchairs and children's paddling pools. He guessed that an estimate of two hundred rioters had probably been on the low side: as far as he could count, there must be three or four hundred or more.

A dark blue ESS helicopter arrived overhead and started to circle the mall at a height of less than two hundred feet, the roar of its rotors drowning out the roar of the crowd below it. Its downdraft twisted the smoke from the three burning stores into three dancing tornadoes, and sent empty cardboard boxes and sheets of newspaper tumbling across the parking lots.

Lieutenant Brodie heard more sirens, but these didn't sound like police or fire department vehicles. Three dark blue Crown Victorias with red flashing emergency lights on their rooftops came speeding in from South E Street, followed by four dark blue SUVs. All of them carried the distinctive ESS logo on their doors.

The leading car stopped beside Lieutenant Brodie with a slither of tires. The other vehicles skidded to a halt, too, and all of their doors were immediately flung open. ESS security agents in helmets and dark blue uniforms and Kevlar vests came piling out of them, more than forty of them, and all of them carrying semi-automatic carbines with their buttstocks retracted. They assembled next to Lieutenant Brodie's officers and stood stiffly to attention.

Out of the passenger seat of the first car Joseph Wrack unfolded himself like a long-legged black spider. He was wearing a black shirt and black pants, and a black combat jacket with the collar turned up. Lieutenant Brodie had met him only a few times before, mostly at seminars when the police and the security agency got together to compare notes on tactics and crime figures, but he had taken an instant dislike to him, for both his arrogance and his skull-like face.

'See you got yourself a little trouble here!' Joseph Wrack shouted, trying to make himself heard over the grinding of the helicopter and the cacophony of glass breaking and bricks bouncing off squad cars and all of the cat-calling and whistling and chanting of the rioters. Three more explosions echoed from the far side of parking lot C, and three balls of orange flame rolled into the air.

'Glad to have some backup!' Lieutenant Brodie shouted back, even though the words tasted even more bitter in his mouth than the taste of smoke. He paused for breath, and then he shouted, 'What I've been thinking is, we should form a V-shaped echelon.'

'A V-shaped echelon?'

'That's right, like a pair of pincers,' said Lieutenant Brodie, holding both arms out wide to indicate what he meant. 'We advance toward the mall's main entrance from two sides which will force the rioters to retreat inside the building. Once we have them corralled in the central vault inside, we can divide them up into arrestable groups of ten or so.'

'And then what do we do with them, exactly?'

Lieutenant Brodie checked his watch again. 'I'm expecting more police backup any minute now. I've asked for six buses, too, so once we've hooked them up we should be able to transport them away from here with reasonable dispatch.'

'And where do we take them?'

'Where we always take our offenders, West Valley Detention Center.'

'Which at this particular moment is overcrowded to the point of bursting and incidentally has no water supply, so all of its inmates are wading around knee-deep in their own excrement. Not that they don't deserve to.'

Joseph Wrack reached into the inside pocket of his combat jacket and took out a black-and-yellow pack of Cohiba Lanceros panatelas. He slid one out and took his time lighting it, narrowing his dark brown eyes against the smoke.

After a while he leaned close to Lieutenant Brodie so that he could make himself heard, because he spoke very hoarsely and softly. Lieutenant Brodie ostentatiously waved his cigar smoke aside with his hand, but Joseph Wrack took no notice.

'The thing of it is, Lieutenant,' he said, and it was clear that he was choosing his words very carefully, 'we have specific orders from Governor Smiley to stop this rioting dead in its tracks. I have to tell you, sir, that those orders apply to *you*, too, because we now have an official state of emergency.'

'I'm aware of that,' said Lieutenant Brodie, but let him continue.

'Governor Smiley is doing everything he can to save as many lives as possible in this drought situation, and in his view, these rioters are a direct threat to the survival of those who are doing their best to comply with his water-rationing plan.'

Lieutenant Brodie frowned at him. 'So? We're going to go in and arrest them. What more does he want?'

Joseph Wrack said, 'If you saw a young hoodlum about to take the lives of an innocent young mother and her children, what would you do?'

'I still don't get it.'

'These young people are sabotaging any chance we have of

sharing out water fairly. Apart from the damage they're doing right here, they've been vandalizing water department pumping stations, trying to turn the water supply back on, and they've been threatening the lives of water department maintenance personnel. By doing that, they're endangering every man, woman and child in San Bernardino, and way beyond. Not to put too fine a point on it, sir, they're potential killers.'

Lieutenant Brodie was still bemused, but before he could say anything else, Joseph Wrack turned around to his security agents and waved them forward. All forty of them advanced, stamping their boots on the ground and cocking their carbines with a syncopated rattle.

'What the *hell* do you think you're doing?' demanded Lieutenant Brodie.

'We're calling this party to an immediate halt,' said Joseph Wrack, turning back to him, and approaching so close that Lieutenant Brodie could smell his breath. 'It would be very helpful if you could deploy *your* officers, too. Maybe on the left there, so they can work their way toward their fellow officers pinned down behind their squad cars over there.'

'You don't have the authority to do this, Mr Wrack. Your men had better stay right where they are.'

'I do have the authority, sir. And how do you think it's going to look, at a future inquiry, if you have to admit that you let a riot continue unchecked because you were concerned about protocol?'

'*Mr Wrack!*' There was a sudden surge of noise from the helicopter, and Lieutenant Brodie almost had to scream.

But Joseph Wrack had turned away from him again, as if he hadn't heard him. He lifted his arm like a starter at an athletics meeting, paused for a second, and then brought it sharply down, pointing toward the rioters. The security guards immediately started jogging toward the shopping mall, their ammunition belts jingling, crossing the parking lot in a ragged line.

'*Mr Wrack! You order those men to come back! Mr Wrack! I'm warning you! You're under arrest!*'

Lieutenant Brodie knew that it was a futile thing to say, and he was glad in a way that the helicopter was making too much noise for his own officers to have heard him, but he was dreading what was going to happen next. He had a reputation for using the maximum force available to him during civil disturbances, but even the most violent of incidents had never called for anything more deadly than tear gas or beanbags fired from shotguns.

'Mr Wrack,' he said, under his breath. 'God rot you, you zombie.'

Some of the rioters had already seen the ESS men approaching. A few of them started to run away, into the mall's main entrance or around the side of the Sears building. Most of them stayed where they were, though, dancing and jeering and waving their arms. Several of them picked up broken lumps of curbstone and hurled them toward the advancing security guards, but almost all of their missiles bounced harmlessly across the asphalt, and the security guards kept up their relentless, menacing jog without a single break in their stride.

Even from where he was standing, a hundred yards away, Lieutenant Brodie could see that more of the rioters were beginning to lose their nerve and scatter. Some of the more aggressive were still jumping up and down and howling and giving the security guards the finger, but he suspected that they were so high or so drunk that they had no concept of the danger they were in.

He walked back over to Sergeant Gonzales and said, 'Come on, Hector. We have to get into this, too.'

'This is all wrong, sir!' Sergeant Gonzales protested. His eyes were rolling in panic and frustration. 'What do they think they're *doing*? They can't just go in like that. There's too many! Hundreds! This way or that way, whatever happens, somebody has to get killed!'

'All the more reason we have to get in there. Wrack's taken the initiative, we have to take it back. We're the law, not him, no matter what he says.'

Beckoning with both hands like a football coach, he summoned his seven officers in riot gear to gather around him. Most of them looked confused, and kept glancing nervously over at the crowds of rioters, and the security agents who were still running steadily toward them.

'I'll make this quick,' said Lieutenant Brodie. 'I've just been informed by the director of public safety from Empire Security Services that he and his agents have been given the authority to assist us in suppressing this disturbance in any way they see fit. I'm not sure what their tactics are going to be, but I want you men to get in there amongst them and make sure that they don't use any more force than absolutely necessary. Even rioters have human rights, and impetuous actions today can lead to very expensive lawsuits tomorrow.

'Got that? I don't want this to turn into a goddamned bloodbath, now or later. OK – *go!*'

The seven police officers immediately went jogging off after the security men. Lieutenant Brodie then crossed over to the firefighters who were waiting beside their fire engines, looking impatient. Their crew boss was short and squat with an S-shaped broken nose and a face that was almost as red as his fire engine.

'So what the fuck's going on?' he demanded.

'You'll just have to hold your horses for a while longer,' said Lieutenant Brodie. 'As soon as we have this riot locked down, we'll give you the all clear to go in, OK?'

'Hey – there could be innocent civilians trapped in there,' the crew boss retorted. 'In fact it's highly likely. What are we going to do, stand here and let the whole mall burn right down to the ground, with them in it?'

'If we have to.'

Lieutenant Brodie looked around. The security agents were now less than a hundred feet away from the rioters, and the rioters were pelting them even more furiously with every brick or piece of concrete they could lay their hands on. Even from here, he could hear the debris thumping and clattering on their riot shields.

'Hey, lookit,' said one of the firefighters. 'What is *that* guy doing?'

One of the leading rioters was walking calmly toward the security agents, his arms held high. He was making two V-fingered signs of peace. He had shaggy black shoulder-length hair and he was wearing sunglasses and a red bandanna that covered his face, a red T-shirt with FING A printed on it, and very skinny black jeans.

He might have been trying to call a truce, but none of his fellow rioters were taking any notice of him. They continued to shower the security agents with sticks and rocks and traffic cones and even a torn-up STOP sign.

'Guy must be totally nuts,' said the fire crew boss. 'Who does he think he is – Jesus?'

The second he spoke, the rioter pitched backward, as if he had been violently pushed, although there was nobody within six feet of him. Then another rioter fell on to the ground, a fat young black boy in a purple hoodie, rolling over twice before coming to rest next to a low brick wall. Then another, a tall shaven-headed Hispanic who flung his arms up in the air as if he were dancing; and another, and another. Suddenly, the rioters started dropping left and right, like puppets with their strings suddenly cut.

Lieutenant Brodie heard no gunfire, but the ESS helicopter was still droning right overhead, and the rioters were still shouting, and he had seen that the carbines carried by the security agents were all fitted with flash and sound suppressors.

More rioters fell, at least twenty of them within only a few seconds. The rest now realized what was happening, because they were scattering in all directions, and their roaring had now risen to a high, hysterical scream. Some of the security agents had gone down on one knee, to steady their aim; and they were not only picking off the rioters who were facing them, but the rioters who were desperately trying to run away.

Lieutenant Brodie said, 'Jesus. I don't believe it.'

He could clearly see what Joseph Wrack was doing – driving the rioters toward the mall's main entrance, so that they could be corralled and captured. It was exactly the same plan that *he* had devised. The only difference was that Joseph Wrack had chosen to forgo baton charges and tear-gas and Tasers, and use deadly force as his first line of attack. When any rioter tried to run around the Sears building to the right, or away to the left past Forever 21 and the barricade of squad cars, he was dropped in his tracks.

'Holy Mary Mother of God,' said Sergeant Gonzalez, crossing himself. 'This is a massacre.'

Lieutenant Brodie said, 'Come on, Hector,' and ran forward to catch up with his own seven men.

'*Cease fire!*' he bellowed at the security agents. '*Cease fire!*'

Even if they heard him, the security agents kept their backs to him and continued shooting. All of the rioters were now scurrying for shelter inside the mall, although three or four of them were running with their heads ducked down toward the squad cars, obviously hoping that the police would give them some protection. The security agents fired burst after burst in their direction, and all of them tumbled to the ground, their arms and legs flailing. Several bullets also hit the fender of one of the squad cars, and punctured its tire.

Breathless with anger, Lieutenant Brodie caught up at last with Joseph Wrack. The ESS director of public safety was standing with his arms folded, still smoking his panatela and watching all of this carnage with no apparent emotion at all.

'Stop them! Tell them to hold their fire! For Christ's sake, Wrack, this is wholesale murder!'

Joseph Wrack took the panatela out of his mouth and was about to say something when a bullet cracked between them, so close that Lieutenant Brodie felt the wind of it against his cheek. The riot officers who were crouching behind the squad cars were firing back in their direction, trying to hit the security agents.

Without hesitation, Joseph Wrack tossed aside his panatela and dropped to the ground, spreadeagling himself as flat as he could, one cheek pressed against the asphalt. Lieutenant Brodie remained standing, waving semaphore signals to the police behind the cars and shouting, '*Hold your fire! Hold your fire! This is Lieutenant Henry Brodie, commander of the Southern Division! I order you to hold your fire!*'

Guns crackled like fireworks for more than five seconds, sending a blizzard of bullets in both directions. Some of the rioters were hit again and again, and performed a strange kind of drunken moonwalk before falling on top of each other in heaps. Three security agents went down, too, and one of Lieutenant Brodie's riot officers.

Lieutenant Brodie stood with his arms still raised, looking all around him in horror. There were so many bodies strewn around that it was impossible for him to count them. There were scores of wounded, too, and he could see people with bloodied faces and bloodied clothes painfully trying to extricate themselves from underneath the dead.

The gunfire stopped, but the helicopter was still roaring so loudly that he couldn't think straight.

Joseph Wrack started to climb to his feet. As soon as he did so, however, another bullet cracked past them, nearly as close as the first. He said, '*Shit,*' and dropped abruptly back down to the ground.

Lieutenant Brodie turned his head to see if he could tell where the bullet had come from. If it had been fired by a police officer, then by God he was going to have his badge. He saw a puff of smoke drifting away from one of the squad cars, and he thought he could make out an officer in mirror sunglasses kneeling behind it with a carbine still pointing in his direction.

He had just started to walk toward him when another bullet hit him in the left eye, blowing off the back of his head and drenching Sergeant Gonzalez in his blood and brains.

THREE

'Look at this, will you – *Baking With Julia*!' Bryan protested. 'You wouldn't believe there's any kind of a crisis going on at all!'

He had switched on the TV and changed to the local public service channel, but so far there had been no updates on the drought, or the water supply, or the riots. All that was showing was Julia Child 'in my own kitchen', baking madeleines.

'There's no question at all that the powers that be are deliberately keeping us in the dark,' said John Wilson, who lived on West Mirada Avenue, opposite the elementary school. 'To my mind, that means only one thing – the situation is a heck of a lot worse than they've been telling us.'

'Well, I've tried calling City Hall more times than I can tell you,' put in Dick Bortolotti, who lived five doors away on West 25th. 'Either they simply don't want to answer, or there's nobody there, or the whole darned place has been burned to the ground.'

'That wouldn't surprise me at all,' said Myron Platt, the association's treasurer. 'Did you see all that smoke, first thing this morning? Looks like the Inland Center could be burning, too.'

'And yet there's not a single word about it on the news. Not one. It's crazy.'

Fourteen of the fifteen committee members of the Muscupiabe Neighborhood Association had gathered in Bryan's living room to discuss what they could do about the sudden cutting off of their water supply. The fifteenth member, Tama Takamura, was away visiting her parents in Kyoto.

'I've tried to get in touch with every city and county service that I can think of,' said Bryan. 'I've tried calling California Water and Power. I've tried calling Cal/EPA. Nobody's picking up. Nobody.'

'So what the hell are we going to do?' asked Corben Myers, his deputy chairman. 'What if you're right, and they never turn the water back on? I have two young grandchildren. How are they going to survive?'

'If they'd only give us some information,' said Luis. 'How can they expect us to cope without water if they won't tell us what's going on?'

As if on cue, *Baking With Julia* was suddenly interrupted by a card which read DROUGHT EMERGENCY: A SPECIAL ANNOUNCEMENT. Bryan switched on the sound in time to hear: '—about the water crisis from Governor Halford Smiley.'

There was a moment's blackout and then Governor Smiley appeared, sitting alone at the end of a long mahogany table. He was dressed more soberly than usual, in a white short-sleeved shirt and a plain green necktie.

'Good afternoon, citizens of San Bernardino. I'm talking to you live from your own fair city which I am visiting in the hope of bringing you reassurance about the water crisis that we're faced with. You already know that we have been obliged to rotate the supply of water from one neighborhood to another, so that our limited resources can be shared out as fairly as possible.

'You won't have failed to notice that a small but selfish minority have reacted to this rationing in a way that I can only describe as extremely negative. They have inflicted willful damage on your city center, setting fires and looting business premises and tying up the emergency services which are already stretched to the limit by the shortage of water.

'I want you to stay as calm as you can. I want you to have courage, and I want you to show that deep sense of civic responsibility on which you the citizens of San Bernardino have always prided yourselves. We are doing everything within our power to share out water equally, but I won't try to conceal from you the fact that this is a very grave emergency, and that all of us will have to suffer.

'In the interests of public safety, though, I must add this. We cannot and will not tolerate any citizens behaving in a threatening or violent manner, or causing wanton damage to public or private property. Some of you may feel that you have a legitimate grievance, and that you have a right to demonstrate, but you will be dealt with by the police and the security services to the utmost extent of the law. For that reason there will be a dusk-to-dawn curfew in the city center and every neighborhood in which the water supply has been temporarily withdrawn. That curfew will apply from tonight onward, until further notice. Anybody found out on the street in those localities after dark will be considered to have unlawful intent, and will be dealt with accordingly.'

He paused, staring at the camera with what he clearly imagined
to be a serious, concerned expression, but he appeared to have
forgotten what he was supposed to say next. Eventually he glanced
to his left and said, '*What?*' and then '*Oh*. Remember,' he said,
'we are all in this crisis together. You have my heartfelt good
wishes, and my promise to be here for you through all of the
difficult days and weeks that lie ahead of us. Let us be of good
cheer, my friends, and pray to the Lord for rain.'

Julia Child reappeared, rolling out balls of dough.

The committee members stood looking at each other in
disbelief.

'A *curfew?*' said Bryan. 'A dusk-to-dawn curfew? They might
just as well lock us all up in the slammer! Maybe some people
downtown have been rioting, but *we* haven't, and we don't intend
to, either. I thought you were innocent until you were proven guilty.'

'Did you see where he was speaking from?' asked Myron. 'That
was the conference room at Verdemont Country Club. No, I'm
absolutely sure. That's where my company holds their annual stock-
holders' meetings.'

'So what are we waiting for?' said Corben.

'What do you mean, what are we waiting for?' Luis asked him.

'I mean, Bryan believes that our association members have a
right to know what's going on and we have a mandate to go to the
authorities and demand they give us some answers. Our water's
been cut off, for God's sake, and our water is our lifeblood! We
need to know how long it's going to be cut off for, and whether
they're going to be cutting us off on a regular basis. So – since we
can't contact the authorities on the phone, let Mohammed go to the
mountain.'

'What the hell does Mohammed have to do with it?'

'I mean let's all go to the Verdemont Country Club and beard
Governor Smiley in his den.'

Bryan felt suddenly inspired, almost brave. This was what the
neighborhood association was all about: action. 'Great idea, Corben,'
he said. 'Let's darn well do it.'

He went through to the kitchen where Marjorie was sitting at the
table watching their portable television. She was wearing pink latex
gloves and polishing their silver cutlery. 'We're going over to the
Verdemont Country Club,' he told her. 'Governor Smiley's there, and
I'm going to ask him a few pertinent questions about our water supply.'

'I saw him,' she said. 'Do you really think you ought to?'

'Of course. Why not? I'm the elected representative of the residents of Muscupiabe. I have a duty to ask him questions, and he has a duty to give me some answers.'

'Well, I think you'd be wiser not to go. He didn't sound very amenable to me.'

'Oh, come on. You heard him say that we're all in this together.'

'Politicians always tell you that. They never mean it. Let me tell you, Bry, I was listening very carefully to what he was saying and that man is not in the mood for being challenged.'

'I don't care what kind of a mood he's in. It's his *job* to be challenged, and I'm going to challenge him.'

Marjorie looked up at him over her the rim of her spectacles. 'Bry,' she said.

'What?'

'No . . . nothing,' she replied, and went back to cleaning the fish knives.

They arrived outside Verdemont Country Club in a convoy of five vehicles. The parking lot was almost empty except for three black Escalades and two Crown Victorias with ESS logos on their doors. The sky was hazy with heat, but cloudless.

Bryan climbed stiffly down from his Range Rover and looked around. Verdemont Country Club was an imposing Colonial-style building with a white-pillared portico, like a house from a Southern plantation. It was set in front of a green, gently rolling eighteen-hole golf course, with the mountains behind it. To the south, almost invisible through the heat, was the San Bernardino valley. Bryan could see palls of dark brown smoke still hanging over the city center, but he could hear no sirens and he could neither hear nor see any helicopters. Apart from the incessant chirruping of cicadas, the afternoon was almost completely silent. No airplanes in the sky, no noise of traffic on the freeways, not even the whinnying of golf carts.

He and his fellow committee members walked across the parking lot to the portico. The air was so hot that Bryan felt as if it were scorching his nostrils as he breathed it in.

As they approached the entrance, two security guards in dark blue uniforms stepped out of the shadows. They were both wearing mirror sunglasses, so that as they came up to him, all Bryan could see in their eyes was a distorted reflection of himself, with his committee standing behind him.

'Help you?' asked one of the security guards. His cheeks were cratered with acne, like the moon.

'Bryan Johnson, chairman of the Muscupiabe Neighborhood Association. These good people are my committee. We've come to see Governor Smiley.'

'Governor Smiley is not here, sir.'

'Yes, he is. We saw him on TV less than an hour ago, and he was here.'

'Sorry, sir. I'm afraid that you're mistaken.'

Myron stepped forward in his blue golfing cap and his flappy blue shorts and said emphatically, 'He's here, young man. Or he *was* here. I recognized the room he was in.'

'Sorry, sir. I'm not at liberty to tell you whether he was here or not. The governor's movements are strictly confidential.'

Bryan said, 'We're elected representatives. We have a right to see him.'

'Sorry, sir. Security.'

It was then that Luis said, '*Bryan* . . . do you see what I see?'

He tugged Bryan's sleeve and pointed to the first green, which was just visible behind the left-hand side of the clubhouse. A sprinkler had suddenly started up, and water was glittering in the air, creating a rainbow.

'They're watering the greens,' said Luis, and his voice was hollow with shock. 'We don't have any water to drink, or to cook in, or to wash in, and *they're watering the goddamned greens.*'

The other members of the committee stared at the sprinkler, too. Corben said, 'That is outrageous. I mean that is *outrageous!*'

Bryan turned to the security guards and snapped, 'Who's in charge here? Who's in charge of this club? I want to talk to the manager.'

'The manager is not available, sir. I'm sorry.'

'Then the deputy manager, or the deputy-deputy manager! Or whoever's in charge of the golf course! The greenkeeper, if I have to!'

'I'm sorry, sir. There's nobody here you can talk to.' The security guard's tone was completely expressionless, as if he were prepared to say the same thing, over and over, for the rest of the day if necessary, until Bryan and his committee members went away.

'I don't believe you for a moment,' said Bryan. 'I'm going in there right now and I'm going to find who's in charge for myself.'

He started to head toward the entrance but the two security guards both took a sideways step and blocked his path.

'I'm sorry, sir. Members only. Unauthorized access is not permitted.'

'The media are going to hear about this.'

'That's your prerogative, sir. But you and your party are trespassing on private property, and I have to request you to leave.'

Bryan turned around to Luis. 'Luis! Go take a picture of that green being watered! I want some proof of this!'

He turned back to the two security men and said, 'Let's see what Governor Smiley has to say when *this* appears on the news!'

But the second security man shouted after Luis, '*Sir*! Sir – you'll have to come back here! Taking unauthorized photographs on country club property is not permitted!'

Luis continued to cross the parking lot and didn't even turn around.

'Sir! You have to come back here!'

Luis waved one hand to acknowledge that he had heard him, but kept on going.

'Sir! This is the last time I'm going to warn you!' the security guard shouted, and unholstered his automatic. The security guard with the acne took out his gun, too.

'Luis!' Bryan called out, in sudden panic. 'Luis! Do as he says! Luis, they're going to shoot you if you don't come back!'

Luis stopped, and raised both hands, although he still didn't turn around. In his right hand, Bryan could see that he was holding up his cellphone, and he guessed that he was taking pictures of the green, which was now less than twenty yards right in front of him.

'Drop the cell, sir, and come back here!' the security guard shouted at him.

Luis hesitated three seconds too long. Bryan thought: *forget the darn pictures, Luis, just do as he says*! But maybe this was the first time in his life that Luis had done something overtly courageous, and he was intoxicated with it.

The security guard's gun went off with a deafening bang. Luis clapped his hands above his head and then fell face-down on to the ground, his cellphone clattering on to the ground beside him.

Bryan heard himself crying out, '*Noooooooo*!!' as if somebody else were shouting in his ears. He launched himself toward Luis, although he felt that he was running in slow motion, and that the air had turned to syrup.

A slurred voice shouted, '*Sirrrr . . . staaaay heeeere*!' but he didn't associate it with himself. All he knew was that Luis had been shot and he needed to reach him as soon as he could.

'Stop!' the voice demanded, but this time it was sharp, and quite clear. Bryan stopped, but stumbled, and as he tried to regain his balance he was punched in the back so hard that he was thrown forward on to the tarmac, cracking his left cheekbone and dislocating his left shoulder.

He lay there, with his face against the ground. He could see Luis' feet, and he could see a window in the side of the golf club with two or three people staring out of it. He could hear the sprinklers going *pishety-pishety-pishety,* over and over, as if they were trying to soothe him to sleep.

Myron was the last to leave. The two security guards had been joined outside the portico by Joseph Wrack himself, as well as three more security guards from ESS. After Myron had opened the door of his Honda Accord he turned around and gave them all a look of absolute hatred, but he didn't speak. Like his fellow committee members, he was too shocked and too frightened to disobey their order to leave the country club immediately.

He sat behind the wheel and closed the door. Before he could drive off, however, Joseph Wrack walked over and tapped on his window with his knuckle.

He tapped again, and Myron reluctantly put the window down.

'Before you go, sir,' said Joseph Wrack, 'please remind your friends what I said about trying to contact the media or mentioning what happened here on Facebook or Twitter.'

'I'm pretty sure they heard you,' said Myron.

'Well, good. Because we will very quickly find out if you do. We know who you are and believe me we will take any and all appropriate action.'

'Appropriate action?' said Myron. 'Does that mean *shooting* us, like our friends here?'

'Sir – this is a state of emergency and in order to maintain public safety we have the authority to use deadly force. So let's keep those lips zipped, shall we? Have a safe journey home.'

A white ambulance from American Medical Response was turning into the country club driveway, without siren or red-and-orange lights. One of the security guards directed it to park close to the two men lying on the tarmac. Neither of them had moved since they had been shot, and it was obvious that they were both dead. A long dark runnel of blood ran all the way from Bryan's body to the drainage grid in the center of the parking lot.

Joseph Wrack raised both eyebrows as if to say, '*You won't forget now, will you, my friend?*' Myron closed his window, started his engine and drove away.

'*Paskudnyak,*' he said, under his breath, as he went out through the country club gates. '*Vi tsu derleb ikh im shoyn tsu bagrobn.*' It was what his grandfather always used to say about people he disliked. 'May I live long enough to bury him.'

Two paramedics knelt down beside Luis, checking for any vital signs. A few moments later, Governor Smiley came out of the country club entrance, still wearing the white shirt in which he had appeared on TV, but now with a salmon-pink linen coat and raspberry-colored chinos.

'Your guys really needed to do that?' he asked. 'I thought you had enough on your plate after this morning. I've just had Chief Williams on the phone. He's deeply upset about the loss of life at the Inland Center, especially Lieutenant Brodie.'

'Oh, he's "deeply upset", is he? So he should be. There was only one person to blame for Lieutenant Brodie getting himself killed and that was Lieutenant Brodie. Chief Williams should realize that this city is totally out of control, and we're not going to get back the upper hand until the police stop acting like pussies. I always said that Williams was a milquetoast, just like the mayor.'

'So who were *these* people?'

'They both came from the Muscupiabe Neighborhood Association. The fat guy, he's the chairman. They were trying to force their way into the country club to confront you about their water being shut off and they were threatening physical violence, so my people had no choice. The skinny Hispanic guy was trying to take pictures of the water sprinklers.'

'Were they armed?'

'Fat guy was carrying a concealed nine millimeter. We'll pass it over to the cops when they get here. If they ever get here.'

'Of course it'll have his prints on it?'

Joseph Wrack took the panatela out of his mouth and looked pained, as if Governor Smiley had gratuitously questioned his integrity.

Governor Smiley said, 'OK. It'll have his prints on it. Stupid of me to ask.' He squinted across at the paramedics as they draped pale green sheets over each of the bodies and then walked back to their ambulance.

After a moment, he said, 'Muscupiabe, that's a real shame.'

'Why's that, then?'

'Well, we only cut off Muscupiabe to show the poorer neighborhoods like Las Plazas that we were being fair, but they won't be off for more than twenty-four hours, if that. They're good people in Muscupiabe. All reliable Smiley supporters.'

'I was going to ask you about that,' said Joseph Wrack, and his voice sounded even drier than usual. 'I was wondering why you cut off University Heights. I mean, that's a pretty affluent area. They must all pay their taxes and their water bills.'

'They do. You're right. But in the last election more than eighty-two percent of them voted Munoz.'

'Oh, so you're not just punishing the poor. You're punishing anybody who doesn't support Smiley.'

'Of course. That's what politics is all about. Sticks and carrots. Or, in this case, water or no water.'

'I see. OK. In that case, I'm glad I voted for you.'

A squad car finally appeared at the end of the country club driveway, closely followed by a brown panel van from the coroner's office.

'Any progress with Saskia?' Governor Smiley asked, as he watched them approach.

'Not so far. Not since we caught up with them at Wildwood Plaza. My guess is that they hightailed it south-west immediately after that and picked up the Riverside Freeway. That could take them all the way to the coast, and LAX.'

'Shit. She could be anywhere by now. She could be in New York.'

'It's possible. But flights have been very restricted and I've had my people checking all of the passenger manifests. No sign of her so far.'

Governor Smiley looked thoughtful. 'If they were filling up with gas last time they were spotted, maybe they're headed east, by road. Maybe they're making for Vegas.'

'Anything's possible,' said Joseph Wrack. 'But my people are keeping a sharp lookout, don't you worry. ESS has eyes just about everywhere. We'll find Ms Vane for you, sooner or later.'

Governor Smiley glanced at him sideways. 'OK,' he said. 'But make sure that you do. Saskia Vane owes me a big, big favor; but you know how things can turn out. Sometimes favors can work in reverse.'

'We'll find her,' Joseph Wrack repeated. 'Have I ever let you down before, Governor?'

Faintly, in the distance, they could hear the drone of a helicopter approaching. A bespectacled young woman in a white blouse and a cream linen skirt came tip-tapping out of the golf club entrance on very high heels. 'Governor Smiley?' she said. 'Your ride is on its way.'

Governor Smiley gripped Joseph Wrack's right arm and squeezed it hard. 'Just find the bitch for me, you got it?'

FOUR

Martin was woken up by the cabin door creaking. He opened his eyes and lifted his head, but all he saw was the briefest flicker of a shadow as somebody walked between the cabin and the early-morning sun.

Saskia was gone, and that had probably been her. The opposite bunk was still empty, so Santos must have slept for the rest of the night in his truck.

He dragged his blanket aside and sat up, wincing from the soreness between his legs. He felt as if he had been fighting all night with a pit bull terrier, because his shoulders and his hips were bruised and he was covered in teeth marks. He looked down. His penis was reddened and he even had bites on the insides of his thighs. He had gone to bed with sexually aggressive women before, but none of them had been as fierce as Saskia. He felt that she had wanted to devour him alive.

He slowly dressed. It was only seven fifteen a.m., but even up here in the mountains, more than six-and-a-half-thousand feet above sea level, it was already warm. He buckled up his belt and pushed open the cabin door. The sky was denim blue and the air was fragrant with the smell of pine. A pair of scrub jays were screeching at each other on the opposite side of the clearing.

As he stepped out of the cabin, he saw that Santos was hunkered down beside their makeshift hearth in nothing but his red stripy shorts, lighting a fire. He was skeletally thin, and his skin was stretched over his bones like parchment.

'Hi, Santos. How are you feeling?'

Santos nodded, without looking up. 'Much better, much better. The pain comes but then it goes. It is always worse when I get tired.' He blew steadily on to the sticks that he was using as kindling, and flames began to spring up. Once he was sure that they were well alight, he stood up and looked around. 'I have to admit to you, Martin, I am glad that this has happened. It has brought me back to the mountains. Otherwise I never would have come here again. My spirit is here. The spirits of my people are here. Here in the mountains is a good place to die.'

'I think there's plenty of life in you yet, Kemo Sabay.'

'"Kemo Sabay"?' said Santos. 'Why do you call me "Kemo Sabay"? It was the Lone Ranger who was called "Kemo Sabay", the white man. The Indian was called Tonto.'

'Oh, yeah? Well, that's where you're wrong. Back in the early days, when it was only a radio show, the Lone Ranger called Tonto "Kemo Sabay" instead of the other way about. It means "trusted scout", which is what you are. I used to be mad about the Wild West when I was a kid, so you can't catch me out. See? You've learned something, and you've been given a compliment, too. That's a pretty good way to start the day.'

Santos was staring at him with narrowed eyes, his head tilted slightly to one side. 'That's a very bad bite on your neck,' he said.

Martin tugged up his shirt collar to cover it. 'Mosquito, more than likely. I *thought* I heard one buzzing around.'

'Maybe it's the mountain air,' said Santos, without a hint of irony. 'It gives the mosquitoes such an appetite.'

Peta and Ella were coming out of their cabin now; and then Tyler and Mikey. Susan was still inside, dressing George and Mina, but Nathan came out with his shirt buttoned up in all the wrong button-holes. There was no sign of Rita yet. Martin guessed that she was either sleeping, or suffering from a catastrophic hangover, or else she had already started on her first Budweiser of the day, and didn't want anybody to see her.

Saskia appeared, however. She had managed to wipe off all of her foundation and her eye make-up and Martin could see what a striking face she had, even if her eyes did look smaller without mascara. She came right up to him and said, 'Good morning, Martin! Hope you slept well?'

'Sure, yes. On and off.'

'Mmm. Me too. And what *dreams* I had! What's for breakfast?'

'We have bagels, with American cheese if you like,' said Santos. He bent over and poked around in the cardboard box full of groceries that they had taken from the Chevron food mart. 'Or here we are – Campbell's chunky chicken, broccoli, cheese and potato soup. Only one hundred ninety calories. Or a strawberry and wheat flake breakfast bar.'

'Good God. Any juice?'

Peta and Ella went over to a fallen log on the opposite side of the fire and sat down together. Peta wrapped a blanket around Ella's shoulders and hugged her. Ella was looking very pale and she was shivering, although the morning was so warm. Martin picked up a carton of cranberry juice and walked across to join them.

'She's OK,' said Peta. 'She has the cramps, that's all. I've given her some painkillers.'

Ella looked up and gave him the weakest of smiles. 'I'm all right, Daddy. Really.'

'You're sure? Here, drink some of this.'

Peta said, 'Ella and I were talking last night. We decided that neither of us want to turn back. I know that Tyler wants to keep going, too. It's not just a question of escaping from the drought, Martin. It's a question of making a fresh start – bringing our family back together again.'

'You're sure about that? I can't guarantee that I've changed all that much.'

Peta looked him directly in the eye. Every time he looked back at her he thought how beautiful she was. He felt as if he needed to look at her all the time, and never turn away, because he didn't want to waste a minute of his life looking at anybody else. It was hard to believe that he had shouted at her, and slammed doors, and smashed furniture, and thrown her violently across the room.

'I've seen you in the past few days,' said Peta. 'I think you've changed much more than you know. You don't take your devils out on other people any more. You face up to them. I don't think you'll ever get rid of them. I don't think that's possible. But I think that you and I could live together again, or try to, at least.'

Martin opened and closed his mouth without saying anything. Whatever he said, he was sure that it was going to come out cock-eyed. How could he tell Peta how he felt about the world, when he didn't really know himself? Yet here she was looking him with such renewed confidence, even though he had hurt her so much; and here was Ella looking at him too, and Ella had such hope in her eyes.

He was about to ask Peta to wait until they had reached Lost Girl Lake, so that they could sit down together and decide how they were going to plan their future, but then Saskia came up behind him and patted him on the shoulder. It was on a spot where she had bitten him very hard, and he couldn't help flinching.

'Martin?' she said. 'I need to talk to you.'

'OK,' Martin told her. 'Give me a couple of minutes, could you?'

'It's urgent, Martin. I need to talk to you right now.'

He was about to insist that she waited until he had finished talking to Peta, but when he saw the expression on her face he said, 'Oh . . . right. Peta – I won't be a moment.'

Saskia walked toward the cabin that she was supposed to have been sharing with Rita and Martin followed her. The cabin door was ajar but she stopped before she went in and turned around to face him.

'I think Rita's dead,' she said.

'*Dead*? Are you serious?'

'I'm sure of it. Go in and take a look at her.'

'Oh, Jesus. When did you realize?'

He went up to the cabin and pushed the door wider. Rita was lying on her bunk with her eyes wide open, staring at the ceiling. Her hair was tangled and her face was a blueish-gray color, almost metallic. Her mouth was caked with orange vomit.

Martin pressed his fingertips against her neck but he couldn't feel a pulse. Then he leaned over her, with his ear almost touching her lips, but he couldn't feel her breathing. She smelled strongly of stale alcohol and bile and although she was tightly bundled up in her blanket, he could smell that she had emptied her bowels.

Saskia said, 'When I got up this morning the blanket was covering her face completely and I assumed that she was still asleep. I came back because I had forgotten my watch and I thought it was time she got up, too, and had some breakfast. I lifted up the blanket and that was when I saw that she was dead.'

'Choked on her own vomit,' said Martin. 'What the hell do we tell her kids?'

Saskia said, 'I'll do it. I'll tell Susan first, and then she and I can explain it to Mikey and Nathan and the little ones.'

Martin drew the blanket back to cover Rita's face. He didn't want her children to see her like this. Strangely, she didn't look like herself at all. Martin had seen more than twenty of his fellow marines killed in Afghanistan, and he had noticed the same thing with them. Once they were dead, they did nothing more than superficially resemble the people they had been when they were alive. That was one of the reasons he believed in souls.

They went back outside. Susan and Mikey were standing there, waiting for them. Susan's eyes were puffy and Mikey's hair was sticking up like a cockerel.

'My mom's dead, isn't she?' said Mikey.

Martin put his arm around his shoulders. 'Yes,' he said. 'How did you know?'

'We saw you go in there, and we kind of guessed that was why.'

Susan said, 'We've been expecting it. She's been sick so much lately. She hasn't been eating anything and after she used the toilet it was full of blood.'

'We'll have to break it to your brothers and your little sister,' said Saskia. 'Do you want to do it, or shall I?'

'I'll do it,' said Susan. 'I don't think that they'll be surprised. They've heard me often enough, telling her that drinking so much is going to kill her.' She paused, and shook her head, and said, 'Stupid, *stupid* woman! She used to be so beautiful. Hard to believe now, isn't it?'

'We can't take her with us so we'll have to bury her here for now,' said Martin. 'Once this drought thing is over, though, we can come back and take her home and give her a proper funeral.'

'Like, dig her up again?' said Mikey.

Martin nodded.

'What's the matter?' Santos called out. 'Nobody coming for breakfast? The bagels were kind of stale, but I toasted them, and I made some coffee, too!'

Using the signboard that said *Camp Knobcone*, and a small yellow plastic bucket which Mikey found in the back of Santos' truck, Martin and Saskia and Mikey cleared the ground of pine needles and then dug a shallow grave in the fine sandy loam.

Martin tightly wrapped up Rita's body in a second blanket, and then he and Santos carried her out of the cabin and laid her gently in the ground. Nathan and George and Mina were all sobbing, and even though he wasn't crying out loud, Mikey was wiping the tears from his eyes with his fingers.

'Want to say a few words, anybody?' asked Martin.

Santos stepped forward and raised both of his hands. 'Today I leave my daughter behind, but not for ever. I will return here to give her the Yuhaviatam ceremony that she deserves, and cremate her in the way that our people have always cremated our dead, so that the smoke of her spirit returns to the sky and the ashes of her body return to the soil.' He looked down at the body wrapped in blankets and said, 'You do not bring children into this world and expect them to leave it before you. My heart hurts, Rita, more than you can ever know. While I am gone, may Taamit the sun and Muat the moon shine down on you constantly, so that you know no more darkness.'

As he said these words, they saw lightning flashing, somewhere to the north of them, over Heartbreak Ridge. After a long pause, they heard the grumbling of thunder.

'Don't say it's going to rain,' said Susan. 'That would be so sad, if it started to rain again, right now.'

More lightning flashed, followed by a long drumroll of thunder that seemed to go on and on for almost a minute.

Martin said, 'It's not going to rain, Susan. That's just static. We used to get the same thing in the mountains in Afghanistan.' He sniffed, and said, 'If it was going to rain, you could smell it.'

They filled up the grave with soil and pine needles, and then covered it all over with large granite rocks, not only to mark where it was, but to prevent it from being dug up by coyotes or raccoons.

Once Martin had lifted the last rock into place, and smacked the soil from his hands, Saskia came up to him and said, 'You and your lovely ex-wife seem to be getting along well.'

'Do we? We have our children to take care of, that's why.'

'But you enjoyed it last night?'

'I'm a little sore, if that's what you mean.'

She reached out and touched his arm and gave him a slanted smile. 'Sore but satisfied, I hope?'

'Oh, yeah, satisfied,' he said, and started to walk back toward the clearing, where Santos and Susan were chivvying the children back into Santos' truck. Thunder rumbled from the north again, but there was still no smell of rain in the air, and the forest remained hot and claustrophobic and utterly still, except for the intermittent dropping of pine cones.

'We'll do it again, then, when we get the chance?' said Saskia, keeping pace with him.

He had reached his car now. Ella was waiting for him in the back seat, and she could obviously see that Saskia was asking him something intense. Ella's eyes darted from one to the other.

'We really need to get going,' said Martin. He opened the passenger door for Saskia and waited for her to climb in. 'We can talk about it later, OK?'

* * *

Santos took them back down the narrow trail that led to the highway,
but they had driven only about five or six miles before he pulled
into the side of the road, and so Peta and Martin pulled in behind
him. He got out of his Suburban and walked back toward them, his
legs as thin as two mahogany walking sticks, his face kept in shadow
by his Panama hat.

'See that turn-off right ahead of us?' he said, pointing to a gap
in the dusty green chaparral.

'Not really, no,' said Martin.

'Take my word for it, Martin, that *is* a turn-off. You won't find
it on the map. You can just about make it out on the satellite picture,
but even so you wouldn't guess that it was a track. It's the path that
the Yuhaviatam used when they traveled between what is now the
Joshua Tree National Forest and Arrowhead Springs. They named
it the Path of the Sacred Bear. Of course that was in the days when
many black bears lived in these mountains.'

'They still do.'

'Not the native bears. Your people killed them all, made them
extinct, just like you tried to make *us* extinct. Didn't you know that
all the bears that live in these mountains now were imported from
Yosemite, as a tourist attraction? For your people, there is nothing
sacred about the natural world. You see it only as an
entertainment.'

Martin said, 'OK, Santos, I think I've had enough of your ethnic
resentment for one day. Are you seriously suggesting we *drive* down
that turn-off? It might be different if we all had off-road SUVs.'

'It will be difficult, yes. But it is the only way that we can descend
from the mountains without anybody understanding which way we
have gone.'

'Right, then. If you're game to do it, then so am I. Lead on,
Macduff.'

'Macduff? Who is Macduff? I thought I was Kemo Sabay.'

Martin stared at Santos narrowly, but he couldn't detect even the
hint of a smile on his face.

'You know something?' he said. 'I'm gradually beginning to
understand *why* we tried to make you extinct.'

Santos returned to his truck, started it up, and turned off the
highway on to the Path of the Sacred Bear. Peta and Martin followed.
Martin could make out some rutted indentations in the ground which
might have been described as a path, but for most of the time he

found that they were driving through dense chaparral, with the branches squeaking and scraping against the sides of his car.

'Daddy!' said Ella, in alarm. 'Are you *sure* this is the right way?'

Saskia turned around in her seat and said, 'Don't worry, Ella. As far as your Daddy's concerned, the rougher the better.'

Martin gave her a quick, sharp look, but Saskia only crossed her legs and gave him the tartest of smiles. Normally he would have come back to her with a smart retort, but he was too preoccupied with wrestling his Eldorado through the scrub. The so-called Path of the Sacred Bear was so deeply furrowed that the car kept trying to steer itself, and the front and rear overhangs repeatedly banged against the ground. Santos had switched his Suburban to four-wheel drive, and so he was plowing steadily forward at nearly ten miles an hour. Peta's Hilux had four-wheel drive, too, so she was keeping up with him; but Martin's front-wheel drive Eldorado was bouncing and jostling and wallowing with every rut and ridge that it encountered.

'Daddy, I feel *sea*sick!' Ella cried out.

'Hold on, sweetheart! It can't be too much further!'

But as they drove further and further south-eastward, the terrain became increasingly rugged. Not only that, it began to slope sharply downward and sideways, at almost forty-five degrees. Martin had to keep his foot jammed on the Eldorado's brake pedal to prevent it from careering into the rear of Peta's pickup.

The ride downhill was jarring and tumultuous, with all three vehicles swaying wildly from side to side. All Martin could see was rocks – sky – trees – rocks – steering-wheel – sky.

Even Saskia had to brace her feet against the floor and cling on to the door handle. 'Oh, my God,' she said. 'This is worse than Goliath!'

The banging of their suspension against the rocks was so loud that Ella started to cry; and Martin had to shout out, 'It's OK, sweetheart! It's going to be OK!' But then his muffler hit a boulder with an even louder bang, and he was sure that it had been knocked right off.

Very gradually, however, the ground began to level off. After a final violent shaking up as they crunched and bumped and slid through a slew of dry gray gravel, they suddenly dipped down into a natural granite trench, with high rocky walls on either side of them. The bottom of the trench undulated up and down, and was ribbed in places like a washboard, but it was much smoother than the ground that they had been driving over so far, and they could drive much faster. Martin guessed that once upon a time, maybe thousands of years ago, it had probably been a watercourse.

He could see why the Yuhaviatam had chosen to come this way. The trench ran with only a few wide curves for more than three miles, and for most of its distance, anyone who was walking or riding or driving along it would be completely unseen from the foothills all around it.

At last the sides of the trench began to fall away, and they found themselves driving out over the scrubby gray desert of Morongo Valley, with the mountains behind them now. They had descended more than five thousand feet in less than two hours, and even though their vehicles had all taken a battering, they were all still running. Martin's muffler was scraping along the ground, but when he stopped and ducked down beside the car to take a look at it, he could see that it was still hanging on by one twisted bracket.

Santos and Peta stopped, too, and all of them got out of their vehicles and stood together and passed round warm two-liter bottles of Mountain Dew and Pepsi. Far to the south-east, in the distance, they could see the occasional glitter of a car traveling along the Twentynine Palms Highway.

'So where do we go from here?' Martin asked Santos. 'Do we take the road, or what?'

Santos shook his head. 'No. All the way to Lost Girl Lake, we will travel along the sacred pathway used by my ancestors.'

'Your ancestors weren't driving Cadillacs. I don't know how much more my poor old car can take.'

'We will get there, I promise you,' said Santos. 'And if your car gives up its ghost, we will find you another.'

'I see. The sacred ritual of grand theft auto.'

'Make no mistake,' said Santos. 'This is a war. Those who have water have declared war against those who have not. In a war, everything is permissible, so you can take whatever you need. It was *your* people who taught us that, again and again. You wanted what we had, so you took it from us, without any feeling of conscience.'

'For Christ's sake,' said Martin. 'Let's just get going again before you start blaming me for Wounded Knee.'

FIVE

Joseph Wrack was standing in his office on the fifth floor of the ESS Building on East 4th Street, holding a mug of Kupi Luwak coffee and staring unblinkingly at the brown palls of smoke that were still rising from the Inland Center further downtown.

He had never been philosophical. To him, there was no difference between right and wrong. All that mattered was the outcome. But he had just received a phone call from the Odyssey Hospice at Riverside to tell him that his mother probably had less than forty-eight hours left to live, and he was wondering what the purpose of her life had been, except to give birth to him.

His mother had never enjoyed much in the way of happiness. Her own parents had both been academics, cold and critical, and her life had been no better when she escaped them to get married. Joseph's father had always spoken to her as if she were an imbecile, although she had been clever and quite pretty and been able to play the piano.

But Joseph thought: *what difference does it all make, in the end?* Even if she had been blissfully happy all her life and played Chopin to concert standard, the outcome would still have been the same. She still would have ended up in the Odyssey Hospice, half-blind and half-deaf and doubly incontinent. *Life's a shit and then you shit.*

There was a complicated rapping at his office door and his operations director Jim Broader bustled in. Jim was a big, busy man. Before joining ESS, he had been a district resource officer for the Los Angeles Police Department, but he had conveniently resigned three months ahead of an official investigation into the misappropriation of departmental expenses. He had a swarthy, coarse-pored face with shaggy black eyebrows and a nose like a blob of modeling clay. His shirt collars curled up because they were always too tight for him, and his belly hung pendulously over his belt. He smelled strongly of Perry Ellis aftershave and cigarettes.

'Morning, boss! You want the good news or the good news?'

Joseph Wrack didn't answer, or even turn away from the window.

He didn't like being called 'boss' and he didn't like Jim Broader very much. Jim Broader however was a bully and everybody in ESS was afraid of him and Joseph Wrack was a great believer in management by intimidation, especially in the security business. In his opinion, his security guards would only be truly effective if they were more frightened of him than they were of being shot by armed robbers.

Apart from that, Jim Broader was a schmoozer. He knew everybody who was anybody, and a great many people who were nobody, but still extremely useful.

'Would you believe it, we've located them! Saskia Vane and that Makepeace character! And we have a pretty good idea where they might be headed!'

Now Joseph Wrack did turn around. He carefully set down his mug of coffee on his desk and said, 'How far have they gone? Have they made it to LAX yet?'

'No, boss, they haven't. And the reason for that is, they're not *going* to LAX. They're headed in totally the opposite direction.'

Joseph Wrack walked across his office to the large laminated map of Southern California that was mounted on his wall. 'So *where*?' he demanded.

Jim Broader came up behind him and pointed to Big Bear City. 'Three times a week we send an armored van to pick up cash from the First Mountain Bank. This morning the crew went to a local bed and breakfast to get themselves something to eat before the bank opened – same place they always go, apparently. But the owner told them he was closed, on account of the water supply being cut off. He complained that it was killing his business.'

'So? What does this have to do with Makepeace and Saskia Vane?'

'Ah,' said Jim Broader, looking deeply pleased with himself. 'The owner happened to mention that yesterday evening he had been forced to turn away a party of twelve, including several kids. They had pleaded with him, but he couldn't risk losing his license.'

'Go on.'

'All of our guys have been given a BOLO for Saskia Vane and this Makepeace character, so they asked the owner to tell them what this party of twelve looked like. He said they were traveling in three separate vehicles: an old Chevy Suburban; as well as some kind of pickup; maybe blue or green; and a bronze Eldorado convertible, with two women in it, apart from the driver. One of the women had short black hair.'

Joseph Wrack continued to stare at the map. 'Shit,' he said, with his teeth clenched together. '*Shit*! That's them all right. Big Bear City, *shit*! So where did they go from there?'

Jim Broader followed Route 247 with his finger. 'East a ways, and then due north is my guess. Barstow, then Vegas, then who knows where? Denver? They might even try for Canada.'

Joseph Wrack was biting the edge of one of his thumbnails. 'If they carried on driving overnight last night, they could be in Salt Lake City by now, goddamnit. Get in touch with Bill McNaughton at SLC Security – ask *him* to put out a BOLO, too, and be sure to let us know the *second* any one of his people catches sight of them. But I also want three choppers out looking for them nearer to home, and three road patrols. They have kids with them, remember. They could have stopped someplace to rest, so they may not have gone all that far.' He still didn't take his eyes away from the map, as if he expected to see three tiny vehicles crawling across it. 'Most likely you're right, and they're headed north. On the other hand, that Saskia woman is very far from stupid and Makepeace is an ex-Marine . . . one of life's survivors. Maybe that's what they want us to think. They could be making east for Phoenix, or even south for Mexico.'

'OK,' said Jim Broader. 'I'm on it.'

'I *want* Makepeace, Jim,' said Joseph Wrack. 'Nobody screws around with me, the way he did. Nobody wrecks my property or hurts my people. I want that Saskia Vane, too. She tipped him off, after all. And not only that, Governor Smiley wants her, and I want to know why.'

'Boss?'

'Smiley says that she owes him, and I want to know *what* she owes him, because he's scared of her, too.'

'I'll tell you who might have an idea – Abelina King. She handles all the publicity for Gold Crescent Pictures.'

'Yes, I know Abelina King. She used to live here in San Bernardino before she went to LA. She did some promotion for us but I haven't seen her in years. Why would she know anything?'

'She used to be very good friends with Saskia Vane *and* with Governor Smiley. I'll see if I can get in touch with her, anyhow. And there's a few other people in LA who might have an inkling.'

Joseph Wrack reached out and drummed his fingertips on the San Bernardino Mountains. 'Where are you, Martin Makepeace? Where are you, Saskia Vane? Let me tell you something, you two . . . I'm going to find you, wherever you are. I'm going to find you, and when I do, you're going to wish that you were never born.'

His phone shrilled. He let it ring six or seven times and then he picked it up. 'What?' he demanded.

'Mr Wrack? This is Nurse Petersen at the Odyssey. Your mother is conscious now. Would you like to speak to her?'

Joseph Wrack kept on drumming his fingertips on the map. 'Tell her I'm busy, would you? No, don't tell her that. Tell her you couldn't get hold of me. I'll call back later.'

'She's heavily sedated, Mr Wrack, because of the pain. She may not be conscious later.'

'I see. I'll just have to take my chances, then, won't I?'

When Halford Smiley arrived back at his office in the State Capitol in Sacramento, he found Lisa Esposito from the Office of Ground Water and Drinking Water waiting for him.

'Lisa, come along in,' he said, crossing over to his desk and dropping the file that he had been reading on the way back from San Bernardino.

Lisa Esposito was a very tall woman, over six feet, and she could have been a model if she hadn't been so large and intimidating. Her hair was a wild torrent of dark brown waves that cascaded right down over her shoulders. Her eyes had heavy green-shadowed lids and her dark red lips seemed to be permanently stretched back to show off her large white teeth. She was wearing a pale lavender suit and although she was quite small-breasted it was carefully tailored to minimize the generous width of her hips.

'Coffee? Lemon tea?' asked Halford. 'I seem to remember that you like your lemon tea. Got to keep your tongue sharp somehow.'

'I'm good, thank you,' said Lisa. Her accent was hard and tensile and she barely moved those stretched-back lips when she talked, like a ventriloquist. 'The EPA will be sending you an email about this, but Douglas thought it would be a good idea if I came to brief you in person.'

'Oh, yes?' said Halford. His personal assistant appeared in the doorway and he waved his hand to her and said, 'Coffee, Nann, would you? And some of those ginger cookies, if you have them. And if you don't, then why the hell not? Ha! Ha! Only kidding!'

He took off his salmon pink coat and draped it over the back of his chair. 'OK, then, Lisa, to what do I owe the pleasure? Please – have a seat. I do like to talk to my women on the same level.'

Lisa remained standing, so that Halford had to continue to look up at her. He went over to his desk and sat down himself.

'So what's this all about?' he asked her, tilting his chair back.

Lisa opened her large purple tote bag and took out a folder. 'You need to know that the President has given the Environmental Protection Agency the power to take overall control of the water supply in every state critically affected by the drought. That, as you know, means every state except for Washington, Oregon, New Hampshire and Maine.'

'What the hell is that all about?' Halford demanded. 'What can the EPA do that I haven't done already? I've cut agricultural irrigation by twenty-two percent. I know that irrigation is still going to use up most of our groundwater, but if I cut it any more we're going to go hungry as well as thirsty.

'I've also brought in a special water rotation system in every major population center, to share out what groundwater we *do* have as fairly as possible.

He picked up the folder from his desk and said, 'You want to see the latest figures, as of Tuesday? So far I've managed to reduce California's total daily consumption from forty-six thousand million gallons to thirty-one thousand million gallons. I'd like to see the EPA get even close.'

Lisa said, 'It's not so much the quantity of water that the President is concerned about, Governor. It's the extreme negative reaction that you've been getting from the public. There's an election next year, and the last thing he wants to do is alienate ethnic minorities and blue-collar workers and women.'

'Oh,' said Halford. 'I thought that he might be more interested in saving as many lives as possible.'

'Of course he is. And that's why he's given the EPA the authority to take over. You've had riots in Oakland, and Modesto, and Fresno, and Bakersfield. You've had even worse riots in San Bernardino, even though you went there yourself to keep the population calm.'

Halford shook his head dismissively. 'You call them "riots", Lisa, but they're nothing more than minor public disturbances. You'll always have your lawless element who are ready to take advantage of any natural disaster. Look at all that looting after Hurricane

Katrina. I can tell you now that we have all of those disturbances totally under control.'

'All the same, Halford, the EPA will be sending in officials from the Office of Enforcement and Compliance, and they'll be handling the drought crisis from now on. You'll be able to read all the details in the email, but Douglas thought we owed you the courtesy of informing you in person, and so did I.'

Halford said nothing for a very long time, but sat with his eyes cast down and his lower lip protruding just a little, like a child who has been told that he can no longer have his own way. Eventually, though, he stood up and went to the window and looked out over Capitol Park. The lawns were scorched yellow for want of watering, and the leaves of the trees had turned brown, but right from the very beginning of the drought Halford had insisted that the state legislature should be seen to be setting an example.

'Is there any message you want me to take back to the EPA?' asked Lisa.

'Message? Yes, I have a message. You can tell the EPA to go fuck themselves.'

'Halford, that isn't going to help.'

'It's not intended to help. I am the elected Governor of the state of California and I am in charge of handling this drought crisis, not the EPA or the OECP or the OW or the OGWBW, or any other goddamned stupid acronym you care to mention. Not the President, either. Especially not the President. He can go fuck himself too, him and his ethnic minorities and his blue-collar workers and his women.'

'Halford—'

Halford went over and looked her straight in the face, even though he had to tilt his head back to do so. 'You can tell the EPA that if any of their officials attempt to exert any authority over the management of water anywhere in the state, they risk being treated the same as anybody who riots – in other words, a threat to public safety. Under the current emergency laws, we can use deadly force to deal with them.'

Lisa looked down at him and started to smile. 'You're not serious.'

'Oh, I'm serious, Lisa. Never more so.'

The smile faded. 'It's true what they say about you, isn't it, Halford?'

'They say a lot of things about me, Lisa, some of them

derogatory, but most of them complimentary. I get things done, that's all, and I don't particularly care how I do it.'

'They say you were going to be twins, but you strangled your brother before you were even born.'

Halford couldn't help grinning at her. 'That's good. I haven't heard that one. I like it.'

Lisa left just as Nann was bringing in Halford's coffee and a plate of cookies. Halford picked up one of the cookies and sniffed it. 'This is orange,' he said, 'not ginger.'

'I'm so sorry, Governor, that's all we have at the moment.'

Halford said, 'Hold out your hand.'

'What?'

'Hold out your hand.'

Nann did as she was told, holding out her right hand, palm upward. Halford laid the cookie on it, and then folded her fingers back until the cookie was completely crushed.

'How long have you been working for me?' he asked her.

'Seven months,' she said, although her lip was trembling and there were tears springing up in her eyes.

'After seven months, Nann, you should have learned that if I can't get exactly what I want, then I don't want anything at all. No substitutes, that's my motto in life. No fucking alternatives. The right thing, or nothing.'

Nann nodded, and swallowed, still holding the crushed cookie in her hand.

Halford said, 'Have I ever told you that you have very sexy ears?'

SIX

By mid-afternoon they were driving up a narrow trail that led them through the Big Morongo Canyon Preserve. The gray sunbaked mountains all around them gave them no sense of scale, so they might just as well have been three tiny vehicles crawling their way across Joseph Wrack's map.

The heat was overwhelming. By three p.m. it had grown so fierce that Martin and Saskia and Ella could hardly breathe, and so Martin closed the top of his Eldorado and switched the air conditioning on full. Even though the interior of the car quickly became cooler, it now felt dark and claustrophobic, especially since it was so dazzlingly bright outside.

They reached the crest of a promontory, overlooking a deep, dry valley, and Santos stopped his Suburban and climbed out. Peta and Martin stopped, too.

'Everything OK?' Martin called out.

'It's the kids,' said Santos. 'My air con needs re-gassing and this heat is killing them. Mina most of all.'

Martin looked inside the truck and saw that all the children were lolling on their seats limp and exhausted. Mina was cuddled up against Susan, sucking her thumb; but even Susan was looking waxy, with her hair stuck wetly to her forehead.

Saskia reached over and lifted Mina out. Mina's eyes were half-closed and she gave a little shudder as Saskia held her in her arms, as if a goose had walked over her grave.

'This kid's sick,' said Saskia. She pressed her hand against Mina's forehead to check her temperature. 'I don't know what she's suffering from, maybe some kind of virus, but she needs to see a doctor.'

'She's been sick on and off for a couple of weeks,' said Susan. 'Sometimes she's been OK but other times she's been throwing up and then falling asleep for hours and hours and you can't wake her up.'

'Didn't you take her to the ER?'

'Mom said she would get better on her own. Besides, if she needed treatment we couldn't pay for it.'

'I see. She could afford booze for herself but no medication for her daughter.'

'Rita has passed now,' said Santos, without looking around. 'There is no honor in speaking ill of those who cannot defend themselves.'

'Let me keep Mina with me,' Saskia suggested. 'I have some ibuprofen which should keep her fever down, and if I give her regular drinks and keep her cool she should start feeling better.'

'You sound like you've done this before,' said Martin.

Saskia took a handkerchief out of her pocket and patted Mina's forehead with it and wiped her runny nose. 'Yes,' she said, without looking at Martin. 'Maybe.'

Peta came up and linked arms with Martin. 'Poor little thing,' she said. 'At least Ella's feeling better. If she keeps on getting cramps, though, the doctor may recommend that she goes on the pill.'

'She's fourteen years old, for Christ's sake.'

'Just because she's on the pill that doesn't mean she's going to go around and sleep with every boy in her class. She's very choosy when it comes to boys.'

'She'd better be, otherwise I'll be going around to their houses and breaking their legs.'

He was suddenly aware that Saskia was staring at him over Mina's shoulder, unblinking, in the same way she had stared at him when he had first met her in Arlene's office. It was almost as if he were invisible, and she could see right through him, to the heat-distorted mountains behind him.

'Come on,' he said, 'I'll take her. Let's get you settled in the car.'

He took Mina and carried her back to his Eldorado. She was hot and damp and floppy and she smelled of stale urine and unwashed hair. Saskia sat in the passenger seat and held out her hands and Martin carefully laid Mina on her lap.

'You and your ex seem to be getting along better and better,' said Saskia.

Martin glanced across at Ella, who was lying across the rear seats with her feet up, prodding at her cellphone. She couldn't make a call or send texts to any of her friends, because there was still no signal, but at least she could play Bejewel. Fortunately, she didn't give any indication that she had heard what Saskia had said.

'It's called parenthood,' said Martin. 'Just because you separate, that doesn't mean that you abandon your children.'

'All right,' Saskia smiled. 'No need to get saintly about it. I believe you.'

Martin closed the door as gently as he could and walked around the front of the car to the driver's side. He was opening his own door when his ears picked up the distant throbbing of a helicopter. He stopped and listened, and after a while he could hear that it was coming nearer. It was probably only a highway patrol helicopter, or an air ambulance, and most likely it was following the Twentynine Palms Highway. All the same, they were parked high up on this exposed, treeless promontory, where anybody in a helicopter could easily spot them from five miles away.

'Santos!' he shouted out. 'Peta! Do you hear that? Chopper coming! Let's get the hell out of here!'

Santos waved and then pointed left and downward. 'Follow me into the canyon! It will be harder for anybody to see us down there!'

Before he closed his door, Martin heard a second helicopter approaching from the west. This one sounded as if it were flying very fast, and much lower than the first helicopter, because the roaring of its engine kept fading, and then growing louder, and then fading again, which meant that it was following the contour of the mountains.

'What's wrong?' asked Saskia.

'I'm not too sure. Two choppers, and I think they might be headed our way. It could just be a coincidence.'

Santos started up his Suburban. He drove along the promontory for another fifty yards and then tilted abruptly off to the left and down a track that was even narrower and steeper than the one they had followed to climb to the crest of the mountain. It was barely a track at all: more like a ridge, knobbly with rock, and Martin thought that it felt like trying to drive down the spine of a genuflecting dinosaur.

The muffler of his Eldorado took more punishment, banging loudly against the rock with almost every bump. Even though the track was so jagged, however, and even though it sloped downward at an increasingly precipitous angle, it was dead straight all the way to the floor of the canyon below, so it would take them only a few minutes to reach the comparative shelter of the canyon's overhanging walls and the twisted pine trees that grew up its sides. Not only that, the deeper recesses of the canyon were thickly filled with spiky chaparral. The rest of the Cadillac's paintwork would probably be ruined, but at least nobody would be able to see where they had gone.

'I feel sick again,' said Ella, clinging on to Martin's headrest to stop herself being thrown from side to side. Saskia was gripping the doorhandle tightly in one hand and Mina in the other, but she kept her lips tightly pursed and said nothing.

'Nearly there,' said Martin. He couldn't hear the helicopters at all now, even though his window was open. He had probably been right, and they had been only police helicopters or flying eyes from one of the TV stations. He could see Santos up ahead of him, just about to drive his truck into the entrance to the canyon, and he thought, *that's it, we've made it.*

At that instant, one of the helicopters came roaring around the side of the mountain, in between them and the canyon, and hovered in front of them, only about twenty-five feet from the ground. It blew up such billowing clouds of dust that it almost disappeared, but Martin could still make out that it was blue, dark blue, and that it carried the silver logo of the ESS.

He slammed on the brakes and the Eldorado slewed ninety degrees to the left. When it stopped, it see-sawed for a few seconds across the top of the ridge, but then with a buckling metallic creak it slid backward, about twenty or thirty feet, until its rear end crunched softly into a thicket of chaparral.

'Out!' shouted Martin. 'Get out of the car, *now*, and hit the ground!'

Even through the dust, he could see that the helicopter's side door was open, and a security guard in a dark blue uniform and sunglasses was leaning out of it, with one booted foot resting on the landing skid. He was holding a carbine across his lap, and he was tilting his head left and right, trying to see where they were. The roaring of the helicopter's rotors was overwhelming, like a sawmill, and Martin could hardly think straight.

He opened his door and knelt down beside the car. First he folded back the driver's seat so that Ella could clamber out of the back. Then he held out his hands for Saskia to pass Mina across to him. Saskia came out last, keeping her head well down, and using her elbows to wriggle across the front seats like a Marine under fire.

Once they were all out, and crouching behind the car for cover, Martin shouted, 'Stay here! I'm going to go check on the others!'

He struggled his way through the scratchy chaparral to reach the back of the car. Opening up the trunk a few inches, he groped around inside until he found one of the Colt Commandos, and then two spare clips of ammunition. He lifted the gun out, and slotted in one of the magazines. Saskia and Ella both looked at him anxiously, but he raised his hand and shouted, 'Don't worry! I'm not going to kill anybody! Not unless I don't have any choice!'

Staying low, he made his way past Ella and Saskia to the front of the car and then cautiously lifted his head and took a look across the hood. The helicopter was still in the same position in front of the canyon entrance, about twenty-five feet in the air, although it was rotating very slowly around and around so that the security guard with the carbine could keep all three of their vehicles covered.

He could see Peta and Tyler, hunkering down behind their Hilux. He shouted to Peta, and whistled, but the helicopter was making too much noise for him to be able to catch her attention.

Santos and Susan and the children had climbed out of their Suburban, but they had made no attempt to hide behind it, or use it as a shield. They were simply gathered beside it, quite openly, with Susan holding little George in his arms, and Santos standing between Mikey and Nathan, with his hands resting protectively on their shoulders.

Martin realized that the helicopter couldn't land here, because the ground directly beneath it was much too stony, and it also sloped sideways at two sharply conflicting angles. In front of the canyon entrance the ground was much more level, and there were far fewer boulders strewn around, but if the pilot tried to bring the helicopter any closer, there would be a serious risk that the tips of his rotors would strike the overhanging rocks.

No – Martin reckoned that this helicopter was simply hovering here to guard them, so that they wouldn't try to get away. The pilot of the second helicopter must have gone looking for a place to land nearby, and a team of ESS security guards was probably making their way toward them, even now.

Martin stayed where he was, keeping his head well down. From the random way that the security guard on the side of the helicopter kept looking around, it was clear that he hadn't spotted him yet.

'What's happening, Martin?' Saskia shouted, from behind him. 'Can't we just make a run for it?'

'We wouldn't stand a chance! Besides – I think the other chopper must have put down someplace, and they'll be sending some of their goons on foot! I want to see which direction they're coming from first!'

That was one of the lessons he had learned in Afghanistan, the hard way. Until you find out what your enemy's planning to do, do nothing. Watch and assess.

He didn't have to wait too long. After only a few minutes, four ESS security guards came jog-trotting around the side of the mountain. They were all dressed in full combat gear, with helmets and face masks, and three of them were armed with carbines. They took up positions on either side of the helicopter, their weapons raised. They could see only Santos and Susan and the children, who were obviously no threat to them, but they kept their distance. It was more than likely that some of them had been in the team that had tried to catch up with Martin at Peta's house, and that was why they were being so wary.

The security guard on the side of the helicopter dropped down a white heavy-duty bullhorn to the leader of the men on foot. He caught it and slung the lanyard around his wrist, and then he switched it on and tested it out. '*One – two – three! Can you people hear me? Put up your hands if you can hear me!*'

Santos and the children looked at each other apprehensively, and then Santos gave the security guard a jerky, reluctant wave. Although the helicopter was roaring so loudly, the bullhorn amplified the security guard's voice to more than ninety decibels. On a quiet day, they could have heard him more than a mile away.

'*OK, good!*' he bellowed. '*We're looking for only two people! You got it? We don't care about the rest of you! The rest of you are free to go wherever you want!*'

Martin glanced over his shoulder at Saskia. She was holding Mina close to her chest, her fingers buried in Mina's greasy hair, and she was frowning with worry. 'She's really sick, Martin! Maybe we should just give ourselves up! I mean, what are they going to do to us?'

'Just stay down,' Martin told her. 'I don't trust these clowns one inch.'

'*We're looking for Martin Makepeace! You got that? Martin Makepeace we're looking for! And Saskia Vane! That's Sas-ki-a Vane! Those are the two individuals we need to locate! The rest of you, you're all free to go!*'

Saskia said, 'Come on, Martin! This is all over! We can't go on running any more! The kids can't take it, and I don't think I can, either!'

'Please, Saskia! Trust me!' said Martin. 'Just stay where you are!'

'What about your own kids – Ella here, and Tyler! What about your ex? You're not going to put them through any more of this, are you?'

'Saskia—' Martin began, but then he was interrupted again by the security guard with the bullhorn.

'*We're not going to wait here for ever, people! We need Martin Makepeace and Saskia Vane to come forward and give themselves up! If they don't, we'll be forced to take punitive measures against you!*'

He paused, waiting for Santos to respond, but Santos did nothing more than draw Mikey and Nathan closer to him. The security guard lifted up the bullhorn again and announced, '*Listen up! Five! I'll give you five! If Martin Makepeace and Saskia Vane fail to show themselves by then, we're going to confiscate your vehicles and take you back to the city under arrest! We have the legal authority and make no mistake we'll use it!*'

Saskia suddenly stood up, still carrying Mina in her arms.

'Saskia – no – for Christ's sake!' said Martin, and snatched at the leg of her pants as she pushed her way past him, but she shook herself free.

She walked out in front of the Eldorado and stood there defiantly. 'I'm Saskia Vane!' she shouted. 'If you want me, you'd better come get me! But you let everybody else go!'

Immediately, with no further warning, the security guard with the bullhorn pointed at Saskia, with his arm held out straight, and two of his men lifted their carbines and fired at her. Saskia dropped on to the rocks and rolled over, and Mina tumbled out of her arms and lay next to her.

Another security guard fired, but the bullets ricocheted off the ground. One of them smashed one of the Eldorado's headlights, and the other pinged off its radiator grille.

Santos spread his arms out wide and tried to shepherd all of his grandchildren back behind his truck and out of the line of fire. Susan stumbled, and fell on to one knee, but she managed to get back on her feet again without dropping little George.

Mikey, however, pulled himself away from Santos and started to run toward Saskia and Mina, as they lay on the ground.

'That's my baby sister!' he screamed. 'Don't shoot! Don't shoot! That's my baby sister! She's sick!'

'Mikey!' shouted Santos. 'Mikey, come back here!'

But Mikey kept running, his eyes wild and his hair sticking up. 'That's my baby sister! Don't shoot!'

He had nearly reached Mina when a single shot cracked, almost drowned by the noise of the helicopter. Mikey stumbled and cartwheeled and then pitched forward on to the rocks. He managed to lift his head up a little, but then he fell forward again, and lay still.

Martin, crouching behind the fender of his Eldorado, felt as if a freezing ocean wave had crashed over him. He was so angry and so shocked that he was shaking. But this wasn't the haphazard rage of post-traumatic stress disorder. This wasn't the blind, illogical fury that had led him to shout at Peta and push her from one side of the room to the other.

This was the same ice-cold anger that he had felt when he was on patrol in Afghanistan, and one of his friends had fallen down right in front of him, hit by a Taliban sniper. You didn't scream and shout and start firing wildly in all directions. You immediately hit the ground and took whatever cover you could find, and even though you were shaking you worked out where the shot had come from, and when you picked out that raghead's position you took extremely precise aim and squeezed the trigger and you blew his fucking face off.

Martin lifted the Colt Commando over the hood of the car and aimed it at the helicopter. It was an AS-50 AStar and he knew exactly where the fuel tank was, under the transmission deck. It was self-sealing and designed to be crashworthy, but even a self-sealing tank wouldn't be able to stand up to a sustained burst of sub-machine gun fire.

The helicopter was slowly rotating anticlockwise, its right flank gradually becoming more exposed, so Martin held back until he could take his best shot. Apart from the helicopter, though, everything else appeared to have become suspended in time. The security guards underneath it were still standing like toy action figures with their weapons raised. The security guard with the bullhorn was still pointing to the spot where Saskia had fallen. Santos still had his arms outstretched, trying to shield his grandchildren. Peta and Tyler were still cowering behind their pickup.

As the helicopter turned side-on, however, the security guard who was standing in its open door caught sight of Martin behind his car. He started to lift his carbine and shouted something to the men on the ground, but they didn't appear to hear him.

Martin fired two three-round bursts at the helicopter, to find his range. He heard Ella behind him scream, '*Daddy!*' but he could see the pattern of bullets hitting the dark blue fuselage almost exactly where he wanted them to, just behind the ESS logo, and he ignored her. He switched to automatic and kept on firing until the thirty-round magazine was empty.

The bullets hammered a ragged star-shaped hole in the side of the helicopter, and its gears instantly seized up, with a scream like a tortured beast. With a grating metallic shriek, its rotors stopped, and it started to drop, but before it could hit the ground its fuel tank exploded. Martin ducked down behind his car again as a tsunami of heat overwhelmed him, as scorchingly hot as his anger had been icy cold.

Fragments of helicopter were blasted in every direction, rattling and bouncing up against the walls of the canyon, clattering against their vehicles, and cracking the windshield of Martin's Eldorado. A huge ball of yellow fire rolled into the air before it was swallowed up by a boiling cloud of whitish-gray smoke.

If any of the security guards had cried out, Martin hadn't heard them. When he cautiously stood up he could see why. All that was left of the helicopter was its skids, and its controls, and the blackened framework of its seats. Its crew were still strapped in, but two of them were nothing more than legs and pelvises and ribcages, while another two were still intact, but with their clothes charred into flakes like burned newspaper and their face masks milky-opaque from the heat.

The security guards who had been standing beneath the helicopter had all been incinerated, too, and three of them were lying amongst the boulders, their arms bent in the monkey-like posture of all serious burns victims, their hair and their uniforms still smoking. There was no sign of the fourth guard, the one who been holding the bullhorn, although the bullhorn itself had been blown almost a hundred feet away, into the chaparral. The falling helicopter had probably landed right on top of him, and cremated him.

'*Mikey!*' wailed Santos, and came hurrying as fast as he could over the boulders. '*Mina!*'

Martin's ears were still ringing from firing his sub-machine gun and the blast-pressure from the helicopter's fuel tank blowing up. Saskia was only a few yards away, lying on her side with little Mina next to her, but before Martin stepped out of cover, he ejected the empty magazine from his Colt and clicked in a fresh one. Wherever they were, any remaining crew from the second helicopter must have heard the explosion, and it was possible that they might send more security guards down to the canyon to find out what had happened.

He went over and hunkered down next to Saskia and Mina. As he did so, Mina opened her eyes and sat up. Dazed, she slowly looked around at the bodies and the smoldering wreckage all around her, and then she burst out crying, with a high-pitched piping sound like a fledgling jay. Martin picked her up and held her close to him, and said, 'Shush now, Mina. Everything's OK now. Everything's fine.'

Santos came hobbling over. 'Here,' he said. 'Let me have her. Come to grandpa, Mina. Come on.' He took Mina in his arms and patted her on the back to comfort her, although his face was gray with shock.

'How's Mikey?' asked Martin.

Santos gave him the smallest shake of his head. 'See for yourself. They hit him in the chest.'

Martin looked over Santos' shoulder to where Mikey was lying face-down among the rocks. The back of his T-shirt was glistening scarlet with arterial blood.

'What kind of monsters can kill a child like that?' said Santos, his voice trembling and his eyes flooded with tears. 'At least you gave them what they deserved.'

Peta and Tyler were coming over to join them. They both looked as shocked as Santos. Peta was holding up her right hand to shield her face like a blinker, so that she wouldn't have to look at all the charred and half-dismembered corpses.

'Saskia—' said Peta. 'Is she dead?'

Martin bent over and looked at Saskia. Her eyes were closed and her face was smudged with soot from the helicopter blast. She was dressed all in black so it was difficult to see if she had been hit by any of the security guard's bullets, so he carefully turned her over on to her side.

At that moment she opened her eyes and stared at him, looking just as bewildered as little Mina.

'My God, Martin,' she croaked. 'What happened?'

Martin helped her to sit up. 'Did they hit you?' he asked her.

'No, no, they didn't,' she said. She looked around her in disbelief.

'My God. It blew up. My God. Just look at it. Those men, they're
all dead.'

'You're sure you're not hurt?'

'No, no, I'm not. As soon as they started shooting at me I hit
the ground. Is Mina all right? Mina's not hurt, is she? I couldn't
help dropping her.'

Santos was still patting Mina's back. She had stopped crying now
and was repeatedly sniffing. 'Mina's OK. It looks like she might
have bumped her head, but at least she's alive.'

Martin took Saskia's hand and she climbed back on to her feet.
She brushed herself down and then she pressed her fingers to her
temples. 'I have *such* a splitting headache. My God.'

Tyler was standing over Mikey's body, clutching himself as if he
were cold. 'What do we do now, Dad? We're not going to try to
go on, are we?'

'I don't think Saskia and I have a lot of choice,' said Martin. 'I
don't know how the rest of you feel. If you give up and go back
to San Berdoo now, there still won't be any water. One way or
another, if we don't keep going, I don't think there's much of a
future for any of us.'

'What are we going to do with Mikey?' asked Tyler. Martin could
see that Mikey's shooting had badly affected him. Maybe he felt
that he should have run out and caught him. He had failed to save
Maria from being raped. Now he had failed to save Mikey.

Martin walked over and laid his hand on Tyler's shoulder. Tyler's
mouth was puckered up with helplessness and grief.

'Come on, Tyler. You can't blame yourself. Most of the time in
life you just have to stand back and admit to yourself that there's
nothing you can do.'

'*You* always manage to do something. Look – you just blew up
their helicopter and killed them all. What did I do? Nothing. I didn't
even shout at Mikey to come back.'

'Tyler, you're in shock. We all are. And for Christ's sake don't
take me as some kind of example. Take it from me, you can't solve
all of life's problems with a sub-machine gun.'

Just then, they heard the whistling sound of the second helicopter
starting up. The roar of its engine grew louder and louder until it
eventually appeared over the crest of the promontory. Shading his
eyes, Martin could see that the pilot was alone in the cabin. He lifted
up his Colt Commando to make sure that the pilot could see it.

The pilot circled around for a few moments, taking a long look down at the burned-out wreckage of the first helicopter below him. Then he veered steeply away, heading west. The roaring quickly dwindled to a distant drone, and then nothing.

Santos said, 'We will have to leave Mikey here. We cannot take his body with us. Let us find a good place and cover him with stones. The Great Spirit will look over him until we can come back for him, just as we will one day return for his mother.'

SEVEN

J oseph Wrack was hunched on the black leather corner couch in his office eating a take-out *chirashi zushi*, Japanese vinegared rice with fish. It had been delivered from Seattle Best Teriyaki on East Hospitality Lane, which had not yet had its water supply cut off, and would probably escape the 'rotational hiatus' because of all the four-star hotels in the area.

He was watching a news update on the nationwide effects of the drought. The President had announced this morning that 'we are now looking at a situation that is considerably more serious than we had first envisaged.' The TV report showed billions of acres of devastation, especially in the Midwest. In Iowa, soybean and corn crops had withered and dried up; wheat fields in Kansas had been blackened for lack of rain; and potatoes in Idaho and Wisconsin and Colorado were far too shriveled to be worth digging up. Apple trees in Oregon had failed even to blossom this year, and in California, broccoli was turning yellow even before it was harvested, and the wetlands in the Sacramento Valley which produced most of the nation's rice looked like sun-cracked deserts.

Joseph Wrack was not watching the news to be told something that he didn't know already. In fact he knew that the drought was at least twice as serious as the President was trying to make out. Governor Smiley had been regularly keeping him informed on the confidential reports that he had been receiving from various agricultural associations like the Visalia citrus growers and the Napa Valley wine growers. Orange groves had produced seventy-two percent less marketable fruit than two years ago; and in Napa, Chardonnay grapes were drying into raisins while they were still on the vine.

Joseph Wrack's interest in the news was to see how many lies and half-truths the President could get away with, just to keep the nation calm. His entire career in security had been devoted to catching people out when they were lying, and he liked to think that he could tell when somebody was being evasive or mendacious simply by their tone of voice, or the way they swept their hair back, or suddenly beamed when they imagined that their audience had actually believed them.

He was chasing a small shred of fish around his bowl with his needle-pointed Japanese chopsticks when there was a knock at the door and Jim Broader barged in. Jim Broader's blood pressure must have been high, because his swarthy complexion was even darker than usual, as if his head were going to burst. One of his shirt tails was hanging out, and he was wheezing.

'Boss!' he gasped, and leaned against Joseph Wrack's desk while he tried to get his breath back. 'Boss!'

'For Christ's sake, Jim. This is my first break all day. I'm *trying* to enjoy a very late lunch?'

'Sorry, boss. It's Martin Makepeace and Saskia Vane.'

Joseph Wrack set down his bowl on the coffee table in front of him. 'We've *caught* them?' he said, hoarsely. 'Don't tell me we've caught them!'

Jim Broader shook his head. 'No, boss. I just received a message from Eye-Sky Five. They located them all right, in the Big Morongo Canyon Preserve.'

Joseph Wrack stood up, and triumphantly punched his right fist into the open palm of his left hand.

'What did I say? What did I tell you? I *said* they weren't going to head north, didn't I? I *said* they weren't going to Vegas. They must have stopped someplace in the mountains overnight, because of the kids!

He paused, and then he said, 'So where are they now? If we didn't catch them, *why* didn't we catch them?'

'We don't know where they are, exactly. Eye-Sky Three eyeballed them first. They had them cornered, by the sound of it, although the terrain wasn't suitable for touchdown. Eye-Sky Five landed as near as they could and their snatch team went down on foot.'

Joseph Wrack circled around the end of the coffee table and slowly approached Jim Broader as if he were a black panther walking up to a fear-paralyzed bullock.

'What happened, Jim? Tell me.'

'We don't know, exactly. It must have been Makepeace. You know that he's armed with a sub-machine gun.'

'What happened, Jim?' Joseph Wrack's voice was lowered to a rasping whisper, so that he was almost inaudible.

'Eye-Sky Three went down, boss. Robbins said that it was totaled. Looked like the fuel tank went up.'

'Casualties?'

Jim Broader was so nervous that he was spitting. Joseph Wrack wiped his saliva from his cheek with the back of his hand, but stayed unflinchingly face to face with him.

'Nine altogether, boss. All of the team in Eye-Sky Three and four of the team from Eye-Sky Five. Robbins was the only survivor.'

'Nine,' said Joseph Wrack. '*Nine.*'

He walked over to his desk, opened up a silver-plated box, and took out a panatela. He lit it, and for a moment his head disappeared into a cloud of blue smoke. Jim Broader watched him anxiously as he went to the window and stood looking out over East 4th Street.

'Boss?' he said, after a while. 'Do you want me to inform their families?'

Joseph Wrack turned around and stared at him as if he had said something blasphemous. 'Do you know how much an AS-50 AStar actually *costs*?' he asked.

'Yes, boss. A couple of million, give or take.'

'Two million three hundred thousand to be more precise. And do you have *any* idea how much we have to pay for insurance?'

'Yes, boss. I have seen the figures. It's, er – it's a hell of a lot, isn't it?'

'Yes, Jim. It's a hell of a lot. It's a *hell* of a lot. And in the space of two days, we have also had to write off one prison bus and two brand-new Cadillac Escalades. Our insurance premiums are going to go through the roof. Not to mention what this is doing to our reputation as the Inland Empire's most efficient and trustworthy security service.'

'Yes, boss.'

Joseph Wrack turned back to the window. There were only a few pedestrians walking along East 4th Street but the way he looked down at them reminded Jim Broader of Harry Lime in *The Third Man* looking down from the fairground carousel at the diminutive people on the ground and asking, '*Would you really feel any pity if one of those dots stopped moving forever?*'

Instead, he said, 'I want a full report on this, Jim. I want to know exactly where and how it happened. I want a detailed cost break-down, including an estimate of how much excess our insurance companies will expect us to pay. I also want a comprehensive marketing analysis. We need for people to be on our side. We need to evoke sympathy. We lost these nine guys fighting to protect our local community. "Our sacrifice for your safety," that kind of thing.'

'How about their families?'

'Yes, those too. Give me all their contact details. I'll talk to them personally.'

'I really don't mind doing it myself, boss. I knew most of those men pretty well.'

'No, no. leave it to me. Breaking the news to a woman that her husband's been killed, that needs *tact*. That needs *compassion*. You wouldn't know compassion if it came up behind you and bit you in your big fat ass.'

Jim Broader stood up straight and tucked in his shirt tail. 'OK, boss, I'll get on to it.'

'I don't need it right away, Jim. Tomorrow or the day after, if you like. There's something else you have to do first, and you know what *that* is, don't you?'

'Boss?'

Joseph Wrack came back across his office and stared at Jim Broader with an idiotic grin on his face.

'You have to find Martin Makepeace, Jim, that's what you have to do first. You have to find Martin Makepeace and waste him. I don't care how you do it. Just bring me back enough evidence that you've done it. One hand would do. Or even one finger. Or one of his eyeballs. If he's not extinct by this time tomorrow, Jim, I will seriously want to know why.'

Once Jim Broader had gone, Joseph Wrack returned to the black leather couch and the TV news, although he didn't turn the sound back on, and after watching it for only two or three minutes, he switched it off altogether. He had seen enough aerial views of drought-ravaged wheatfields and interviews with politicians who were all furrowing their brows to appear as if they genuinely felt the nation's pain.

'Goddamned hypocrites,' he said, out loud. He hated hypocrisy. If there was one thing that he had learned from his father, it was that if you are going to be a shit, then act like a shit. Don't go around smiling and clapping people on the back, pretending that you're Mr Appreciative Guy.

He was also too angry to think about the drought. He was so angry that it was knotting up his stomach, as if he had acute diarrhea. He had built up Empire Security Services on the principle of absolutely no compromise. His guards were trained to open fire first and worry about the consequences afterward, and would-be bank robbers and jewel thieves knew that they would, which is why ESS-guarded businesses reported fifty-six percent less attempted crime than businesses guarded by their competitors.

Over the years, Joseph Wrack had tirelessly developed contacts in state and county and city government, as well as the DA's office and the judiciary. Even when his men caused collateral casualties, or shot somebody who simply had the misfortune to look like a robber, they were very rarely prosecuted and even more rarely found guilty.

He stood up, and then he sat down again, biting his knuckle. He felt like calling for a helicopter and going out in search of Martin Makepeace himself, and then strangling him in person. How had Makepeace *dared* to wreck his bus and his SUVs and his helicopter and put ten of his men out of action? Jesus – he was only some pissant social worker in the children's department.

There was another knock at the door. *Not Jim Broader again with yet another of his dumbass questions.* But a smart young black woman in a pink floral blouse and high-waisted white slacks came in. She had a short shiny bob streaked with pink and she was immaculately groomed, her cheekbones emphasized with rose-colored blusher, her lips painted in a cupid's bow, her long nails perfectly polished. She wore heavy-rimmed, upswept spectacles, which made her look academic as well as sexy.

'Abelina!' said Joseph Wrack, standing up again. 'Haven't seen you since *when,* for Christ's sake?'

Abelina King waved one hand from side to side and wrinkled up her nose. 'Still smoking those cat turds, Joseph?'

'It's the coffee that comes from cat turds, Abelina. What I smoke is the finest Havana panatelas.'

'Whatever you say, J.W. They still *smell* like cat turds.'

'What the hell are *you* doing in town?' Joseph Wrack asked her. 'I thought you were permanently based in LA these days.'

'I am, J.W., I am. I only came back to get my mother. I heard about the riots and I thought it was time to get her out of here. Mind you, we've had riots in LA, too. Six people got killed in Crenshaw only the day before yesterday. There was nothing on the news about it, but my friend told me. It doesn't seem like there's *nothing* on the news these days except "don't use too much water and everything's going to be fine". Yeah, right . . . just as soon as it starts to rain again.'

'So, how can I help you?' asked Joseph Wrack. 'Sit down, why don't you? How about a cup of coffee?'

'Cat turd coffee? No thanks. Anyhow, I've come here to help *you*, not the other way about.'

'Oh, yeah? And how are you going to do that?'

'Your man got in touch with me. What's his name, the guy with the breath that smells like onions. Jim something. Used to be a cop.'

'Jim Broader? He's my deputy. He's OK, Jim, apart from the breath, and he's not exactly Einstein. But he keeps the troops in order, and he's wily enough. After all, what we're looking to do here is keep banks from being robbed, not work out if we can travel backward in time.'

Abelina King sat down on the edge of the black leather couch and crossed her legs. 'A glass of water would be good,' she said. Joseph Wrack went across to the fridge in the corner of his office and took out a bottle of Arrowhead.

'You want to drink this slow, and savor every drop,' he told her, as he poured it out for her. 'This is worth its weight in water.'

'Thanks,' said Abelina King. 'Jim Thing said you were interested in Saskia Vane, and whatever involvement she might have with Governor Smiley.'

'That's right. Halford told me that Saskia Vane owes him some kind of a favor, but he wouldn't tell me what it is.'

'And what makes *you* so curious?'

Joseph Wrack gave her a tight, humorless smile. 'I'm curious about everybody and everything, Abelina. It's my job. The more I know, the less I get taken by surprise. And you know me. I don't like surprises. They give me heartburn.'

'Well, I don't know everything, J.W., and what I do know I don't know for certain. But Saskia Vane used to be married, not too many years ago. Her maiden name I think was something like Kaminski or Kaplinski or Kaplonski, something Polish anyhow. She was an attorney, and she met David Vane when she was defending him on a charge of possession. He was a record promoter. You've heard of Mind Explosion? Lenny Lucas and the Angels? Kathy Rose Duncan?'

'Yes, I've heard of them,' said Joseph Wrack, impatiently. 'Mind Explosion were crap. But go on.'

'During his trial, Saskia became *totally* besotted with David Vane and after he was acquitted they got married. From what I heard, though, it wasn't an easy marriage. A broken plate special, if you know what I mean. David Vane was an irredeemable cokehead and very generous with his affections to all of the teenage girls who used to come backstage at his concerts, while Saskia on the other hand was domineering and *very* possessive and always needed to take control.'

'So – OK – where does Halford Smiley come into this?'

Abelina lifted one cautionary finger. 'This I got third- or maybe even *fourth*-hand, so I can't swear to you, J.W., that it's true. But I do know for certain that Halford Smiley and David Vane had known each other since college, or even further back than that. They had hung out together, shared girlfriends together, smoked pot together, like who didn't?

'Halford Smiley as you know ended up marrying Mona Van Pelt, and I don't think anybody is under any illusion as to *why* he married her. It begins with "m" and ends with "y" and rhymes with "honey". Mona was amazing looking, no question. She still is. But she's always been a frigid stuck-up society bitch who has no interests in life except for her charities and her Chihuahuas. The only things that really turn Mona on are her dogs' undying devotion and other people's abject gratitude.

'Whenever Mona was away on one of her charity trips to Africa, or wherever, Halford Smiley would throw parties and have his friends around, as well as quite a few girls. S and M parties, that's what I was told. Leather and whips and handcuffs, that kind of a party.'

'Yes, I heard about those,' said Joseph Wrack. 'I seem to remember that *The National Enquirer* were all ready to run a story about them, weren't they, but Halford managed to get an injunction.'

'Not without a little help from Saskia Vane,' said Abelina. 'Apart from the fact that she was a hotshot lawyer, she and her husband had been to those parties, too. I think she was just as anxious as Halford Smiley that the details wouldn't come out.'

'I still don't get it,' said Joseph Wrack. 'From what you're saying it sounds like Halford owed Saskia Vane the favor, not the other way about.'

'I know . . . and like I say, I was never told about any of this first-hand. I'm a studio publicist, J.W., not a news reporter. I wasn't going to go digging to find out what really happened. All I know is that about six months after *The National Enquirer* thing, David Vane was found dead. He was discovered in his own home, but what the news reports *didn't* say was that he and Saskia had been to one of Halford Smiley's parties the previous evening.'

'So what was the cause of death?'

'The coroner said auto-erotic asphyxiation. Strangled himself to get his jollies. You know, like David Carradine maybe did.'

'I'm still at a loss here. What exactly are you suggesting? Do you think that David Vane might have died at Halford's party, and that they might have smuggled his body back to his own home, so that Halford wouldn't be implicated? *That* wouldn't have done Saskia any favors.'

'I'm sorry, J.W., that's all I know,' said Abelina. 'If you want to find out more, you'll have to find it out for yourself. Me and my mother are leaving town. She's waiting for me downstairs, in reception.'

'OK,' said Joseph Wrack. He sat there for a moment, thinking, and then he stood up. 'Thanks for coming in, Abelina. It's been great to see you again, whatever.'

Abelina stood up, too. 'I can't tell you something that I don't know, J.W. No point in making it up, either. You make things up, you always get found out, in the end.'

Joseph Wrack opened the door for her, and kissed her on both cheeks. 'Safe journey back to LA,' he told her.

When she had gone, however, he went over to the map on the wall, and stood in front of it, breathing hard. He traced his finger across it until he found Big Morongo Canyon Preserve. Then he punched it so hard that he made a triangular tear in the map itself, and dented the plaster wall behind it.

EIGHT

'I'm dying,' said Saskia. 'In fact, I wish I *could* die. Just close my eyes and never wake up.'

'Have another drink,' Martin told her. 'You're probably dehydrated. Dehydration lowers your blood pressure, makes you feel depressed.'

'If I have to drink any more warm Mountain Dew I'm going to throw up, I swear it.'

'Just try to hold on. Santos said that we should get there pretty soon.'

'I don't care any more, Martin. I really don't. I'm dying.'

They had been jolting across the desert of the Joshua Tree National Park now for over five hours, while the sun sank behind them and the sky turned scarlet, so that Martin felt as if they were driving through a 1950s' sci-fi movie like *Forbidden Planet*. There were mountains in the distance which never seemed to come any closer, and all around them stretched mile after mile of desiccated creosote bushes and the weird fuzzy shapes of Joshua trees. Ella was asleep on the back seat and little Mina was sleeping, too, with her head resting in Saskia's lap, whistling through one blocked nostril.

Although it was still so warm, Martin lowered the Eldorado's top. Three turkey vultures were circling high above them, keeping up with them as they slowly crawled eastward.

'I guess you have to admire the Indians who first came this way,' said Martin. 'They wouldn't have known where the hell they were going, or what they were going to find when they got there. All they had to guide them was some legend about the arrowhead.'

'Do *you* know where the hell we're going?' asked Saskia. 'I just hope to God Santos does.'

From the position of the sun behind them, Martin realized that Santos was gradually leading them north-eastward instead of due east. He knew that there were several camping grounds in the park, and ranger stations, but even though they were probably unoccupied, because of the drought, Santos was making sure that he gave them all a wide berth, so that nobody would be able to report that they had seen them passing by. They had crossed over one narrow tarmac road as they made their way further into the desert, but they had been careful to ensure that no other vehicles were in sight in either direction.

The mountains at last appeared to be coming nearer. After another half hour, the ground began to rise, and they found themselves bumping over bare, rectangular slabs of granite, like giants' paving stones. Their engines began to labor as their ascent grew steeper, and the suspension of Martin's car was knocking so loudly that he was sure that one of his rear shock absorbers had collapsed. Eventually, however, they reached the opening to a wide dry wash. Its bed was filled with smooth oval pebbles which had been sluiced down it over thousands of years by recurrent floods, but its gradient was far less punishing, and it formed a natural pathway up toward the skyline.

It took them at least fifteen more minutes to reach the crest of the slope, their engines still whining and their tires crunching and slithering on the pebbles. When they finally got to the top, Santos stopped his truck and Peta and Martin pulled up close behind him. They didn't have to get out to ask Santos where they were, and how much longer they would have to keep driving. They could see the valley ahead of them and they knew that they had arrived.

The valley was very deep, and because the sun was now so low it was filled up with shadow. Its sides were sheer but its lower slopes were covered with teddy-bear cholla and creosote bush and bursage, all growing so thickly and so close together that there must be water there, under the ground. A pungent smell of desert vegetation was rising from the darkness as the air began to cool.

Ella opened her eyes, sat up and looked around. 'Are we there yet?' she asked. 'Is this it?'

'I guess so,' said Martin. Although they had arrived at their destination, he was suddenly feeling tired and dispirited and very far from any kind of civilization. This valley was spectacular, but he had never imagined that he could miss his apartment in Hummingbird Haven so much. Right now he would have given anything to pry off his shoes, take a beer out of the fridge, and collapse into his armchair in front of the television.

Santos started up his truck again and they began a slow, unsteady descent. The cholla cactus and the creosote bushes were so dense that it was like submerging beneath the surface of a dark, prickly ocean. They all switched on their headlights but even then they were driving through such a mass of branches and cactus stems that it was almost impossible to see where they were going. Martin realized now why so few people knew about the existence of Lost Girl Lake, and how much they had needed Santos to guide them here. The noise of the cholla scraping against the sides of their vehicles set his teeth on edge. They appeared to be soft and furry, which was why they were called 'teddy bear' cholla, but what looked like fur was sharp silvery spines.

Ella reached out to touch one, but Martin glanced across and saw what she was doing. 'Ella – no! Don't!' he warned her. 'Those cholla prickles, they're like fish hooks! Once they're stuck to your skin you can't pull them off!'

'Oh, my God,' said Saskia, immediately taking her bare elbow from where she had been resting it on top of the door. 'And we're supposed to make *camp* here?'

'Well, if nothing else, the cholla will keep other people away,' said Martin. 'Desert rats collect cholla balls and pile them up around their nests to protect them from predators.'

'Really? How do you *know* that? That's so – I don't know – *ethological.*'

Martin gave her a smile. 'The Marine Corps trained us for Afghanistan in the Mojave Desert. One of my friends threw a cholla stem at me and it stuck to my back. They had to use a hair-comb to pull it off and then tweezers to pick all of the rest of the spines out. It hurt like hell. My back was sore and all swelled up for days.'

The bushes began to thin out, and at last they reached the end of the valley – a triangular area of scrubby open ground, about the same size and shape as a baseball infield, but walled in by two sheer cliffs of whitish-gray granite, at least three hundred feet high, which met together almost at a right angle.

They parked their vehicles side by side, and switched off their engines, and this time everybody wearily climbed out. Santos left his sidelights on because here on the valley floor it was almost completely dark.

Martin looked up to the purple evening sky high above them and saw that the stars were coming out, which made him feel even more isolated from the real world than he had before. The valley was silent, except for an occasional scrabbling noise in the bushes, which could have been anything from wood rats to a desert night lizard.

Santos came over, wiping the sweat from his forehead with the back of his hand. 'We made it,' he said. 'I was beginning to think we never would. Welcome to Lost Girl Lake, everybody.'

'So, where's the lake?' asked Tyler. 'I don't see any lake.' His face was as pale as a *Twilight* vampire and he had dark shadows around his eyes. In fact, looking around at all the surviving members of their party, Martin could see how much their escape had taken out of them. They all looked exhausted and dirty and demoralized.

George sat down on the ground and folded his arms and announced, 'I wanna go *home* now!'

'I want to go home too,' said Nathan. 'I don't *like* this place. It's too dark! It's too spooky!'

Martin said, 'Come on, guys. It's much too far to think about going back tonight. And besides, we're having an adventure!'

'I don't *like* deventures,' said George, emphatically. 'I want Mom to come back, and Mikey.'

Santos patted the boys' shoulders. 'Come, and I will show you the lake. Then you will all understand why we have come here, and be glad that we did. Martin – can you bring your flashlight? We're going to need it. Oh – and bring your cellphones, too. They will give us a little more light.'

He turned and started to walk across the triangular open space, directly toward the angle where the two granite rock faces met.

Peta looked up at Martin and said, 'Where's he going? That's a total dead end.'

'Oh, it's just a bit of old Indian medicine-man magic,' said Saskia. 'They can walk through solid rock, didn't you know that? I just hope we palefaces can do the same.'

Santos reached the sheer granite walls, and without any hesitation stepped to the left and disappeared.

'Where did he go?' asked Ella. 'One second he was there and then he was gone.'

'What did I tell you?' said Saskia, although she sounded just as surprised as Ella. 'Magic.'

Together, they all approached the two rock faces. As they came closer, and Martin shone his flashlight on them, they saw that there was a crevice where they met, about ten feet high and two feet wide. Deep inside the crevice, they could see the beam of Santos' flashlight dancing against a low ceiling of corrugated granite.

'Come on!' called Santos. Although the crevice was so narrow, his voice was echoing and distorted and oddly amplified, as if he were shouting through a megaphone.

'I think you'd better go first, Martin,' said Peta.

'Yes, Martin,' put in Saskia, linking arms with him. 'You can protect us, can't you?'

Martin's flashlight caught Peta turning her head and giving Saskia a quick, quizzical frown; although she didn't say anything.

Martin pushed his way into the crevice, inching along sideways because the space was so tight. For the first twenty feet he felt severely claustrophobic, especially when the granite walls came even closer together, so that they scraped against his shoulders and his elbows He looked back and saw that Peta was following him, and then Ella, and that Saskia had picked up little Mina so that she could carry her. This wasn't really the time to be thinking about it, but Martin found Saskia such a contradictory character – sarcastic and vexatious and domineering one minute and then tender and considerate the next. He had been involved with several messy and complicated women before he had met Peta, but none as complicated as Saskia.

As he edged his way further, the crevice began to widen, and after a few more feet it opened out into a cavern. With only two criss-crossing flashlights to illuminate it, it was difficult at first for Martin to be able to judge the scale of it, but it felt and sounded vast.

He had come out on to a wide flat ledge, about seventy-five feet wide. Santos was standing on the opposite side, shining his flashlight to guide him. Beyond the ledge there was a lake. Its water was so still and so clear that it looked as if there were no water there at all. There was no wind to ripple it, after all, and no fish swimming in it. Martin went over to join Santos and shone his flashlight into it, and he could clearly see the bottom of it, even though it must have been at least thirty feet deep.

He directed his flashlight upward. He could just about make out the ceiling of the cavern, which rose higher and higher in a series of rectangular granite pillars, until it disappeared into a darkness which his flashlight was unable to penetrate. He thought that if men in the Stone Age had attempted to build cathedrals, this is what they would have looked like.

The cavern felt cool, and he could detect a very faint current of air blowing through it, like somebody breathing against his face when they were deeply asleep. Apart from the shuffling of their feet and their awed conversation, it was utterly silent.

'Lost Girl Lake,' said Santos. 'Like Big Bear Lake, its water all comes from melting snow. But *this* water is filtered through layer after layer of rock, until it is completely pure, and it is never polluted by boats or oil or sewage or weeds. Not even by birds, or rats, or people's dogs, or even by people. Who knows how many millions of gallons of water are here? The caves go back under the mountains, maybe for miles. Nobody has ever explored them. There is probably enough water here to supply the whole city, at least until it rains again.'

Ella went to the very edge of the ledge, knelt down and scooped up a handful of water. She drank some, and then she splashed some in her face. 'That's wonderful,' she said. 'Can we wash in it?'

Santos pointed his flashlight off to the left. 'Over there is a small pool which is separated from the main lake. When my people first settled here, they used it for washing themselves, although the Yuhaviatam men went naked and the women wore mostly deerskins or rabbit fur, so they had no clothes to wash.'

'So what are we going to do now?' asked Saskia. 'I vote we make ourselves something to eat and then try to get some sleep.'

'Seconded,' said Martin.

'Thirded,' said Tyler. 'I've never been so bushed in my life.'

Martin and Tyler went out into the darkness to collect cholla stems and creosote bush to make a fire. Meanwhile, Santos and Peta and Ella carried their food supplies into the cavern. They also dragged in all of the blankets that they had brought with them, and folded them into sleeping bags.

It took Martin and Tyler several minutes of strenuous pushing and pulling and silent cursing, but eventually they managed to force enough cactus and wood through the crevice in the rock to build a good fire. They stacked it up in the center of the ledge and Martin flicked his Semper Fi Zippo to set it alight. The cholla flared up first, spitting and crackling with bright white flames, almost as bright as magnesium.

'My God!' said Saskia, holding up her hand to shield her eyes. 'I never would have guessed that you could start a fire with a *cactus*! Aren't they full of water?'

'They are, yes,' said Martin. 'But teddy bear chollas are

incredibly combustible. In fact they're so combustible they're dangerous. Apart from their goddamned prickles, of course.'

They sat around the fire and made themselves a meal of Manhattan clam chowder and meatballs and rigatoni, which they ate from a motley assortment of plastic plates and bowls and coffee mugs, which Martin and Peta had once taken on picnics. The smoke from the fire rose steadily upward and disappeared into the darkness of the cavern's ceiling, and although he couldn't see one, Martin could only suppose that there was an opening up there somewhere, between the rocks. If there was, it would probably be unwise of them to light a fire during the day, in case somebody spotted it.

'How long are we going to be able to live like this?' asked Peta. 'We'll have run out of supplies in two or three days.'

'The Yuhaviatam lived here for several years,' said Santos. 'It is surprising to many people how rich the desert can be for food, even today. There are many seeds and buds that we can eat. For meat, we can survive on bighorn sheep, or jackrabbits, or kangaroo rats.'

'*Rats?*' said George, disgustedly. 'I'm not eating *rats!*'

'A barbecued rat, George, when you are very hungry, is a great treat,' said Santos. 'Especially if it is basted in agave syrup.'

Once they had eaten, they wrapped Nathan and George and Mina up in their blankets, and then they quietly talked together for a while, before taking turns to go over to the washing pool.

Once he had taken off his clothes and eased himself up to his neck in the cool, slightly mineral-tasting water, Martin's confidence began to return. If the Yuhaviatam had happily lived like this, then he was sure that they could, too – at least until the drought was over. He rinsed out his clothes and then stood up, so that he could wring them out. Although he was mostly in shadow, he could see Saskia sitting cross-legged by the embers of the dying fire, her blanket wrapped only loosely around her so that her cleavage was exposed, staring at him.

Peta had her back turned, talking to Tyler, but Ella saw Saskia looking at him.

Martin remembered what a Marine sergeant had said to him once, when they were talking about losing their nerve during firefights with the Taliban. 'You can run away from the world as far as you like, Makepeace, but you can never run away from yourself. Wherever you go, there you fucking are.'

*   *   *

He was bone-tired, but Martin couldn't sleep. He lay on his side, watching the sparks in the fire winking out, one after the other, trying to relax his mind and his body. *Calm*, he told himself. *Think of an ocean, lapping on the shore. Think of that monotonous rubab music they used to play in Afghanistan.* But every tendon in his body felt as tense as piano wire, and he couldn't help worrying that Joseph Wrack's men might have picked up their trail, and be coming after them even now. One of his Colt Commandos was folded into his blanket next to him, although he didn't relish the idea of firing a sub-machine gun fire in a confined space like this, with innocent women and children all around him.

At last, just as the first faint light was beginning to creep in through the crevice, Martin fell asleep. He didn't dream of anything at all. He just fell into a dark, bottomless well, and kept on falling.

He was woken up by a loud scuffling noise, followed by a piercing scream. Then another scream, and a cry of 'Mommy! *Momm-eeeeee!*'

He sat up instantly and turned around. By the light from outside and from Santos' flashlight, he saw two large beasts with yellow eyes and flailing tails. Coyotes. One of them was snarling and jumping excitedly from side to side. The other had its teeth in Mina's shoulder and was dragging her across the floor of the cavern, toward the crevice.

Mina was crying and kicking and struggling but the coyote had its jaws firmly locked and kept pulling her further and further along the crevice. It was clearly determined not to let go of her.

Martin's blankets were twisted tightly around his legs but he tugged himself free and clambered to his feet, bending down to pick up his Colt Commando. Everybody else was awake now, and shouting, and George was letting out an ear-splitting shriek of terror that was almost continuous.

'Shoot it! Shoot it!' Susan was begging.

'Martin – do something!' said Peta. 'Make it let her go!'

'I can't shoot it yet!' Martin told them. 'We'll get ricochets every which way! I'll end up killing all of us instead!'

The coyote dragged Mina right through the crevice and into the open. Martin followed, with Tyler close behind him. Outside, it was already warm, and the sky was the color of orange juice. What made the morning seem all the more unearthly was that apart from Mina's screaming and Susan's panicky shouting there was another, blood-curdling sound in the air, echoing from one mountain-top to another – the dawn chorus of coyotes howling.

As the coyote jerked Mina across the rough open ground in front of the cavern entrance, Martin hurried after it. Mina was kicking and flailing so violently that he didn't want to risk a shot from anything except point-blank range.

'*Momm-eeeee!*' she kept on screaming. '*Momm-eeeee!*'

Martin caught up with them. The coyote stared up at him balefully and bared its lips but it still kept her teeth firmly embedded in Mina's shoulder. Mina's eyes were rolling with shock and she was panting for breath. Martin slowly and cautiously stretched out his left hand, keeping eye contact with the coyote all the time. If he could seize the scruff of its neck he could hopefully hold the animal still for long enough to force the muzzle of his sub-machine gun into its ribcage and blow its insides out.

Just as he was about to grab a handful of fur and skin, however, the other coyote gave a harsh bark and came running at full pelt toward him. It stopped two or three feet short of him, but it kept barking and snarling and leaping up at him.

He swung the Colt Commando around and squeezed the trigger. Nothing happened, only a complicated click. He tried to eject the round in the chamber but it was jammed tight. There was no time to work out what had gone wrong with it. Faulty ammunition, broken extractor spring, it could have been anything. All he could do was grab the Commando's barrel and try to club the coyote with it. It was futile. The coyote kept dancing and dodging around him, still snarling, but making sure that it stayed well out of his reach.

Mina screamed again, because she was being dragged even further toward the bushes. Martin tried two or three times more to hit the other coyote, but each time it sprang back, and he missed it. In the end he hurled the gun at it as hard as he could. The coyote bounded to one side, and the gun clattered uselessly on to the ground.

'*Mommeeeeee!*' screamed Mina.

Martin had once been told by an Army dog handler how to tackle a pit bull when it goes berserk. He had never tried it, and he had no idea if it really worked or not, but he didn't know now what else he could do. Turning away from the second coyote, he ran back over to the one who was pulling Mina away. He came around behind it, and even though it tried to twist itself away from him, he managed to throw one leg over it and straddle its back. He sat down on its spine with all of his weight, clenching its body tightly between his knees. It struggled and thrashed with all of its strength, and it was stronger than any man he had ever wrestled with. What amazed him was that it still wouldn't open its jaws and release its grip on Mina's shoulder. It was going to keep hold of its prey at any price.

He bent forward, catching hold of both of its upper front legs and then gripping them as tightly as he could, even though it was furiously scrabbling to break free. But just as he was about to deliver his *coup de grâce*, the second coyote came running up again and launched itself on top of him, snarling and biting and scratching and tearing at his shirt. He heard a crunch as it bit into his right biceps, and instantly he felt a searing red-hot pain, as if somebody had branded him.

'*Yaaaah!*' he shouted, as the coyote went for him again. 'Get off me, you monster! *Yaaaah!*'

The coyote tried to tear at his face, and its front teeth collided with his right cheekbone, as hard as a punch with a knuckleduster. He ducked his head down and lifted up his shoulder in a bid to protect himself, but then he felt it tearing into his ear. He thought at that moment that he would have to release his hold on the first coyote's legs, just to stop the second coyote from ripping half his face off.

Suddenly, though, he heard a dull, heavy thud. The second coyote yelped and leapt away from him, keening in pain. As it circled away from him, he saw that Tyler was standing only a few feet away from it, holding a large granite rock in his hand. Tyler pivoted his foot in the classic pitcher's move that Martin had taught him when he was only five years old, and threw a knuckleball, hitting the second coyote in the flank.

Martin didn't hesitate. With all of his strength, he wrenched the first coyote's front legs sideways and upward, as far as they would go. He heard muscles and tendons and connective tissue ripping apart, and the coyote dropped flat to the ground underneath him, as promptly as if he had hit it on the head with a baseball bat. *Pull the dog's front legs wide apart and you'll have a good chance of stopping its heart*, the Army dog handler had told him, and he thanked God that it had worked on this coyote.

Tyler pitched another rock at the second coyote, and it barked and whined and ran off into the bushes.

Martin carefully pried open the dead coyote's jaws and lifted out

Mina's shoulder. Mina was still conscious but she was deeply
shocked and whimpering and her lips were blue. He gently picked
her up and carried her over to Susan, who had her arms outstretched
already. Her cheeks were glistening with tears, and all she could
do was say, 'Thank you. Thank you. Both of you. Thank you.'

'Let's just get her inside and wrap her up and give her something
to drink,' said Martin.

As they all started to make their way back into the cavern, Saskia
came up to him and gently touched his bloodstained shirtsleeve with
her fingertips. 'You're hurt, Martin. We should clean that up for
you.'

'Nah, it's nothing. Just a coyote bite. I've had worse bites than
that, believe me.'

Saskia lowered her eyelashes and then gave him a long, sugges-
tive smile. 'Really?' she said. 'What could bite you worse than
that?'

Martin turned to Tyler, and laid his left arm around his shoulders.
'Think you earned your stripes there, soldier. That was real quick
thinking. Not to mention some very impressive pitching. Knuckleball's
the hardest there is, especially with a rock. You probably saved little
Mina's life there, and my life, too.'

Tyler nodded and said, 'I did, didn't I?'

Martin scruffed his hair and slapped him on the back. He knew
for himself that there are few feelings in life more uplifting them
redemption.

Back inside the cavern, in the gloom, Susan washed little Mina's
bites and dressed her in a clean pink dress. She gave her a drink of
lake water and wrapped her up tightly in her blankets, so that she
could sleep to get over the shock of her attack.

Peta said, 'I should clean your bites, too, Martin. You don't know
what you can catch from coyotes.'

Santos, who was standing close by, said, 'Coyote is the demon
of bad luck. He is the demon of everything going wrong. If you
kill his running-dogs, then you risk all kinds of misfortune.'

'Oh, thanks, Santos,' said Martin. 'But there you go. Shit happens.'

NINE

They ate a scrappy breakfast of cold hot dogs, dry Cap'n Crunch cereal and half-melted Ding Dongs. Then they lifted the tents out of Peta's Hilux and began to set up a camp on the flat ground outside the cavern. By ten, the morning was roastingly hot, with another cloudless sky, and although the high walls of the canyon gave them plenty of shade, there was no breeze at all. The greatest relief as they worked was to go back inside the crevice and kneel by the lake to take a drink of water and splash themselves.

Peta had brought their three Wenzel lightweight tents, two four-man and one two-man. They pitched them at angles to each other and when they had pitched them they covered them thickly in heaps of bursage and creosote bushes so that they would be camouflaged from any passing helicopter.

Mina was already looking much better. She was sitting on a rock in her bright pink dress, playing with two of her Barbie dolls and singing to herself.

'My God,' said Saskia. 'I wish I was that resilient.'

Nathan and George had caught a collared lizard. They had put it into a cardboard box with two plastic GIs and were pretending it was a dinosaur. George was talking in a low growl which was what he obviously thought dinosaurs sounded like, when they spoke.

Martin and Tyler dragged the body of the dead coyote deep into the bushes and built a cairn over it, because the ground was far too hard to dig a shallow grave and bury it.

'I've seen stories about that on the news, coyotes making off with children,' said Tyler, as they stacked on the last few rocks. 'Never thought I'd ever see it in real life.'

'Coyotes, they'll eat anything,' Martin told him. 'They like cats, especially. Friend of mine, when we were training, a coyote came into his tent and ate his tennis shoe.'

'Jesus,' said Tyler.

'I'll have to find out why that gun jammed,' said Martin. 'We have a spare, and there's no question that you're a world-class pitcher, but next time there could be a whole pack of them.'

They made their way through the cactus and the chaparral back to the camp. Tyler went across to help Ella, who was trying to hammer in a tent peg, while Martin edged his way back through the crevice to find his Colt Commando.

As he entered the main cavern, he suddenly felt chilled, and he gave a violent, involuntary shudder. He stopped, and blinked. He felt freezing cold, but at the same time he was sweating profusely. He could feel his shirt clinging wetly to his back and when he blinked the perspiration stung his eyes.

Santos was standing on the opposite side of the ledge, with his unlit stogie in his mouth, folding up blankets. He looked across at Martin and said, 'Martin? Are you OK?'

Martin took two steps forward, and then stopped again. Santos' voice had echoed as if he were calling to him down a long empty sewer pipe, and the ledge beneath his feet felt as if it were tilting sideways. The interior of the cavern began to grow darker and darker, and even colder.

'I'm – I feel kind of—'

He sank slowly to his knees, reaching out with one hand to steady himself, because the ground was rising and falling underneath him and he didn't want to lose his balance and fall over sideways.

Santos came across and bent over him, frowning. 'You look sick, Martin. Wait – let me get my flashlight. Open your eyes wide, let me look at your pupils.'

Martin was shaking now, and he felt an agonizing pain all the way up his spine. Santos shone his flashlight into his eyes, left and then right. 'Very dilated. You are sick. Stick out your tongue.'

'What?'

'Stick out your tongue. Yes – see, furry. Well, you can't see it, but it *is* furry.'

'I feel so *cold*, Santos. What the hell's wrong with me?'

Santos went over to the blankets that he had been folding and brought four of them back. 'You need to keep warm, Wasicu. Look, I will spread these out for you.'

Martin lay down on the blankets and Santos covered him up, right up to the neck. He was juddering uncontrollably, so that he could barely speak. He had been beaten and tortured by the Taliban, but even then he had never felt as bad as this. That had simply been pain. Now he felt as if some icy cold demon had seized him by the shoulders and was trying to shake the skeleton out of his body.

Santos lifted the blankets at one side and took a look at his upper arm, where the coyote had bitten him. He chewed at his stogie thoughtfully and then he said, 'Yes, you see, it's already infected. Let us hope that it isn't rabies.'

'*Rabies*?' croaked Martin. 'That's lethal.'

'Yes, it can be. About twenty years ago one of my uncles was bitten by a raccoon and he died of rabies. But, I think you're lucky. Rabies doesn't usually show itself for days, sometimes weeks, even months. This is nothing more than blood poisoning.'

Martin closed his eyes. He didn't actually care at that moment why he felt so bad, he knew only that he did.

Santos stood up. 'Another reason you are lucky,' he said. 'Outside there is so much chaparral, so much creosote bush. The creosote bush has great medicinal properties. If you lie still here, and keep yourself warm, I will pick some leaves from the creosote bush and make you some tea, which will cure you.'

Martin nodded, without even opening his eyes.

'Well – it *should* cure you,' Santos added. 'Unlike the bacon stealers, I do not like to make false promises.'

Martin could do nothing but huddle himself in his blankets and shiver. He wished that he could keep still, but the icy cold demon wouldn't stop shaking him and shaking him, until he felt that even the thoughts in his brain had been shaken apart.

After a few minutes, though, he felt a soft hand touching his cheek and a voice said, 'Martin?'

He opened his eyes. Peta was kneeling next to him, frowning at him with concern.

'Santos told me you were sick. He said your arm was infected, where that coyote bit you.'

Martin nodded. 'Not rabies, anyhow. That's what he said.'

'How are you feeling?'

'Cold. So cold. I just can't get warm.'

'Would you like some more blankets?'

He nodded again. Peta went over and brought him two more blankets, which she folded over double and spread on top of him.

'How's that? Any better?'

'Still cold. I can't stop shaking.'

Peta hesitated for a moment, and then she tugged off her candy-striped sneakers, lifted the blankets and lay down next to him, putting her arms around him and holding him close. He still couldn't stop himself from shivering, but now he could feel the warmth of her body up against his, and feel her hair against his cheek, and he began to relax, and his mind began to reassemble itself.

'Santos is making you some medicine,' she breathed, close to his ear. 'He said it will take him a little while, because he has to pick some leaves and grind them up. Maybe you should try to get some sleep.'

'I'm not tired,' he said. 'Just cold.'

She held him even closer so that her breasts pressed against his chest. It had been so long since they had lain together like this, but now it seemed as if no time had passed at all. Peta's skin was just as soft, and she smelled the same as always, even though she was wearing no perfume. He had always thought that she smelled faintly of clover.

Martin gradually stopped shivering. He felt drained, and battered, but the icy demon had given up trying to shake out his skeleton, and the pain in his back had eased off into a dull, tolerable ache.

He opened his eyes and looked at Peta, and she looked back at him, not blinking. He had never met another blonde with such dark blue irises. He lay there, not saying anything, wondering what she was thinking, but her expression gave him no clue at all. He realized that he was familiar with every single freckle across the bridge of her nose. He could have drawn a pencil-sketch of them from memory.

'Better?' she said, at last.

'Yes,' he said. 'Much better.'

They continued to lie there together without speaking. Martin felt that they didn't really need to. What more did they need to say to each other? He closed his eyes again and after a few minutes he found himself falling down the same dark well that he had fallen into last night, when he had dropped off to sleep out of total exhaustion. He kept on falling, but he wasn't afraid. He wondered if this was what it felt like, when you died.

Peta closed her eyes, too, although she didn't fall asleep. With her eyes closed, however, she didn't see Saskia coming into the cavern.

Saskia walked toward the heap of blankets, but when she saw Peta's tousled blonde hair lying next to Martin's, she stopped. She stared at the two of them for a while, with her eyes narrowed, and a muscle in her left cheek flinching repetitively as if she were grinding her teeth. Then she turned around and walked out into the sunshine.

By the time it grew dark, Martin was already able to sit up and eat a few spoonfuls of rigatoni. He was still feeling weak, but his temperature was almost back to normal. Santos had brewed up a strong infusion of creosote leaves for him, and he had been sipping it regularly throughout the day. It tasted exactly like diluted fence preservative, but that is how it had come by its name.

'The creosote bush has a strong toxic in its leaves which keeps other plants from growing too close to it and stealing its water,' Santos explained, as he stirred up another mugful. 'That is why it kills bacteria, and makes you well.'

'You should have your own TV show,' said Martin. '*Santos Murillo, M.D.*'

'When the land is yours, you know what it can do for you,' Santos retorted, and spat out his stogie.

Martin and Peta and Tyler and Ella sat together in the same tent all afternoon, talking and reminiscing about the times they had gone camping, back in the days before Martin had been sent to Afghanistan. Through the open tent flap, Martin could see Saskia playing with Mina. He remembered what she had said when Mina had been taken ill, and he had asked her if she had ever taken care of a child before. '*Yes,*' she had said. '*Maybe.*'

Peta saw him staring outside and leaned her head against his shoulder so that she could see what he was looking at.

'What is it with Saskia?' she asked. 'She seems to like you and despise you, both at the same time.'

'I don't know. I think she has issues. Something in her past that she still needs to deal with.'

'She's very attractive, in a scary kind of a way.'

'Yes. Maybe "scary" is the word for it.'

The heat was so intense that they spent most of the day resting. When it grew dark, they went into the cavern and lit a fire. They made hamburgers with canned beef patties which they toasted on sticks, and bread that was already becoming dry and stale, so they toasted that, too, and melted cheese slices on top of it.

Afterward, as the fire gradually died down, they sang songs, and Santos told them a Serrano Indian story about Wiyot, the first god of humanity. Wiyot's power over all creatures went to his head, and he became cruel and careless, so Frog mixed up a potion and poisoned him.

Santos was still telling the story when he was interrupted by the sound of an engine starting up, right outside the cavern. Martin immediately reached for his Colt Commando and stood up.

'*Dad* – they haven't found us, have they?' said Tyler.

'No – that sounded like one of *our* vehicles. Maybe somebody's trying to steal it.'

He hurried across to the crevice and elbowed his way out into the darkness. He was just in time to see the red tail lights of Peta's Hilux disappearing into the bushes.

Santos came out with his flashlight, followed by Tyler, and then Peta.

'My *pickup*!' she wailed. 'Somebody's stolen my pickup!'

'Santos,' said Martin, 'let me borrow your truck. I'll get after them.'

'OK,' Santos told him. He handed over his flashlight and said, 'The keys are still in it.'

Martin went across to Santos' Suburban. He tried to open the driver's door but it was locked, and when he shone the flashlight inside he could see that there were no keys in the ignition.

'Santos! It's locked! You must have taken the keys out!'

Santos spread his arms wide. 'I swear – I left it open with keys still in it. What was the point of locking it, way out here in the desert?'

'*Shit*,' said Martin. He would have to take his own car, even though its suspension was shot and if he drove up the valley and over the desert at anything more than a snail's pace he would probably wreck it altogether. But whoever had stolen Peta's pickup had to be stopped. If they managed to drive it as far as the open highway, and any cops or ESS agents saw it, and identified it, they would be bound to flag it down and ask where it had come from.

He opened the Eldorado's door and immediately saw that his keys had gone, too.

He looked up the valley. He could still hear the Hilux whinnying and crunching its way through the bushes and over the rocks, but he could no longer see its tail lights.

Santos came up to him and sniffed. 'Hey – you could always run after it,' he suggested. 'You were once a Marine, weren't you? You must still be fit.'

Martin knew that he was only half serious, but he shook his head. 'The way I feel at the moment, Santos, I'd probably have a heart attack.'

'I will brew you up some more chaparral tea before you turn in tonight. You should feel much better in the morning.'

'I'm sure I will. That's if our pickup-jacker doesn't get stopped by the cops, or some of those goons from Empire Security. They must have a BOLO out for all of our vehicles.' He paused, and listened. All he could hear now was a coyote, howling and yipping at the stars. 'Who the hell would have wanted to steal a clapped-out five-year-old Hilux?'

Ella was looking around, frowning. 'Where's Saskia?' she said. 'I saw her go out earlier. I thought she was going to the bathroom.'

'We're out in the middle of the desert, OK, and she talks about going to the bathroom!' Tyler mocked her.

But then Martin looked around, too, and said, 'You're right, Ella. Where *is* Saskia? She's not in the cave, is she?'

'I'll go take a look,' said Tyler, and disappeared into the crevice. A few seconds later he came back out and said, 'No – she's not there!' He went from tent to tent, too, lifting up their flaps and checking inside. 'Not in any of these, either!'

Peta said, 'My God, that was *her*, wasn't it? She's taken my pickup!'

They all looked at each other. Martin didn't know what to say, or what to think. This could have been Saskia's intention all along – to find out where they were going, and once she had done so, to go back and tell Joseph Wrack. Maybe she thought that would earn Joseph Wrack's forgiveness for tipping Martin off about West Valley Detention Center and the prison bus. With a woman like Saskia, who could tell?

'What are we going to do now, Daddy?' asked Ella.

'There's not too much we *can* do, sweetheart, not tonight. We'll just have to stay here and hope that Saskia doesn't tell anybody where we are.' He looked back up the valley. 'It's my own goddamned fault,' he said. 'I should never have trusted her. She worked for Governor Smiley, for God's sake, and she owed him some big favor, although she wouldn't tell me what it was.'

Santos said, 'Maybe she just didn't like the idea of camping out here. She was a city type of woman, after all. Maybe she *won't* tell anybody where we are.'

'You're very optimistic for a man who can't forget that most of his people were hunted down and massacred so that strangers could steal their land.'

Santos shrugged. 'Suspicion wears a man down, like sandstone.'

'Sure. Yes, I know. And a constant stream of wise Indian sayings has just about the same effect.'

TEN

'**S**omebody to see you, boss,' said Jim Broader. He sounded strangely excited but Joseph Wrack didn't turn around to see why. He wasn't interested in what made other people excited, except if it gave him leverage over them.

He was standing at his office window, eating a bowl of muesli and staring fixedly at the thick brown smoke which was drifting across the city from last night's riots. Last night had been even more violent than the day before. Although he wouldn't openly admit it, Joseph Wrack was quite aware that the police and ESS had lost control. Even with the use of deadly force, he knew that it was going to take the most uncompromising of law-enforcement operations to restore order. They may even have to wait for the rioters to start dying of thirst. Normally, in hot weather like this, an adult would succumb from lack of fluid in only two or three days. But the rioters had pillaged thousands of bottles of soda from supermarkets, and water was still to be found in car washes and ponds and municipal fountains, so it could take anything up to a week before they started dying in significant numbers. He had done the math. His only consolation was that death from thirst was agonizingly painful.

In a last attempt to contain the chaos, the mayor had wanted to call in local units of the Army National Guard, but Governor Smiley had overruled him. He had deployed them instead in downtown Los Angeles, in Compton and Gardena and Pico-Union and other neighborhoods where the water supply had been cut off and the riots were now so violent that even the heavily censored TV news reports had described them as 'hellish'.

Jim Broader coughed, and said, 'Boss?'

'What?' said Joseph Wrack. 'I thought I specifically told you to cancel all of my appointments this morning.' He continued to stare out of the window. He had decided that he quite enjoyed watching buildings burn.

'With me, you don't *have* an appointment,' said a woman's voice. 'You can't very well cancel something that you don't have, now can you?'

Joseph Wrack turned around, a spoonful of muesli half lifted toward his mouth. There, in the doorway, stood Saskia Vane. She was still dressed in her black silk blouse and her tight-fitting black jeans, but her black hair was gleaming and she was wearing full make-up, including blusher on her cheeks and shiny scarlet lip gloss.

'Well, well,' said Joseph Wrack. 'This is a surprise, Ms Vane. So where the hell have *you* been? My people have been looking for you.'

'Don't let me interrupt your breakfast,' she told him, walking up to him so that he could smell her perfume. 'A boy needs his strength, doesn't he?'

Joseph Wrack put down his bowl on his desk. 'Do you know something?' he said. 'Suddenly I've lost my appetite. Just like I lost it yesterday, when I lost a two-point-three million dollar helicopter, and nine of my security guards.'

'I'm glad to hear you have your priorities right,' said Saskia. She went over to the window and looked out at the smoke, which was even thicker now, and filled with whirling scraps of white ash. 'Holy moly. The whole city's on fire, almost. It always confuses me, though. When people riot, why do they always destroy their own neighborhoods? You think it would be more sensible to burn down somebody else's neighborhood. Talk about cutting your nose off to spite your face.'

'I thought you'd run off with that Martin Makepeace,' said Joseph Wrack. He circled around the back of his desk, but Saskia circled after him.

'I did. You're right. I did run off with him. But you know what they say about flogging a dead horse.'

'So what does that mean? You and he aren't buddies any longer? I never understood why you were in the first place.'

'We never were. But I've always had a thing for knights in shining armor.'

'He's not a knight in shining armor. He's a fucking post-traumatic trigger-happy nut-brain.'

'Maybe I wanted to get back at Halford Smiley.'

'Oh, *I* see. Now I'm beginning to get it. This is all about you and Governor Smiley, isn't it? And I don't suppose it has anything to do with your late lamented husband David?'

Saskia gave Joseph Wrack the most hostile stare that anyone had ever given him in his life. He wouldn't have been surprised if sharp steel blades had come flying out of her eyes and pinned him to the wall. 'I'm not saying anything to you, you creep. The only person I'm going to speak to is Halford.'

'You're not even going to give me a *hint* where I can find Makepeace? He has to be out in the desert someplace. If you don't tell me now, we'll still find him, you know. We have heat-seeking sensors on all of our helicopters. We'll find him. Nobody does what he did to me and gets away with it. Nobody blows up a two-point-three million dollar helicopter and expects me to turn the other cheek.'

'You forgot about the nine men.'

Joseph Wrack pointed one finger at her and said, harshly and hoarsely, 'Don't you fuck with me, Ms Vane! Don't you ever try and fuck with me!'

'I wouldn't dream of it,' said Saskia. 'I don't like scrawny men with cigar breath who eat muesli for breakfast.'

Joseph clenched his teeth to rein himself in. Then he said, even more hoarsely, 'Where is he, Ms Vane?'

'I told you. The only person I'm going to speak to is Halford.'

'He's hiding in some Godforsaken canyon, isn't he, someplace in the Big Morongo? That's where he is!'

'I'm not telling you. I'm only telling Halford. Nobody else.'

Joseph Wrack stood with his lips pursed for a moment, looking down at his desk. Then he picked up his half-finished bowl of muesli and threw it across the room, so that it spattered all over the carpet. Saskia smiled the small, confident smile of a woman who knows that she's winning.

'Halford's back in Sacramento right now,' said Joseph Wrack. 'I'll have my assistant set up a video link.'

'Oh, no. I need to talk to Halford face to face. In person.'

'Read my lips, Ms Vane. He's in Sacramento. He has a statewide emergency on his hands, in case you hadn't noticed. And even if he has some kind of unresolved issue with you, he doesn't give a rat's ass about Martin Makepeace. Unlike myself, of course.'

'This is about *much* more than Martin Makepeace, I can assure you, and if Halford doesn't get to know about it until it's too late, he's going to be very, *very* sore about it. Let me give you a clue. This is about water.'

Joseph Wrack opened his box of panatelas and took one out. 'Go on,' he said, reaching for his lighter.

'Are you hard of hearing or something? I just told you twice that the only person I'm going to speak to is Halford. I want him here, in person.'

'How about I fly you up to Sacramento to see him?'

'No good. Too much security, too much media attention, even if the media are being gagged. I need to talk to him here, in San Bernardino, in private.'

'And if I *can* arrange for him to come here?'

'Then I will tell you exactly where you can find Martin Makepeace. However much you bluster that you'll be able to track him down, Mr Wrack, I can assure you that you never will. Not without my help.'

Joseph Wrack sat down and lit his panatela; but almost as soon as he had puffed it into life, he crushed it out in his ashtray. He flicked the switch of his intercom and said, 'Mandy? Get me Governor Smiley, will you? I don't care where he is, or what he's doing. Tell his PA that it's an emergency. Make sure she lets him know that Saskia Vane is here – Saskia Vane. No – *Saskia*, you moron!

He sat back, lacing his fingers together across his stomach. 'Satisfied?' he asked.

'We'll see. It depends if he agrees to come back down here to San Bernardino or not. But I'm quite confident that he will, once I've told him what the deal is. If this goes according to plan, all of us should get what we want.'

'What plan, Ms Vane?'

Saskia gave him that smile again, that smile that meant she was two steps ahead of him.

'So we're staying?' said Peta.

Martin was sitting on the trunk of his car with his feet on the back seat, his Colt Commado across his knees. He was keeping watch for any sign of ESS guards making their way down the valley, and staying alert for the sound of any helicopters coming their way. It was almost noon. The sky was cloudless again, and the temperature had reached 121 degrees.

He shrugged. 'I don't really see that we have any choice. At least here we have a chance of survival. Better than the city, anyhow.'

'Do you think that Saskia will have told ESS where we are?'

'I have no idea. When you think about it, why should she? And even if she does, it doesn't seem very logical for them to send out any more choppers after us, does it? I don't think they're going to risk losing another one, just for me. Besides, they must be pretty much overstretched right now, with all of those riots.'

'I guess so.'

She stood next to him in silence for a while, and then she said, 'This drought can't go on for ever, can it? I mean, what's going to happen to us, if it does?'

'Don't ask me. But I don't see how a whole continent can go for year after year without *any* rain at all. Maybe it's something to do with global warming. Who knows? But if it does go on, God knows how many people are going to die.'

As if to emphasize what he had said, there was a distant crumpling sound of thunder. The dry desert air was highly charged with static, and last night it had thundered for nearly an hour, without a single drop of rain.

Peta said, 'I think you know what I'm going to ask you, Martin.'

He turned to look at her. 'What you're going to ask me is, can I keep those djinns bottled up?'

'You still have them?'

'I think I'll have them for the rest of my life, darling. I could back to Dr Vaudrey, I guess, but I wouldn't hold out much hope. Maybe I need an exorcist, rather than a shrink.'

'I miss you,' she said. 'I miss you more than I can tell you, and sometimes I almost manage to persuade myself that those rows we had weren't all that terrible. But they were, Martin. You almost broke me.'

He reached out his hand to her and said, 'Come here,' but she stayed where she was.

At that moment Nathan came running up to them, holding up both hands, and jingling something shiny in each of them.

'Your keys! We found your car keys! And grandpa's, too!'

'Found your car keys!' panted George, running up close behind him.

Martin swung off the trunk. 'Thanks, Nathan. You're amazing.'

'Our dinosaur got away and we chased our dinosaur into the bushes and there they were.'

'Brilliant. Tell your dinosaur he deserves a medal.'

Nathan followed Martin around to the back of his car. 'Why did Saskia go away?' he asked him.

Martin unlocked his Eldorado's trunk and lifted the lid. He looked down at Nathan with his sad brown squint and his curly black hair which badly needed cutting. He was wearing a faded orange T-shirt with a ragged hole next to the collar.

'I don't know, Nathan. I wish I did.'

'I really liked her,' said Nathan. 'She said that when I grew older I could be whatever I wanted. And she said she was sad about my mom. And she gave me a hug.' Suddenly he was blinking back tears. 'I miss my mom. And I miss Mikey. I miss them so much.'

Peta came over and put her arms around him. It was then that George started crying, too, and she had to put her arms around both of them. *God*, thought Martin, *these are people, these are two small people with emotions and ambitions and their whole lives in front of them, and Halford Smiley is quite prepared to let them die of thirst.*

He lifted the second Colt Commando out of the trunk, as well the last two thirty-round magazines. He was just about to close the lid when he realized that he couldn't see the second M-67 fragmentation grenade which Charlie had given him. He lifted the spare-wheel cover, but it hadn't rolled under there. Maybe Charlie had taken it with him when they had stopped the prison bus, and had dropped it. Most likely he had still been carrying it when he had blown himself up, either in his pocket or hooked to his belt, and it had blown up, too.

Whatever had happened to it, it was no longer in his trunk, which was a relief, in a way. Martin couldn't think how he could have used it, except to pull out the pin and keep on holding it tight, as Charlie had suggested, if life ever got too boring.

Susan came out of the crevice and called out, 'Lunch! Come see what I've cooked! Chicken and pumpkin surprise!'

Halford was in a foul temper when he returned Joseph Wrack's call. Although it hadn't been reported on the news, the rioting in South Los Angeles had degenerated into an orgy of burning, looting and shooting. Halford had brought in the National Guard from three different armories – Long Beach, Van Nuys and San Bernardino – but even they had been forced to retreat. Now they were doing nothing more than holding the perimeter around those areas where the water supply had been cut off, trying to prevent the chaos from spreading.

The Chief of Staff of the West Los Angeles National Guard, Colonel Hank Spanner, had reported to the governor and the mayor that the rioters were 'almost as well armed as we are, and certainly much readier to open fire'. In the 1992 riots, Korean storekeepers with rifles had positioned themselves on rooftops to protect their property. This time, the Korean storekeepers had joined the rioters – Hispanic, African American, Asian and white.

Governor Smiley had been asked by an NBC News reporter why he simply didn't order the water supply to be turned back on. Wouldn't that end the riots immediately, without any further damage or loss of life?

Halford had looked at him as if he were retarded. 'The reason I'm not going to turn the water back on is because there isn't enough water to go around, and if you think that I'm prepared to give those people water just because they've threatened us with violence, then you're out of your cotton-picking mind. Most of them never pay for their water . . . why should we deprive hard-working families who do? Jesus. Now you'll be telling me you were in favor of Proposition Thirty-four.'

Saskia could hear Halford barking at Joseph Wrack over the phone. It reminded her of those coyotes yipping, back at Lost Girl Lake. Joseph Wrack said, 'OK, your honor. I agree. But she won't talk to anybody else but you. She flat-out refuses.'

At last he came over to the couch and handed the phone to Saskia. His expression was grim. While Saskia and Halford talked, he went back to his desk and lit another panatela. He would have preferred a nostrilful of Colombian blow, but a panatela would have to do for now.

'Hel-*lo*, Halford,' Saskia purred. 'It's your favorite persuader.'

'So – you came back! Don't tell me that you grew tired of Mr Makepeace that quickly? I thought he was just your type. Muscular, stupid and pliable. That's how you like them, isn't it, my darling?'

'He's muscular, yes. But he's not at all stupid, and he's not very pliable, either. He's just a bit too sentimental for me. Too hearts and flowers, would you believe? He's still carrying a torch for his ex.'

'So what the fuck does that have to do with me? I'm a busy man, Saskia. I've got five major cities on fire, I've got the President threatening to send in troops under the Insurrection Act, I've got Mona whining that she hasn't seen me for a week, and I'm trying to keep everybody in a state that has absolutely no fucking water.'

'I know where there's water, Halford. Lots of water. Maybe not enough to supply the whole state, but enough to make you a hero.'

There was a very long silence. Then Halford said, 'Where? What are you talking about?'

Saskia spoke slowly and carefully. 'I know where you can find water, Halford. That's where Martin Makepeace and his family are now.'

'You're serious?'

'Have you ever known me *not* to be serious? Just because you've always been a clown.'

'Well, OK, if you're serious, where is it?'

'Halford – do you think I came down in the last shower of rain? Come to that, the last shower of rain was so long ago that maybe I did.'

'Where is it, Saskia? Have you told Joseph where it is?'

'Of course not. Not before you and I have been able to discuss terms, and Mr Joseph Wrack has given me his solemn and binding assurance that he'll stay off my back.'

'What terms are you talking about, Saskia?'

'I think you know what terms. But I'm not going to discuss them over the phone. It has to be face to face, in private.'

'All right. So come up to Sacramento. Joseph will arrange a flight for you. What's the time now? You could be here by three.'

'No, Halford.'

'So how the fuck are we going to discuss these terms of yours face to face unless you come here and meet me face to face?'

'Don't lose your cool, Halford. There's nothing so ridiculous as a clown stamping his foot. *You* are going to come *here*. It's going to be you and me, that's all. No entourage. No PAs. We're going to go someplace private together and have a little discussion and I don't want any security men with their hands folded over their cocks or anybody asking what we're talking about or why we're talking at all.'

'You're shooting me a line here, Saskia. What the hell are you after?'

'Come here and find out, Halford.'

'I can't! How can I? I have a million people screaming questions at me that I don't know the answer to. I have a strategy meeting with the National Guard and the Highway Patrol in two hours' time. We're having an emergency hearing in the Capitol at nine o'clock. I haven't even eaten breakfast yet.'

'You have a Lieutenant Governor, don't you? Kenneth Korven? What's he doing, sitting on his hands? Have him fill in for you, while you're away.'

'Kenneth Korven is an asshole. Worse than that, he's a Democrat.'

Saskia said, 'OK, Halford, if I can't persuade you to come, then I can't. But I'm not lying to you about the water.'

Halford was silent for a long time. Saskia stayed silent, too. Joseph Wrack sat at his desk, tilted back in his chair, smoking. He was beginning to look amused. The smoke shuddered up toward the air-conditioning vents, hovered for a moment, and then was suddenly sucked away. Through the double-glazed windows they could faintly hear shouting and sirens in the streets below.

Halford must have been talking to somebody, with his hand over the receiver, because Saskia heard him say, 'No – like, now! What's the ramp-to-ramp time, that's what I want to know!'

'Does that mean you're coming?' she asked him.

'Yes, you bitch, it does. In actual fact, you've probably done me a favor. Kenneth Korven can stand there and fail to answer all of those millions of questions that I don't know the answer to, which won't do his political reputation any good at all.'

'Good,' said Saskia. 'So when can I expect you?'

'Four thirty, thereabouts.'

'And you know what to bring with you, don't you?'

'Saskia, whatever you think of me, I'm not totally dumb. Nobody in this world gives you anything for nothing, especially you.'

'OK,' Saskia. 'I'm going back to my hotel, but I'll meet you back here at Empire Security Services.'

She stood up and handed the phone back to Joseph Wrack.

'You're not looking for a job, are you?' he asked her. 'I could use a woman like you.'

'A job? With you? I'd rather go and work for the sanitation department. But if you have a car I could borrow, I'd appreciate it. I drove here in a somewhat battered pickup.'

Joseph Wrack opened his desk drawer, took out a car key on a leather fob and tossed it over to her. 'Silver Buick Lacrosse, if that's not beneath your dignity. Second level, left of the elevators as you come out of them.'

Saskia leaned across his desk, took the key, and blew him a kiss.

ELEVEN

Santos said, 'When I die, you will make sure to burn my body, won't you?'

Martin looked across at him in surprise. 'Santos, you're not going to die on my watch. This drought can't go on for ever and by the time you die we'll be back in the city and you'll have a regular cremation at a regular crematorium. Is there a special ritual for Yuhaviatam funerals? Any gods we need to invoke?'

Santos looked back at him from under the shadow of his Panama hat and Martin could see by his eyes that he was in pain. 'Just ask the Great Spirit to take me to my Juanita, that's all. She was my wife.'

'Santos—'

Santos raised his hand to stop him, whatever he was going to say. 'I have nearly had my time, Wasicu. Now it is the children's time. I think we did the right thing, bringing them here. They will get to know their real mother now, which is the earth. They will get to know the land that is rightly theirs.'

In the shade that they had erected outside one of the tents, Nathan and George and little Mina were sitting cross-legged on the ground while Ella was singing their alphabet to them. '*G is for gorilla . . . guh-guh-guh gorilla!*'

Somewhere in the distance, they heard the beating of a helicopter. Martin listened for a while. It didn't sound as if it were coming any closer, but all the same he reached across for his sub-machine gun.

'I told you that woman had a dark shadow around her,' said Santos.

Martin didn't answer, but continued to strain his ears. After a few minutes, the sound of the helicopter faded, and then there was nothing but Ella singing, '*M is for monkey . . . muh-muh-muh monkey!*' and the endless chirruping of insects.

'OK, maybe you were right,' Martin admitted. 'But they haven't come after us yet, have they? Every hour that goes by, I trust her a little more.'

'There is only one person you need to trust,' said Santos. 'That

is yourself. The day that you can do that, on *that* day you will begin
to be healed.'

Martin laid his sub-machine gun down.

'I'll burn you, OK, if it comes to that. I promise. I'll burn you,
and I'll ask the Great Spirit to reunite you with Juanita. I won't
even charge you. Not like your usual mortician.'

Saskia was waiting in the parking lot of Ontario International Airport
when Halford appeared. The sun was reflected so brightly from the
glass roof of the terminal entrance that she was almost dazzled, but
she could see that he was accompanied by two security men in light
gray suits and sunglasses and a girl in a pale blue suit who looked
like one of his personal assistants.

The parking lot was almost deserted because all scheduled flights
had been canceled, and only private jets were flying in and out.
Because she had been able to park so close to the terminal, Saskia
could clearly see that Halford was arguing with his security men.
She guessed that they were deeply reluctant to let him out of their
sight, especially since he wouldn't have told them why he needed
to come here to San Bernardino so urgently, and what he was going
to be doing when he got here.

She couldn't help smiling to herself as she watched him shouting
and gesticulating, although she couldn't hear what he was saying.
She had always enjoyed dominating other people, but she could
understand now why real power was so addictive. She had called
him, and Halford had been obliged to come, whether he really
wanted to or not. She actually found that she was aroused.

After a while, the security men went back inside the terminal
building. Halford spoke to the girl in the pale blue suit for a moment.
He kissed her on the cheek and then she went back inside, too.
Halford was now standing alone on the sidewalk in his cream linen
suit and his canary yellow shirt, impatiently looking right and left,
waiting for Saskia to make an appearance. Saskia let him wait there
for over a minute. She was almost tempted to drive away and leave
him stranded, but she wanted to do more than humiliate him.

She blew the Buick's horn and flashed its lights. Halford lifted
his arm to acknowledge that he had seen her, and came hurrying
over the pedestrian crossing to the parking lot. He climbed into the
passenger seat, slammed the door and said, 'Hallo, Saskia. I can't
say it's great to see you.'

Saskia started the engine and backed out of her parking space.
'One day, Halford, the people of California will thank you for this.
Like I said, you're going to be a hero.'

'So where's this water?'

'All in good time, Halford. I'm going to take you to Joseph
Wrack's office and then I can show you both where it is. First,
though—' she said, and held out her hand, palm upward.

'Oh, no,' Halford told her. 'You don't get the DVDs till I know
where this water is.'

'You swear on your mother's life that you're going to give me
every single copy? Because if I find out that you haven't, Halford,
I'm going to have your balls for Rocky Mountain oysters, with
Tabasco sauce.'

'When did you get so aggressive, Saskia?' said Halford.

'When I found out what a self-indulgent, pompous, unfeeling
sack of shit you really are. That's when.'

Halford laid his hand on her thigh. 'You shouldn't talk dirty like
that. It gets me horny.'

They were driving over the high concrete curve where the San
Bernardino Freeway met the Riverside Freeway, and turned northward into the city. Saskia said, 'How about I drive right off the
ramp here and kill us both? Because I will if you don't take your
hand off me.'

Halford was not at all happy about Saskia driving him through the
downtown area to the Empire Security building. As she steered her
way around the burned-out vehicles and tipped-over trashcans, he
shrank down in the passenger seat and held up his right hand to
blinker his face. The streets were mostly empty, but every now and
then a small gang of looters would come running past, whooping
and shouting, and as they reached East 4th Street, some of them
ran alongside them, and banged on the roof of the car with their
fists. It was only when they heard the wail of a police siren that
they all scattered.

'Jesus, Saskia. Supposing one of them recognizes me?'

'Then they'll probably tear your door open and kill you. Look
at this city, Halford. You did this. You and your rotational hiatuses.
You hypocrite.'

'You were prepared to promote them for me.'

'I wasn't happy at all. I had no choice, and you know it.'

She opened the electric gate outside the Empire Security building and drove down into the underground parking structure. Halford said, 'This won't take long, will it? As soon as this is a done deal, I need to get back to the airport.'

Saskia didn't answer, but climbed out of the Buick and walked briskly toward the elevator. Halford heaved himself out and followed her. He wasn't used to being treated like this, opening his own car door and having to run after people. As they went up to Joseph Wrack's office in the elevator car, he made an effort to stand up very straight, so that he looked taller, and much more in command, but Saskia's high-heeled ankle-boots made her just as tall as he was.

'God, you're a bitch,' he said, under his breath, but all she did was smile at him.

Joseph Wrack was on the phone when Jim Broader showed them through to his office. Jim Broader was deeply impressed by meeting the governor of California, and kept smacking his hands together and letting out little girlish giggles. 'Can I get your honor anything to drink? Coffee, soda, something stronger?'

'Do you have water?'

'Sure. Sure we have water.'

'Then you're better off than most of the poor fuckers in this Godforsaken state. I don't want anything, thanks. I just want to get this done and get the hell out of here. I have a plane waiting.'

'OK, your honor. Fine. Sure. Sorry.'

'I'll have a vodka tonic with a twist,' said Saskia. 'Plenty of ice.'

Joseph Wrack put down the phone. 'There's a major riot at Riverside Plaza. Chief Delgado wants to know if I can send him some reinforcements for crowd control, but regrettably we don't have any more men to spare. None at all. Not one. Not even retirees.'

He paused and then he smiled and held out his hand. 'Anyhow, how are you, your honor? Good to see you, if a little unexpected. You got here real quick. What kind of plane are you flying these days?'

'Let's just get this over with, shall we?' said Halford. 'I have a disaster to take care of.'

Saskia said, 'Switch on the TV, would you, Mr Wrack, and click it on to maps? We're looking for a satellite picture of Joshua Tree National Park.'

The park appeared on the screen, dry and rugged. Saskia took the remote control from Joseph Wrack and enlarged the image, and then she gradually followed the trail along which Santos had led them. She could have focused on the valley immediately, but she wanted to build some suspense.

'How the *hell* did you drive all the way out there?' asked Halford. 'I can't see even a jackrabbit track.'

'We had a Native American to guide us. Most Native Americans still know this country a whole lot better than we do, Halford. They're good for more than running casinos.'

She shifted the satellite picture further and further north-eastward, until at last she reached the valley. She magnified the image as far as it would go. Although it was blurred, she could distinctly make out the thick bushy undergrowth and the triangular area of open ground where they had pitched their tents.

She pointed to the sharp angle where the two rock faces met, and said, 'There.'

Halford approached the screen and peered at it closely. '*There?* Where? I thought you said there was water. I don't see any water.'

'It's all underground, Halford. It's an underground lake, and that is where you can get through to it. The Serrano Indians found it in eighteen-something-or-other when they were on their way to Arrowhead Springs. I don't know how far it extends underneath the surface, but this Native American who took us there said it could be bigger than Big Bear Lake. And – because it's underground – all of the water is one hundred percent pure. I've tasted it, Halford. It's the best water you ever tasted in your life.'

Halford kept staring at the satellite image. He didn't say anything, but Saskia came up to him and spoke for him, in a low, growly imitation of his own voice. 'People of the state of California, I have an announcement to make of great importance. As the drought has worsened, and you have been suffering more and more, I have been sending out teams of geologists to discover new and untapped sources of fresh water. This morning I am delighted to be able to tell you that I have already located an underground lake in Joshua Tree National Park which will very soon alleviate the critical water supply problem in San Bernardino County, and possibly beyond.'

Halford turned and stared at her. She found it impossible to read the expression on his face, because she had never seen any man look like that, ever. He reached into the inside pocket of his yellow jacket and took out a plain white envelope. He handed it to her and said, 'Those are the only copies. On my mother's life.'

Joseph Wrack stood a little way back, watching and smoking. Halford turned to him and said, 'I expect you'll be itching—' He had to stop, and clear his throat before he could carry on. 'I expect you'll be itching to get out there to find that Martin Makepeace.'

'Oh, yes, your honor, you can count on it. I'll be putting a team together at first light tomorrow.'

'I thought you didn't have any men to spare,' put in Saskia. 'Haven't you forgotten? Rioting? Riverside Plaza? Or is getting your revenge on Martin Makepeace much more important than saving some tacky suburban shopping mall?'

Joseph Wrack couldn't stop himself from grinning one of his skeletal grins. 'That job offer's still open, Ms Vane. But even if you really don't want it, there's one thing you *can* maybe do for me.'

'Oh, really?'

'There are some children in that little escape party of yours, aren't there?'

'Yes, Mr Wrack. One of whom your men shot and killed in cold blood. A mischievous little boy called Mikey who never did anybody harm in the whole of his life. You're complaining that nine of your men got killed? They killed Mikey, that was why.'

'Well, I'm real sorry that happened. I am. And I'm very anxious that no more children get hurt. What I'm suggesting is that you come out with us tomorrow morning and talk to Martin Makepeace. See if you can cajole him into giving himself up. The very last thing we want is bullets flying around, with little children in harm's way. ESS is a security company, Ms Vane. It's our avowed mission to protect the lives of innocent people, not to put them in jeopardy.'

Saskia knew that Joseph Wrack was talking his usual insincere bullshit, and that he was anxious only to avoid a firefight in which more of his own men might be killed, and in which he might even lose another helicopter. Apart from that, killing children was very poor PR, especially since the ESS brochure showed one of their security guards holding the hands of two smiling toddlers, one white and one Hispanic, underneath the caption 'First Steps To Safety'.

But then she thought of Mina, sweaty and feverish; and grumpy little George; and Nathan, grieving for his older brother, unable to understand why the world was being so horrible to him.

She thought of Martin, too. She had felt so strongly attracted to him that she didn't really want him to come to any harm, but at the same time she wanted to punish him for not feeling as aroused by

her as she had been by him. He deserved to be punished, one way
or another, like most men. Bitten and beaten and scratched and choked
until they begged her to stop; and then begged her to do it again.

'All right, Mr Wrack,' she said, at last. 'I'll talk to him.'

'It'll have to be pretty early,' said Joseph Wrack. 'We need to
leave no later than a quarter after five so we'll arrive at sunrise.'

He looked at the satellite image more closely, tracing the tips of
his fingers over it as if he could almost feel how prickly the cholla
was. 'This is where they're camped out, is it, in this open space
here? In that case we can't land there. We might accidentally hurt
the kids and apart from that Makepeace could open fire on us before
we'd even get our skids down. No . . . we'll have to touch down
here, at the head of the valley, and then make our way down on
foot. We can wave a white flag to show that we've come for a
powwow.' He turned back to Saskia. 'Where are you staying? I'll
send a driver for you at four forty-five.'

'The Hilton. Meanwhile . . . I think I should take Halford back
to the airport. He looks like he has ants in his pants.'

'Don't worry, Jim Broader can drive him. It's about time Jim did
something useful around here.'

'No, I'll take him,' said Saskia. 'His honor and I have a couple
more things to talk over before he goes back to Sacramento.'

'We do?' said Halford, irritably.

They made their way back to the freeway through the rubble-strewn
streets. Every now and then Saskia had to back up and turn around
because the street ahead of them was barricaded with burning
vehicles.

'I think you're taking me this way on purpose,' said Halford, as
they came nearer to the Inland Center, from which a huge column
of smoke was rising into the afternoon sky.

'Maybe I am. Maybe you need to have your nose rubbed in what
you've done.'

'Saskia, for Christ's sake. You have your DVDs back now. What
more do you want?'

'I don't really know, Halford. You caused me so much pain.'

'Listen . . . I know how much you loved David. You didn't mean
that to happen. It was his own fault, as much as yours.'

'Oh, terrific. You can say that now. You didn't say that when you
were threatening to hand over all of your videos to the DA's office.'

'I had to protect myself, Saskia, as well as you. It was always a two-way arrangement.'

They were on South E Street now, with only a few blocks to go before they reached the freeway, but Saskia slowed the car down and then drew into the curb. On their right-hand side, in the Burger Mania parking lot, at least five cars were on fire and another six or seven had already been reduced to blackened skeletons. The restaurant itself was gutted, with all of its windows smashed.

'What are you stopping for?' asked Halford. 'Come on, Saskia, I just need to get back to the airport. My security people are going to be having kittens as it is.'

Saskia turned into the parking lot. Although so many cars were burning, there was nobody in sight. She looked around, frowning, for exactly the kind of space she wanted, and then she backed into one, stopped, and applied the parking brake.

'What the *fuck* are you doing?' Halford demanded.

Saskia turned to him and said, 'You know, Halford, I blame myself, mostly, for David. He always wanted more and I should have said no. I blame myself for what *you've* been putting me through, too. I should have told you to do your worst, and hang the consequences. But maybe I enjoyed you treating me the way you did, thinking you could fuck me whenever you felt like it, and everything else you made me do. You're such an irredeemable bastard, Halford, and you have such terrible taste in clothes, but maybe that's why you turn women on so much.'

Halford closed his eyes for a moment, as if he had a migraine. Then he said, 'Saskia. Put a lid on the psychoanalysis, will you, honey, and just drive me to the airport?'

'There's only one more thing, Halford. I have a little souvenir for you.'

'Souvenir? What are you talking about?'

'It's in the trunk. I'll get it for you. We won't be seeing each other ever again, will we? So it's something for you to remember me by.'

'I don't *want* anything to remember you by. I'd rather have something to forget you by. Can't we just get going?'

Saskia took no notice. She took the keys out of the ignition, climbed out of the car and went around to the trunk. She opened it up and took out the spherical M-67 fragmentation grenade that she had wedged between the spare wheel and the side of the trunk, to

stop it from tumbling around. With the trunk lid still open to mask
what she was doing, just in case Halford happened to turn around,
she pulled the pin out of the grenade. Then she slammed the trunk
shut, and opened up the offside rear door.

'*Saskia*—' snapped Halford. But without a word to him, Saskia
dropped the grenade into the footwell behind him. The safety spoon
fell off it, and because she had deliberately parked on a slight slope,
facing forward, it rolled right under his seat.

'Saskia, what in *God's* name are we waiting for?'

Saskia shut the door and started to run, pressing the central
locking button on the Buick's remote as she did so. She wasn't
waiting for anything, because she knew that she had only a few
seconds to escape from the blast.

She sprinted across the Burger Mania parking lot to the low wall
that divided it from the Shoe City parking lot next door, and threw
herself flat down on the tarmac behind it. She closed her eyes and
stuck her fingers in her ears, so she neither saw nor heard Halford
as he shouted at her and tried to get out of the car.

Two tugs at the Buick's door-handle unlocked it, but the fuse on
the M67's six-and-a-half pounds of Composition 4 explosive was
only four-point-four seconds. The car was blown apart with a shattering explosion which echoed and re-echoed from all of the buildings
around it, and on the opposite side of the road. A blizzard of metal
and plastic fragments flew over Saskia's head and were scattered
more than five hundred feet away, in all directions.

After a few seconds, the clattering stopped, and Saskia dared to
look up from behind the wall. The Buick was in flames, and it
would only be a matter of time before the gas tank blew up, too.
There was nothing left of Halford's seat except for springs, and
there was nothing left of Halford but an empty sack-like figure that
was hugging a deflated air-bag. It looked more like a blood-soaked
nightdress case than the Governor of California.

Saskia could see Halford's head resting on the front steps of
Burger Mania, although thankfully he was looking in the opposite
direction.

She didn't wait any longer. She started to walk briskly back
toward the city center. The way things were, with rioting all across
the county, it would probably be days before anybody discovered
what had happened to Halford Smiley. Who would notice one more
burned-out car in a parking lot crowded with burned-out cars?

It was still so hot that the road in front of her was shimmering, and she wished that she had had the foresight to bring a bottle of water with her and worn more practical shoes, because she was starting to hobble. But she had only walked as far as SoCal Super Trucks, a quarter of a mile further up the road, when a bullhorn blew loudly behind her, and a fire engine pulled up beside her.

The driver leaned out of his window and called out, 'Need a ride, pretty lady?'

She crossed over the road. 'Thank you! You saved my life!'

The firefighters opened the door for her and held out their hands to help her climb up the steps. Inside the crew cabin it smelled strongly of smoke and rubber and sweat. Five soot-stained faces grinned at her as one of the firefighters shifted himself sideways to give her enough space to sit down.

'I had a little car trouble,' she said, loudly, as the fire engine pulled away with its engine bellowing. 'Something I should have fixed a long time ago.'

TWELVE

Night fell and the stars came out and there was still no sign that Joseph Wrack had sent out a team to hunt them down, but Martin stayed where he was, sitting on the trunk of his Eldorado, with his Colt Commando across his knees.

Peta came over with a mug of Manhattan chowder for him. 'Maybe she hasn't told ESS where we are,' she said. 'Maybe she just didn't relish the idea of living in the desert with a bunch of kids.'

'I don't know,' said Martin. 'I think we'll have to give it two or three days before we're totally sure. The Taliban used to do that to us . . . launch an attack and then disappear for days on end, until we thought that they must have moved on someplace else. Then, when we were all relaxed, they'd hit us again, even harder.'

'This isn't a war, Martin.'

'Oh, yes it is, sweetheart. All human life is a war, and it always will be. So long as somebody has something that somebody else wants – so long as somebody believes in something different from somebody else – there'll always be war. Always. It's never going to end. Never. Not until this planet splits apart.'

'You shouldn't be such a pessimist,' said Peta. She pointed to the stars and said, 'Look . . . Cassiopeia.'

Martin squinted upward. 'Oh, yeah? They all just look like stars to me. You were always telling fortunes. What does that mean?'

'Cassiopeia is the goddess of riches and good fortune. If she shines on you, it means that one day, you'll strike it rich.'

'Like I'm going to win the MegaMillions?'

'Maybe not *literally* rich, but your life is going to turn out well.'

'Oh. I see. To tell you the truth, I don't give a damn, so long as it starts raining again. What's the point of being rich if the whole country is nothing but a dried-out desert?'

In the early hours of the morning, just before the false dawn began to light up the sky, Martin folded back his blankets and crossed over to the opposite side of the tent, where Peta was sleeping. He carefully eased himself in beside her and put his arms around her, and kissed her cheek. She stirred and said, 'What? It's not time to get up yet, is it?'

Abruptly, she woke up, and opened her eyes. Martin could see them glistening in the darkness.

'Ssh,' he said, and touched her lips with his fingertip, then kissed her.

They made love strongly and urgently, and then lay together silently for a long time afterward. Peta stroked the stubble on Martin's chin as if it were Braille, and she was a blind woman trying to discover what he looked like. Gradually the tent began to fill with dim blue light.

Martin returned to his own blankets. He looked across at Peta and she looked back at him, but he had no idea if this meant that they would get back together again. After a while she turned her back on him, and fell asleep again. At least he assumed she was asleep. Maybe, like him, she was just lying there thinking.

The blue light grew brighter. He picked up his wristwatch and peered at the time. Six eleven. It was than that he heard the faraway *whack-whack-whack* of a helicopter; and then another; and they were coming closer.

By the time he saw the white flag waving in the distance, he had already made sure that everybody else was safely inside the cavern. He kept himself shielded behind Santos' Suburban, holding one of his Colt Commandos, and with the other propped up close beside him, with the last of his magazines in it.

This morning seemed even hotter than ever, and he heard persistent thunder from the east, over the Coxcomb Mountains, which were the driest, most craggy and most inhospitable mountains in the whole of the Joshua Tree National Park.

The white flag came nearer. At last he heard a voice calling. 'Martin! Martin, can you hear me? Martin, this is Saskia!'

Shit, he thought. *So she has betrayed us, after all. Thank you, Saskia, I love you, too.*

'Martin! I just want to talk to you, that's all!' She came out of the bushes and walked across to the center of the open ground, still flapping her white flag from side to side. 'Can you hear me, Martin! I just want to talk!'

'What about, Saskia?' he called back. 'How to rat out the people who saved you?'

'I'm sorry, Martin! I really am sorry! But you can't go on living like this, out in the desert! Think of the kids!'

Martin said, 'Are you alone?'

'There are two men from ESS a little way behind me, in case I need help. But I promise you I've only come to talk.'

Martin stayed where he was, behind the Suburban. No matter what assurances Saskia gave him, there was no way that he was going to step out into anybody's line of fire. If he had been one of Joseph Wracks' men, he would have dropped him as soon as he got the shot. *Efaqa*, they had called it, in Afghanistan. It sounded like Arabic, but it was an acronym for 'eliminate first, ask questions afterward'.

Saskia walked a few paces further toward the entrance to the cavern. She still couldn't see where he was.

'I'm over here,' he told her, but when she started to walk toward him, he said, 'Stay where you are. Don't come any closer. Don't even look at me.'

'Martin, I'm sorry. But this is insane, hiding out here.'

'What's it to you?'

'You have children with you. Nathan and George and Mina. Your own kids, too, Tyler and Ella. How long do you think they're going to last, living off seeds and jackrabbits?'

'As if you care. You don't give a bent cent for anybody except yourself. Why did you do it, Saskia? If you didn't want to stay here nobody was forcing you. You didn't have to tell Wrack where we were.'

Saskia said, 'I wanted you, Martin. Don't you understand that? I wanted you from the very moment I first saw you.'

'Is *that* what this all about? Jealousy? And you're calling *me* insane?'

'You don't understand. I had to get even, Martin. Not with you. Well, yes, I admit it, maybe with you. But mostly with Halford Smiley. I did a deal with Halford to tell him where the water was.'

'You're a very sick woman, Saskia. Did anybody ever tell you that?'

Now she turned to face him, and she tossed her white flag on to the ground. 'How sick is it to want to be happy, Martin? How sick is it to want to forget your past, and all the people you've hurt, and all the mistakes you've made? I killed my own husband, Martin! I strangled him, and I loved him more than you can ever imagine! And then I met you.'

Her fists were clenched and there were tears running down her cheeks. She stood there, incapable of saying any more.

Martin glanced quickly up the valley. He could see one of the ESS security guards standing about two hundred feet away, next to a teddy bear cholla. He was armed with a carbine with a telescopic sight. He couldn't see the second guard.

He knew that his position was hopeless. He had only sixty rounds of ammunition left, but even if he had a whole arsenal of weapons he wouldn't be able to hold out against ESS. Not only that, ESS security guards obviously had no compunction about shooting children. He was quite sure that if he tried to put up a fight, they would all be killed, all of them, and their bodies buried here, and who would ever know?

'What's the deal?' he asked Saskia.

Saskia took a moment to smear the tears away from her eyes. Then she said, 'Wrack only wants you, Martin. He doesn't want to hurt you, he just wants to see you handed over to the police, because of all the damage you've done.'

'And I'm supposed to believe that?'

'Martin, whatever I think about you, I wouldn't have come here if I thought that he was going to do you any harm. I'll admit that he's a very vengeful man, and he wants to see you punished, but he's not going to break the law to see that happen.'

'And everybody else here, he won't touch any of them?'

'It's only you he wants, Martin. If you give yourself up, that's it. It's all over. Everybody else here can do anything they want. Stay here, go back to the city, whatever. Wrack came here today in person. He's up at the head of the valley, in his helicopter. He can give you his promise face to face.'

'He came here himself? Jesus. He *must* be mad at me.'

'He is. You cost him nine men and a very expensive helicopter, and a whole lot of prestige, too.'

Martin stayed where he was for over a minute, weighing up the odds, although in truth he knew there was nothing more to think about. He didn't trust Saskia and he trusted Joseph Wrack even less, but what alternatives did he have?

He carefully propped his sub-machine gun next to the second one, and stepped out from behind the Suburban with his hands held up.

As he came up to her, Saskia said, 'I'm so sorry, Martin. Really.'

But even though her mascara was streaked from crying, he could see a look in her eyes that was almost triumphant, and she was actually starting to smile. *Think you could reject me, did you? Think that I was nothing but a sadomasochistic slut? Well,* now *look at you.*

Her nostrils flared and he wouldn't have been surprised if she told him to get down on his knees.

A shot cracked out. A bullet sang past his head and ricocheted off the rock face thirty feet behind him. Immediately, he lunged forward, seized hold of Saskia and pulled her roughly in front of him.

'*Martin!*' she screamed.

Over her shoulder, he could see both security guards standing amongst the cactus, their carbines raised and pointing in their direction. Gripping both of Saskia's arms, he started to heave her back toward the Suburban.

'*What are you doing?*' she shrilled, trying to twist away from him.

He heard a second shot, and this was so close that it shattered one of the Suburban's rear windows, showering them with fragments of glass. Then, just as he reached the back of the truck, where his sub-machine guns were propped up, there was a third shot, and he felt Saskia jolt against him as if she had been punched very hard in the chest.

Her knees gave way, and she slowly sagged to the ground. He managed to drag her out of the line of fire, but when he gently laid her down he saw that the front of her black silk blouse was wet with blood.

Her face was white and she was staring up at him with unfocused eyes. '*David?*' she whispered, and a runnel of blood slid out of the side of her mouth. '*David, is that you?*'

Martin grabbed one of his sub-machine guns and quickly ducked his head around the back of the Suburban. The two ESS security guards clearly thought that they had hit both Saskia and Martin, because they were emerging from the bushes at a leisurely pace with their carbines lowered. One of them was talking on a two-way radio, and although Martin couldn't hear what he was saying, he could guess. *Targets down.*

He waited until they had made their way between the tents and were halfway across the open ground. Then, stepping out from behind the truck, he opened fire, one quick automatic burst for each of them. For a split-second, each of them danced like two life-size marionettes and then they pitched to the ground, dropping their carbines, and lay still.

Martin went over to them, keeping them covered, and keeping half an eye up the valley in case there were more security agents concealed in the bushes. His ears were singing and he didn't hear Santos coming up behind him, so that when he touched Martin's arm, Martin spun around and pointed his sub-machine gun at him.

Santos lifted both hands and said, 'This is bad, Wasicu! This is very bad! They will send more!'

'What?' said Martin 'I can't hear you!'

'I said, this is very bad!' Santos shouted. 'They will send more men and they will kill us!'

'It's pretty clear that they were intending to do that anyhow,' Martin told him. He bent over and examined each of the security guards closely. They were both dead. One of them had been shot in the neck and a large bubble of blood swelled out of his throat and quietly popped.

'So what can we do?' asked Santos. 'There is nowhere for us to run to.'

Martin went back over to Saskia. Her eyes were still open and she was staring at the morning sky but she was dead, too. *My God, Saskia,* he thought. *You brought this on yourself, didn't you?* He gently closed her eyelids with his finger and thumb.

'I thought that if I gave myself up they wouldn't harm you and Peta and the kids,' said Martin. 'But now I don't believe that they're going to let any of us get out of here alive. If they could shoot Mikey in cold blood like that, they're not going to have any qualms about the rest of us, are they?'

Santos looked across at the bodies of the two security agents, and then back at Saskia. 'You are right, Wasicu. And it is not just revenge that they are looking for.'

'What do you mean?'

'Think about it. Because of this dark-shadow woman, they now know of the existence of Lost Girl Lake. Can you think how much profit they will hope to make out of it, in the middle of this drought? They will not want anybody to tell the world how they found it. They killed our women and children to take our land. They will not hesitate to do the same to take our water.'

'In that case, I guess there's nothing else we can do. It's the Alamo, all over again.'

They edged their way through the crevice into the cavern. Peta and Tyler and Ella and the children were all standing clustered together, their faces pale with fright.

'What was all that shooting?' said Peta. 'We thought they might have killed you.'

'They damn nearly did,' Martin told her. 'They sent Saskia down with a white flag of truce, to persuade me to give myself up. As soon as I broke cover, they took a potshot at me. Saskia's dead, I'm sorry to say, as well as two of their men.' He paused, and then he said, 'There's no easy way to say this, but we're pretty sure that they intend to kill all of us. I don't have much ammo left, so we can't hold out for very long, but I'm going to do what I can. There's only one way into this cavern, and that's through the crevice, so it's not too difficult to defend. I think all we can do now is hope and pray.'

George and Mina both silently started to cry, their mouths turned down and tears rolling down their cheeks. Nathan pressed his hand over his mouth and squeezed his eyes tight shut. Susan put her arms around them and said, 'They can't kill the children. They *can't.*'

'I'm sorry, Susan. They're very hard-hearted people, who don't value anybody's life. Probably not even their own. But I'm going to do everything I can to protect you.'

Tyler said, 'What can I do, Dad?'

'Not too much, really. If it comes to fighting them at close quarters, I guess you could always use that camping mallet. Santos, you have a knife, don't you? I wish I knew where that hand grenade disappeared to. That would have been pretty useful, right about now.'

He ushered Peta and Susan and the children over to the washing pool. There was a hollow behind the pool, and if they kept themselves crouched down inside it, there would be less likelihood of them being hit by stray bullets.

Peta was holding Ella's hand. She looked up at him and said, 'Supposing we all just gave ourselves up? They wouldn't just kill us in cold blood, would they?'

'I'll try, but I don't hold out much hope.'

There was nothing they could do now but sit and wait for Joseph Wrack's men to try to come in after them. The batteries in Martin's and Santos' flashlights were slowly dying, so that their bulbs glowed dull orange; and apart from that the only illumination was the sunshine reflected through the crevice from the rock wall outside.

Santos began to sing, very softly, in his native language, and at the same time slap his thigh and nod his head in time to the words. When he had finished, he said, 'That was a song my grandmother taught me. It is like a hymn, I suppose. I was asking the Great Spirit to lead me safely up the mountain, so that when I reached the top the rest of my life stretched out before me, all the way to my distant death. I was also asking that the Great Spirit should protect my people from harm, and as far as I am concerned, you are my people now, all of you. The enemy is not red or white. The enemy is greed.'

They waited for over another hour. It was too much to hope that Joseph Wrack had given up and taken his men back to the city. If he had gone to the trouble of coming out here in person to hunt Martin down, he wasn't going to be satisfied until the job was done. They hadn't heard the helicopters lifting off, so they could be fairly sure that the ESS men were still at the head of the valley and preparing themselves for another attack. Maybe they would even wait until nightfall, when the children were all tired, and they could blind them with flash grenades. That was what Martin would have done, if he had been planning an assault on a Taliban camp.

A few more minutes went by, however, and Santos suddenly lifted his head up and sniffed and said, 'Smoke. I smell smoke.'

Martin sniffed, too. 'I don't smell anything.'

'Wait, it will come to you. It is creosote bush burning. Creosote bush and cholla.'

Martin kept on sniffing, and soon he began to pick up the distinctive aroma of burning chaparral. Mina coughed, and George started coughing, too, although he was deliberately trying to cough louder than his little sister.

Before long, gray clouds of smoke began to drift in through the crevice, with shafts of reflected sunlight playing through it. Fragments of white cactus ash danced in the sunlight like moths.

'What are they trying to do, Dad?' asked Tyler. 'Smoke us out?'

Martin took hold of his Colt Commando and stood up. 'It sure looks like it, doesn't it? I think now is the time to see if I can do some kind of a deal with them, if that's possible.' He pointed to his second Colt Commando, which was lying next to their cardboard boxes of food. 'If anything happens, you know how to use that, don't you, Tyler?'

Tyler gave him a queasy nod.

'Martin,' said Peta. 'Please . . . be really careful, won't you?'

Martin gave her a tight humorless smile and walked across to the crevice. The smoke was billowing even more densely now, and it was so acrid that it burned his nostrils and the back of his throat. He tugged his filthy khaki bandana out of his pocket, the bandana that he had been using to clean his sub-machine guns, and tied it around his nose and mouth. It smelled of cordite and gun oil but it saved him from breathing creosote and cholla ash.

He shouldered his way through the crevice and then cautiously put his head around it. As he did so, he heard a loud howling sound, and a geyser of flame spouted toward him, out of the bushes. He jerked back into the crevice, hitting the back of his head against the rock, and even though the flames didn't reach as far as the valley walls, he felt a searing blast of heat, and he could smell gasoline, too.

He waited a moment, until the howling had abruptly stopped, and then he gingerly looked out of the crevice again. He could hardly believe what he saw. The whole valley was on fire, and almost completely hidden in smoke. The teddy bear cactus were blazing white and fierce and the chaparral branches were glowing red through the gloom like a network of overheating electrical wires.

Out of the smoke three ESS security guards were walking toward the open ground where their tents were pitched, two of them armed with carbines but one of them toting what looked like a rocket-propelled grenade launcher. They were all wearing face masks and respirators, as well as body armor with the ESS logo on it.

At their head was Joseph Wrack. Martin recognized him instantly, even though he was wearing a face mask, because of his iron-gray flat-top haircut. Strapped to his back was an Army-issue flame-thrower, with three khaki tanks on his back, two for gasoline and one for nitrogen gas propellant. He let out a short spurt of fire as he approached, and the last of the bushes burst into flame. He raised the nozzle a little more and let out another spurt, sweeping it quickly from left to right over the triangle of open ground. All three tents instantly caught fire, and were burned into skeletons in a matter of seconds, with blackened fragments of fabric flying up into the air.

As soon as he saw the flame-thrower, Martin knew for certain that there was no point in them offering to give themselves up. Flame-throwers were designed for one thing only – and that was to set fire to people, especially people who were hiding in caves or tunnels or other places where it was difficult to gain access.

Joseph Wrack had now stepped out on to the open ground, with his three men close behind him, and although Martin couldn't tell if he had seen him or not, he was walking directly toward him. He raised his flame-thrower again and Martin urgently shuffled his way back through the crevice and into the cavern. He shouted, '*Get back!*' to Santos and Tyler, who were both standing in the center of the cavern, waiting for him. He grabbed Tyler's sleeve with his left hand and barged Santos with his right elbow, so that they both stumbled with him toward the washing pool. He jumped straight in and they both followed him, splashing water over Peta and Ella and Susan and the children, who were crouching in the hollow in the cavern wall.

There was another howl, much louder than before, and a sheet of blazing gasoline roared through the crevice and exploded in all directions. For a few seconds, even the walls and the floor were on fire. Mina screamed and George started crying again.

About half a minute passed, and then another torrent of fire came through, longer than the first, and so powerful that the wall of the cavern directly opposite the crevice, over a hundred feet away, was set alight. Martin stayed waist-deep in the washing-pool, keeping his sub-machine gun pointed toward the crevice, while Santos and Tyler climbed out to join Peta and Susan and the children.

More time went by. They could hear the security guards outside talking to each other, and also talking on their two-way radios. They could also hear some clanking noises.

'What's happening?' asked Santos. 'What are they waiting for?'

'Wrack is probably filling up his gas tanks. Flame-throwers only last for six or seven seconds before they run out of fuel.'

'So what do we do now?'

'We don't do anything. They'll probably keep on blasting away for a while, but they can't easily bring that thing inside here because the entrance is too narrow for anybody to make their way through while they're wearing it, and we can pick them off as soon as they appear.

'During World War Two, they used flame-throwers against the Japs when they were hiding in caves and tunnels. Not to set fire to them, because they couldn't reach them, but to burn up all of the oxygen, so that they suffocated. But of course they can't do that to us here. This cavern's way too big, and way too well ventilated.'

Another few minutes went by, and then they heard a harsh amplified voice. It was Joseph Wrack, speaking through a bullhorn.

'Makepeace! This is Joseph Wrack, from Empire Security Services. I'm giving you a last chance here, Makepeace. I don't know what happened when Saskia came to talk to you, but it was all an unfortunate accident. My men thought that you were threatening her life, that's why they opened fire. They were under the impression that they had shot you, too, but – well – obviously not.'

He paused, and through the bullhorn Martin could actually hear him licking his lips. It was smoky inside the cavern, but it must have been even smokier outside.

'That's eleven men of mine you've taken down, Makepeace. Eleven. All with wives or partners and families to take care of. Plus, of course, one helicopter. I think I have every justification for being pissed with you, don't you? However, if you all come out of there now without giving me any further grief, I'll let everybody go, unharmed. You, I'll have to take you in to the cops, that's my legal duty under *posse comitatus*. But you did the crime, Makepeace, and sooner or later you'll have to serve the time.'

Martin looked around at everybody huddled in the hollow. All the gasoline flames had guttered out now, and their flashlights had died, so that he could barely see their faces through the gloom. Just their eyes, glittering.

'What do we think?' he asked them. 'Maybe I *should* give myself up. Even if I have to go court, I can call you as witnesses, can't I? I can probably get away with justifiable homicide. Self-defense.'

Peta said, 'No. Don't even think about. I thought before that you might be able to make a deal with him, but what has he been doing? He's been doing his best to burn us all to death. Any one of these children could have been standing in the way, when he fired that thing. I don't trust him one inch.'

'Me neither,' said Santos. 'He is making this offer only because he doesn't know how he is going to get us out of here. We have food here, we have water. We could survive here for many days. Don't tell me that he can afford to stay out there for very much longer.'

'Do you have an answer for me?' Joseph Wrack called out. 'I'm not going to wait too much longer. Are you coming out peacefully, or not?'

'We're agreed then?' said Martin. 'We're going to try to hold out?'

Nathan nodded enthusiastically. 'Absolutely. Tell him to go fuck himself.'

He looked around, but nobody said anything to him. It was probably the first time in his life that he hadn't been told to watch his language.

'What's your answer?' Joseph Wrack demanded. 'Come on, Makepeace! What's your answer?'

THIRTEEN

As it was, Martin didn't answer at all.

Over the next twenty minutes, Joseph Wrack appealed to him twice more to give himself up, sounding angrier each time. When Martin still didn't reply he said, in that hoarse, amplified voice, 'OK. Have it your way, you obstinate bastard. Don't say I didn't warn you.'

They heard a scratching sound as he switched off his bullhorn and then a lot more clattering outside.

'What do you think he's going to do?' asked Ella.

'I don't know, sweetheart. In the Marines they taught us to think like the enemy thinks. Put ourselves in their shoes, if you see what I mean. Or sandals, rather, with the Taliban. But this Wrack guy . . . I can't get a grip on the way that his brain works. He promises to do something and he knows you don't believe it but he doesn't seem to care whether you believe it or not, because he was never going to do it, anyhow.'

Tyler said, '*What*?' but Santos said, 'Never mind, young Wasicu. That is white man's logic. Explains nothing, excuses everything.'

Martin climbed out of the washing pool. The bush fires in the valley must have almost burned themselves out by now, because there was very little smoke eddying in through the crevice. He went over to the edge of the lake, knelt down and scooped up several handfuls of water. He drank some, and splashed the rest on his face and on to the back of his neck.

Peta came over and said, 'I'm sorry about Saskia.'

'Yes, well, so am I. But I'm much more sorry for the rest of us. Saskia got what she deserved. These kids don't deserve any of this, and neither do you. Your dad always used to say that you and I should never have gotten married, didn't he?'

'My dad had black days, just like you. He was in Vietnam.'

'I never knew that.'

'Yes, he was in the Medical Corps. They had a serious shortfall of surgeons in those days, and he saw a lot of young men die who didn't have to. So I think he understood what your djinns were all about.'

Martin stood up. He put his arms around her and said, 'I love you, Peta. I never stopped loving you, even when I was going crazy. Maybe even more when I was going crazy. If we manage to get through this—'

She eased herself free from him. 'Let's get out of here first, shall we? Do you know how *frightened* I am? Do you know how frightened Tyler and Ella and all of those children are?'

Martin said nothing as she went back to the hollow behind the washing pool. Then he bent down and picked up his sub-machine gun. He had heard stories of Muslim fathers in Bosnia shooting their own families and then themselves, rather than let the Serbs get their hands on them, to torture them and rape them. Would he consider shooting Peta and Tyler and Ella and Santos and all of his grandchildren, rather than let them be burned alive, or whatever Joseph Wrack planned to do to them?

He wondered for a moment if Wrack would simply seal the crevice with concrete, in the way that the Serbs had sealed up Muslim mosques and cemeteries during the Bosnian conflict, but that would mean sealing the entrance to the lake, too. If Santos was right, the lake was more important than all of their lives. There had been gold in the Joshua Tree National Park, and there probably still was, but in the middle of this drought, Lost Girl Lake was worth much more than gold.

He walked back over to the hollow. 'Anybody hungry? How about we all have something to eat? I know that none of us has much of an appetite, but we need to keep our strength up.'

The first explosion was devastating. It made a flat, hard sound, as if two bricks had been banged together very close to their ears. The shock wave that followed it made the surface of the lake ripple, all the way into the darkness of the inner cavern, and then splash fretfully against the ledge. They were all stunned, and the little ones stood with their hands pressed to their ears, temporarily deafened.

Dust and smoke rolled into the cavern through the crevice, but as it dissipated they could see much more sunlight streaming in than it had before, and they could also see that the floor of the cavern was strewn with thousands of fragments of broken granite.

Martin realized at once what Joseph Wrack was doing. He had ordered his men to fire their rocket-propelled grenade launcher at the entrance to the crevice, blasting open a much wider hole for them to attack the cavern. He should have guessed that was what

Wrack would do, because he had done the same in Afghanistan to penetrate Taliban fortifications. Each grenade contained over 700 grams of high explosive, and it would take only two or three to open up the crevice to three times its original width.

'*Everybody, get right down!*' he shouted, just as a second grenade exploded. This time, granite chippings rained down on them and bounced across the floor like hailstones, and the sound of the blast echoed deep in the unexplored depths of Lost Girl Lake.

Martin was lying flat, and he lifted his head to make sure that the others were all doing the same. Susan was actually lying on top of George and Mina, while Peta and Tyler and Ella had their arms around each other. Santos was lying a few feet off to his left, and lifted up his head, too. They exchanged looks that both meant: *this is it. Whoever we believe in, God or Gitche Manitou, please don't let any of us suffer.*

There was a third explosion, and this time huge lumps of rock thundered down, and part of the rock face collapsed, so that the sun came bursting into the cavern as dazzling as an A-bomb test. Shielding his eyes, Martin saw Joseph Wrack stepping over the rubble with his flame-thrower in his hands, and his three men following behind him, two with their carbines raised and the third with a pistol.

'Throw that weapon away, Makepeace!' said Joseph Wrack, hoarsely. 'Far as you can! Don't get up! Just throw it!'

Martin took hold of the Colt Commando by its barrel and slung it sideways across the cavern floor. Immediately, one of Joseph Wrack's men came crunching through the grit to pick it up.

Joseph Wrack looked down at them, lying prone, and reached out with his left hand for the flame-thrower's igniter safety-catch, which was just behind the nozzle.

He walked right up to Martin now, and he spoke so softly, as he usually did, that only Martin could hear him.

'Ever heard that expression, "you're toast"?'

Martin lifted his head and looked up at him. 'I'm asking you, Wrack. No, all right, I'm not asking you, I'm *pleading* with you. You can cremate me if you want to. But please don't hurt my family. Please don't hurt any of these children. They're totally innocent. They've done nothing. They're only here because I brought them here, for the water.'

'Oh, yes,' said Joseph Wrack. 'The water.'

He looked across at Lost Girl Lake. Now that the sun was shining into the cavern, the water was even clearer than ever. Joseph Wrack walked slowly over to the edge of the ledge and stared down at it. He craned his neck to look up at the cathedral-like ceiling, with its tier upon tier of granite, and then he looked back into the water again. He seemed to be mesmerized, as if he were thinking of all the power and wealth that this lake could give him. *Lake Wrack.*

After a moment, he knelt down on one knee. Holding the hose of his flame-thrower well out of the way to one side, he dipped his left hand into the water and brought it up to his lips to taste it.

'*Not you!*' shouted Santos.

Joseph Wrack turned, frowning. Santos had climbed to his feet and was stalking toward him, shaking both of fists in fury.

'Not you! That is sacred water! That water belongs to my people, and to the people my people choose to share it with! And we would never share our water with you, you murderer of children!'

Joseph Wrack stood up. 'You listen to me, you old coot, you'd better lie down again, right now, or else it's going to be the worse for you. And that's a promise.'

But Santos continued storming toward him, throwing aside his Panama hat.

'You murdered my grandson! You will not drink even one drop of our sacred water!'

Joseph Wrack's security guards raised their carbines but Joseph Wrack lifted his left hand, palm raised, as a signal that *he* was going to take care of this, himself.

Santos was still at least twenty feet away from him when Joseph Wrack lifted up the hose of his flame-thrower and pointed it at him. He pressed the firing button on his igniter, and then the firing trigger. There was a high-pitched screech of pressurized gas and then Santos was enveloped in a two-second fountain of fire.

Santos stopped and stood still, blazing from head to foot, The flames were so fierce that Martin could only dimly see him, a shadowy outline with his fists still raised. He was burning, but he didn't scream, and he didn't fall to the ground. It was like watching one of those Buddhist monks burning, stoical to the last, in spite of the agony.

Martin was about to stand up himself when Santos took one lurching step forward, and then another. Joseph Wrack backed away from him, but then Santos suddenly rushed at him, like some terrible fiery nemesis, with a soft but audible roar of flames. Joseph Wrack was right on the very edge of the ledge, and Santos hurled himself on top of him, so that he toppled backward, with Santos clutching him tight. As they hit the water, there was a crackling and hissing of steam, and Joseph Wrack let out a *crawwwkkk!* that sounded more like a crow than a human.

Joseph Wrack's three security guards ran to the edge of the lake, but for a moment they all stood there helplessly, not knowing what they could do. The water was so clear that they could see it was over thirty feet deep, and they were all dressed in combat gear. One of them, however, started to unbuckle his body armor.

Santos was charred black, and his clothes were in tatters, but he continued to cling on to Joseph Wrack, head-butting him whenever he tried to lift his face out of the water. Joseph Wrack was thrashing and struggling wildly but his flame-thrower pack was weighing him down, too. When its fuel tanks were almost full it weighed over sixty-five pounds.

Martin stood up and crossed quickly over to the side of the cavern, where they had stacked their boxes of food. As he did so, he prayed that none of the security guards would see what he was doing and take a shot at him. By now, however, the security guard who had taken off his armor had also unlaced his boots and kicked them off, and was preparing to dive into the water, while the other two were kneeling by the edge of the water, stretching out their hands as far as they could to see if they could catch hold of Santos's legs.

Martin picked up his second Colt Commando and walked back toward the edge of the lake. By the time he got there, Joseph Wrack had managed to roll over, so that Santos was underneath him, but he could see that Santos' arms were still clamped around his waist. The flesh of Santos' fingers was seared black and scarlet, and some of the bones were exposed, like barbecued ribs. Martin couldn't even imagine what pain he was in.

Joseph Wrack was spluttering and gasping and grunting but he was doing everything he could to keep Santos' head under the surface.

The security guard dived into the water next to them, surfacing and shaking the water out of his eyes. He was about to seize hold of Joseph Wrack's ankle when Martin shouted, '*Freeze!* Don't move! Any of you!'

One of the security guards kneeling by the edge of the ledge lunged toward his carbine, which he had left lying on the ground beside him, but Martin snapped, '*Freeze*, I told you!' and he froze. Martin stalked around him, picked up his carbine and tossed it well out of reach. He then picked up the other guard's weapon, and the holstered pistol that the guard in the lake had left behind him, and threw them after it.

'Tyler!' he called, and Tyler stood up and collected them.

'Mr Wrack's *drowning*, for Christ's sake,' said one of the security guards, in a panicky, strangled voice. 'You can't just let him drown!'

'I don't intend to,' said Martin. 'You,' he told the security guard in the water, 'pull them to the edge here.'

'Help me!' blurted Joseph Wrack. 'Help me!'

The security guard took hold of the leg of Santos' pants, but as he did so, Santos released his hold on Joseph Wrack and sank. His lungs must have been filled with water, because he went down as quickly as a sinking rowboat, and the lake was so clear that they could see him dropping slowly all the way down to the bottom.

Joseph Wrack rolled over again, now that he no longer had Santos underneath him, acting as ballast. His eyes were closed now, and his lips were purple.

The security guard in the water said, 'Roy! Vernon! Help me get him out here! He needs CPR, and quick!'

He dragged Joseph Wrack to the ledge and his two companions reached down and heaved their boss out of the water, and laid him on his side.

'Get this goddamned flame-thrower off of him!' said one of them. Hunkering down beside him, he unbuckled the belt around his waist. He was starting to wrestle off the shoulder straps when Joseph Wrack shuddered, and convulsed, and blurted out half a lungful of water. He opened his eyes and looked up at the security guard who was trying to take off his flame-thrower harness, and then he tried to sit up.

'It's OK, Mr Wrack, let's just get you out of this thing, shall we?'

But Joseph Wrack pushed him irritably away, and coughed up more water.

'*Sir* – you almost drowned – you need to—'

'Get the fuck off me, will you?' Joseph Wrack grated. He turned his head around, trying to orient himself. 'Goddamned lunatic – pushing me into the water like that – what the fuck did he think he was doing?'

'He was burning to death, that's what he was doing,' said Martin, very loudly. 'He was burning to death and he wanted to take you with him.'

Joseph Wrack looked up. When he saw that Martin was holding a sub-machine gun and that his own men were unarmed, he said, 'What? What the fuck is going on here?'

The security guard who had dived in to save him was just climbing out of the water. 'Sorry, Mr Wrack,' he said. 'We were more interested in saving you. We didn't realize he had another weapon.'

Joseph Wrack's lips slowly stretched back to bare his long, narrow teeth, and he actually snarled. The security guard who had been trying to take off his flame-thrower was making a second clumsy attempt to unfasten his buckles, but again Joseph Wrack pushed him away, so ferociously that the man staggered backward and almost lost his balance. He picked up the nozzle of his flame-thrower and pressed the igniter button, and then he took hold of the firing grip and swung the hose around so that it was pointing toward Martin.

Without hesitation, Martin fired a burst of five shots at him, and he jolted with the impact as they hit him. The fifth bullet was a tracer round, which flared bright red as it flashed out of the barrel of Martin's Colt Commando and ripped into Joseph Wrack's chest. All of the bullets went right through him and punctured the gasoline tanks that were strapped to his back – Martin heard the metallic bang as every one of them hit home. But the tracer round, filled with incandescent magnesium, ignited the gasoline instantly.

Joseph Wrack blew up. Martin, half-deafened by firing his Colt Commando, heard almost nothing but a dull, reverberating thud. But blood and body parts and shrapnel and pieces of twisted harness were blasted in all directions. There was an extraordinary roar as his body was engulfed by fire, almost as if the fire were some voracious animal that wanted to devour what was left of him.

His three security guards were all knocked to the ground by the explosion. It looked to Martin as if the one who had been trying to remove his flame-thrower was dead. The other two were lying side by side, their faces blackened and their hair scorched, but one of them was already trying to sit up, and the other was stirring.

Martin turned back to Peta and Tyler and Ella and Santos' grandchildren. None of the children were crying. They all looked too shocked.

He went up to Peta and put his arm around her.

'My God,' she said. 'You saved us. All except for poor Santos. You saved our lives.'

Martin looked back at the grisly remains of Joseph Wrack, still burning fiercely like an effigy that had fallen from the top of a bonfire. He didn't know what to say. As soon as he had seen Joseph Wrack coming down the valley with his flame-thrower, he had thought that none of them could expect to survive. Now the smoke from Joseph Wrack's body was drifting out of the cavern and into the morning sunshine, and they were still alive.

He walked over to the edge of the ledge and looked down into the lake. He could see Santos lying on the bottom, but he knew that it wouldn't be long before he would rise back up to the surface and they could lift him out.

He went across to the two security guards and said, 'How many choppers did you bring in? I heard two.'

One of the security guards nodded, and coughed. 'Two, yes.'

'Any more of you goons still up there?'

'Only the pilots. There was only five of us altogether, not counting Mr Wrack.'

'Can you get in touch with them?'

The security guard held up his two-way radio. Looking at his soot-smudged face more closely, Martin could see how young he was. Only a kid, underneath that body armor and that military-style uniform. But Martin remembered that when he and his buddies had first been sent to Afghanistan, they had all been kids, too, even though they had believed that they were men. You never see yourself as others see you.

'Tell them that everything's going to plan. Tell them to wait a while longer. You have some mopping up to do, that's all.'

The security guard hesitated, but Martin pointed his Colt Commando at him and said, 'Look at me. Go on. Just look at me. Do I look like I'm in the mood for you to piss me off? People have died here today. You do what I tell you or I'll shoot you between your legs and then see how your life turns out.'

The security guard clicked his mike and said, 'Eye-Sky Two. Eye-Sky Two.'

A crackly voice said, 'Eye-Sky Two, Go ahead, Rick.'

'Everything's good down here. We just have to tidy up some.'

'How long's that going to take?'

Martin held up one finger and the security guard said, 'Maybe an hour. Just hold on there, OK?'

'Let me talk to Mr Wrack.'

'Mr Wrack? Sorry, Lief. Mr Wrack's kind of involved right now. I'll have him get back to you.'

Martin patted the security guard on the back and said, 'Good for you. Well done.' Then he tugged the radio away from his shoulder, dropped it on the ground and stamped on it. He kicked the crushed remains in the direction of Joseph Wrack's smoking corpse.

'Just in case you go off message, if you know what I mean.'

He went back to Peta and the children.

'I don't know about you, but I don't think we can stay here any longer, not the way we are now. They've burned our tents. They've opened up the cavern to the elements, and any stray coyotes that might want to come prowling in here. These security guys know where Lost Girl Lake is located now, and we can't just kill them in cold blood, or expect them to keep quiet about it when they get back to the city, because they won't.'

He reached out and took hold of little Mina's hand. 'Apart from that, we've lost the only person who knew how to survive out here in the desert. I don't know which plants you can eat and which ones you can't. I don't know how to toast flower seeds and make them into cakes.'

'I can cook,' said Mina. 'Mommy teached me how to make brownies.'

'That was out of a packet, stupid,' said Nathan. 'They don't have packets in the desert.'

Peta said, 'You think that we should go back?'

'Wrack's dead, and so I don't think that anybody's going to be looking for me any more. I don't think the police are going to be worrying about Tyler, either, not now.'

'But what about water, Martin? That was the whole reason we came here, for the water. How are we going to survive without water?'

'We tell the water department where this lake is, and that should help. Come on, there are millions and millions of gallons here, and it would only take them a few days to set up a pipeline. In Helmand, we laid five miles of pipe in a single afternoon.'

Peta looked around, and smiled at the children. 'You're right, I suppose. We'll just have to fight for our water like everybody else.'

As soon as she had said that, they heard thunder. It rumbled on and on, like a distant artillery barrage.

'Hear that?' said Martin. 'The voice of God.'

FOURTEEN

After an hour, Santos' blackened body rose silently to the surface of Lost Girl Lake. The two security guards pulled him into the side and then lifted him out.

Grimacing with effort and disgust, they carried him outside, and then went back for the body of their fellow security guard. They laid them side by side with Saskia and the two security guards that Martin had shot. Peta made Nathan and George and Mina sit in Santos' Suburban, with Susan to look after them, so they wouldn't have to see.

There was no question of taking five bodies with them back to San Bernardino, and that was excluding the grotesquely cremated remains of Joseph Wrack. They couldn't bury them, however, because the ground was solid granite, and it would have taken pneumatic drills to dig even a shallow grave. Most of the bushes in the valley had been reduced to fine gray spidery ash, and the blankets in their tents had been burned, so they had nothing to cover them, apart from stones, and building a cairn for them, like they had for Mikey, would have taken hours.

'We can come back for them,' said Martin. He looked up at the turkey vultures wheeling around on the thermals that rose out of the valley. 'Meanwhile, I think we'll have to leave them to Mother Nature.

He stood over Santos' body for a few moments. 'Hey, Kemo Sabay,' he said, quietly. 'You did ask me to make sure that you were burned, didn't you? I know this wasn't exactly what you had in mind, but I hope it's enough for you. You'll be going back to your land now, anyhow. Meeting all of your people. I'm sorry for what happened to you. I'm sorry for what happened to all of you Yuhaviatam. I really am.' He paused, and then he said, 'Gitche Manitou? Can you hear me? If you can, then take this guy to meet his Juanita, will you?'

Peta said, 'Come on, Martin. We need to go.'

He checked his Eldorado to make sure that he hadn't left anything in the glove box, and then he put up its roof and locked it. He didn't

know whether he would ever be coming back for it. Their trek along
the Path of the Sacred Bear had wrecked its suspension and its
muffler and ruinously scratched its paintwork, but he might be able
to salvage it one day.

Tyler drove them up the valley in Santos' truck, with Martin
sitting in the back to keep the two security guards covered. When
they reached the head of the valley, they saw the two dark-blue ESS
helicopters, one on either side of the wash, a Robinson Raven and
an AStar. Their pilots were sitting on a rock together a little way
away, smoking. Tyler brought the Suburban to a halt and Martin
climbed out, with his sub-machine gun raised, and both of them
stood up in alarm.

'Hi there, gentlemen!' Martin called out. 'This isn't as threatening
as it looks, so I'm asking for a little calm. No – relax, you don't
have to put up your hands.'

'Where's Mr Wrack?' asked one of them. 'How come you left
Mr Wrack behind?'

Martin said, 'Mr Wrack has had an accident. That's why we had
to leave him behind. Let's just say that he's not in very good shape
right now. What you're going to do now is fly us all back to your
base in San Bernardino – all of us. After that we're going to part
company, as friends, I hope.'

'What kind of an accident?' said one of the pilots, in a strong
South Carolina accent. 'What – you mean he's *dead*?'

'Yes, he is, I'm afraid. I guess that's what you get for playing
with fire.'

'*Told* him he shouldn't have brung that flame-thrower,' said the
pilot. 'Didn't like having that dang thing aboard with me one bit.
Plus all of that extra gas.'

The other pilot shrugged. He seemed completely unperturbed. 'Far
as I'm concerned, Dooby, it couldn't have happened to a nicer guy.'

They lifted off from the head of the valley and tilted south-westward,
back across the Joshua Tree National Park and Desert Hot Springs
until they reached Highway 19, which would take them back toward
Redlands, and then to San Bernardino.

Martin and Peta and Ella and Mina were in one helicopter, with
one of the two surviving security guards, while Tyler and Susan
and Nathan and George and the other security guard were in the
other.

Martin had given Tyler the pistol that he had taken from the ESS man who had dived into the water, but neither of the security guards seemed to be interested in giving them any trouble. Lief, their pilot, appeared to be positively jubilant that Joseph Wrack was dead.

'Don't get me wrong,' he said. 'Assholes I can tolerate. If a guy's an asshole he's an asshole. We all behave like assholes now and again. It's the human condition. Darwin's Origin of Assholes. What I can't tolerate is assholes who behave like sons of bitches, and Joseph Wrack was the meanest son of a bitch I ever came across, ever. Don't know what's going to happen now. Maybe his deputy's going to take over – Jim Broader. He's an asshole, I'm telling you. But a son of a bitch, no.'

He talked non-stop as they flew along the highway, and Martin was glad that he was the only other person in the cabin wearing headphones.

Far ahead of them, on the horizon, he could see lightning flicker. As they neared Redlands, however, and veered north-westward toward San Bernardino, he was sure that he could see gray clouds building. He turned around in his seat and pointed them out to Peta. 'Haven't seen clouds like that in over a year!' he shouted.

'What?' she shouted back.

'Clouds! Over there!'

The wind was beginning to rise, and buffet the helicopter, and the pilot stopped talking as he concentrated on keeping them on course. The roaring of their engine rose and fell as they circled at last around the ESS helipad off East 3rd Street, on the northern perimeter of San Bernardino International Airport. Martin turned his head around to see where the other helicopter was. It was close behind them, off to their starboard side and slightly higher, but it was struggling against the wind just as much as they were. The two helicopters dipped and danced like two dragonflies before they finally settled on to the concrete landing pad.

Almost at once, four ground crew in fluorescent orange overalls came hurrying out of the helipad building to anchor both helicopters with hooks and cables.

They all climbed out, and by now the sky above them was heavy with low gray clouds. The speed with which they had rolled over was astonishing. There was another flicker of lightning, and a grumble of thunder, and then, like some kind of Biblical miracle, it began to rain. They all stood looking upward. The children had their arms outspread. At first, the rain was nothing more than a few warm spots, but then it started to come down harder.

It thundered again, much nearer and louder.

Martin turned to Peta. Her blonde hair was wet and straggly, and raindrops were running down her cheeks like tears.

'What did I tell you?' he said. 'The voice of God.'

It rained for only twenty minutes before the clouds passed over and the sun came out again, so that steam rose from the sidewalks and the whole city shone blurred and bright.

But it thundered and rained again, during the night, much more heavily this time. Peta turned over and said to Martin, 'Are you awake?'

'I haven't slept yet,' he told her. 'I can't stop thinking about everything that's happened, and I still can't believe that I'm here.'

In the darkness, she touched his face with her fingertips, as if she were blind. 'It will be different this time, won't it?'

'Yes,' he said. 'I promise you.'

It kept on steadily raining for over two hours and he could hear it chuckling in the gutters and filling up the rain butt in the back yard. He still couldn't close his eyes, but he put his arm around Peta and held her while she fell asleep again. He didn't know what was going to happen to him now – whether the police would come looking for him for killing Joseph Wrack or Joseph Wrack's security guards, as well as destroying one of his helicopters. Then there was the question of him springing Tyler from custody, when Tyler had already been charged with felony homicide. In a strange way, though, he felt completely calm about it – for tonight, anyhow. He knew that a kind of justice had been done, and that once the truth was known, he and Tyler stood a good chance of being exonerated. Most of all, though, he was back with Peta, and Tyler and Ella were sleeping in their own bedrooms, and it was raining.

The following morning, on NBC News, it was announced that Governor Halford Smiley, who had unaccountably been missing for over twelve hours, had been discovered dead in a parking lot in south San Bernardino. Apparently he had been the victim of a car bomb, although there was no indication as to who might have wanted to blow him up, or why. No terrorist organizations had claimed credit for killing him, although an extreme group of environmental activists calling themselves Thirst For Action had said that they would 'line-dance on his grave' because his 'rotational hiatuses' had been tantamount to class genocide.

For the time being, Lieutenant Governor Kenneth Korven would be taking over the running of the state of California. He had already agreed that the Environmental Protection Agency should temporarily take over the rationing of water, at least until the drought emergency was over. That would mean that all of those neighborhoods whose water had been permanently cut off would have their supply restored, at least every alternate day, and that those neighborhoods who never had been cut off would have to suffer the same restrictions.

Lieutenant Governor Korven also announced the fortuitous discovery of a 'substantial' underground aquifer in the Joshua Tree National Park. It was possible that this water could be used to alleviate the drought crisis in San Bernardino County and surrounding areas.

After the first rainfall in well over a year, weather forecasters were cautiously predicting a gradual return to normal precipitation. There had been intermittent rain all across the Midwest, and in parts of Louisiana there had even been flooding. Several tankers stranded on the bed of the Mississippi had been refloated.

For the first time in days, there was no serious rioting in downtown San Bernardino, and no more fires, although some looting continued. That evening, it rained again, very softly and gently, and the air began to cool. The following morning, very early, Martin and Peta heard a gurgling noise coming from their bathroom, and it was their toilet cistern filling up.

On the third day, Martin took a taxi down to the office in Carousel Mall. The downtown area was still a scene of devastation, although burned-out cars were being lifted up on to low-loaders and crews of men in high-visibility coats were sweeping the broken glass and rocks and trash from the streets.

The only person in the office was Brenda, the receptionist, her hair still tightly French-pleated, scowling as always.

'I think Arlene will be wanting a word with you, Martin,' she said, as soon as he walked in through the door. 'She's not in today and I haven't been able to contact her at home, but I'm quite sure that she'll have something to say.'

Martin smiled. 'That's OK, Brenda. I'll come in tomorrow and if there's anything eating her I'm sure we can sort it all out. For now, what staff cars do we have in the parking garage? I need to borrow one.'

Brenda opened her desk drawer, took out three sets of car keys, and said, 'We have a Sonic or a Cruze. Or a Prius.'

'I'll take the Prius. I don't want anybody saying that I don't do my bit for climate change.'

Once he had gone down to the parking garage and picked up the car, he drove home to Fullerton Drive. Home. He liked the sound of that. There were two things he had to do first. One was to go to his apartment at Hummingbird Haven and collect all his clothes and the rest of his stuff. More important than that, though, he had to take Tyler to San Bernardino Community Hospital.

Maria was sitting up in bed when Tyler rapped at her door, watching TV. Her face was still swollen, but the bruises around her eyes were turning yellow, and her lips were healing, although she still had several scabs.

'*Tyler!*' she said, and her eyes widened. 'They told me you'd been arrested. What are you doing here?'

'Is it OK?' Tyler asked her. 'If you don't want to see me, I'll go.'

'No,' she said. 'Stay. I wanted to tell the police that you didn't shoot Papa. I asked the nurses but they said that no cops could come to see me, because of the riots. I asked again yesterday because I thought you were in prison but they still said no.'

'You will tell them that I didn't shoot him, though, won't you? I mean, when all of this rioting is finished and they can come see you.'

She held out her hand to him. Her wrist was bandaged and two of her fingernails were missing. 'Tyler . . . of course I will tell them. It wasn't you. It was that Big Puppet. I can tell the police what he looked like, everything.'

Tyler was tempted to tell her what had happened to Big Puppet, but decided it was better if he said nothing at all. He took her hand between his. Although her face was so bruised, he thought that she still looked beautiful. 'The other thing,' he said, with a catch in his throat.

'What other thing? What do you mean?'

'What I did to you. What that Big Puppet made me do to you. I'm so sorry. You must hate me for it. I'm really so sorry.'

Maria shook her head. 'It wasn't your fault, Tyler. I know that. In fact I'm glad you did it because he would have killed both of us, like my Papa.'

'Is it OK if I come see you tomorrow? I'm sorry . . . I didn't bring you anything. Most of the stores are smashed up so there's nothing to buy.'

Maria smiled at him. As she did so, rain sprinkled against the window, and as they both turned their heads to look outside, they could see clouds tumbling hurriedly across the sky, as if they had an urgent appointment to keep.

Martin picked up the last box of books and looked around his empty apartment. He had left the TV because it was eight years old and in any case it had been given to him by Shirelle in the office because she no longer needed it and otherwise she would have sent it off for recycling.

This was one place he wasn't sad to be leaving. All it reminded him of was lonely evenings and Hungry Man dinners and one-night stands with girls who had known that he was never going to get serious with them.

He heard the front door open. 'Tyler?' he called out. 'Just coming!'

He carried the box of books out into the corridor. There was somebody standing in the open doorway but it wasn't Tyler. It was a skinny, unshaven Hispanic man with wild black hair and a sagging green linen coat, underneath which he was bare-chested, with thick curly chest-hair. He wore baggy gray pants that hung down so low that Martin could see the waistband of his Calvin Klein shorts.

He was toothlessly grinning and he was pointing a gun at Martin, which he was holding sideways in approved gangsta fashion.

'Jesus,' said Martin.

'Catched up with you at last,' said Jesus. 'I been looking and looking but I couldn't find your ass noplace. Friend of mine knew that you lived here, gave me the heads up that you was back. You probably know him. Juan, the janitor. I always razz him, call him the Juanitor.'

'What do you want, Jesus?'

'What do I want? What do I want? What do you *think* I fucking want? You pushed my head down the john and I want what's-it-called? Retro-bewshun. That's it. Nobody pushes my head down no john and lives to laugh about it, man. Ezzie told everybody about it, of course she did. If there hadn't been no drought, man, you could have drowned me.'

'So now you've come to get even?'

Jesus shook his head so that his earrings waggled. 'I want more than even. I want to make sure that you never stick your nose in my life never again, nor nobody else's life, come to that.'

He cocked the automatic and aimed it directly at Martin's head. Martin tensed, ready to throw the box of books at him, in the hope of deflecting his aim.

'Any last words, Mr Social Service loser? How about an apology? How about, "Sorry, Jesus, for pushing your head down the john"? Not that it would make no difference. I'm still going to waste you, whatever.'

What Jesus didn't realize was that Tyler had now quietly come up the steps to Martin's apartment and had appeared right behind him. Martin remained expressionless, but Tyler indicated that he was going to make a grab for Jesus' gun.

Martin said, 'Yes. Good idea.'

Jesus was taken aback. 'What does *that* mean, man? "Good idea"? It's a good idea that you apologizes? Well, if it's such a good idea, then do it. Like, apologize. "Sorry, Jesus, for pushing your head down the john."'

Tyler reached out and grabbed Jesus' wrist, wrenching it upward. Jesus fired one shot into the ceiling before Tyler twisted his wrist around so violently that he had to let go of the gun. Martin dropped the box of books on to Jesus' feet and then punched him in the face so hard that he dislocated his jaw.

Jesus was left standing there with his mouth gaping open and his tongue hanging out, gagging and choking, unable to speak.

'Now get the hell out of here, Jesus!' Martin barked at him. 'And don't ever let me see your miserable face ever again. The water supply's back on, so next time I *will* drown you, I swear to God!'

Martin and Tyler stood at the top of the steps watching Jesus scuttle across to the parking area, where he had left his yellow Mustang.

Tyler handed Martin the automatic. 'Something to add to your armory, Dad.'

Martin turned the automatic this way and that. It was a battered old Browning, with duct tape wound around the butt because it had lost its wooden grips. 'Thanks. And thanks for saving my life.'

'You saved my life, Dad. You saved *all* of our lives.'

Martin said, 'I'll tell you something, Tyler, I'm so tired of all this. Sometimes I think, this is the twenty-first century. Why the hell do we have to keep fighting each other, just to stay alive?'

'I don't know, Dad. I don't know the answer to that one. I don't think anybody does. Maybe God, but He's not telling.'

EPILOGUE

No bodies were ever found at Lost Girl Lake.

Park rangers came across three burned-out tents outside the entrance to the cavern, and over the following weeks and months they found items of clothing and personal possessions including wallets and keys, all of which were scattered over a very wide area.

They also found respirators, belts and Kevlar body armor, all of which were identified as belonging to Empire Security Services in San Bernardino, although ESS representatives insisted that they were unable to explain how they had got there.

Inside the cavern they discovered several boxes of canned and dried food. Most incongruous of all were the twisted remains of an M2A1-7 military flame-thrower, which was illegal for civilian use in California.

The evening before Thanksgiving, three young Chemehuevi Indians from the Twentynine Palms Mission reservation were flagged down by highway patrol officers on the Utah Trail because they were driving a Cadillac Eldorado convertible with a broken headlight. They were unable to produce driving licenses or any documents relating to the vehicle, but they protested that they hadn't stolen it.

They had found it abandoned in the Joshua Tree National Park and considered that it was 'a gift from Mother Earth'.

kE 12/15

Lightning Source UK Ltd.
Milton Keynes UK
UKOW04f0133211115

263168UK00002B/10/P

9 781847 515193